HOW I SPENT THE APOCALYPSE

APOCALYPSE

Selina Rosen

For Roland and Zeb.
I hope this isn't the future you inherit

How I Spent the Apocalypse
Selina Rosen
First Edition Copyright © Selina Rosen 2011
Second Edition Copyright © Selina Rosen 2016

Published by Yard Dog Press Create Space

Second Print Version ISBN 978-1-937105-96-9
How I Spent the Apocolypse
First Edition Copyright © Selina Rosen, 2011
Second Edition Copyright © Selina Rosen 2016

Yard Dog Press
710 W. Redbud Lane
Alma, AR 72921-7247

http://www.yarddogpress.com

Edited by Tania Mears
Copy Editor & Technical Editor Lynn Rosen
Cover art by Mitchell Bentley

First Print Edition October 15th, 2011
Second Print Edition July 15h, 2016
Printed in the United States of America
0 9 8 7 6 5 4 3 2 1

For Roland and Zeb.
I hope this isn't the future you inherit
from all of us dumb-f---s.

CHAPTER 1

Don't Leave Home Without It

Don't try to travel during the disaster. *Unless you have days to get the hell out of Dodge you're much better off to stay put and hunker down. In other words, if you waited till the last minute to try to make it through the apocalypse you're probably already screwed, so you might as well stay put where at least you have some stuff.*

If you have to leave because a river of lava...or just a river...is headed your way, then take your survival kit, all your food, as many blankets and sensible clothes as you can, and get while the getting is good. But if you leave empty handed you will be as screwed as you would be if the lava hit you.

Don't wait till the last minute to go when every other idiot is trying to get away. You'd be better off on a rubber raft than stuck in traffic 'cause even if it's a river of lava at least you'll go quick— without having to hear idiots honking their horns as if that could magically clear sixty miles of bumper-to-bumper traffic. And then there's all the screaming as the lava consumes them.

And for God's sake when evacuating don't be one of the idiots who runs out of gas. Turn the car off if traffic is stopped. Carry gas with you. Real survivalists always keep their gas tanks in all their vehicles full and have an extra five-gallon can full at any given time.

If you're on any coast and you hear something apocalyptic may be happening then if you're smart... Well if you were really smart, you would have already moved years ago... But if you're still there just load up all you can and head inland. Find a nice park with cabins or get a hotel room in a small town. Hell, move in with family or friends.

Our most likely doomsday scenario will be caused or made worse by climate change. I know—every right winger in this country seems to think this is something liberals made up to scare us into regulating big business and doing without all that big crap you just have to have—but just because some idiots refuse to believe in something doesn't mean it isn't real. I mean come on! People were convinced the world was flat—some still are—that doesn't make it flat. If you're on one of the coasts and you want to sur-

vive—get inland. If you're in a big city—get out. You might have done everything right but your neighbors won't have and they will kill you and take your shit.

Inner-city gangs will likely be killing everyone else to live. If anyone survives in the big cities they will most likely be exactly the sort of people we least needed to have survive. They will have survived not because of their wits but because there is strength in numbers and they will be willing to kill to get what they need.

The only trouble thugs might have is that they are all idiots. Let's face it; smart people don't buy into the things a gang promises. With no one to inhibit them, the morons will most likely do their drug of choice till they die. Of course, in the meantime, they won't have any trouble at all killing you to take your food, water, or prescription meds.

Now as soon as you land someplace if the worst hasn't happened yet—and if you're smart you saw the signs and got out in plenty of time—take any credit cards you have, go to the store, and max them out. Buy all the dry goods you can. If you're afraid you won't have a way to cook beans and rice or other grains, then get peanut butter, canned meat and honey—lots of honey—even sugar. Both give you quick calories. Max your cards out buying sleeping bags and other survival-type stuff. After all, if the worst happens you won't have to worry about paying it off. Even if civilization does survive enough for debt to still be a problem, well... Would you rather be dead or have a little debt?

Grocery stores have already been emptied when you get there? Head for a feed store. They sell several animal products that can be consumed by humans. Wheat bran, rice bran, and ground corn come to mind. Use your head. Only get full-grain products and stay away from pelleted feed with chemical additives.

So there are reasons to evacuate even at the last minute, but for the most part if you've waited till the apocalypse begins to leave the coasts or the cities it's probably too late for you anyway. As a basic rule, don't travel once the apocalypse has started. Look, Flo Jo couldn't outrun cancer, and you won't be able to outrun the tidal wave, the hurricane, the tornado, or the blizzard, either.

Yep, that's the kind of sound advice that I used to hand out on my weekly podcast entitled, *Living Through the End dot com*. A long title I know but sort of catchy and not the sort of thing people easily forgot. It had over three million loyal listeners. Their donations didn't make me filthy rich, but they did give me more than enough money to quit my job about eight years before the end of the world as we knew it and allowed me to devote all of my time—and all their money—to preparing for the coming disaster.

Although I'll be completely honest and tell you that I didn't need their money or the time because I'd been preparing for the inevitable since I was a kid, and it turned out that what I had without all the cool shit I managed to put back would have been enough. Having money just let me do it bigger and better. It allowed me to help other people, too. The truth is without the money me and mine would have made it, but lots of other people wouldn't have.

And having all the really cool shit... Well it really livened up the ole apocalypse for me.

As a kid I started doing things like hording batteries and food. Soon I'd escalated to spending time my teachers thought I should have spent studying, playing sports, or socializing with my peers trying to figure out where the safest place in America was.

Of course the joke's on them because turns out I really *didn't* need to learn any of that crap I told them I didn't need to learn, and I'm alive and most everyone else is dead. So na na na boo boo.

About now you might be asking yourself why I knew. How I knew. Am I some modern-day prophet, a psychic?

Nope. If I was, my own life wouldn't have had so many snags, would it? What I am is obsessive compulsive and crazier than a shit house rat. I've had recurring nightmares of the destruction of the world for as long as I can remember. I have no idea what started the dreams. Maybe it had something to do with the fact that my parents loved disaster movies and I'd seen way too many of them from my crib. Or maybe I was one of the few people who paid any attention at all to the news. But the dreams were what started my obsession with doomsday.

Also... Well, I'm really smart. I know that makes me sound egotistical, but it's also true. I heard what people were saying about global warming—later changed to Catastrophic Climate Change in the hope that stupid people would quit saying, "Where's my global warming?" every time it was colder than shit. And I read too much—or so my trailer trash family would say over and over. I swear what really saved me—and through me a big slice of mankind—was my family disowning me. I never would have amounted to shit if they hadn't kicked me out on my ass when I was sixteen.

Anyway, I read a lot, so I knew what was going on in the Middle East. While we were farting around over there trying to keep our fingers on the pulse of one of the biggest oil veins in the world, stirring up all those idiot, radical religious fucks in Iraq, Iran and Afghanistan—giving them someone besides each other to hate—Pakistan and India were on the verge of a full-out nuclear war that was also driven by religious dissent.

Any idiot with a TV should have been able to see that our government had been taken over by people whose own religious beliefs said we were way past Armageddon and who were mostly into stuffing their already-full pockets. They didn't give a good God-damn what happened to the people, the economy, or the world when they were done with it.

Our government at that time was made up of two kinds of people. The first were rich idiots who used the ultra religious to get them into power so that they could hand the world over to mega corporations. These same corporations somehow managed to pay huge bonuses to executives who had apparently run their companies and the country into bankruptcy but were still considered by the CEOs of their companies to be the BEST people for the job. The second type were rich idiots who talked a good game about making things more fair and who were all for throwing money at problems but who never gave up their big houses or cars or quit jetting all over. They looked down on everyone who wasn't wealthy even as they said they wanted to help those less fortunate. They made it clear that they thought we "less fortunate" got that way because we were uneducated and uninformed. In other words, they thought we were just too stupid to dig out of poverty and better our lives without their help. They never understood—how could they when most of them were born to money, privilege or both—that some people just weren't as fortunate. That it had *nothing* to do with being uneducated or stupid, and *everything* to do with the fact that so many of us were just handed a big shit sandwich. They really thought you could make everyone happy and... You can never do that, not when everyone has been brainwashed to think that success is measured in how much shit you own.

And all the while it was getting either hotter or colder depending upon where you were on the globe, and everything was crazy and... No one seemed to give a damn as long as they could drive their cars as big as houses and live in there houses as big as churches and go to their church that was as big as a stadium. They just watched sitcom reruns on their seventy-inch plasma screen TVs and sucked down their micro-waved, processed food packets in their climate-controlled homes and ignored all the warning signs.

Yuppies and religious morons are equally responsible for the destruction of the world, make no doubt about that. Everyone having to have more than everyone else and not caring about the cost to the environment or whether our people were being sent to fight a war against terrorism that never would have started in the first place if we'd never allowed ourselves to become so reliant on oil. We played right into those idiot religious zealots in the middle East's hands who, like the radical Christians wanted Armageddon because they all thought it would be a happy thing. Well they all got their wish, didn't they?

I wonder if any of them got sucked up into that heaven they were always talking about. If not, Armageddon wasn't what they thought it was going to be.

I didn't get to go to college. In fact, I barely made it through high school because as I said my parents kicked me out of the house when I was sixteen and I had to fend for myself. Of course with my family I'd always had to fend for myself anyway, so no big difference except that I had to put a roof over my head and buy a car. That meant working every night and weekend at a quick mart. And like I said before, the time I was supposed to be studying I spent reading all about everything that people should never know if they don't just want to make themselves as crazy as... Well, as I turned out to be.

Now you might be asking yourself how I can say that I'm so smart and all-seeing since I didn't have any high-falutin' education and I keep admitting I'm crazy. Well I've read a lot—and not stupid shit, the important stuff, the stuff you need to know to survive through any disaster. I read about history, what we did wrong, what they did wrong. You study enough history you find out two truths. First, it's absolutely true that humans are so God-damned dumb that history ALWAYS repeats itself! Second, anything that ever got done that was worth doing or wasn't worth doing was done by some super-smart, crazier-than-shit person just like me.

Crazy Katy. Folks started calling me that back when I started building what people called The Bunker. It's not a bunker; it's my house. Alright, it's a really secure house, but it's not a bunker.

Though considering everything that's happened, it wouldn't have been so crazy if I was building a bunker.

Those stupid fucks! You ever just wish you could get super-famous and rich so that everyone who had ever put you down had to eat shit and die? Well everyone who was a real thorn in my side and tried to cause me any real trouble, they all died in the global disaster.

Everyone that is except for Lucy Powers.

I was way busy getting ready for the coming apocalypse. I was also trying to talk my sons into giving up on riding it out in my son Billy's home in Fort Smith and come home. I had my cell phone in one hand and a stack of wood in the other. See, you keep getting ready right up to the point you can't any more once you know a storm or disaster is imminent. You never say, *Well that's enough*, and stop because what if that last arm load of wood is the difference between living and dying? Then you're going to be feeling really stupid—and cold—while you're dying.

My oldest son, Billy Ray, sighed that sigh I knew meant he was just trying to shut his crazy mother up. Then he said, "Mom... I've got my survival kit and plenty of toilet paper, dried beans, rice, and enough kerosene to last a week all in the basement. Jimmy Dean..." My youngest son. Don't blame me; I didn't name them. "...is on his way over here right now."

There was no sense in arguing with him, and the truth was I just flat didn't have time to waste trying to convince him that this time I was sure. I'd hauled those boys into storm shelters and run them through drills so many times that they no longer even got upset. They thought I was full of shit, and the youngest one... Well, he'd given up long ago even pretending to have a survival kit or any extra food or fuel put back. He'd told me to my face that I was a nut job and that I had ruined their childhood scaring the shit out of them that at any minute the world as we knew it was going to vanish.

My son Jimmy Dean is often quoted these days as saying, "Just because Mom is crazy doesn't mean she isn't right."

Ah vindication, sort of makes me understand why all the religious idiots kept working for the end of the world. I would have just looked really stupid to everyone, and my sons never would have really respected me if the apocalypse hadn't actually come.

Anyway, my son Billy was pretending to take me seriously while telling me they could ride it out in town, which I knew was a crock, and I was trying to get the door open so that I could put the wood away. That was when the alarm went off telling me someone had opened the front gate. I jumped, dropped the wood, and damn near shoved the phone right through my head, so I was already in a mood when I saw what had become the bane of my existence—a freaking news team—coming through the front gates. I could have kicked my sons' asses because if it wasn't for them I would have had the front gates locked down tight already.

How did I know it was a news team? Because it was a shiny new car. I didn't have many friends left, and the few friends I'd actually managed to keep over the years didn't drive anything that wasn't at least ten years old

"Fucking beautiful," I mumbled.

"What?" Billy Ray asked.

"Not you son," I said. "Fucking news crew is here."

Billy chuckled. "What do you expect, Mom? You got on your

podcast two days ago and this time no *maybe*, no *might be*, this time you flat-assed announced the end of the world. You should have known they'd show up."

"Yeah... Well I know you think I'm just crying wolf once again, but this is it, Billy. Don't you forget that, and don't you or your stupid brother forget everything I taught you. I love you; I have to go."

It sucks when you can't get your kids to do what you need them to. Sucks when they won't listen to you when you're right and they're... Well, stupid. Still I wasn't too worried about my boys. They did know how to survive, they were only about twenty minutes away from me, and I had purposely moved to the hell which was Northwest Arkansas because it was one of the safest places in the country to be. All we had to worry about were tornados and ice storms as natural disasters went. We're too far north for hurricanes or the people fleeing them to reach us. Too far south to get really hammered by a bad blizzard. Just out of reach of both a Yellow Stone Caldara eruption and the New Mandarin Fault. That didn't mean it wasn't going to get bad here; it just meant that we had a better shot at survival than most people.

I looked down at the scattered pieces of wood. I had too much to do to waste time dealing with these idiot yuppie scum.

I watched as the girl and her cameraman got out and then frowned, trying to think how to get rid of them the quickest. There's a lot to do when you're just minutes away from the end of the world. This time it was just the girl and a cameraman; I usually got inundated with a full news crew. I assumed that because of all that was happening they were spread a little thin.

I knew the reporter. It wasn't the first time she'd been here, and she'd never once masked her obvious disdain for me and all I stood for. I also knew she had to be really bitter about being sent to talk to the crazy woman instead of getting a "real" assignment.

Of course as much as Lucy annoyed me, and as much as I did NOT want to see her right then, she was at least in part responsible for my "success." You see, I didn't come by the over three million listeners by accident. When I started out I probably had only a handful of listeners. Then of course they told others and pretty soon there were a few hundred. Few of those donated, though, so the income mostly just kept up my computer equipment at best. I guess what really opened it up, what got me all the loyal followers who gladly donated enough money for me to finish building, stocking and fortifying my home the way I wanted to, was the news coverage.

See, when the second of the mega hurricanes hit the gulf coast and several of the survivors explained that they had survived because of what they'd learned on my podcast, my audience just grew overnight. Then, three months later a family that made it through a group of three F4 twisters that tore up greater Memphis and killed thousands of people said that their survival was completely due to the fact that they listened religiously to my podcast and took my advice. That was the first time the news people came. Of course the fact that I was on the news just got even more people listening.

After that... Well the weather got progressively worse, didn't it? When flood survivors, fire, hurricane, and tornado survivors all started saying my podcast was the reason they were alive, the number of listeners kept growing and the donations kept rolling in and getting bigger. Some of them gave me a butt-load of money. There was a lesbian couple owned a bed and breakfast and a natural gas well who sent me thousands of dollars. Do the math people. You have three million listeners. If only a third of them give you a dollar and some of them give you butt loads... It's a lot of money.

But you know what? It takes a lot of money to build what I built, and it takes a lot of money to set up the system that I set up.

Every time I would sound any sort of alarm like telling one area of the country or another to hunker down or get out, whether I wound up being right or being wrong, here came this sexy little tight-assed reporter to ask ole Crazy Katy questions—her tongue all but poking a hole right in her cheek.

"Too busy. Can't talk," I said, waving my arms in front of me. The camera was already rolling, and no matter what I said these dick heads would discount it. I think she lived for the sole intent and purpose of making me look like the biggest nut job in all of North America. "Listen... End of the world as we know it is coming and I've got a lot of crap to do, so..." I waved my hand dismissively, which... Well she might have been a grade A yuppie bitch, but she was hot as hell and me? Well I'm as queer as they come and had been mostly single for years, so the fact that I was in such a big-assed hurry to get rid of her tells you just how sure I was that the world was about to go boom.

"Ms. Sanders, always before you have said 'maybe' in your reports. You've pointed to this area or to that, and..."

"Are we live?" I asked.

"We can be," she assured me as I went to take the windmill down. It's really cool by the way. I just undo the cables and belts, push a couple of buttons, and it goes right into a hole in the ground. Then I push a button and the steel door closes over the top of it. I had just got them closed and locked when the camera guy said...

"Going live in three...two...one..."

"I'm Lucy Powers reporting from just outside Rudy, Arkansas. I'm here with Katy Sanders, the owner and operator of *Living Through The End dot com*..."

"We don't have time for any of this shit. Listen people, all hell is about to break loose on a global scale. Maybe you think what happened yesterday is all the way across the globe. The Pakistanis threw half a dozen nukes at India, and India threw twice that many back and... It's just them. Well it's not going to be just them. Do you have any idea how much dirt was thrown into the atmosphere? Besides, that whole area is sitting on a huge fault. Look, everything has been out of balance for a long time. Climate change has been kicking our ass, and unless I'm dead wrong we're about to see a chain reaction of disasters. So if you're still in a big city put your head between your knees and kiss your ass good bye..."

The camera man started to shut down the camera, so I took the gun out of my pocket, pointed it at his head and cocked it. I didn't even lose my train of thought.

"If you aren't in a city, fill everything you can get your hands on with water. Get to a store, stock up on non-perishable food items. Everyone find some way that doesn't include utilities running to keep warm. If you are on the coasts, get to higher ground. I'm going to keep running all through the apocalypse, so if you can get a radio signal, go to one ninety-eight AM, I'll be there telling you what I can at eight AM and eight PM US Central every day. You have a ham radio? You can contact me at T-H-E-E-N-D-one-four-seven."

I uncocked the gun, put the safety back on, and put it back in my pocket. I looked at Lucy, whose jaw just hung open. Then I ran off to check that the barn door was locked—which of course it was—that the solar panels where in their hiding hole just like the wind mill—which of course they also were. In my head I was checking off a list of all the things I might have forgotten. When I came back and started picking up the armload of wood I'd dropped, the sky was already looking black, and Lucy was saying something about the number of times I'd been wrong about other disasters. I pointed at a dip where a dark sky met a merely gray one and told her. "See that? That's cold air hitting hot air. It's a hook. There will be at least one tornado in this storm. You best find shelter quick."

With that I walked inside, closed the door, and started broadcasting. I had to get the word out, warn as many people as I could. After all, those people had helped me build the perfect home to protect me and mine—if I could get mine to come home—from the coming apocalypse and I owed them. Besides, unlike so many other survivalists, I didn't really see much sense in surviving if no one else did. I podcast at the same times every day. Then I powered the radio transmitter up for the first time. Radio was the most reliable thing we'd have left, and I had bought equipment strong enough to send and receive from around the globe. It was ready to go, too. I'd have to compete with other stations now, and I guess if the world didn't blow up I could be arrested for breaking any number of FCC regulations, but first off I was sure this was it and second... Well I'm crazy and I had plenty of money, so I wouldn't do any real time.

When I had warned everyone I could and had given them all the information I could think of to give them I set it up on a loop so that it would play over and over again. Then I went in to the living room, turned on the TV, and started watching the news. After all, the way I figured it this might be the last time I got to watch news.

I kept switching channels back and forth trying to see what everyone's take was on things. They were all mostly still keeping their heads planted up their asses. The weather channel was having a field day. Let's face it, even with all the bad weather of the last few years their jobs were mostly trying to make things like rains storms sound exciting. It was clear by the expressions on their faces when they went from thinking this was all just very exciting to "we're all fucked."

Someone was actually getting a tornado on film as it ripped apart a house and barn and then it was pretty obvious that whoever was holding that camera wasn't any more—in that "he's dead" sort of way. There were a few seconds that we actually got to see up in the funnel and then nothing. Then some red-faced news guy who no doubt knew it was the end of the world was warning everyone to take shelter and...

I knew that wasn't going to be enough. I was worried about my boys, so I called them on the cell phone.

"Don't worry, Mom. We're in the basement and we've got all our stuff. We're going to be alright," Billy said. In the background my younger son was screaming hysterically.

"I'm sorry mama! I'm sorry! God I'm sorry!"

"Billy?"

"Yeah, Mama?"

"Slap your brother's face, and then tell him I love him." I could hear a slapping sound and then Jimmy screaming, "What did you do that for?" Then Billy telling him it was because I loved him.

"You boys remember everything I taught you."

"We will, Mama. We're sitting good, so don't worry about us."

"I love you, Billy."

"Love you, too, Mama."

Don't worry about them! What a stupid, fucking thing to say. I wouldn't have had to worry about the stupid little fuckers if they had been in the house with me, but no... They just had to be all independent. I seriously wonder how the world got so God-damn overpopulated. I mean why do people want kids? What makes them have them? Hell, some people went out of their way to have them. Why is the need to procreate so strong? Kids are nothing but a heartache and a worry. You fix everything for them so that they'll be safe during the apocalypse, and what do they do? Decide you're a crackpot and move into the city to get away from you.

The city!

I switched to CNN. They were reporting a massive quake that was shaking all of Pakistan and most of Turkey and had caused a volcanic eruption. Santa Anna winds were fueling fires that were raging all across Southern California as gale-force winds struck the entire Pacific Coast. Hurricanes were forming all across the Atlantic seaboards. They were predicting a strong arctic blast descending on Canada, and that was of course the real problem. The real problem for the US was that this was happening in November—winter—which meant things were going to get really nasty, especially up north.

I had just stood up to go make another announcement and tell my listeners what CNN was reporting when I heard someone knocking on the door. Now I knew it wasn't my boys, and I would have had to kill them both if it was because traveling in this shit would have meant that they broke my very first rule. But I have to tell you that part of me hoped it was my boys, and I was damned disappointed when I opened the outer door and it was that fucking reporter.

CHAPTER 2

It's Yours Not Theirs

Your supplies are for you, and your shelter is for you. *You can't let anyone else in. If you let those who didn't prepare for this eat your food and drink your water, then you and your family will die just like the dumbass who never even put together a plan or a survival pack.*

The average apartment dweller in the big city doesn't have enough food to last a week.

If you are close to a large city you will most likely have to defend yourself against all the stupid fucks who didn't realize that twenty pounds of dried beans and rice can go a long way. A drawer full of jerky could last months if you ration it with all your other foods, and everyone should just always keep a three-year supply of multi-vitamins for each member of their family. Cycle them out so that they don't go bad, but put them back and make sure you always have a three-year supply in your survival kit.

Don't wait till your food and water supplies get low to start rationing. Ration from day one. If anyone bitches explain that they can eat their portion of the rations and be happy or they can go hungry for a day and see what it really means to be starving to death.

These will not be easy times. It will be hard to turn friends and neighbors away. I suggest if you have the room and money you might put back some supplies just so you can help your friends and neighbors. Also it might be beneficial for groups of people to make plans to all stay at one residence which may be better suited for the apocalypse. You can group together and share resources. For instance, if it is super cold it will be easier to heat one room in one house than twenty rooms in twenty houses. More people means more body heat, too, but you must make sure that each person brings food and water with them. If sharing your supplies and your space with other people is not beneficial to you, if all it will do is tax your already meager larder, then you must turn them away.

Yep, wise words. Of course Lucy Powers didn't give me much choice. The wind was horrible, and she didn't wait to be asked in. I didn't wait to put my whole body into it and shut and bolt the exterior door, either. I hurried her through the interior door that opens into the corridor which connects the house to the barn, the shop, and my primary storage facilities.

Did I mention my listeners gave me a LOT of money?

She was crying, saying incoherent things, and there were little cuts all over her face and hands. I gently guided her into the house and into the bathroom where I helped her sit down on the commode and started to treat her wounds.

"I didn't know where else to go!" She cried. "The whole world's coming apart out there... Grayson." She sobbed. "He's just gone, sucked up by it. God! He's dead and I just ran. I just ran." She kept crying, which made it hard to treat her wounds, and the whole time I was just going over what I'd told my listeners a dozen times about the evils of taking someone in who had nothing to give you.

And she literally had nothing. Even the clothes on her back were ripped to shreds. To make matters worse I was pretty sure she had no skills that would be useful. She probably didn't even know how to wash a dish without a machine to do it for her.

And I knew she thought I was a lunatic.

Of course I *am* a lunatic, so I didn't really think it was much of a reason to hold a grudge, and it wasn't like I didn't have enough supplies.

"What's happening?" she asked. When she looked up at me with those big, blue eyes, I suddenly thought of something she might be good for.

She made a face as the hydrogen peroxide hit the cut by her eye that I was treating. It wasn't bad. It didn't need stitches, which was almost too bad because I know how to stitch people up real good. None of her cuts were deep, but they all needed to be treated if for no other reason than I had all the stuff to do it with.

"What's happening?" she asked again.

"Tornados, hurricanes, fire storms, earthquakes... I'm just going to go out on a limb and once again say... End of the world!"

Then we could hear it, that awful sound that tornados make. People say it's like a train, but it's not. It's more like they let every demon out of hell at once and the train was running over all of them at the same time. Even in my house under two reinforced domes of concrete I had this feeling of impending doom, and I was really worried about my boys.

The tornado touched down on my place briefly and then it jumped and just sort of stayed right over us, taunting us before it went on its destructive way leaving so-called straight-line winds—which will do a hell of a lot of damage all by themselves. As the giant hail started smashing into my house I cringed. All my stuff was put up, locked down, and hopefully tornado proof, but somewhere out there that stupid girl had parked that God-damned rental car.

"Where's your car?" I screamed over the crashing roar that was just getting louder.

"It went with the twister and Grayson." She cried again, but I had new respect for the girl's survival instincts because she had obviously run here from God only knew how far. I looked down and saw she was actually wearing running shoes and decided she wasn't as stupid as I had previously thought.

"Good, at least we don't have to worry about it being slammed into the house," I said. I was done treating her wounds. She needed a bath, but that could wait.

"It couldn't be that bad... I mean the lights are still on."

"Ah huh," I said, thinking I could explain that the whole place ran off its own power supply later.

She said she needed to use the bathroom, so I left her to it and cringed when she flushed the toilet. We never flushed unless there was a turd in it. You certainly don't waste water during a disaster. Of course I had more than enough water, but I don't believe in wasting it.

I don't believe in wasting anything.

When she came in and sat down she had obviously combed her hair and washed her face and hands, which more or less undid everything I'd done. She sat down on the couch nowhere near me and watched the TV with a sort of blank stare. I had turned the local news back on. It didn't sound good. There were at least six funnel clouds that had been spotted, and one had hit the ground in Rudy proper. The hail was golf-ball to soft-ball sized, and what the tornados and wind weren't destroying it undoubtedly was. Oklahoma City and Tulsa also had tornado warnings. The few pictures they had of Fort Smith were so bad that I couldn't even tell what part of town they were picturing.

My cell phone rang. It was my boys, and this time Jimmy was on the phone.

I was never so glad to hear anyone's voice in my life. "Mama, we're OK how are you?"

"Great now that I know you're alright."

"It hit us. Billy's really upset. He's sure his house is completely gone. We can't get the basement door open."

"Put Billy on the phone, honey."

"Mama..."

"Billy, don't even try to get out of the basement tonight and don't worry about the damned house. Ain't none of it gonna matter now anyway. You enjoyed it while you had it, and hell, boy, the bank owned more of it than you did anyway."

"What should we do, Mama?"

"Did you bring your chain saw and axe down in the basement with you?"

"Yep."

"Is it wet in there?" I asked, quickly making a mental note of how far they were from the river and deciding they were safe.

"Not really. House was on a cement slab."

"Then get comfortable. There is another storm right behind this one, and it's full of tornados, too. In the morning if the storms are gone saw your way out. Remember not to use the chainsaw if it's going to take you more than a few seconds to get out because you'll wind up with carbon monoxide poisoning. If you can find your four wheelers, pack what you can and get your butts home because you are only going to have a very small window of time before the next storm front hits. If you have to, you hike out, you hear me?"

"Will do, Mama."

"Be careful. I already broke one of my rules. Don't make me break another by making me come after you."

I said good night to my sons and then closed the phone. I needed a drink. I got up to go to the fridge and get a beer and then I'd get back on my blog and start answering some of the thousands of questions that would be coming in. I'd try to pick the ones that were asked most, the ones that seemed most urgent, but the truth was I couldn't answer them all, there was just no way. There would be people on the edge needing an answer that I could have provided that would be the difference between life and death, and I'd miss them, and I just couldn't worry about it. I was all wireless, and I had the radio station and the ham station up, so I'd do all I could, hope that at least some of the people I was answering were able to get the answers they needed some way, and just work till I dropped.

"You have kids?" Lucy asked.

"Two boys."

"Why aren't they here?"

She might as well have spit in my face her question made me that mad. "Because they're grown men now who think they know every God-damned thing and they don't listen to me because people like you have gone out of your way to make them believe that I'm fucking out of my tiny little mind."

"I'm sorry," she said in a mere whisper. I just ignored her apology, got my beer and went in to try to help "my people," not really giving any thought to what I was going to do about Lucy. She would be a waste of food and time, and I just knew she was going to be nothing but trouble. In short I was sure that girl was going to ruin the apocalypse for me.

A thunderclap sounded loud enough to make me jump. I ignored that, too, and just started answering questions.

Ted in Illinois said there was already a foot of snow on the ground. But the ice had come first—two inches of it—and it had broken every tree and power pole as far as he could see. He had plenty of food and had just finished filling everything that would hold it with water. He had a fireplace, but he wasn't sure he had enough wood, and his house was already getting cold. They were projecting wind chills as low as twenty below over night.

His question was the same as many of the ones I was getting from the northern states. They were used to long, cold winters, but not prepared to be off the grid at all and certainly not during record cold temperatures. And I knew this winter was going to be colder and longer than anything even they were used to.

I went right to the radio and computer. I told them everything that I knew was going on. Then I read Ted's question out loud and told them, "Use utilities to heat and light your home till they all go out. Only then get into your wood supply. It may be that some people will keep services all through the apocalypse. Other places it could last for days. If you have a wood stove or fireplace, pick that room. Otherwise pick the smallest room in the house with the least windows. Only heat this room. The more people that do this the longer the power will last. Fill any cracks around the windows with plastic wrap or aluminum foil then hang several layers of blankets or stack mattresses or furniture over any windows in the room. This will help you insulate that room. Hang a blanket over the door you intend to use to come and go. Bring all your food blankets and clothing into this room. Bring any of your firewood into the house and put it in an adjoining room. When the utilities give out, then and only then, start burning your wood. Ration it like you do your food and water. The idea is to make the space habitable while wearing several layers of clothes, not cozy enough for shorts and a tank top.

For those of you without any combustible-type heating stove, if you have a tent pitch it in the middle of the room and cover it with blankets, clothes, anything that will insulate. If you have a Coleman stove or a lamp and fuel, use it only sparingly as you could get carbon monoxide poisoning. Candles are great. They will warm something as small as a tent more than you think and don't have the problems of the gas-burning camping appliances, but you will need that type of appliance to cook on, so if you don't have one and a supply of fuel get it now. You will basically be treating the room like the outdoors and the tent like home...

I don't know how many more I had answered when she

walked into the room.

"This place is a little claustrophobic."

It's true. The house is small. My office is the largest room in the house, and it's only sixteen by sixteen. Less space means less to heat and cool—not that it took much to heat and cool anyway because of its construction—it also took less material to build it smaller.

"I didn't build it for you," I said, and just kept working.

"CNN is reporting tornados in Georgia, ice storms in Kansas and Missouri, and a tidal wave off the coast of Washington extending as far south as Baja."

"Well at least that will put those fires out," I mumbled and continued writing.

"It's not funny; it's horrible. Thousands are dying and..."

"None of those people are me. Look, chick, hundreds of thousands died yesterday in India and Pakistan, did you cry for them?" Her silence told me she hadn't. "You know why you didn't cry for them?" I didn't even give her time to answer. "Because it wasn't you, and it wasn't anyone you knew. You weren't there, and you didn't see it, and part of you said they deserved it because they had done it to themselves. Well this—all of this—was caused by that action, but we also did it to ourselves. We have been pushing everything out of balance. We are parasites, and there are too many of us. We are killing our host, and now it's shaking like crazy to get rid of us. The only ones that are going to make it, the only ones that deserve to make it, are the ones who are going to hang on tight for dear life. Now I don't have time to talk. You can condemn me later, but right now I'm trying to save who I can."

She didn't go away, but she was quiet, just standing there, which of course bugged the living shit out of me.

"What?" I asked.

"I lost my cell phone. Can I use yours?"

"Key-rist!" I pulled it out of my pocket and threw it at her. I was surprised some when she caught it. "Go someplace else to call. I'm trying to work."

She left the room, but I could see her hovering just outside the door, which was annoying to say the least. Now the truth is I don't really like to be alone. I've spent a lot of my life that way since the boys left home because crazy people—even famous crazy people—don't generally have many friends. I had a few, but I'd spent most of my time alone working. I'd never had any trouble at all picking women up, but keeping them was another matter altogether. They were all over in love with me till they realized how crazy I really was, then it was, "Bye! See ya." It was a shame, really, because I'm not really bad looking, I have lots of money, I've been told I'm a really good lover, and I was their best chance for making it through the apocalypse. Of course they'd all thought that the fact that I believed we were headed for doom and was preparing for it was the craziest thing I did. So, there you go. All except Cindy. she'd known I was crazy, and really wasn't all over the whole apocalypse thing, but she loved me and stayed with me no matter how much grief her family and friends—or even I—gave her. She saw my obsession with surviving a coming apocalypse the way most women see their husband's fishing, hunting or sports-watching habit. You know, irritating, but if that's the worst thing he does...

Of course she didn't listen to me any better than those boys of ours did. About ten years before the apocalypse she was driving home from work. It was raining hard and we'd had a bunch of flash flooding. How many times had I told her, how many times had I warned everyone else? Hunker down till the storm or disaster passes; don't try to go anywhere. But Cindy wanted to come home, and she drove through what she thought was just a few inches of water. It washed her right off the bridge and into the swollen creek. They said she drowned quickly. At the funeral people even told me that drowning was a painless way to go. I'm sure that's mostly shit, and that they think that because they've never drowned.

To this day I have nightmares seeing the tow truck winch her car out of the creek, seeing her dead, lifeless body floating inside and sinking lower as the water ran out of the car till she was out of sight.

My boys think that's what pushed me over the edge. They think I wasn't really crazy till their mother died, but I was just as crazy just not as driven. And maybe I started the whole podcasting thing because I needed something to fill my suddenly empty life. Does the reason why I did it really matter now?

Love will make you crazy, and losing someone who loves you unconditionally... Well, it's a bitter pill to swallow, but I had her boys to raise by myself and nightmares of the destruction of the world, so I just threw myself into my work. Actually that was when I went to working only part time because I got two-hundred-thousand dollars in life insurance from Cindy, and I knew the apocalypse was right around the corner, so I started working hard on the new house. I'll admit it now; part of me wanted the new house because I couldn't stand being in the house I'd shared with her. It was too weird not seeing her there and even weirder when I did, because she was dead and that just ain't right.

Anyway, like I said, I don't really like to be alone. But right then I certainly didn't want that girl around, so I wasn't happy when she walked back in and handed me my cell phone saying, "The head of CNN wants to talk to you."

"What?" I say into the phone. I'm not impressed by money or power or freaking titles—never have been. Sure to hell wasn't after the shit hit the fan. Show me that you can make something useful from old newspapers, sticks, and duct tape, and then I'll be impressed.

"Lucy tells me you have enough equipment there to send us feed." I looked around me at all the equipment. I knew I did. Hell, all I had to do was send him a live video blog from my computer.

"Yeah."

"You hook us up, and I'll put you on the air live. I don't care what you say, and I won't stop you." I'm thinking he'd just become a true believer.

I spent the next six hours telling anyone who could watch or listen—because I had the radio transmitter going, too—how best to survive any and all the disaster scenarios I could think of. I was completely drained by the time our link with CNN just died. When we ran in the living room and turned on the TV, NBC was reporting that a line of massive tornados had ripped the CNN building and most of Atlanta to pieces.

Lucy had been standing, helping me work the equipment, too keyed up to sit the whole time we'd been transmitting. Now she flopped onto the couch next to me and just stared at the TV as if someone had punched her in the gut, and she just couldn't wrap her head around the why of it.

I got up silently and went to put some wood in the stove and shut it down for the night. It's a nice one—airtight with a catalytic converter and a fan that blows the heat through pipes in the front. I'd only ever really had to fire it at night until the apocalypse because... Well I'll explain that later.

"Thank you," Lucy said, suddenly standing right behind me.

"For saving your life or making you the most famous reporter on earth?"

"That's not really going to be worth much now, is it?" she said, an angry note to her voice that I figured I deserved.

"Sorry, I'm tired and I have a bad headache. I'm going to pop a couple of ibuprofen, get a shower, and go to bed."

She looked panicked then. "I don't want to be alone."

"Well you can bunk with me if you like, but I'm going to bed."

"Alright. Can I get a shower?"

"Yes, but its water on, water off, soap up, rinse, and get out."

She made a face, but nodded, so I think maybe she was starting to realize what sort of world it was going to be. Of course being the gentlewoman I am, I got my shower first. I had just finished putting on my pajamas in the bathroom, and already I was seeing what a huge imposition she was because normally—even if my boys were there—I would have just walked naked to the bedroom and gotten into my night clothes there. When I stepped out of the bathroom she was waiting there, which was flat-assed annoying.

"I... I have no clothes except what I'm wearing," she said.

I laughed then, momentarily getting my sense of humor back. "Well, dear, this may be the worst part of the apocalypse for you. You're going to have to wear my clothes." The look on her face said she didn't think that was going to work. I'm six feet tall, and she was maybe five-five tops, I weighed one-hundred-eighty pounds, she might have weighed one-twenty soaking wet.

I got her some boxer shorts and a T-shirt and she looked at me like I was from Mars. I shrugged, handed them to her and went to bed. It had been a long, hard day, and I no sooner lay down than I was asleep. I woke up because the cell phone was ringing. To tell the truth, I was sort of surprised it was still working. I guessed some towers must still be up. I answered it.

"Hello, Billy."

"How'd ya know it was me, Mom?"

"No one else calls me, and certainly not during the Apocalypse."

"We got out of the basement no problem. But listen, Mom. Both of the four-wheelers were trashed so we took parts off one of them and got the other one running, but both of us are going to have to ride it and there's no room for anything but us and our guns."

"You see any of your neighbors?"

"The Simpsons are out milling around. There's nothing left of their house, though, except the closet they were hiding in..."

"Tell them to get your wood stove if they can find it and set it up in your basement. Should be stuff that will work for stove pipes all around there. Tell them to stack as many shingles—those should be everywhere—on the cement slab as they can. Let them have your survival kit and all your supplies. I have plenty for us all here." And that was when I remembered that I had all sorts of clothes for Jimmy, and he was a lot closer to Lucy's size than I was. It wasn't like me to forget things. I guess the end of the world had me a little off my game. "Give them everything."

"Herbert's saying they're going to try to walk to Mountainburg, and..."

"Mountainburg got hit just as bad, and they'll never make it. You offer him what you've got and my advice and then get the hell out of there. Get home and sooner is better."

I gave him a few more instructions then hung up, looked at the clock, saw it was nine and moaned. I'd gotten all of four hours sleep, but I still had to get up because I had too much to do to just sleep all day. There would be plenty of time to sleep when the next storm rolled in. People didn't know it yet, but this one had just been the warning.

I got out of bed and realized that I hadn't been alone. Lucy was in my bed and still sound asleep. I had been kidding when I'd said she could bunk with me. I certainly never thought Miss Prissy Pants would do it, but what the hell? I'd only slept on the one side of the bed since I started living with Cindy anyway.

I dressed, got my milk bucket and headed for the barn.

The goats were restless and hard to milk. Normally I just went to the milk room, they got in line, came in one at a time, let me milk them, and left. Even the rabbits seemed more skittish than normal, and the chickens and guineas started screaming as soon as I stepped into the barn. Now I could have said they knew something was going on, but it was probably closer to the truth to say that they weren't used to being locked in the barn. The door was usually open, and they could come and go as they pleased. Being locked in the barn was different for them, and you know what? Probably that big storm the night before had spooked them because I didn't get as much milk as I normally did, either, now that I think about it. There was light coming in the skylights, but it was overcast outside and there wasn't enough light, so I turned on the low-wattage, compact fluorescents that mimicked sunlight that were the only bulbs I used. I had just finished feeding the animals when I heard a noise behind me and turned to see Lucy standing there in a pair of my boxers, a knot tied in the side to keep them from falling down, and one of my T-shirts knotted up to keep it up. Her hair, which had no doubt had too much spray in it the night before, was standing up all over her head, and her make up was smeared all over her face. She looked a sight but I didn't laugh. Took everything I had, but I didn't.

"I heard the most ungodly noise," she said, rubbing her eyes and only making the mascara thing worse. I'm guessing that trying to shower my way and finding no cold cream—since I didn't own any—she hadn't even tried to get the makeup off.

"Guineas," I said pointing.

She just nodded silently. She was shivering with cold—and it *was* cold—which wasn't usual for the barn and certainly not the greenhouse. That's right, the corridor that leads from the house to the barn is filled with a stream and a greenhouse, and this is why I normally didn't have to light that stove until night. See, as long as the sun was shining that greenhouse and stream heated the entire house. Water is a perfect heat sink—it grabs the heat, hangs onto it, and then lets it go slowly. Of course the same was true of the concrete floor and the walls until they met the glass.

Now how did a greenhouse stand up to a tornado and giant hail? Well about eight years ago one of my listeners who knew I loved to recycle and knew that I was specifically looking for "aquarium" glass called and told me they were redoing a part of the aquarium he worked in and that they were getting rid of all the old "glass." I bought it for a fraction of what it costs new and hired an eighteen wheeler to move it here for me.

Do I have to keep reminding you that the listeners gave me a bunch of money?

Anyway, once I had that I sort of built to it. The top of the greenhouse used to be a walk-through that went under a shark tank and the "glass" in the rest of the house was formerly pieces of the front of a five-hundred-thousand gallon Beluga Whale tank. It's fifteen-inches thick and reinforced. It isn't going anywhere unless something none of us could hope to live through hits it.

The whole place—the corridor, the house, the shop, the storage building, the barn—is all under the ground five feet and then gets its height in the domes which are all above ground. It's an engineering marvel that I for one am quite proud of considering I had no formal education and learned everything I know from reading books, listening to people, and hands-on experience. I worked construction. That's right, you didn't know I was a construction worker. Well I was. I worked every kind of construction—road crews, bridge crews, metal crews, framing crews, excavation—you name it; I did it. And I paid attention and asked questions. Think about it. I got paid to get an education in engineering and construction.

I grabbed the milk bucket and headed for the house where I closed the door between the barn and the corridor. It is a Dutch door; the bottom is solid and there are actually two top doors, one is solid and the other is wire because the truth is the greenhouse warms the barn and the barn warms the greenhouse.

But today it was cold. Too cold for the plants to be happy.

I turned the lights on in the greenhouse, too. I only ever use them when the sky is dark because otherwise the plants get plenty of light. But the lights won't heat the greenhouse. So I open the door to the house and leave it open. I strain the milk, put it in the fridge. and when I turn around there is Lucy again, freezing and shaking like a dog shitting peach seeds. I don't say anything. Me, I would have wrapped myself in a blanket as I got out of bed, or I'd go back to bed when I realized it was cold, but I was a survivor and this girl wasn't. If she'd been anywhere but right here she'd be dead already. She was... Well, not stupid, but she had not a lick of common sense. Or probably closer to the truth was that she'd been raised with a silver spoon in her mouth, had everything she'd ever wanted handed to her on a big, gold platter with a side order of diamonds, and just had no idea at all how the real world worked. Now she was going to have to find out the hard way, and I might have felt sorry for her if her all-but-crawling-up-my-ass wasn't driving me nuts.

I walked into the living room, opened the damper, and started messing with the stove. I stirred up the coals and decided I didn't need to take any ash out. Then I stoked it full of wood and in minutes I had a roaring fire. Lucy showed her first signs of intelligence for the day when she moved closer to the stove and started to glean its warmth.

I let the stove get going really good and then I walk across the room and turned on the fan. Heat rises. This fan forces hot air into an insulated duct that runs into and through the greenhouse where it has a vent and then into the barn. I had the storage room and the shop vents turned off because I don't need heat there if I'm not in there. The shop also has its own heater that I can crank up if I'm working in there.

When I turn around there is Lucy again, not by the stove but only inches away from me. I lose it. "What the hell are you doing?" I demand of the woman who jumps about a foot in the air.

"I... I'm scared," she says.

"And standing five inches from me at all times, what's that doin' for ya?"

"I... I... You're the only one here!" She started crying. I felt bad then because she, of course, had every right to be scared. Her whole world had just for all intents and purposes blown up, and she was in the company of a strange, crazy woman stuck in... alright I'll quit calling it a house, a bunker alright? There you go. Now are you happy? I live in a bunker, but don't you all wish you had been? All things considered is it so crazy to live in a bunker?

"I'm afraid... I lived in Atlanta. I'm sure my family, all my friends, my boyfriend... They're all dead. I just saw the guy I've worked with for the last six years ripped away by wind and then I'm just running, and I know you don't understand that I'm upset because I doubt you get upset about anything, but I'm just a mere mortal and I have no idea how to even begin to find a place in my head to put all the hateful stuff I know right now. I'm just scared, alright? And as long as I can see you I'm not so scared. I know that doesn't really make any sense, but at least if I can see you I know I'm not all alone. That I'm not the last person on earth."

Boyfriend? That just didn't sound right to me because I was pretty sure that she'd been putting off this totally gay vibe every time I'd seen her before. Of course I've often thought that whole Gay-dar thing is screwed completely up by wishful thinking. I only half heard everything she said after "boyfriend." See, if she'd had a boyfriend she really wasn't of any use to me. *Oh well*, I thought, *maybe she'll give the boys something to play with*. To have to put up with her and not be able to fuck her... Well I'm here to tell you that did not help my mood one damn bit. I almost asked her right on the spot if she was at least bisexual or even curious, and then just put her right outside in my shorts and shirt looking like death warmed up if she wasn't.

Useless. She was useless to me, and likely as not she'd get my boys to fighting since they fought most of the time anyway and they were both as horny as the billy-goat in full rut and never had been able to just share a damn thing... Which was why they were always fighting.

The apocalypse was looking worse and worse to me.

Then I remembered the truth about women, or at least the truth the way I see it. All women are bi, all of them. I'll explain this more later for all of the guys who are reading this and saying, BULL SHIT every woman really wants some cock.

"Why don't you go wash up and comb your hair? I'll get some of Jimmy's clothes for you. I think you and he are about the same size."

Scraping her off me long enough to get her to change clothes and do something about the mess which was her face and hair had been like trying to scrape the white out of chicken shit, and she left the bathroom door open a crack I guess so she could hear me?

While she was in the bathroom I started cooking breakfast. I cooked it on top of the wood stove as I often did in the wintertime. There just wasn't any sense in wasting the electricity, and my stove—even though it was the most efficient one on the market—used a lot of power.

The wind generator and the solar panels were off line and we were running off the battery bank. I could always start up the methane-operated generator and recharge them, but I might as well save where I could.

Where did my methane supply come from? Where do you think? My toilet flushed into it for a start. Rabbits and goats both have nice little round-pelleted shit that will roll. I built sleeping platforms for the goats that are slanted enough that most days you don't even have to sweep the shit into the trough. The trough runs down hill into a big sewer pipe that runs directly into the collection unit. The rabbits have a piece of tin under their cage that runs into a large sewer pipe and then right into the collection unit. There is a sliding door between the collection unit and the actual methane chamber. One batch is always cooking while they next batch is getting ready to go. About every six months I have to release the sludge in the methane cooker. I open a big valve and the goopy shit gravity feeds into a big pit out in the garden. The pit is a cement basin with holes all in it and the cement basin is surrounded by three feet of rock. I throw a bunch of ashes from the stove on the top of it just to keep it from stinking so bad then I leave it alone. In about three months all the pathogens that might have been left in it are dead and I use it in the garden the orchard and the pastures for fertilizer.

See I told you. I don't like to waste anything.

We have a machine that pressurizes the methane and then I use it to run the generator, my car, and our four wheelers.

Hey I might have been set up better than most everyone else to ride out the storm, but I hadn't been part of the problem. I'd always lived as green a life as possible. Having more money had just allowed me to buy the technology necessary to make me even greener.

That was the problem. The rich people had all the money and the people who would have used it to make the world better didn't.

Now the rich people are all dead and the world is better off without them. See the mega rich have always been the problem. They consume so much and share so little so that when the end came no one gave a damn what happened to them. They were totally unprepared because the rich idiots never really believed that anything could happen to them that they couldn't buy their way out of; therefore, none of them took their money and used it to build something like—oh, I don't know—a self-sufficient bunker in the middle of one of the safest parts of the country. No, they just bought more and more pollution-spewing crap.

They couldn't buy their way out of the apocalypse, so I imagine—maybe hope would be a better word here—that they were some of the first to die. You can't hire someone to save your ass from sure death, not when it's obvious that money isn't going to be worth a good damn when the smoke clears, and let's face it... What survival skills did rich people have? None. They were incapable of doing anything on their own. They deserved to die, because they're the ones that destroyed the world, not poor people. The rich—with more money than good sense and certainly more money than conscience—milked the world for all it was worth, more often than not using the poor as slaves. The only bitch was that the rich and greedy didn't just kill themselves—of course they never had.

The thing that really sucks, though, is that give us a couple of hundred years and greedy fuckers will have figured out how to get rich again and then all the crap will start all over. But it will take them a long time to completely fuck the world over again and... By then I'll be good and dead so... Not my problem.

I had just finished making breakfast when she walked out. She had obviously washed her hair, her long, thick dark-brown hair, which had probably used more water than I did in a week.

As if reading my mind she said quickly, "I just got it wet, and then I shampooed it, and then I rinsed."

I didn't get into the fact that she'd showered last night. After all I was just being picky. We had plenty of water; the well was full, and after that rain last night all of the cisterns would be as well. I just don't like waste. Waste was one of the things that caused all the problems in the first place. Screw that, it wasn't one of the problems it was THE problem. If we hadn't wasted all our gas, or had worked on becoming less oil dependant way before it was necessary, we wouldn't have needed the Middle East and they could have just kept shelling each other and we wouldn't have given a shit. So everything that happened was the fault of waste and stupid-assed religion.

And the eighteen-plus nuclear warheads. We'll probably never know exactly how many of them were launched in the Middle East or who fired what at whom, when.

I set the table and we sat down to eat a hot breakfast of scrabbled eggs, sausage, toast, and coffee. I momentarily felt guilty about all the people who were probably freezing to death, drowning, dying in a pool of lava, or lying under a piece of fallen debris. I even felt bad about people who weren't getting to eat a nice, hot breakfast of fresh eggs in a nice warm house, but I pushed all that out of my head. Everyone could have prepared. They might not have been able to prepare as well as I had, but they could have all survived in some form of comfort with very little effort. Alright that's bullshit because some places were literally no longer on the map when all was said and done. But certainly more could have made it than did.

We ate breakfast in silence, so I think maybe she was thinking about everyone who wasn't eating and everyone who just wasn't anymore, too.

"When do you think I'll be able to go home?" she asked, and

I thought but didn't say, *Never, no one's ever going to be going home again because it isn't going to be there. At least not like it was when you left it.*

I shrugged. "Weeks, maybe months..."

"What!" she shouted, and she didn't even let me get to years or decades.

"Domino effect," I said with a shrug, thinking that explained everything to anyone with half a brain.

"Domino effect?" So at that point I decided she was a half-wit.

"Chain reaction, whatever you want to call it. We have been just teetering on the edge of global annihilation for decades. When something is tipping so precariously, when so many things are just barely holding on, it only takes one thing to start everything sliding. Once one thing goes so does everything else... The domino effect," I say again, but she's still just got that blank, lost expression on her face. I stood up. "Come on, I have a chart in my office."

She just looked at my chart—the one I'd been making, adding to, and taking away from for twenty years, covered with news pictures and clippings and lines and calculations and estimates that covered most of one wall—with an expression that said it wasn't actually helping.

"Look." I started pointing to things on the chart as I talked. "Birth of religion started all the crap which caused, or at least helped to fuel, almost every war since. To make matters worse, most of the religions said that the more kids you have the better—this led to over population. Advances in agriculture, the invention of penicillin—yet more population because all the advances to modern medicine kept an older population alive longer at great cost to our social and economic structure, and drove up the cost of medical care. Older people lived longer, younger stronger people in the working class died because they couldn't afford proper health care, this means that as the end of the world as we know it hits, there are actually more people over the age of sixty-five in this country than there are under twenty-five. Old people are not going to be able to survive this, and if they do they won't be any help rebuilding."

"The invention of the combustion engine, the American Dream, the industrialization of China, all good things, right? No. All of them contribute to our ultimate problem, which is climate change. The industrialization and the democratizing of China... All those people wanting to live the way we live in America... They started to pollute as much as we were and that further accelerated the problem. At that point it didn't matter how many light bulbs we changed or how low the emissions from our factories and cars were because China was just belching huge plums of coal smoke into the atmosphere as fast as they could. And what could we say to them really? *Don't be like us* just isn't very convincing.

"All these things, every one of them, are the dominos that all got set up. Jesus' followers write down his words, split from Judaism, start a new sect; Mohammad reads the New Testament, decides to write his own bible, starts his own religion. The Germans start WWI then WWII—this causes all the mega powers to freak out so they all go after and eventually get nuclear weapons. The AIDS virus devastates Africa, causes more problems there, and more land gets cleared. The Brazilians switch to ethanol, good thing? Wrong. Mass deforestation to clear the jungle to plant sugar cane. Burning all that jungle, burning the sugar cane to make the ethanol, all leaves a huge carbon footprint. Slash and burn. Bio diesel—what a crock of shit. Growing the crops to make the fuel causes even more toxic chemicals to be released into our air and water. It's not efficient. Crops into fuel causes the cost of feed to double, which causes anything to do with meat or dairy to double in cost. Everything else doubles because of gas prices. The cost of medical just keeps going up and up. America is thrown into an economic depression which only effects what used to be the middle class and isn't any more.

"Stealing freedom, starting wars that can't be won, stirring up the entire Middle East, all those dominos were already lined up. Then they put that asshole in charge of what was at the time the strongest nation in the world and that was when the dominos started tipping. At first they tipped slowly, but they gained momentum as they fell. Everyone is driving a car that burns enough gas to run a city, building houses so big fifteen families could live in them, burning copious amounts of energy. Energy that they are getting from the freaking Middle East! Using more and more, and wasting more and more. And then the Muslims want a holy war and the Christians just want the world to end so that *their* god can be right, and the Jews want the West Bank at any cost, on and on and on and... Katrina hits and no one really takes notice and snow storms get worse, and tornados are stronger and there are more of them, and there are more forest fires, and the Santa Anna winds just keep burning Southern California, on and on and... A million indicators that there is global warming and that we're at least helping and no one will stop all their bullshit to even try to slow it down. Not if it means they might have to go without even one of the useless things they think they must have or life just won't be worth living. And all the time people just keep popping out more kids, covering more ground with big-ass houses, and there is bird flu and monkey pox and AIDS, and all these indicators that there are just too damn many of us, but no one does anything. They just keep setting up the dominos.

"Then Pakistan falls into the hands of a fundamentalist Muslim group and within months they make a nuclear strike against India. India makes a strike against them. Next thing you know both countries are smoking holes. This starts those dominos falling hard and fast. The bombs aggravate the fault line that runs through both countries as well as Turkey. Massive earthquakes and after shocks aggravate a volcano which blows and erupts. The lava runs into the sea, super heating it. Massive fish kill and typhoon hits the coast of Egypt. Between the bombs and the volcano they spew thousands of pounds of dust into the atmosphere. This cools the planet as quick cold-fronts hit a planet that's been too hot for years. It spawns tornados in record numbers and ferocity, hurricanes, gale force winds, and blizzards— lots and lots of blizzards.

"There is a storm coming down from the north right now. An arctic blast, a strong one. It's dumping snow, lots of it, everywhere and causing record cold temperatures. When it hits us I expect we will have the worst winter we have ever had, but it will be bearable if you have shelter and food. I'm not so sure about the northern states.

"But the world will right itself eventually. Could be weeks, most likely months, and maybe years. After that humans will have to dig themselves out and go on. There may be fighting, maybe even wars over food and land to grow crops. That depends on how many people actually come through this, and what sort of people survive."

"I can never go home," Lucy said in a hollow voice. I hadn't come right out and said it, but she'd guessed.

Just then I heard the alarm on the front gate. My boys were finally home.

CHAPTER 3

Please Don't Flush

Don't flush the commode! Water will be precious in the post-apocalyptic world. *Every time you flush you are wasting vast amounts of water. Have a bucket on hand and learn to use it. Or if you're able to go outside build yourself an outhouse. Just dig a hole, put a shelter over it, shit in the hole and cover it with dirt. It ain't rocket science.*

Keep the shit away from the general population. Urine smells bad when it ferments but is mostly sterile; the problem is the shit. So take it as far away from people as possible. Try not to dump it in a runoff area or anywhere you will likely have to walk later. Bury it if you can. If you have a septic tank you could open the lid and dump it in there, again it ain't rocket science

You could prepare by buying a fifty-five-gallon drum and a bunch of garbage sacks. Stick the garbage sack in the bucket, use it all day, and then tie it closed tightly and put it into the drum. I suggest putting this drum someplace where you will just never have to touch it again. In time the planet will right itself and then you can build an outhouse or maybe go ahead and use that toilet. But through the worst of it, fight the urge.

You will want to use the toilet. You will want to watch your refuse washed away like you always have. But if your water runs out you will be screwed. If you have plenty of water from melting snow or rivers or streams, then flush it with a bucket by pouring the water directly into the stool. You can flush more with less water this way, oh, and you could bathe with the water before you use it to flush with, so it gets two uses.

Now I know you're all freaking out from all the shit talk. You like to sit down, go, and then just flush; anything else seems intolerable. This is one of the big problems. You've all been flushing that shit all this time, and if you don't have a septic tank, guess what? All that shit has to be treated and then do you know where that water goes? Into our rivers and streams, then out to the ocean.

If you're in a city that is flooded, guess what? You will be adding crap to the filthy water that already surrounds you every time you flush. As a general rule don't flush. If your area is flooded, then boil and strain not only the water you drink but also any

*water you bathe or brush your teeth with. Try to stay out of the
flood water. If you get in the water, bathe and wash anything
that gets wet. Flood water is full of shit and dead bodies and
every kind of toxic bacteria. If you are in an area that floods, when
the worst passes pick up and try to get to higher drier ground.*

My boys were cold and near tears as I hugged them and then
hustled them to the stove to shed their clothes and warm up.

"Temperature's dropping like a rock," Jimmy said through
chattering teeth. Jimmy is blond-headed, blue-eyed and homely.
The fact that Lucy fit into his clothes perfectly tells you he's not
a very big man and what God didn't give the boy in size or beauty
he didn't give him in brains or charm, either. Yep, Jimmy came
from the short end of the gene pool. Let me tell you just how
stupid this boy was. When he was in his teens I used the
phrase—I still often use these days to explain the cold—"colder
than a well digger's ass." Jimmy asked me why anyone would
want to dig on a whale's ass and if that was why we needed to
save them. Nope, not the brightest crayon in the box, my boy
Jimmy. Of course that was in part because from the moment
he'd sprouted his first pimple he didn't even try to pretend to be
interested in anything he couldn't eat or slip on his penis.

"The Simpsons were all ready to go when the wind just got
colder and then they decided to try to hold up in my basement.
I'm glad my supplies won't go to waste," Billy said, his skin was
red from the cold. Now Billy was everything poor Jimmy wasn't.
He was a huge guy, six-foot four, with black hair and baby-blue
eyes, good looking, and though he sometimes did stupid things
he wasn't actually stupid. That boy could charm the birds right
out of the trees.

You try not to have favorites, but it's hard when the kids are
so different. Hard when one of them judges you harshly and the
other just loves you even when he thinks you're a flake.

Of course the sad truth was that Jimmy was my favorite.

They both seemed to notice Lucy at the same time and got
this stupid-assed look on their faces as they both said to her at
once, waving like morons, "Hi, new Mommy."

And this might have been yet another reason I'd had so much
trouble keeping a woman after their mother died, to have two
grown boys calling you Mom? Well it near screamed that I was
older than dirt, and they loved to tease the living shit out of
whoever I was with, too. In fact, meeting the boys had sort of
been the acid test for girls I was dating. Up to that point none of
them had passed.

"Hello, I'm Lucy." If she knew what they meant she didn't
show it, and I didn't bother to tell them any different. The longer

I could keep them from finding out she was a single, straight chick, the less I had to contend with the two of them running around with hard-ons trying to bed her and fighting with each other. Billy started crying then and he hugged my neck. I hugged him back. Soon I had his brother on the other side. I knew they'd been through hell before they started talking.

I'd put them right on the radio, too. I figured it was more than safe now. I was pretty sure there wasn't going to be any FCC when this was all over. I can't take credit, though, it was Lucy's idea. She said she sort of had it figured that we were the news at that point and that people needed news.

I didn't know how important it was for anyone to do the "news," but figured that hearing what the boys had been through and how they'd made it home might help someone.

"All the streets on the whole north side of town were flooded," Billy started. "There weren't many buildings actually standing and even less that still had roofs. Just like you said, Mom, the steel buildings fared the worst and the old cement-block houses did the best... Though most of those didn't have no roofs. Just like someone came along and opened them up like a giant opening up can after can. There were a few houses didn't look like they got hit at all, but not many. We didn't see many people..."

"But there were bodies everywhere," Jimmy interjected. His voice got a little choked as he continued. "This one guy was naked, just sort of hanging on a tree limb. I don't know if he was naked to start with or if the tornado ripped his clothes off, but there he was just as naked as a jay bird with a big ole limb sticking right out of his chest. Terrible."

I patted his back as I said, "Leave the bodies alone, people. Unless they are in your way don't waste your time with them. Take care of what you need first. The dead don't need food or shelter, so shove them out of your way and get yourself taken care of. It's going to get cold if it isn't already where you are, and it will be easier and safer to move those bodies when they freeze anyway. Don't waste time. Get anything that will burn and bring it into shelter with you. I don't care how much water you have, get more. Even if your town has been flattened there will still be water running out of busted lines for several days till the water towers empty. Don't dwell on the dead; worry about living." I nodded at Billy and he started talking again.

"We had trouble even finding the roads and we couldn't have gotten out at all if we hadn't had the four wheeler. It was slow going because I didn't want to pop a tire on a nail or something else sharp. We were just about out of town when this guy comes up with a shotgun and tries to stop us. I sped up and drove behind a van that was sitting on it's top. I knew a guy pointing a gun at us trying to stop us... Well, he couldn't want anything but to take our rig so he could get the hell out of Dodge. He took a couple of shots at the van. I grabbed my hunting rifle, aimed, and put one through his head. We made sure he was alone and good and dead and then we took his shot gun, just like you told us, Mom."

I patted his shoulder. He was a big-hearted boy, and I know that must have been hard for him. "That's right, people. Listen and listen good. Someone approaches you with a weapon you better shoot first and ask questions later. There are a whole lot of survivalists out there who really believe they're the only ones that deserve to survive. And when people get desperate, people that normally are fair and decent will kill you to get your food or your shelter. And don't ever leave weapons behind. It's that kind of world now, people."

"After that Jimmy just held the rifle in his hands where people could see it and we didn't have any more trouble like that, but the roads didn't get any easier to move on. Seemed like everyone was trying to leave town and they were having to move stuff to do it because so much was in the way. There were people who pulled their cars off the road, gave up, and started walking. There were people fighting over stupid shit like a gas can, and others were helping each other move stuff so they could all get out, but most were just screaming and fighting. Scared I guess. There was a hotel we passed in Van Buren hadn't taken any damage, but they obviously didn't have power and their parking lot was so full of cars you couldn't have gotten another one in there."

Now that is some stupid shit. Move a bunch of people into a small area with no food and no way to get heat with a blizzard on the way. They'd never make it. There was a grocery store close by and even if it was damaged if they gathered the food up and stored it someplace safe, if they carefully rationed the food and water... Well they'd still most likely be screwed because someone always has to be in control and it usually winds up being the biggest asshole with the most guns instead of the guy with the brains and... Unless I was wrong—and I hardly ever am—there was going to be a lot of cannibalism going on. And no need for it. If people used their heads and congregated in places like schools and other buildings with big common rooms, if they found wood heaters and all worked together to find all the food and blankets and stuff that they could, anyone who had made it though the storm would have a really good chance of making it. But the whole trying to get out of town trying to go someplace else... All those people would die tonight. If you got stranded in what was coming in with no shelter and no heat... Dead by morning. And there was no need for it because there were still lots of buildings still standing, if people had just stopped to think for a minute.

"Lots of bodies all around the road, like maybe people just freaked out and started killing each other. Not a cop, not a national guardsman, no ambulances to be seen, just people going ape-shit crazy everywhere I looked. I think some of them people were thinking they could get someplace else and be safer. After the first tornados a lot of people had left. A bunch of them were caught by the second wave of tornados when one of the twisters obviously decided to just go right down Grand Avenue, just sort of tangling the cars up in the buildings," Billy continued. "There are trees down all over the roads. Power lines were down all over the place, and I know for certain that a couple of them were live but we treated them all like they were. I don't know if they are even going to try to fix things, but if they do it's going to take them months. I was never so glad to see anything as I was that gate. By the way, Mom, it's pretty bad bent. We need to fix it."

"And the whole time we were traveling it was getting colder," Jimmy said. "It was colder when we left the house than it had been when we got up, and it just got progressively colder all day long. Just now when we came in, the thermometer in the air lock said it was thirteen degrees." I had a little weather station out there—everything with sensors outside. It was more like a mudroom than an air lock, but the boys liked to call it that because it had two doors and had all that high-tech equipment in it. Yet they thought they weren't kids anymore. Thirteen degrees—explained why it had been so cold in the greenhouse before I stoked the fire up. It was getting cold quick and we were running out of time.

"Listen up and listen up good. All indications, everything I've heard, all that I know from my own instruments says that it's about to get a lot colder very quickly all over the US and Canada, so find a place and hunker down. Don't waste a minute. You don't have shelter? Find or start making it wherever you are and start gathering food from wherever you can. If you can't make yourself warm in the next few hours you won't make it through the night. Right now we have to get ready ourselves. I'll be back in a couple of hours."

I fed the boys a hearty meal and then we all got dressed as warm as we could and walked outside.

I hadn't been outside since the storm, and I wasn't really ready for the devastation. My trees... So many of them were just destroyed, bent and twisted, broken and uprooted. It made me sick, so I ignored it. The perimeter fence had held. It was made of concrete block laid so that there were six-inch holes every foot—sort of checkerboard style. I'd had a footing poured and I'd had a six-foot T-post stuck into the holes in the blocks every four foot and cement poured into it to the top. The blocks went to four foot and then on top of that we strung barbed wire up the T-posts every two inches so it was a six-foot fence. It had taken a crew of ten men six months to build, but it was worth it because all me and the boys had to do was dress warm, run around on the four-wheelers, and fix a couple of holes in the wire part of the fence. We also fixed the gate and I padlocked it. This was it. If anyone wanted in now they were going to have to ask for entry, crawl over or cut the fence, and they'd better not do that.

Lucy had insisted on going with us, so we'd given her warm clothes. She'd mostly stood around right in my way and crowded me on the four-wheeler, freezing her ass off until we had finished. I made a mental note of where big trees were down. If things got really bad we might be digging them out of the snow and cutting them for fire wood later.

At one point Billy pointed to the six sets of metal doors seemingly buried in the side of a hill that was covered in what was new grass. "What's that?" he asked. Which was a good question because it hadn't been there the last time he'd been on this part of the property. It was, in fact, a fairly new addition.

"Insurance," was all I said. "Go on back to the house. We're done." Billy and Jimmy headed back up to the house and Lucy and I headed for the "Insurance." I got off the four wheeler and started checking the doors, just making sure they were all still closed and locked.

"What sort of insurance?" Lucy asked while I was checking the latches.

"When I realized it was going to happen at any time I still had nearly two million dollars in the bank." Lucy looked a little shocked. "Turns out there was all sorts of money in the crazy-doomsday-lady business. Who knew? Any way, I bought six brand new inter-mobile cargo containers. Had a small hill knocked down. Had the boxes put here and then I had them covered in rebar and steel mesh and covered them with six inches of fibered concrete, leaving only the doors free. Then I had the bulldozer come back in and cover it with the dirt from the hill we moved. Now do you want to stand around out here in the cold or get back to the house?"

I got on and she got on behind me but screamed in my ear as I took off, "But what's in them?"

"Insurance."

I let Jimmy and Billy put my four-wheeler away and Lucy

and I went in the front door. The thermometer in the "air lock" read ten degrees, and it was nowhere near dark yet. Lucy immediately ran to the fire to try to get warm. The boys standing next to the stove shucking their outer layers of clothing. I headed to my bedroom to do the same. I turn around as I'm taking off the last of my outside clothes and there's Lucy, still dressed for the outside, and I had to tell her, "You'll get warm quicker if you take off your coat and all the shirts and extra socks you're wearing." She started peeling off layers, and I didn't even ask her why she was still following me around even though the boys were there to pester all piss out of. I decided it was like some take on Stockholm Syndrome and tried to just ignore her. "You should strip by the stove."

We warmed up by the fire, and then I went to check the computer. As you might have guessed Lucy had followed me. I had a text message. At first I thought it was from the mayor of Rudy asking for my help, and I damn near deleted it. Then I saw the "junior" after the name and knew it was his son.

Why did I damn near delete it? Because the mayor of Rudy had never done anything but make fun of me and glare at me like he thought if I looked at small children they'd wind up wall-eyed or hump-backed. Hell, once he'd even called the cops and tried to have me hauled in because he said I threatened him. All I did was tell him if he wasn't ready he was going to die with everyone else, and I wouldn't have said that if he didn't insist on telling me that I was crazy. If that old son of a bitch wasn't dead, he should be, and I sure wasn't going to do anything to save him.

But it was his son who was asking for my help, which meant the old son of a bitch was probably dead, which served him right. The boy wasn't his father, though, any more than my boys are me, so I took a deep breath and read his message.

Katy,
Thirty-four of us have made it through the storm last night. I am trying to get them to work together, and they are trying, but none of us really knows what to do. Can you help us?

Please,
Roy Cockrun JR.

A guy like this kid's dad should have a name like Cockrun. Though Running Cock would have suited him better, but then he wasn't an Indian.

I was hoping the kid was a nice guy who didn't deserve the

name.

I guessed he had a satellite phone. Everything else would have likely been useless already.

Where are you now? I asked and was surprised when he answered right away.

We are in the old Baptist church. It didn't take much damage.

It was an old rock building, not too big, with a full basement. Less than a hundred feet from a big hill—that would have protected it. My mind worked quickly.

Send five people to gather up all the blankets, clothes, and mattresses you can. Doesn't matter if they are wet now; they'll dry. Send five to gather all the food you can. Everyone should dress in layers and take turns being inside. Find a wood stove. There was one in the general store. Get it. Send ten people to start gathering wood. Get all the wood you can gather—pieces of houses and fences—anything that will burn. Drag everything up close. Worry about cutting it later. Stack the stuff that will go in a stove now in one pile and the long stuff in another. Get them started, but you stay here. I'm not done yet.

"What's going on?" Lucy asked at my back.

"Thirty-four people are holed up in Rudy; I'm trying to get them lined out."

Roy's message came back, *Done.*

Josh Wintery had all those blue plastic barrels for sale. He got them from the baby food plant and all they had in them was banana purée. Send five people to collect as many as they can find. Do you still have water?

Yes, in the tower, but I don't know for how long it's running out of broken lines everywhere.

Have your barrel brigade find some hoses and hook them up somewhere. Put the barrels in the basement and fill them with water. Did the town ever win their bid to get on natural gas?

No.

I remembered the church had a huge propane tank.

Turn the gas heater on in the church and start warming it up now. Send someone out and tell them to turn off all the tanks they can find before anything has a chance to make a spark and blow one up. Is the general store still intact?

No, but part of it's still there and the boys just hauled over the wood stove and they found plenty of stovepipe.

Good have them put it in the middle of the church against an outside wall preferably on the south wall... No wait, it's an old building. Look and see if there isn't maybe a chimney that's been covered up.

We found it.

Make sure it's clear. Hook up the stove and get a fire going immediately. The gas isn't going to last long if you use it to heat. If I remember right there is a small kitchen in the church with a gas cook stove. As the blankets come in hang them over all the windows. Use the wet ones; it doesn't matter. It's going to get cold, colder than any of us have ever seen before. Get everything you can from the store and from the other houses, wet or not—medicine, candles, all the food... Don't leave any food out of the church; bring everything you can find in. You're going to need it all. Candy... Anything the least bit edible... Everything. Drag up all the wood you can find. Break it up, saw it up, get as much inside as you have room for and pull the rest up outside and keep doing it till you run out of wood or strength or daylight or it gets too cold.

And then I told him about not flushing and the importance of letting the light in if the sun was shining outside and pulling the blankets closed again when it wasn't. He said they were going to build an outhouse.

"Don't flush?" Lucy asked at my shoulder.

"That's right. I need to fill you in. Around here we don't flush pee; we only flush shit. Four squares of toilet paper per job and the TP goes in a waste can and gets burned in the stove. It doesn't go in the toilet."

"You have rules for using the bathroom?" she said in disbelief.

"Sugar, we have rules for everything."

CHAPTER 4

Don't Eat the Yellow Snow

You can melt ice and snow to get water *if you have a heat source. Ice takes longer to melt but you get more bang for your buck. You're melting snow... Well it takes a lot of snow to make just a little water. Another problem with melting it on your stove is that bringing that much ice or snow in is going to cool your space, so you may want to do it in small amounts.*

The snow will not necessarily be clean. It may be filled with dirt particles and may even be radioactive depending on what has happened. So boil and filter even the water you make from ice or snow. Boiling and filtering won't take care of any radioactivity, but nothing will, so if that happens we're all screwed anyway.

Just before the sun set it actually warmed up several degrees and then the snow started to fall. At first just a few flakes and then it was as if they were blowing it up against the west windows. There was so much coming down so fast that it didn't look real. It looked like movie snow in a Christmas movie... The old one where Rudolph the red-nosed reindeer saves the day. The boys and I were all sort of psyched. We'd always liked the snow. We used to get at least a good six-inch snow every winter till climate change screwed us and all we ever got was freezing fucking rain. Snow was fun, but freezing rain just sucked for everyone, and I was glad that on top of everything else we didn't have ice to contend with.

We were warm and cozy and I was so glad to have my boys home that I didn't even really notice when they started fighting over who was going to cook dinner. I think Lucy was a little surprised because they weren't arguing about who was going to have to cook dinner but who was going to get to.

"They both like to cook," I explained.

"They don't look alike," she said conversationally.

"They had different fathers," I said. I was answering blog questions. There weren't many new ones, and I knew that meant that most people had lost the means to run their computers, but it didn't mean they were dead. "And before you say neither of them looks like me—they aren't biologically mine."

She nodded as if to say she had guessed that, but I could

tell by the puzzled look on her face that she hadn't.

The arguing from the kitchen had reached a crescendo, so I yelled, "Jimmy, you cook dinner! Billy, why don't you go take care of the animals?"

There was a moment of triumph from Jimmy as Billy grumbled something about the size of his brother's penis and went off to the barn. Of course Lucy just sat there as I answered e-mails.

Wireless communications... satellites... well there were just enough booster towers to keep that going indefinitely if you could keep your system charged. Of course I was reaching a lot more people and they were reaching me by radio. I couldn't be getting the satellite images I was getting without the super high-tech equipment I had. Of course I almost wished I couldn't. It didn't look or sound good. From what I was getting from the few people still talking and what I could see with the satellite images, hurricanes had wiped out most of the Atlantic seaboard and the Gulf Coast. Tornados had torn up Arizona and New Mexico and torn holes all through the south. A tidal wave and then strong straight-line winds had pounded the Pacific coast. I didn't even bother to look and see what was happening to the rest of the planet, but I doubted they were faring much better.

See, the planet is all connected, and all of these faults and volcanoes... Well they have been rumbling and not going off and a big one could happen at any minute and... Dominos. People seem to forget that the world is all connected. That when you're talking fault lines or major volcanic eruptions... Well islands have been born or died all the way across the globe from major geological events. You get more than one started by man-made stupidity, and you've got instant Armageddon. It was going to take the Earth a while to settle from this, and even I didn't know how long it might take or even when the dominos might stop falling.

Suddenly Lucy was franticly digging through my left pocket.

"What the fuck!" I said, making an off key stroke that had me telling someone to shit tight.

"Can I use your phone?" Lucy asked, as she fished it from my pocket.

"Yeah, but I think you need to kiss me now," I mumbled, and fixed the whole shit problem.

Lucy started hitting numbers. She must have realized that cell phones would still work for a while and that she knew people she could try to call. I half watched her as I worked. No one was answering. That was obvious because she was either saying nothing or leaving messages and giving out my number. Every time she looked a little closer to absolute panic.

See? That's what grief does to you. It's not about the dead

person. It's about you, what you've lost, and that feeling that you're all alone in the world. That's what Lucy was finding out as she went through those numbers of people she called so much she had their numbers memorized. I'd had no friends like that in years. I hated my family because they hated me, but when Cindy died... Well let's just say I knew how she must be feeling calling people who weren't answering and probably weren't ever going to.

The world was coming to an end, and we might survive—in fact I was pretty sure we would—but the world would never be the same again. It was all sort of surreal then, me just going through what I'd planned to do for years. Fixing what had to be fixed, staying warm, trying to help those who could still be reached. Billy was taking care of the stock, Jimmy was cooking, and everyone and everything I really cared about in the whole world was there with me. But I knew how she felt. That's why I turned into a total coward, mumbled some lame-assed thing about checking on Billy, and took off.

Of course I ran away from Lucy's grief and right into Billy's because when I got to the barn Billy was milking Spot and crying like a baby, which was sort of making all the animals a little jumpy.

"Oh baby," I patted his back, "What's wrong?"

He looked at me like I was crazier than I am, "What's wrong, Mom? What's wrong? The world's coming apart. People are just dead everywhere and more of them are going to die in this cold, aren't they? I remember, Mom. I remember what you said. Watch out for rising water, fire and cold. Everyone was trying to leave the city, Mom, everyone trying to get to relatives' or friends' houses. Cars were mostly useless. I killed a guy, Mom. I killed a man who was just trying to get out of there like everyone else was."

"He would have killed you and your brother..."

"And maybe we'd be better off. Who wants to live like this in a damn bunker? No one wants to live like this except you."

And this is my good kid, so again I say... Why do people think they have to have kids?

"I'm sorry, Mom, I'm sorry, I didn't mean that." He stood up and hugged my neck. Spot kicked the milk bucket over, wasting a lot of milk and making a God-awful mess, but I just held my boy who dwarfed me and patted his back. "You were right. I think I'm mad because you were right. I was happy. Life was good. I liked my house, Mom. I know you always thought it was a waste, but I loved it and all my stuff, and now they're just a huge pile of crap and... Well you were right and living like that destroyed the world and now everyone's paying because I wanted a seventy-inch plasma screen TV."

So they do eventually learn. Of course it took the apocalypse, but there you go.

"You know what I keep thinking about, Mom? There was this girl named Cherry who worked at the Waffle Hut. She was nice and always friendly and I really liked her, but you know how I get around girls I really like..."

Did I ever. Both of my boys suffered from a not-so-rare malady of young men I like to call penile stupidia, in which the victim can look across a room full of attractive, intelligent young women and fall hopelessly and completely in love with the one truly psychotic bitch there. Billy was always with some trampy-assed, drug-addicted or alcoholic psycho bimbo because he didn't have any trouble talking to them or picking them up because they were nothing but trash. But a nice girl with a job and brains? Well he could talk to them all day but he couldn't bring himself to ask them out.

"... So I never went out with her and I don't even have her number and I have no idea where she lives and... Well I called the Waffle Hut when the shit started to hit the fan to tell her to come over, but she wasn't at work and they wouldn't give me her home number, so if she isn't dead already she will be and..."

I pushed away from him. I let the goat out of the head gate and put her out of the milk room. "Come on." I took his hand and lead him back into the office.

"What are you doing, Mom?" Billy asked.

"I have equipment that can crawl up a gnat's ass in Detroit. If that girl's out there, we can find her."

In the office Lucy was still trying to call people, tears running down her face. But her people were in Atlanta, and this girl Billy couldn't quit thinking about was in Fort Smith. If she had hunkered down somewhere she might still be alive and she could make it if she really was smart. Since he'd never fucked her I figured she probably was, because if she was some brain-dead piece of trailer-trash he would have already screwed her and she would have taken a bunch of his money and slept with his best friend and hocked his sound system to buy crank... like the last one had.

And he's the keeper. Remember that when you get to thinking that you just have to start repopulating the world.

If she had a cell phone and if it was on we might be able to reach her and if I could reach her I could talk her through this thing.

"What's her last name?" I asked Billy, ignoring Lucy.

"Summers."

I gave him a look. "Cherry Summers? Her name is Cherry

Summers. You've got to be fucking kidding me." With a name like that it was more likely he'd met her hanging on some pole at a strip club than a Waffle Hut.

"I swear, Mom, that's her name."

I typed in the name and not too surprisingly got only one entry in Fort Smith. I gave the number to my son who hammered it greedily into his phone. Apparently he got the answering machine because he got that same look on his face Lucy got every time she made a call and got it—or worse yet nothing. I took the phone from my son.

"If you get this message call us back at..." and I gave her the number. "Find someplace still standing with a wood stove or fireplace. Stay warm. Dress in layers. Grab whatever food you can, find bring it into that room with you, cover the doors and windows with blankets or stacked furniture. Burn whatever will burn for heat."

I hit the end of the message so I closed the phone and handed it back to Lucy. Between you and me, I figured the girl was dead or would be soon. Hypothermia is a bitch. Hypothermia with a big dose of shock and not enough food or water will kick your ass quick. But it put a look of relief and hope on Billy's face, and that was reason enough to do it.

Lucy handed me my phone back, and I realized that she hadn't followed me out to the barn, no doubt fully consumed with trying to reach someone... anyone. However when I said I'd finish up in the barn Lucy followed. In fact, she followed so close that if I'd stopped she would have run into me, and it dawned on me that since she couldn't reach anyone she was probably going to be stuck to me worse than before.

She tried to help me clean up the mess Spot had made... Why do I have a goat named Spot? Because she has spots, of course, and when I finish milking her I get to say, "Out damn Spot," which I always think is funny no matter how many times I say it.

As I was saying, Lucy tried to help me clean up the milk and tried to help take care of the chickens and guineas and rabbits. Mostly she just got right in my way. I grabbed a handful of fish food on the way back to the kitchen and threw it into the river where the fish greedily snapped at it. The waterfall was running at the far end against the wall to the house which meant either Jimmy was washing dishes or more likely the cisterns were all full of run-off and groundwater was seeping into them. When the cisterns are full a pump kicks on and the overflow runs down the waterfall into the indoor river. The waterfall helps to aerate the water. The water runs into the three-foot deep, two-foot wide trough that runs the length of the greenhouse. When it hits the wall to the barn there is a spillway that runs into another trough which runs into the barn to water the animals. The overflow there runs under the floor in pipes and runs all the way out to one of the outside ponds.

Now the water trough that goes through the greenhouse is filled with fish and plants and snails. Not cod, but perch and channel cats. All our bathwater, washing machine water, and sink water runs down the waterfall and into a box filled with lava rocks and water plants. The roots and rocks filter the debris and what comes out of the rocks the fish and snails eat. We have to watch what shampoos and soaps we use, but you know what? You ought to anyway. The trough has two-foot walls in it every three feet and this helps to hold the water while the fish and snails and plants clean it before it gets to the animals in the barn.

I stopped and was just watching the fish snap up the food. I didn't have to feed them much; there was enough food that got washed out in the dishes, off our bodies, and out of our clothes that they had their own little eco-system going on here. The snails ate the algae and food particles, the fish ate the snails and the algae and the food particles and picked at the plants. The plants filtered the water naturally.

"They're pretty," Lucy said, and I probably would have laughed at her if I didn't think sun perch were pretty, too. "And hungry."

"I don't know that they're actually hungry. I think they're just like my boys and will eat anytime there's food whether they're hungry or not."

I stepped into the "air lock" and checked the temperature. It was now eight degrees; the wind chill was ten below zero already. Anyone stuck out in this—even in a house—if there was no heat source they wouldn't make it through the night unless they near smothered themselves in blankets and coats. I couldn't imagine how cold it was getting to the north of us if we were this cold. I did know the front was covering most of Canada, the United States, and part of Mexico.

"It's really cold in here," Lucy said, and she was right. It was damn cold in the air lock, which was alright. That was what it was for to stop the real cold from getting in the house, but it had never been really cold before.

My mind got this weird picture of a dozen humans with popsicle sticks up their asses in a box marked human-sickles. I shook the image from my mind and hoped that the people in Rudy proper were watching their fire and keeping it hot. I hoped that somewhere the girl with the stripper name had found a place to keep warm.

Thinking about how cold it was made me decide to fill the wood box, so I turned and walked back into the barn, opened the door and walked into the hallway. It is ten feet wide, twenty feet long, and right then all but a two-foot path down the middle was filled floor to rounded ceiling with wood.

"Wow!" Lucy said at my back.

"There's more in the shop." I pointed to the closed door at the end of the hall.

Lucy held out her arms, so I filled them up and grabbed an armload myself. Now the hall was damn near as cold as the airlock, and it is two layers of concrete and all that wood is insulation, too. All but the domed top of the hallway is underground just like the rest of the house.

I need to clarify something now. When I say it was cold I mean it was about forty. So it was cold, but not freezing. Because of the way the building was constructed, even without heat it kept a constant forty in even the coldest weather and a constant seventy in even the hottest.

We easily filled the wood box and then I stoked the fire completely up and got it blazing before I shut it down. I opened the door between the greenhouse and the house so that more heat would reach the plants. I went back into the greenhouse and checked the temperature. It was fine. Of course anything above freezing would be fine, and I was sure I could keep it that warm, but part of me was worrying because the temperature was dropping so fast. We'd be fine, and I wasn't even worried about the plants, but there were people out there struggling and it was just dropping too fast for most of them to have time to prepare if they hadn't already.

Jimmy made a dinner of sausage and eggs and a fresh salad he'd just picked from the greenhouse.

"This sausage is really good, guess we better enjoy it while we can," Lucy said. The boys looked at her like she'd sprouted a second head. "I mean when we run out that will be it."

"No it won't. Mom makes it all the time," Jimmy said. I shot him a look, but he didn't get it 'cause subtlety is mostly wasted on Jimmy. "Rabbits have plenty of feed and they aren't likely to stop breeding just because there's an apocalypse."

A look of horror crossed Lucy's face. "You mean this is made..."

"From rabbit meat, yes it is. And you ate it this morning and you ate it just now and unless you're an even bigger dumbass than I think you are you'll eat it whenever it gets put on the table. You eat meat obviously?"

"Well yes but..."

"But what? You never had to see it when it was cute and

furry, that's what. Hypocrites! An entire society that wanted everything that isn't clean and easy done by people they don't have to go to the club with. How do you think that society is going to fare now, shitting in buckets and scrounging for food? Don't judge me!"

"I... I wasn't judging you. I wasn't going to judge you."

"That's all you've ever done is judge me. Well guess what, everyone who believed me has a fighting chance of making it, and everyone who believed you is going to die."

"Wow," Billy said, grinning at his brother as he figured out why Lucy looked so familiar. "Mom's banging the news lady."

Jimmy grinned back, "You know what Mom always says. Any port in a storm."

"I'm not banging her you dumbasses!" I said. "She was here when the tornado hit, so we're stuck with her and she's stuck with us."

The look on Lucy's face was hard to read right then. She either wanted to storm out in the snow and die rather than stay there with me or she wanted to smack me in the head and tell me off—or she was close to just having a complete mental break down. Might have been all three now I think about it.

I felt like a shmuck, so before she did any of those things I said, "I'm sorry. You'll have to excuse me, but I'm crazy."

"You aren't crazy," she said, looking at her plate.

"Yeah I am. There's paperwork around here somewhere to prove it," I said.

This brought a smile to her face that quickly faded.

"You're right. If I hadn't slanted my reports, maybe more people would have listened and..."

"Did you think I was crazy?"

"Sure she did, Mom, you know she did. Everyone did. I know we did," Jimmy said with a laugh.

"I didn't ask you, shit head."

I looked at Lucy. "Did you think I was crazy?"

She took a deep breath, obviously not wanting to answer, but she finally did. "Yes, yes I did."

"Then it would have been wrong for you to tell people I wasn't. Besides because of you lots of people did listen. Lots of people started to listen to me after you started reporting on my predictions. A lot more than ever would have known about me and what I thought. So the truth is you will have saved millions."

"You think lots of people will survive then, Mom?" Billy asked hopefully. No doubt because of the girl with the stripper name.

"I do. I had three million listeners, and there are places that just won't be hit as hard where people with half a brain will be able to make it."

CHAPTER 5

The Importance of Shelter

After water and food, the most important things for your survival will be shelter and fire. Without those two things you will never make it through the apocalypse, and you can't just assume that your house will get through the disasters intact. You should check out your area. What disaster is most likely to befall the area? Be best prepared for that. Fortify your house however you can. Dig a storm shelter. Keep a boat.

Let's say something happens and you are stuck with nothing but a car. Turn the car into an igloo. Cover the car with blankets, dirt, tree limbs, whatever you can find to cover it with. Put all your food in the trunk but then put a hole from the passenger compartment into the trunk so that you can cover the trunk completely. Block all airflow underneath. Grab debris, whatever you can find, and encase that sucker. Leave only one door unblocked. Build a break around this door and put a fire pit inside the break. It should be protected from the wind and you need to roof it with whatever you can. Then fill this area with as much wood as you can. Is this a fire hazard? You bet, but that's the least of your worries right now. Find bricks or stones—preferably not from a river because if they get too hot they can explode. Always keep your fire going. Warm the stones or bricks and then take them into the car with you. Lay all the seats down flat and put all the blankets, clothes, and whatever you can find in it to make yourself a nest.

You will cook, do your business, and feed the fire in the windbreak you've made. Who knows? If you build something tight enough—except for the smoke hole, come on people everyone knows you're going to need a smoke hole—it might be warm enough to stay out there during the day and you might even be able to have it heat the car during the day, but get into the car with rocks or bricks at night and close the door.

Because of course when the sun goes down the temperatures drop even lower. Even in my house I could feel the temperature drop with the sun. When I checked the temperature in the "air lock" at nine o'clock, it was minus ten, and the wind chill was twenty-six below zero.

I'd just heard from Roy Jr. and they were fine. They'd even found a generator—they had plenty of gas between vehicles and what was in the gas tanks at the store—and were running some lights and a small TV with a built-in DVD system and they were all watching a movie. Believe it or not I was glad to hear that. It might seem frivolous, but thirty-four people stuck in one place for God-alone knew how long, they needed that TV. He said the fire was going good, they had plenty of wood, and as long as they stayed under blankets they were even cozy.

I took a hot shower. Not a long one but a hot one, because the little bit I'd been out in it that day had left me feeling chilled. Besides, when the stove's going it heats our water. A set of coils in the stovepipe does the job, so it wasn't like I was taxing the battery bank to do it. When I crawled into bed, Lucy was already there and already asleep. I turned off the light—the last one on in the entire complex—and realized how dark it was. There was a window in my room that pointed towards the road, and usually I could see some light—a star, someone's headlights, my neighbor's security lights. Nothing. Just pitch-black nothing. Now here's the thing. The neighbors' security lights had always annoyed me no end, a waste of electricity and visual pollution that broke the dark, made the stars less bright, and screwed with fire flies. But as I looked into the black abyss that night I missed those lights.

"The sixth mass extinction," I mumbled to myself, except of course I wasn't alone.

"What?" Lucy asked sleepily.

I was lying with my back to her, staring out the window, and I didn't turn around. "You know that the planet has gone through five mass extinctions. I was just thinking this is the sixth one. Environmentalists have been saying we were in the middle of the sixth for years, but now... Well, this is it. Whole species will die off in this."

"It doesn't seem real to me. Does it seem real to you? I mean you are ready, more than prepared, but can you ever really be prepared emotionally for the end of... everything?"

"No, and it doesn't seem real to me, either. And here's the thing. I would have always just been that nut job in the bomb shelter, ole Crazy Katy, if this didn't happen, but... Well I know you won't believe this, but I never wanted the end of the world. I didn't want it for me, and I sure didn't want it for my boys."

"No, I do believe you. Having just spent a little over a day with you I can already see that your biggest problem fitting in was that you just care too much. Most people don't give a damn about anything. I certainly didn't. My job, my car, and climbing the ladder." She sighed. "What you said at dinner, it really struck home..."

"I'm sorry I just..."

"No you were right. Everything you thought was important was. Everything I thought was important, all of it, everything I ever wanted, everything I worked for, is now and forevermore completely unimportant. I want to help because I know I'm using up your stuff and..."

"I have more than enough stuff, Lucy."

"I want to help and all I do is get in the way and... I don't know how to do anything that's important *now*. I thought I was a Renaissance woman, but I can't do anything."

"But you'll learn, Lucy, because you aren't stupid. You're also trying, and that means something."

She was quiet for a while and then she said in a voice that was barely a whisper, "I called twenty people, Katy. Twenty. In seven different states. Not one of them answered. Most of the time there was just nothing. The whole system is breaking down. Last night when I could have still called anyone I wanted to, whom did I call? The news station. Even then I was still thinking about my God-damned job, and now I'm never going to get to talk to them again. Not my mother or my brother or my sister or my nieces and nephews." She started to cry, and I did turn over then. I took her into my arms and patted her shoulder.

"You did your job. That's instinct, Lucy. It's what everyone did last night. They did what they thought they were supposed to do. Whether they were prepared or not they all just did what instinct told them to do. You just have to find a place to put it. I know that sounds stupid, but it's true. You just have to not think about it and when you do you just have to stick it someplace in your brain and think about something else."

She nodded against my shoulder silently as if what I said made sense to her, and I really figured I was the only person it made any sense to because the shrink had told me that it wasn't healthy. That I needed to deal with my grief. I don't think he understood that was the way I was dealing with it.

"What happened to the boys' mother?" she asked, so I guessed she had figured everything out.

"She drowned in a flood. Before you jump to conclusions, no, that wasn't what made me crazy. I've always been crazy, but it sure as hell didn't help."

Lucy quit crying then and pushed away from me, so I let her go and turned back over onto my good sleeping-on side. "So you don't have any problem sleeping with a queer woman?" I asked.

"Are you going to force yourself on me?" she asked, a hint of laughter in her voice.

"Not tonight. My butt's dragging my tracks out," I said.

"So I'm safe for tonight anyway. Besides, who's going to talk, and if they did who would they talk to?"

I don't know if I woke up because Lucy was spooning me or because it was a little chilly. Like it wasn't cold under the covers but my nose was cold and so was my arm where it lay out of the covers. Now, up to that time I'd never had to feed the stove during the night. In fact, I've always said I could damn near heat the place with a match. I peeled myself away from Lucy—who didn't wake up—and got out of bed, grabbed a flashlight, and went into the living room to feed the stove. The living room wasn't as chilly as my room. I opened the damper, stoked the stove, and then went to the bathroom. When I came back the stove was roaring so I shut it back down and started back for my bedroom. In the doorway I ran into something that my flashlight revealed was Lucy, but not before we both jumped and I screamed like a fucking little girl. Billy came running out of his room, and I just waved him back in for which he seemed glad. See, like I told you I'm crazy, and I have these terrible nightmares, and I have roused the whole house screaming more than a few times. I think Billy was just relieved that I hadn't had a nightmare and wasn't going to run around the house all freaky for thirty minutes to an hour checking all the windows and doors with my gun in my hand.

"Sorry," Lucy said in a whisper. "You were just gone and I got worried."

"It's alright," I said. "Let's just go back to bed."

"I have to go to the bathroom," she said. I started to hand her the flashlight and she looked at me. "Could you go with me?"

Now I know you're thinking I threw myself a little fit right then, but I didn't. Any time I got woke up I have to pee, too. And for months after Cindy died I didn't let the boys out of my sight and I went and checked on them four and five times a night.

When we got back in bed the house was already starting to warm up but when I got comfortable Lucy still wound up spooning me. I didn't complain; it felt good. It had been a long time since I'd had anyone else in bed with me, and I was starting to think that boyfriend or not I'd been right about that gay vibe.

When I woke up in the morning Lucy was still wrapped around me and the house was toasty warm. Still I wasn't in any hurry to get out of bed.

"Mom," Billy said from the door in a whisper. "Mom?"

"What?" I answered, also in a whisper.

"I need to charge my phone."

"In my office on my desk," I said. I had no idea how long the cell phones might work, even the ones with the new satellite technologies. The satellites all ran on solar power and if they didn't get hit with space debris they'd all keep working long after we were dead, but there had to be towers and dishes down all over the planet, and they still needed those to work.

"Thanks," he answered, and he was gone. I wondered how much sleep he'd gotten. Worried about that girl and whether she would call. I felt for him, he'd worked hard for the things he had. He'd had nice things, and now the world was all fucked up and he was back to living with his mother. He just really needed to save this girl because if he could then he wouldn't feel like he'd lost everything.

"What's wrong?" Lucy asked in a sleepy voice.

"Nothing, my son's just trying to find a silver lining in this dark cloud," I mumbled back.

"Do you... do you think everything happens for a reason?" Lucy asked, and she still wasn't letting go of me or moving away from my back which... Well, let's face it, the girl was just looking less and less straight by the minute.

"Not really," I said. "Most things that seem odd aren't even that big a coincidence when you think about it." I didn't want to have this conversation. I'd been on the outs with God and fate and everything else ever since Cindy died, and the end of the world certainly wasn't warming me to them. If there was someone pulling our strings it just seemed to me that they'd have to be pretty damn sadistic to just always make bad crap happen to good people and let assholes rule and rape the world and everything on it. Then to wipe out the whole planet because you let the assholes run it into the ground... Well, that didn't make any sense either. It made God seem like a really bad parent. You know, tell a kid not to do things, then make the kid do them, and then punish them for doing them.

Lucy was looking for answers, and she was looking in that place that way too many people looked where, in my opinion, all the trouble had started. People would live who wouldn't deserve to and people would die. Lots of people would die that didn't deserve to, and if there was some power that makes that sort of crap happen then not only am I not going to worship them, but I have a bone to pick with them as well.

Come on... if someone can save you without working up a sweat and they don't do it then you'd call that person an asshole, right?

The house wasn't cold at all now, in fact it was nice and warm. But it was still really dark and the clock said it was eight-thirty. It wasn't hard to see why it was so dark. The window was covered with snow, and judging from how little light was coming through, it was either still snowing or really overcast.

"So you think everything that happens just happens by chance?" Lucy asked.

I got up and started to get dressed, still not wanting to have this conversation. "Yes, mostly. And mostly when you check out even the most bizarre coincidences... Well they aren't all that bizarre at all."

"Mom!" Billy came screaming into the room while I'm standing there in my bra and boxers trying to pull my thermal underwear on, and I damn near fall over. "Sorry but," he held out his phone, "it's Cherry, Mom. On the phone. It's Cherry."

Lucy gave me a smug look. I won't pretend to know why.

I took the phone from my son. "How are you?"

"Fine. Long story short, after talking to Billy at the Waffle Hut one day I looked up your website and me and my room mate Evelyn are hold up in my car. We made it into an igloo. We have water and heat and food, but... I don't know how long the food will last, and we aren't really warm."

"I'll tell you what... You have the charger line for your car?"

"Yes."

"You can keep your phone charged off your car battery. As soon as there is a break in the weather me and Billy will come get you. In the meantime you need anything you can call and I'll try to talk you through it. You even just need to talk, you call. If you don't leave the phone on more than five minutes a day that car battery ought to last a long time. Is there anyone else around? Anyone that you could pool stuff with who maybe has a better shelter?"

"My part of town is just gone. We didn't see anyone, and I mean no one. the whole time we were putting up our shelter and gathering food and stuff. I heard a chainsaw going, but that was way in the distance. When we came out of my bathroom yesterday morning, my bathroom and a couple of closets were the only things standing as far as the eye could see, just rubble... a couple of bodies." Her voice was a little choked as she said that last bit, something about seeing dead people just reminded people how close they'd come themselves. "Everything here is just a tangle of wires and wood and brick and cars. It took the garage off clean and Evelyn's car was just gone, but mine was still sitting there not a scratch on it. Really..." Her voice was choked again. "I don't know what happened to all the people."

"Billy said a lot of people were leaving town." I gave the phone back to Billy. "Don't keep her on the phone too long."

Billy nodded and left the room nearly floating on air. "Stupid-assed people. If they'd all just stayed put, worked with what they had," I mumbled, and finished putting on my thermal underwear bottoms. Lucy was just looking at me. "Everyone is so pathetic. They were just looking to get someplace with electricity and running water because they can't even begin to imagine how you can live without it."

"So... that's just a coincidence?" Lucy says.

"That people are fucking idiots?" I ask.

"Your son's girlfriend?"

I turn to look at her, some annoyed by her willful ignorance because I know the bitch isn't stupid. "Listen... Arkansas is one of the safest places in the country, except for the damned tornados. That's why I'm here. Billy met this girl. He talked about his crazy mother with the bunker and the multi-million-dollar-making web-site because let's face it, if you had a crazy mother who kept preaching the end is near that's what you'd talk about, too. So she looked the web-site up and read it and she's using what she learned. There isn't anything mystical about that."

"Come on I'm sure your son has dated other girls. What are the odds?"

"He didn't date this one, which means she has a brain. Someone with a brain looks at the web-site. They may not have bought the whole thing, but they at least do like Billy did and they get a survival kit together and pick out the safest place in the house and put it there. Shit starts happening so she gathers water and food and brings it in that hole with her and when the coast is clear she takes an idea she read on my site and she does it.

"The brain is a computer. It logs in items and then uses the data when it needs to. No magic, no giant puppet master in the sky pulling our strings. If there is a God—and believe it or not I usually think that there is—then he's not this guardian, father, punisher, the Bible-thumping idiots have created. God doesn't make things happen. God creates and then walks away. Otherwise, if I believe God can hear prayers, then why doesn't he answer them? If God is everything the zealots think he is, then he sits on his throne and passes judgment, decides who deserves help... saving, and who doesn't. And it's all arbitrary because assholes get everything they want and nice guys finish last and they always have. He tests us? What the fuck is up with that? If that's the way God really is then fuck'em. And if fate guides our destiny then why do we even bother to get up in the morning? Won't the same thing happen whether we get up or lie in bed and do nothing?"

I finished dressing quickly and stomped out.

See I told you I didn't want to have that freaking conversation.

I was taking care of the animals when I realized Lucy hadn't followed me, no doubt because she had to get dressed or she was just that pissed off by my little speech. Here's the thing with me, don't ask the question unless you're ready to hear the answer.

Billy came out and just started helping me, his brother was probably still in bed. Jimmy would rather sleep than eat or get laid. He was lazy. On top of every other flaw that boy had, he was so damn lazy he thought rolling over was a work out.

"Thanks, Mom. Cherry says she wouldn't have made it if it hadn't been for you," Billy said. He pulled a couple of books of hay out and stuffed them into the goat feeders. "She said she can't wait till we can come and get her."

"Yeah," is all I say because I know it's a bad idea to go get a couple of more people, and I just seemed to be working really hard at doing all of the things I'd so carefully told everyone else not to do in this situation for years.

Being a nice guy sucks. And yeah I know I'm a chick but in my head I'm a guy, alright? Not a man trapped in a woman's body, not a man at all, but a *guy*.

"So... you get a little last night?" Billy asked, grinning like a shit-eating dog.

"No I didn't. The girl had a boyfriend. She's straight. Now you or your stupid brother..."

"Mom!" Billy held up his hand and made a face like I'd told him to kiss a pig. "She's really old."

"Old?"

"Yeah she's as old as you are." He made that face again.

"Oh she is not, she's maybe thirty-five," I said. I was forty-five at the time. "And thanks a whole fucking lot. Old! Why don't you do me a big favor and go check the power in the batteries and if it's dropped below half crank up the methane generator?" He nodded and, chuckling, went off to do my bidding. I was blissfully alone for all of three whole seconds and then there was Lucy. I could tell because when she walked in the barn the billy goat bleated, telling me that he had decided that she was one of his girls. She guessed I was in the milk room and of course couldn't get in without letting Spot in and I wasn't done milking Harriet so there was a little goat scuffle, but no spilt milk.

"Sorry," she said. I was thinking that she needed to be smarter than the goats to handle them, but I didn't say it just shrugged and kept milking.

"So what is this insurance you were talking about?" she asked.

I was so glad she didn't want to talk about God and fate and shit like that, that I gladly answered. "One of them is filled with toilet paper..."

"Yet you're making us wipe with four sheets."

"I'll tell you what. When you build a bunker and I crash on you just before the apocalypse you can make all the rules. Until then I make them, you got that?"

She nodded, looking dully chastised.

"Listen, I don't mind hard work, and I don't mind roughing it or doing without certain comfort items, but I want to wipe my ass with something I can throw away. Now you're thinking that's a hell of a lot of ass wipe out there, but I've done the math and it will only last three people about forty years. Now you're here and I've got to go pick up two more—and girls wipe every time they pee and... Unless someone starts up a toilet-paper factory, when the smoke clears we're going to run out of paper eventually. Then I'm going to have to do without something I didn't ever want to do without."

Lucy nodded. I put Harriet out and Spot in and started milking her. "So what's in the other ones?" she asked.

"Lots of different stuff. Dry goods, animal feed, beans, rice, flour, corn meal, seeds—lots and lots of seeds. All sealed in plastic wrap. Literally tons of nails and screws, nuts and bolts. I've got six four-wheelers in boxes. Twenty chain saws. Every kind of hand tool you can think of by the gross. Anything that won't get hurt if it freezes. Books and chain and rope, prescription drugs, other medical supplies..."

"How did you..."

"You have enough money you can get anything," I answered. "Clothes, lots of clothes of every kind, blankets, cast iron pots and pans. If a civilization can be cultivated from the ashes, it's going to be a very different economy with very different values and wealth. And I'm going to be the richest person on the planet."

She looked at me through squinted eyes suspiciously. "What is your IQ?"

"Don't know," I answered. It was mostly a lie I hadn't had an IQ test since I was thirteen. My IQ had been one forty-seven then. It had immediately caused me nothing but trouble—teachers expecting me to do better in school than I was. Parents who thought I was acting all uppity because I was smarter than they were. Hell, there are loud farts that have more intelligent things to say than they ever did. Besides, it's a stupid-assed test, and I knew a guy with a higher IQ than I have who believed climate change was a hoax and that Jesus was the son of God... Such stupid shit as that.

"I bet you're off the charts," she said, as if I was committing a capital offense by being smart, and I knew why. I have a Southern accent and walk around in animal shit and build things. I'm not supposed to be able to have intelligent thought. Let me tell you something; it takes some brains to build stuff, not just any idiot can do it, not just any idiot can even learn how to do it.

Hell, Jimmy still can't hammer a nail straight or level a board. Poor Jimmy.

"Well, sorry to disappoint you," I said with a smile. "If it helps, I am crazier than a shit-house rat."

Lucy laughed then. It was the first time I'd ever heard her laugh, and it wasn't a bad sound at all. "Why do you keep saying that?"

"Because it's true." I shrugged. Having finished milking Spot I stood up, hung my milk bucket on it's hook on the ceiling, and waited for Spot to finish her feed. When she finished I took her out of the head gate, opened the door, and said, "Out damned Spot!"

When Lucy laughed at my joke I was in love.

It doesn't take much for me, and let's face it, she was the only woman besides me and she has an amazing rack.

"You don't strike me as the sort of person who reads Shakespeare," she said. No doubt again because I had a South-ern accent walked around in animal shit and built things. How-ever her statement did explain why my boys had never laughed at my really great joke.

"Yep, I kin read an' even wipe my own ass on occasion," I said, making an idiot face and trying to sound like the "special" kid who used to pump gas down at the general store even though it was self-serve and no one paid him to do it.

"That's not what I meant," she said quickly.

"Yes it is," I said, grabbing the milk bucket and starting back for the house. "It's exactly what you meant. You're surprised that I'm smart and surprised that I know Shakespeare because I look and sound like a hick. The whole damn world all caught up in how things sound and how they look, what makes things high class and low class. You know in his day Shakespeare was not celebrated as a literary genius. He was considered the worst sort of hack.

I heard the generator start up and Billy came walking out of the hall that went to the shop. I handed him the milk and shook my head toward the kitchen. He took it and went without a ques-tion. He could tell I was mad. I started to fill the rabbits' hay feeders; I had pellets for them, but I was already rationing those and that meant they'd need more hay.

"What makes someone who's a professional—like say your-self—better than someone who's working class like myself? Money? Hell, I had more money than I could spend, more money than you, that's for sure. Smart clothes, a house that's too big, and a car that burns more gas than a semi? People like you who thought being green meant you changed the four-hundred bulbs in your energy-eating home from iridescent bulbs to compact fluorescents, who were willing to conserve only as long as it didn't get into your comfort zone—what makes you better? What makes anyone better than other people? Really better. Is it how much money they have, what they think is entertaining, what education they have, what job, how they dress, whether they are respected by other people who only respect such things as money or power? Maybe what makes someone better than someone else is that they live within their means, that they are entertained by the things around them, what they actually know, whether their job pays the bills and they are proud of what they do, that they dress for comfort not to impress, and that they respect everyone until they prove they don't deserve anyone's respect."

I had finished haying the rabbits, and I turned to face her. She looked startled, so I'm guessing she was starting to understand that I really was crazy, and I had one of those moments where I wanted to quit screaming at her. Where I knew that the things I was saying were just mean and irrelevant at the time, but I just couldn't keep words from pouring out of my mouth.

"Maybe, Lucy Powers, the thing that makes some people better than other people is that some people actually *care* about something besides themselves and their stupid-assed shit!" I was screaming then, and Lucy seemed to be on edge like maybe she could see that I was capable of violence. Which I am, and... Well I don't know why I was so mad right then. Maybe because I had just caught myself starting to have feelings for her and then she once again as much as called me an idiot or... Well she wasn't calling me an idiot but she was saying that she was surprised that I wasn't one, and now I think about it what pissed me off was that I *was* starting to have feelings for her and she represented everything that I hated about people.

"You judged me before you ever met me. Well, do I look like such a crack-pot now, do I?" I demanded.

"No," she said. "I'm sorry, but you are way over-reacting. Do you think maybe you could stop yelling before you start a stamped?"

"No! Because I told you... I'm fucking crazy! And goats don't stampede especially not in the barn when there are only six of them." I turned on my heel, walked to the hall that went from the barn to the shop, and opened the door. I tried to slam it but Lucy was in my way. "God dammit! I'm trying to get away from you so that I can go somewhere and calm the fuck down. You want me to stop screaming, don't you?"

"Yes... but I don't want to be alone."

"Then go help Billy in the kitchen or go crawl in bed with Jimmy."

"But... I don't know them."

"You don't know me!" I thundered in disbelief. If she had looked around at the animals right then, she would have known I was prone to such fits over seemingly nothing at all because the animals didn't even take notice of my bad temper. Normally animals will run in terror when idiots start yelling, but mine were so used to it that they didn't pay any attention to me unless I was yelling at them. And, yes, they do know the difference.

She started crying then, really crying. Even more than she had cried last night after she'd tried to call everyone and no one answered. Crying... Well the way I had expected her to cry all along. You know, like the world was coming to an end.

I know that women cry to get what they want. It's manipulative, and do you know why they do it? Because it works. She threw her arms around my neck, rested her head on my chest, and just cried long, racking sobs. I hugged her and patted her back.

"I'm sorry Lucy."

This only made her cry louder and harder. I scooted us back out of the hallway into the barn and shut the door because it was cold in there and I hadn't really had any reason to go to the shop except to get away from Lucy and... Well it didn't look like I was going to be getting away from Lucy any time soon.

The crying made my mad go away, so I guess it was a good thing. "Look... I'm sorry, Lucy. That was just me being me. Remember I told you I was crazy."

She sobbed and then she was mumbling things into my chest that I couldn't actually understand but that she obviously thought I could and something must have been a question because then she was looking at me, her eyes already red and puffy, and her nose running and I had to say, "I couldn't understand a word you said."

As I wondered how much of the wet on my shirt was tears and how much was snot, I pulled a handkerchief out of my pocket and wiped her nose like I would do a kid. It wasn't exactly clean, but hey if she could put her snot on my shirt a little of my DNA on her nose wasn't going to hurt anything.

"Do you hate me?" she cried, and then she was crying on my shirt again.

"No, I don't hate you."

"But you don't like me," she cried, and it took me a few seconds to translate it but I finally did.

"Sure I do... Well, at least as much as I like anyone. Hell, you're my best friend."

She laughed through her tears and then made those sounds that let you know someone is about to stop crying. She pushed away from me and held out her hand. I knew what she wanted so I handed her the handkerchief. "I'm sorry that I made you mad and sorry that I cried on you and I'm just... plain sorry." Then she was making that sound that people make when they are going to start crying again.

"Now don't start up again," I begged. I pointed at myself. "I'm manic-depressive, obsessive-compulsive, all right? In short, crazy. And I don't take meds for it. I tried it once—turned me into a zombie. So I live with it, and the people around me have to live with it, too. I try to control it, but sometimes... lots of times... it controls me."

She nodded like she'd already figured that out, and then she said, "But you aren't crazy." She forced a smile then. "My dad, now he was crazy. Voices talking to him, running naked down the street during the Saint Patty Day's parade, whacking off at the breakfast table—insane. You aren't even starting to be crazy."

I almost took offense at that.

She blew her nose on the over-used handkerchief then wiped her face on her sleeve. "Truth be told, it's probably why I had no patience at all with you or what you thought. I thought you were crazy just like my old man, and he ruined our lives with his crazy shit."

I smiled at her. "And I'm sure when you talk to my boys they'll happily tell you that I ruined their lives with my crazy shit."

"Yeah, but they're alive because of your crazy shit."

CHAPTER 6

Stay Out Of the Cold

When temperatures drop into the teens or below you need to stay in your shelter, leaving only when you absolutely have to and, for no reason—even to look for food—venture far from your shelter if it's super cold. If you can't see your shelter, then you are way too far away from it.

Hypothermia will kill you faster than hunger will. Never leave the shelter at night, and try to wait for a break in the weather to leave it at all.

Keep your wood supply close.

If anyone gets sick it will be that much more important that they keep warm. If the sniffle turns into a sinus infection you will be screwed unless you have antibiotics, and if you get too cold you DO increase your risk of a minor illness becoming a more serious one. The colder you get, the more calories you have to take in just to keep warm, which will tax your food supplies.

If you are very smart you will get some antibiotics and keep them on hand. Now we all know you can't get antibiotics over the counter for humans, but you can for animals. It's the same stuff, so stock up. It will work in a pinch.

For the next few days we had just done what we had to do to keep things going. Once a day we'd all go out and shovel the snow off the windows. The first layer of snow was dirty, but even it wasn't more radioactive than normal when I checked it. The rest was pretty clean, so at least the air was starting to clear. Yep, I have a Geiger counter and a full chemistry set, and yes I know how to use them.

Cherry called once a day and so far they were doing fine. She'd built a heater out of bricks and mud and hooked up a stove pipe. The only time she'd really sounded freaked out was the second time she'd called—she hadn't been able to figure out how to cook. They had a few cans of food which heated up just fine on top of the bricks, but it wasn't hot enough to cook beans and rice, which was what she had as her emergency supply because... Well, she's a smart girl.

I explained she needed to soak them in water over night

and then put them on and leave them on all day. It worked and now she was calm... Well as calm as you can be living in a car igloo after an apocalypse when the snow just keeps coming down and it never gets warm enough to melt it.

I'd lived in the area most of my adult life. In all that time the most snow we'd ever gotten was seven inches. Now there was two feet of snow out there and the wind wouldn't stop blowing, which was why we had to clean the windows every day, not that they let in much light. Even during the day it wasn't exactly light outside. Dust was blocking the sunlight, which was why it was so cold.

Only the day before the last broadcast channel—which had been running news—blinked out. The end of an era. They'd been broadcasting out of New York. The last thing they reported was that I was up and running and was giving out both weather info and helpful hints on survival and to tune their radios to one ninety-eight. I did news and weather reports at eight A.M. and eight P.M, and I had taken to letting them repeat till I did another one. This way whenever they turned it on they'd get something. And I was still getting questions—not many, but some—and I answered as many as I could.

The last broadcast said that all attempts to reach the capital had failed and as far as they knew neither the president nor vice president could be reached. The last act of the president was to declare marshal law. Stupid since most of our military—including the National Guard—was actually still in the Goddamned Middle East. You know the Middle East, which was now most probably nothing but a smoldering, radioactive hole. They also said that New York and the entire northeastern seaboard had been without power for five days because of the hurricanes, and the ice storm that followed that. It was snowing again on top of the five feet of snow they already had and the people who hadn't been killed and who hadn't left the city were apparently all fighting amongst themselves over food and shelter. They didn't know how much longer they could broadcast because for days people had been trying to get to their generators, and it was only because of the police that they were able to be on at all.

I'd managed to contact them the day before and I tried to line out a plan for them. Told them to quit worrying about broadcasting, pool all their resources, and get as many people as they could into buildings like theirs and hospitals with generators. They told me that there was not a hospital in the city that was operational because gangs had shown up in force and stolen the generators and taken them... Well, no one knew where.

Like I said all along, if you were in a city when this hit, you were as good as dead. All the scum rises to the top when something like this happens. They don't have things like right or wrong to stop them from doing what they think they need to do to survive. However, meanness alone won't help you survive a long-time disaster. You have these morons stealing and killing to live, and guess what? They will steal and kill till there is no one left alive because they aren't smart... just mean. They'd rather everyone die than share, and...

Let's just cut through the crap right now and say what we all know. No one in the big cities survived. They all died. The ones who didn't die of natural causes died in the gang wars.

When the TV just went blank as we were watching it that night, I think we all felt a sick little twist in our guts. Lucy, though, felt it more than me or the boys, because those were her people. I'd turned the TV off, got on the computer and radio, and had done my broadcast, and Lucy had been unusually quiet. She'd been helping me do them the last few days, but that night she didn't say a word, just sat in the office. Yep there, she was always there, but I was getting so used to having her shadow me that I think I would have been disappointed if I'd turned around and she wasn't there.

Anyway we were all sort of quiet that morning when we got up and went about our chores. It was still bitter cold, eighteen degrees with wind chill of five degrees. We were all already getting tired of being cooped up in the house with each other. Every day I had to break up a fight between Jimmy and Billy, and we were reading a lot and watching a lot of movies just to be someplace else for awhile.

I was checking my messages, and I must have looked as unhappy as I was because Lucy asked, "What's wrong?"

"The six-year-old is getting worse," I said. Two days ago Roy had written to tell me that one of the children was sick—a little girl named Karma whose parents had been killed in the twister. They had treated it like a cold, mostly on my instructions, but now I realized that, likely as not, the child had some internal injury and we were talking about a serious infection at this point. One that needed treatment with antibiotics, and they didn't have antibiotics—not even for animals. Antibiotics might not be enough, but they might be, and I didn't think she had a chance without them. I had them. I had them in abundance. But it was dangerous cold out there, and the usual ten-minute trip to Rudy could take as much as an hour. I had good gear. It was supposed to be rated for the Arctic Circle, so it should be good enough but God-dammit, you aren't supposed to get out of sight of your shelter in the cold. It's just stupid.

"I have to go and bring supplies," I said mostly to myself.

"You can't go out there. You'll freeze to death," Lucy said, in a near panic.

"No I won't. I have Arctic gear."

"Well you aren't going alone," Jimmy said from the door. I had no idea when he got there.

"Well you boys aren't going with me, that's for damn sure. You're staying here where you're safe."

"I'm going with her," Lucy said matter-of-factly.

"No you're not," I said, shaking my head as I stood up. "I'm going alone, and if I don't come back ain't no one going to be stupid enough to look for me, you hear me?"

"I'm going with her," Lucy told Jimmy. Jimmy left, no doubt to get his brother so they could double-team me. The whole time I was putting the skids on the front of my four-wheeler— that's right, it has a snow attachment—hooking up the trailer and loading it, the three of them had been arguing with me— and each other—about who was going with me. I mostly tried to ignore them as I loaded the trailer with medical supplies, beans, rice and cheese—lots and lots of cheese—milk and eggs. Why? Because five goats give a lot of milk and we can't drink it all, so I had made a lot of cheese. The same is true of eggs and twenty-four chickens. We were trying, but there was no way even my always-hungry boys could eat that many eggs or that much cheese. See, before the apocalypse I'd had customers who bought eggs, milk and cheese. Now our surplus would help the folks in Rudy. I had to pack the food and drugs that would freeze in ice chests to transport them.

Apparently Lucy had won the argument with the boys because Jimmy had given her a set of his arctic gear and she was dressing in it as I was dressing.

I just kept saying, "You aren't going."

"I am it's stupid to go alone. I can hold the gun."

"Do you know how to shoot one?" I asked hotly. And I mean hotly. I wasn't really mad yet, but it was hot in all that gear in the house.

"Yes. I'm not a moron you know." Billy handed her his shotgun and told her how to use it.

"She's not going," I told Billy.

"Then I am."

"No you're not," Lucy and I said together.

"You aren't going," I told Lucy, point blank.

"If you let me go, I'll sleep with you."

"You already do," I laughed.

"You know what I mean," she said.

I smiled roguishly, thinking pissing her off would work better at this point than anything else and said, "So this is what it's really all about. You don't really want to go with me, you just want to have your wicked, wicked way with me."

She didn't miss a beat but just smiled back. "No, I said you could have your wicked, wicked way with me."

I thought about it way longer than I should then said, "You aren't going."

"I am."

"You aren't."

And of course thirty minutes later when I roared out of the gates—we had been opening them every day at least once because it's easier to move six inches of snow than it is to move three feet—Billy held them open for me, and Lucy was strapped to my ass holding Billy's shot gun.

The gear was everything it said it was, but it was still cold, and my no-fog goggles kept fogging up even with the face mask I was wearing, so they mostly sucked but I had to wear them. The going was slow. Heated socks and heated gloves, they are worth their weight in gold—everything fogless goggles aren't.

We moved quicker than I thought we would. In fact, in about fifteen minutes I was looking at the bridge that crossed the creek. The creek was frozen all the way across, which was a good thing because the tornado had mostly destroyed the bridge. It might have been nice if they'd bothered to tell me that.

I stood there for a second and just looked at what was left of the town I'd lived near most of my life. It was mostly just sticks poking up through the snow, nothing but the church against the hill was still whole. It sort of drove the whole apocalypse thing home. It was the first time I, or Lucy for that matter, had seen the actual devastation. For a minute as I looked at it my heart just sank, and it just felt hopeless. But I shook it off. What choice did I have?

Now it was cold and the ice was probably safe, but I couldn't be sure because the water was still running under that sheet of ice, and springs and warm pockets can make ice treacherous. The last thing we needed was me and Lucy and the four wheeler wet in this cold.

I stopped the four-wheeler and got off. "Lucy, I'm going to have to check the ice. You stay here."

She nodded.

"I mean it Lucy, stay with the four wheeler."

"I will," Lucy said hotly, and this time she was cold, so I mean she was mad.

"Come on, Lucy, you don't really think I'm going to make you screw me?"

She laughed. "I'm mad because you talk to me like I'm a child, Katy."

The ice was sound and we drove across, me wondering if

later on I might be able to convince Lucy that a promise was a promise and she had said she would if I let her go with me.

Roy and the other survivors had done a good job. The pulpit was now a TV stand and the choir pews were now set up like a movie house. The rest of the pews they had stacked against the west wall to hold the mattresses they'd covered the windows with in place. They had stacked mattresses three high for people to sleep on and separated couples and family groups with sheets and blankets strung on ropes. They had plenty of wood. They had built a nice outhouse and had even fashioned a hallway of sorts to it from the building so that you didn't have to go out in the snow to get to it. They had plenty of water, but when I got there they still had several number three tubs—new so I guessed they got them from the wreckage of the general store—sitting around the wood stove with snow in them.

"We use it for washing and then we flush the toilet," Roy JR explained. "Mind you, the adults take the long cold walk to take a dump, but we all pee in here, and the kids... Well, we have one sick as it is."

Now there were thirty-four survivors and twelve of them were kids and twelve of them were women. Only ten men, which was good. No, I didn't say that because I'm a man hater. I have two sons. I'm not a man hater, but men burn twice as many calories as women and kids.

"No other wounded?" I asked Roy.

"No... people tried to get their families out, especially those with injured. They wanted to get to the hospitals." Roy shrugged. "Weren't many of them, Katy. The twister, it wasn't natural. A bunch of folks, well they were at a prayer meeting at the Assembly of God church, my folks included, and they just kept praying. Dad tried to get me to take Belinda and our two kids and come there with them. Said it was the only place we'd be safe. But I remembered all the things you said, Katy, and I didn't dismiss you the way he did. That twister killed everyone in that church, and me and mine were safe holed-up in our storm shelter."

"Hum," I said, "Must have been a real shocker for them when judgment day came and they weren't all lifted into heaven... But then again, maybe they were."

"Katy, for God's sake," Lucy said in a rebuking tone at my shoulder.

"Let's get the stuff in and then let's look at that sick kid."

The kid was running a real bad fever and looked jaundiced. I gave her a good look over and found a tender spot on her ribs and around her liver. "Does it hurt here?"

"Yes," Karma said. I thought her name was kind of ironic

since she was the only one sick and both her parents had been killed.

"What about here?"

"Yes." A tear came to her eye.

I covered the child back up and turned to Roy, his wife, and Lucy. "Now mind you I'm not a doctor, but I am an EMT." Roy nodded like he remembered that about me, yet another job I did to get paid for training. "But I'd say she's bruised her liver and has an internal infection."

"I didn't know you were an EMT," Lucy said.

"Two years," I answered Lucy.

"Is that bad?" Roy's wife asked in a whisper.

"Well it isn't good, but I think we can give her a vitamin D supplement for a couple of days, and I'll give her a shot of anti-biotics and leave you a script. Do we know if she's allergic to amoxicillin?" They shook their heads no. "Then I'll have a pen ready to go."

"Pen?" Roy asked.

"Adrenalin to counteract anaphylactic shock," I said.

I got in my EMT bag and pulled out a bag with some mullein leaves in it. I handed them to Roy's wife. "Take those, wrap them in a small towel, dunk the towel into some hot water, and then bring it all back." She nodded and took off. See, I believe in mixing the new with the old. Some of those old remedies work better than the pills doctors loved to shove down people's throats.

"So, Karma, do you know what you want from Santa?" I asked as I readied the shot.

"No," she said.

"How about I tell him you want a doll. Would you like a doll?"

Lucy chuckled. "God you're such a sexist pig. Maybe she'd like a truck; wouldn't you have liked a truck when you were a little girl?"

I glared at Lucy. First off I was never a little "girl." I was a little what-ever-the-hell I am. Second off, hell yes I wanted a truck, but I always got a fucking doll.

"I'd like a doll or maybe..." She smiled, forgetting about the approaching shot and how sick she was for a moment, "...a teddy bear. I like Teddy bears."

"Alright I'll tell the big guy."

"You know Santa?" She obviously thought I was full of shit, though at the time I didn't know why.

"No, but I'm sure the old fat fart listens to the radio and I'll broadcast out a list of what you and all the other kids want," I said. I showed her the needle. "Pull down your pants and let's get this shot over with." Lucy pulled the covers down and then helped the kid roll onto her belly.

"Is it going to hurt?" Karma asked.

"Sure it is, but you aren't a pussy are you?" I pulled her pants down a little and rubbed a fleshy spot with some alcohol.

"Katy for God's sake!" Lucy scolded.

"Well you aren't are you?" I asked the kid.

"I don't know," Karma said with tears in her voice.

I held the empty needle where she could see it. "All done."

"Really?" she asked.

"Really," I said. I had the pen ready just in case.

"That didn't hurt at all," she said.

"Then, see? You aren't a pussy," I said.

Roy was just laughing.

When Roy's wife walked in with the poultice I checked to see that it wasn't too hot and then I lifted up Karma's shirt and stuck the poultice where she said the pain was and covered her back up.

"How are you, Karma?" Roy's wife asked.

"Better." Kids will do that. They'll be at death's door—or think they are—and the minute you do something they'll decide they're healed and perk right up. Want to go outside and play. I didn't know whether she'd make it or not, but I thought she had a good chance, and a little hope will go a long way towards making someone feel better.

"Were you good for Katy?" Belinda asked, and it was pretty obvious that she'd already decided to raise this one with her own.

"Yeah, I'm not a pussy," Karma said, and of course Roy and I thought this was hysterical and Lucy and Belinda did not think it was funny at all.

I lined Belinda out on the medication and the vitamins, and then I went to unload the ice chests as everyone—adult and child—gathered around in anticipation of what I had. When they saw the milk, cheese, and the eggs they all actually let out a cheer. But I became everyone's hero when I pulled out the bag of chocolate kisses.

"We have chocolate!" Lucy hissed in my ear as if I'd been making her eat dried turds.

"Yes, loads of it," I said. "I'll get you some when we get home. That is if you want to go home with me." It was one of those things that you don't want to do, but you know it's the right thing to do. There were more people here, people who weren't crazy, and they were warm and had food. If I were Lucy Powers I thought I'd probably rather stay there just to not have to put up with me.

"What do you mean?"

"You could stay here with them," I said.

"Is that what you want, Katy?" she asked, looking right in my eyes.

"No," I said, probably too quickly.

"Then I'm going home with you," she said matter-of-factly.

I just nodded like it didn't matter to me one way or the other, but it obviously did because... Well I'd just said so, hadn't I?

Before we left I told Roy, "You get the kids to write letters to Santa, put up a tree, decorate a little. It would be good for everyone."

"And what happens when there is nothing for them on Christmas morning?" Roy asked in a whisper. "That's just going to make it worse."

"No, because you're going to radio me and tell me what each kid wants. I have bunches of toys at the house, and I'll come back Christmas Day with some more supplies, and I'll do my best to fill that list. Just try to steer them clear of stuff that needs batteries and electricity and the likes."

"Why do you have toys?" Roy asked.

I looked at him like he was a moron and said, "Why not?"

On the way back we were making lots better time because it wasn't actually snowing and I was able to drive in our old tracks. I was still having trouble with my goggles fogging up, but it wasn't too hard to follow the trail.

We were only about a mile from home when something came out of no where and hit me hard in the chest. I went flying off the four-wheeler, the wind knocked out of me, and I might have even blacked out for a second. I had no idea where I was much less where Lucy was. My ribs were burning as I tried to get to my feet, and something landed in my already-burning ribs knocking me onto my back. I looked up into the faces of Greg and Berry Burkholder, Rudy's very own "military" survivalists.

Greg threw down the huge tree branch he'd no doubt used to launch me off my four-wheeler. They both had guns, and I knew I was fucked, probably both ways if you get my drift.

"So, Katy... Tell you what, you take us to your secret bunker and maybe we'll let you live."

"It's not a secret bunker, fuck stick. Everyone knows where it is." I was trying to think of a way to get my hand in my pocket and grab my revolver.

"You get us in then and..."

"So, let me guess, you dumbasses were ready for the military to come raining on your little Nazi parade and try to take all your stupid-assed guns, but you weren't ready for Mother Nature to fuck you right up the ass."

"Shut up, get up, and take us to the house."

"You dumbasses hurt me pretty bad." I groaned for effect. I was trying to kill time. I wondered where Lucy was, if she was alright, and if she was smart enough to not bring attention to herself. I figured if they tried anything with me they'd have to kill me to rape me and then... Well I wouldn't really care. Lucy was another story. If she was smart and quiet she could get back to town. I was sure I could take at least one of these fuckers down with me.

"Just get up and..."

BOOM! Greg quit talking as his face exploded all over me and the snow around me. I didn't wait; I pulled my gun and shot Berry three times in the forehead.

We were wearing the arctic gear with the facemasks and goggles, and mine was suddenly covered in blood, so I couldn't see her face when she ran over to me.

"Are you alright?" we asked together.

"I'm fine. It hit you, you hit me, and I just flew right off the back of the ATV into the trailer," Lucy said. "I don't even think they knew I was there. They hit you full on, though, how are you?"

She was lucky the four wheeler had an automatic kill switch. When there was no one in the seat the engine died otherwise God alone knows where she might have ended up.

I wiped the blood and brains off my goggles. "I'm alright let's just..." When I went to get up I really couldn't. My ribs were at least bruised, and there isn't much hurts worse. "Alright, I'm hurt pretty bad. Help me up and let's just get back to the house."

Lucy helped me up. "You want me to drive?"

"Can you?"

"Yes, I think so. I've watched you do it enough."

"Then get their guns and let's go." My ribs and back were suddenly killing me. I was hurt, and thinking that I was hurt much worse than I had initially thought. I leaned against Lucy as she drove, which couldn't have made it easy for her. The pain was so bad I thought I might pass out, and I knew then that the ribs weren't my only problem. My lower back had gone out. In fact, it felt like I might have actually hit my tail bone on something. Thank God I was wearing all that arctic gear or I most probably would have been broken all to shit—or dead.

Billy must have been watching the gate on the monitor because he was there when we got there, and when he saw Lucy was driving he immediately asked, "What's wrong with Mom?"

"How do you know anything's wrong?" I hissed.

"You were with Mom for twelve years, and in all that time you never let Mom drive you on or in anything. Now what's wrong?"

"It's cold and I'm hurt. Shut the fucking gate and meet us in the shop."

The shop's big. Big enough that the door is just big enough for the Isuzu truck to fit in, which means you have to drive and maneuver to get everything I've got in there in and be able to get it out—and it's not a problem. The door slides sideways on tracks into the wall. Billy ran in behind us, closing the doors, and then Jimmy was there and the two of them were near pulling me in two trying to help me off the four-wheeler.

"God-dammit boys! One of you on each side. Lock your hands under my ass and pick me up."

"What happened?" Billy demanded as he and Jimmy lifted me.

"The Burkholder boys ambushed us. I'd be dead right now if it wasn't for Lucy," I said as they carried me in the house. "My ribs are cracked and my lower back is out. Other than that I'm fine, I'm not going to die or anything, so you can stop looking at me like that."

"I'm going to kill those fucking assholes," Jimmy swore.

"We already killed them. Can't you see I'm wearing part of old Greg here? See? A little blood and a little brain, not much brain 'cause he didn't have much to start with."

"Damn." Lucy rushed past us and into the bathroom where as the boys lay me on the bed I could hear her throwing up. "Lucy killed Greg. Shot him right in the back of the head."

"Wow, I didn't think she had it in her," Jimmy said.

"Me, either. I don't think she could have done it if she'd had time to think about it." I frowned then. Someone like Lucy shouldn't be forced to do something like that. I knew it was going to bother her. It already was.

"Help me get out of my clothes, Jimmy," I said. Because you see Jimmy, for all his other faults, has a gentle hand. Billy goes at everything like he's killing snakes. When Jimmy was a kid his favorite thing to do was put together models. The more intricate the design and the more pieces there were, the better he liked it. Billy didn't have the patience for something like that, but Jimmy did.

"I'll do it," Lucy said, walking into the room. She had already started shedding her own Arctic garb.

"You alright?"

She just nodded.

It wound up taking all three of them to get me out of the suit without killing me. At one point Lucy suggested we cut my clothes off of me, and I exclaimed, "Over my dead body!" When we were down to just my thermal underwear the boys left. I couldn't sit up. All I could do was lie there on my back—which by the way didn't feel too good on my ass. I realized at that moment it was my right ass cheek that was bruised and not my tail bone, for which I was glad.

"What now?" Lucy asked.

"Don't know, give me a second to think," I said. "Sit on the end of the bed where I can see you." She was standing beside the bed, and I had to push my head back to look at her. Even that hurt. Lucy sat on the bed and I could see her better. She looked near tears and nervous as a cat. "Lucy, you saved my life. If you hadn't killed him, we'd both be dead now."

"I know, I'm not thinking about that, that's not what I'm thinking about at all. I suppose I will and maybe I should, but that's not why I got sick and that's not why I'm upset. I'm worried about you and... You almost got killed, and you're all I have. And... Katy why did you want to leave me in that town, why?"

"I didn't *want* to leave you in town," I said honestly. "I just thought you should have the option."

"Don't you think if I had wanted to stay there I would have said so?"

"I don't know," I said, shrugging, which was a way bad move because it hurt a lot.

"Maybe I should look at it?" Lucy asked more than said.

"Maybe. Hell, I don't know, Lucy. If it was someone else I'd know, but me, fuck..."

"Tell me what to do."

"I think... I think my ribs are just cracked at the worst. They hurt like a mother fucker, but the longer I just lay here the more I realize that it's my back that's killing me. It's out and I could probably get it back in myself but not without killing my ribs."

Lucy crawled over on the bed and lifted up my shirt. She made a face. "They are really bruised already. Can you... Well, can you lay on your side? The other one of course."

"If you help me."

She did, and then she slid in to lie on her side behind me. She pulled up my shirt and started to feel around with her fingers on the small of my back. It felt good, and almost immediately the shooting pains that were going down my legs stopped. It was obvious she knew what she was doing before she said, "I used to date a chiropractor."

Her breath was touching the back of my neck and making me momentarily forget about my pain. Who knows, maybe that was her intention? She put one hand on my stomach just under my belly button, and sort of pulled me back into her other hand where her fingers seemed to be moving my spine. Then there was a popping noise and all my back pain was gone. It felt so good I think that if my ribs didn't hurt so bad I might have had orgasm right there on the spot.

"Did I get it?" she asked.

"Yes," I said, and I must have sounded as relieved as I felt because she chuckled.

"So, I'm not completely worthless then?" she asked.

"Not at all. I feel like you saved my life twice now."

"So we're even," Lucy said. "So what about the ribs?"

"You know what? Now that you fixed my back I can live with the ribs and there's nothing that can really be done with them anyway... No, wait. There's some massage oil with arnica in it on the bedside table. Grab that and rub it on my ribs."

She did so, rubbing so gently it hardly hurt at all.

"So what about your ass?"

"What about it?" I asked.

"Doesn't it hurt?"

"Yeah, but..."

"Maybe I should rub some oil on that bruise."

I wasn't going to argue with her.

"Ouch," she said. "It looks terrible."

"My ass or the bruising?" I asked with a laugh.

"The bruising. It's not a bad ass at all."

"You are the damndest straight chick I have ever met."

"And you're the damndest queer chick I've ever met," she said, but I didn't get to question her about it because then she said in a really serious voice. "Was that the first time you killed someone?"

"In self-defense, yep, but I murdered a man once."

She quit rubbing my ass so I was already sorry I said it.

"What?"

"He needed killing," I explained.

"Why what did he do?"

"You can't tell the boys," I said in a whisper.

"Alright." She got up then and closed the door to my room, I guessed just to make sure they couldn't hear. Then she took the blanket off the foot of the bed and used it to cover us both up as she lay beside me, facing me. She looked at me expectantly.

"When I first met Cindy she was pregnant with Jimmy and she had Billy and he was just a little over a year old and she was a screwed-up mess. She had been a stripper and was on crank when she got pregnant with Billy and she had cleaned up her act and had worked very hard to make a better life for her and for him. She got off the drugs, stopped smoking, got a job at a drug store, got a nice little apartment, and then one night she's closing the drug store and this fucker forces his way in and rapes her. She turns him in, he gets convicted, she winds up pregnant, and her head is just a mess.

"I met her and we fell instantly and completely in love, and then none of it mattered. Jimmy was our baby, and we were going to raise our kids and build a home and have a life. We did and everything was great for five years. Then this dickhead gets out of prison and he starts the paperwork to get visitation rights with our son."

"You're kidding!"

"I'm not. He violently raped my wife, he only served five years for it, and then was going to try to have partial custody of our son. It looked like the state was going to give it to him because he had been "rehabilitated," and they thought it was a good idea for Jimmy to have a male influence in his life since we were both women. We were queer and so it was better for him to have contact with a convicted rapist to learn how to be a man.

"I wasn't about to let that happen, so I started tracking the fucker till I knew what he ate, what he drank, where he went, and what he did. So one night I pull in across the street as he pulls up to a quick pick. I see him trying to be the last guy in as a girl is closing up. As he grabs her and pulls her inside I start the car, pull up to the pumps, and park. I grab the aluminum baseball bat off my seat, knock the glass out of the door, run in and this guy is so caught-up in what he's doing to this girl that he doesn't even hear or see me, so I just run up behind him and I clock him in the back of the head right at the base of his skull good and hard. Hard enough to sever his spine. The only problem is that he dies too quick. I pull the girl out from underneath him and she's bruised and battered, but not raped yet and just amazingly grateful and... Well the whole thing's on tape and I tell the cops I swung in to get gas hoping, that I wasn't too late, and when I saw what was happening I didn't think, I just acted."

"You saved that woman, how is that murder?"

"Oh, better than murder, it was premeditated murder. See, a rapist never gets "cured," there is no rehabilitating a rapist. I followed him because I knew it was only a matter of time before he had to do it again. See, rape is a compulsive behavior and I know all about compulsive behaviors. I hit him where I hit him because I knew it was the best and quickest way to kill him. I never told anyone that before, even Cindy just thought it was fate." I smiled. "You would have figured it out, but she never did. And I don't feel guilty. Didn't even on the day I did it. The reason I don't want the boys to know is that Jimmy has enough problems without finding out his father raped his mother. He thinks Cindy and I decided to have him. That we went to a sperm bank and had him that way. It makes him feel special. I don't want either of the boys to know their mother was raped. What would be the point?"

Lucy nodded silently.

"Do you think I should feel guilty?"

"No, I think you did what you had to do. The system was going to screw you. And I don't feel guilty about shooting that guy today, just sort of sick inside. Maybe because I don't feel guilty, maybe because it was so easy. I'm a journalist; I've seen it all. But it's always been something happening to someone else, and I was just reporting on it I wasn't part of it. Now... Well I'm part of the shit that's happening to everyone. I'm not reporting on the events, I'm living them."

I was suddenly tired; maybe the injury, maybe just being so cold and the workout we'd done that day. I felt like I could go to sleep if I could get comfortable, which didn't seem likely.

I must have groaned or something because Lucy asked, "Don't you have some pain killers in your store of ill-gotten pharmaceuticals?"

"Well fuck, yes," I said, feeling like an idiot. "I've got Lorcet. Write me a prescription and send the boys to get them."

"I can get them. I can read, and I know where the medicine is now."

When she came back with the Lorcet and a glass of water she said, "See, I'm getting better. I went all the way to the storage unit and came back without you." She helped me sit up so that I could take the pill then helped me lie back down again.

"And just when I need you to take care of me, too," I mumbled, trying to get comfortable. Truth was right then I didn't want her to get to the point where she didn't have to be around me all the time.

"Katy, don't you believe in fate at all?" she asked, sounding some agitated because she knew my answer.

"No I don't."

"It's just a coincidence that I'm here, that I went with you today..."

"No, better than that, it makes perfect sense." I yawned. "You're a reporter, you've been reporting on me for years. I was saying the end was upon us, so of course you were going to be here. As for today... You *insisted* on going with me. The Burkholder brothers had made a "bunker" out of old tin and dirt in the lowest spot on their property. Even if the fucking piece of shit didn't blow apart in the storm it would have flooded. Still they knew enough about survival to make it a few days. We drove right past their place on the way to Rudy. There isn't another sound out there, so they would have heard that four-wheeler loud and clear, and then they laid in wait for me to come back. It wasn't even a coincidence much less fate."

"Hard head," Lucy mumbled. "Mind if I take a nap with you?"

"Nope, but I don't know if I can actually sleep on this side," I said, only half joking. My good sleeping-on side was all screwed up after all.

She crawled into bed behind me. "Maybe it will help if I'm where I usually am."

I yawned. I have no body chemistry for pain pills. Any of them just knock me out, and these were starting to work their magic. "Lucy, what did you mean when you said I'm the damndest queer chick you ever met?" I asked in a drug-induced haze.

She laughed and ran her hand down my arm. "Where do you keep the chocolate?"

"So you drugged me and crawled into bed with me just to get at my stash." I don't know if I told her where it was or not after that because I just sort of passed out.

CHAPTER 7

Never Go Back or After Anyone

There will be a time when you will feel like you are safe *and your mind will turn to friends and family that may not be in as good a shape as you are. Don't go after them. Never go after anyone. If you leave your safe shelter and food supply and go out to save others, you will most likely do nothing but get yourself killed. Chances are they will already be dead, and then even if you make it back alive you will have risked your life and that of your family's—because it will be hard for them to make it if the strongest member of their team goes off and gets themselves killed trying to save grandma, and uncle Chuck, or God help me, the family pet—for nothing.*

Those that are not prepared have been willfully ignorant, and they deserve whatever happens to them, not you and yours. So as much as it may pain you, stay put and try not to think about them. Allow them to live or die on their own merits; they are NOT your responsibility. You told them to prepare, they didn't, that's their problem.

I didn't wake up till ten o'clock the next day. My ribs hurt and so did my butt, but my back was fine, and I was able to get out of bed myself though I was glad no one was there to watch me do it because it put me into several less-than-flattering positions.

I heard someone moving around in the kitchen so I made my way in there and found Lucy cooking. I smiled and sat down.

"Jimmy took care of the wood stove and brought in wood and is doing the news cast right now." He knew enough to answer questions about survival and tell them what the weather was doing because I had taught him. "Billy is taking care of the animals."

She handed me a cup of coffee, and even though my ribs were killing me and I still had little bits of Greg Burkholder's brains in my hair, I felt something I hadn't felt in a very long time. I was actually happy. I couldn't tell you why really, but I was. Maybe it's true that being close to death makes you feel more alive.

"Thanks. How are you this morning?" I asked. Sometimes something like killing a guy takes a while to soak in.

"Fine, how about you?"

"Sore," I said, and smiled. "Really, really sore. Anyone call back?" I asked her because I had dreamt that her boyfriend called and that he was living with us, too, and that had irritated me no end.

"You mean the people I called?" she asked turning back to the stove.

"Yeah."

"No, no one's going to call, you know that, Katy," she said, and she was sad. But the news just made me that much happier, which I know makes me a terrible person, but I just don't care and the truth is the truth.

"Sorry," I said.

She set a plate of eggs and cheese with some slices of tomatoes in front of me.

"You found a tomato?"

"Two actually," Lucy said. "In fact, the plants seem to be doing fine even with mostly artificial light. You want another pain pill?"

"No, my God I'll be out for a week. Maybe some ibuprofen... You know you don't have to wait on me."

"I'm sponging off of you. I think I should do something. You took care of me, so it seems only right I should at least try to take care of you while you're healing."

"Well you just flat-assed fixed my back," I said. I started eating breakfast as the boys came in, no doubt smelling food. Turned out Lucy was a good cook, at least as good as me or the boys.

"I'm not as good at reading that satellite thing as you are, Mom, but it looks like there may be a break in the weather," Jimmy said.

"Then we can go get Cherry and Evelyn," Billy said excitedly.

"First off let me take a look at the satellite. Second, I'm not going to be able to go anywhere for at least a week."

"We can go, Mom," Billy said. "Jimmy and I can go. We'll put a snow machine kit on one of the other four wheelers, take two, carry lots of guns and ammo, and wear flack jackets."

"You have flack jackets!" Lucy asked in disbelief.

"Mom has damn near everything." Jimmy laughed.

"It's too dangerous. I have to go..."

"Why, because you're bullet proof?" Lucy asked, suddenly obviously really pissed off. "You damn near got killed yesterday. And why weren't we wearing flack jackets if you had them?"

It was a damn good question. If I'd been wearing one I probably wouldn't have gotten my ribs cracked at all, but the truth was I just really didn't think they were necessary. And when the Burkholder boys were standing over me with their guns the flack jacket really wouldn't have helped because... Well they can shoot you in the head, and that close the jackets aren't much good anyway.

"She's right, Mom. Jimmy and I can do this. If there is a break in the weather we should go before it gets bad again," Billy said. "We're grown men, Mom; we can take care of ourselves."

"We shouldn't go after them at all," I said, angry because they were all ruining the good happy I'd had going on. "You never go back for people, never go after them. It's stupid and..."

"But we're set up to do it, Mom. You say that, but then we're set up to do it. You went to Rudy yesterday to take care of those people and, don't take it personal, Mom, but they all hated you. They would probably all be dead if it wasn't for you, and you went there yesterday to bring them supplies and work on that sick kid even though they have always treated you like the devil's own sperm."

Devil's own sperm. It warmed me to hear him use that because it was one of my own little sayings. Ah, tradition.

In all the hubbub I'd forgotten about Karma... Which, well talking about that kid just sounds weird because of her name, doesn't it?

"You aren't going. You certainly aren't going without me. They are doing fine, so it's a stupid risk for nothing. I'll be well soon and then we'll go if the weather's good enough. We'll bring a bunch of supplies to the group holed up at Northside High, too. Yesterday morning I picked up a distress call on the short-wave radio. A cop is holed up there with about sixty people. He said they'd been able to get a couple of wood heaters going and that there was quite a bit of food in the cafeteria but they could use a little more and they are in bad need of light. But we aren't going till it's clear and then Billy, you and I will go and your brother will stay here with Lucy."

"Oh I'm going," both Jimmy and Lucy said.

"Yes, that's smart. Let's risk everyone's life and shut down all the good we're doing here to go and get these girls. Billy and I will go. You two will stay here and we'll go when there is a break in the weather and I can go. Now, I don't want to talk about it anymore. I was in a good mood and you're all ruining it."

There was silence around the table and I ate my breakfast in peace and then went to check and see if there was any news of my patient. There was. Roy thanked me said everyone was in better spirits than they had been since the tornado hit and that Karma was already much improved and couldn't quit talking about Christmas. He sent me a list of the toys the kids wanted and as luck would have it I had nearly all of them. What I didn't have we could substitute or build.

Lucy walked in the office. "Well?" she asked.

"Roy says Karma is on her way to recovery."

Lucy sighed with relief. "Good. What about the weather?"

"Well it looks like Jimmy is right. There is going to be a break in the weather, but it won't last more than twenty-four hours and then there is another storm." I pointed to it on the screen. "A big, bad-assed one."

"I know why you don't want them to go," Lucy said. "But they are both grown men and..."

"They aren't going, Lucy."

"But what if this is the only window, the only break for... Well what if it's months till there is another one?"

"Then they'll all just have to survive by the skin of their own teeth, that's what. I'm prepared, I shouldn't have to risk my life or my sons' lives for them, and maybe the fact that I did almost get killed yesterday on my mission of mercy is making me realize that there isn't much out there worth leaving here for."

"But you'd go," Lucy said in an accusatory fashion. "You'd go if your ribs weren't absolutely killing you."

"Let me see if you can understand this, Lucy. I'll risk my life before I'd risk my sons'—or yours for that matter."

"I know that, I just don't understand why you think you're expendable."

"I don't."

"But you act like you do, Katy," Lucy said.

Did I? I didn't think that I did. It was just that I couldn't stand to lose anyone else that I loved, and if I did something and got killed... Well then I wouldn't have to worry about any of them anymore would I? My sons could do all the stupid shit they wanted after I was dead.

I spent most of the day giving weather reports. At least for a change I had some good news. It would be short-lived, and it would only be from eastern Oklahoma through Arkansas and parts of Louisiana, Tennessee and Mississippi, but it just might be enough time for people to get out and get some more supplies, reinforce their shelters, make things a little more secure, and get more wood. I was telling them to make sure things were safe and if they were then now was the time to check out their area and try to find more supplies and more water sources. I kept checking the satellite images and just kept updating the weather. Unfortunately for anyone from Illinois east, our "warm" front was pushing an even colder front on top of them.

By five o'clock that afternoon I was spent and my ribs were killing me. Lucy had been helping me all day, and I'd been teaching her how to use and read all the equipment. She seemed to be most in her element in the office. I even let her do one of the broadcasts, thinking people would be getting tired of listening to me by now.

I kept starting to get up or sit down myself, but I really couldn't, and Lucy would run over and help me without being asked.

Seriously, I was really enjoying the attention.

The boys made dinner and then we all sat around and watched a movie. I sat in my chair, reared back, and found I was actually comfortable. At one point Lucy had left, gone to my bedroom and come back with the arnica oil. She rubbed it into my ribs while the boys made teasing noises.

I ignored them.

So did Lucy.

When the movie was over I just wanted to go to sleep, but was more than ready to wash the brains and blood out of my hair.

I wasn't sure about taking my thermal underwear off, though, so I kept putting it off till I couldn't stand it any longer. Then I steeled myself and put my legs down. It hurt a lot, but I got up, went to the bathroom, and started to get undressed. Outside the bathroom door Lucy asked, "Do you need help?"

Yes, yes I fucking did. Bending over was excruciating, but I didn't want Lucy to see me naked.

"No I've got it thanks, could you bring me some pajamas?" Because of course I had forgotten those.

"Sure."

I got in the shower and broke my own rule about the shower. It wasn't a problem. The waterfall was running, which meant the cisterns were all full to running over with snow melt. Yeah, against the domes even in this cold the snow was melting and running into the cisterns, which was just one of the reasons I checked it for radioactivity.

I let the water run, the hot water feeling good on my battered body, because now I could see dozens of bruises all over my frame, not just the huge ones on my ribs and my ass. I washed Greg's DNA out of my hair, glad that I kept it short because it meant it would dry fast. I finally turned the water off and got out then I just looked at the towel. I dreaded trying to dry myself.

"Do you need help?" Lucy asked again from outside the door.

Yes, of course I did, but in my mind my ever-so-slight chance of getting Lucy into the sack was never going to happen if she saw my fat, sagging, forty-five-year-old body naked in good light.

I must have been quiet too long. "Do you need help, hard head?"

Undressing had just about killed me. Drying myself off and putting on more clothes... I just didn't want to even think about it.

"Jimmy or Billy could..."

"Fuck, Katy, you don't have anything I don't have."

"Oh yes I fucking do. Cellulite and flab, and my boobs are on my knees."

"You're fucking ridiculous." And then she just walked in.

I tried to grab the towel and cover myself, but moving too fast sent a pain through me that caused me to jerk my hand back, which wasn't much better.

Lucy laughed, grabbed the towel, and just started drying me off. I was glad I didn't have a dick because if I did I no doubt would have gotten a boner.

"Thanks," I said, feeling my face was about as red as it could get without blood pouring from every pore.

"Maybe we should wrap those ribs?" she asked, helping me put my pajamas on.

"Maybe." Truth is there have always been two schools of thought on wrapping cracked ribs. On the one hand, wrapping them might make them feel better. On the other hand, when you breathe your ribs move, and pushing against the wrappings could actually make them worse. "Not right now."

"Hey, Mom, I made some hot chocolate. You want some?" Billy asked from outside the door.

"Yeah sure," I said, thinking it would help me sleep. I sure as hell wasn't taking another Lorcet if I could help it. I didn't like being that out of it and had never understood why anyone would want to be.

"Me, too," Lucy said. She looked at me and smiled. "You know... You actually have a pretty good body."

I smiled back, embarrassed, but said, "I bet you say that to all the butch dykes you have to spend the apocalypse with."

She left and I combed my hair. Even that hurt.

The minute I finished that hot chocolate I was done in, so I brushed my teeth and headed to bed. Lucy wasn't far behind me, and I hardly remembered her coming in.

When I woke up at ten o'clock the next morning with Lucy still beside me I knew what the little fuckers had done. They had doped us. I shook Lucy awake.

"What, what!" she hollered.

"Help me up. Those little fuckers," I said as an explanation.

I wasn't wrong. The boys were gone, and I found a note on

the kitchen table.

> *Mom,*
>
> *I know you're going to be pissed as hell, but we had to go. There may not be another chance. I loaded up with supplies*—and here there was a list of all they had taken, and not too surprisingly he had taken everything I would have. *We are armed and armored and we will be careful.*
>
> *We have taken care of all the animals and with any luck we should be back in time to do the evening chores as well.*
>
> *You were both sleeping so soundly we didn't want to wake you up to fight with us.*
>
> *Billy and Jimmy*

But it was in Billy's handwriting.

"Wake us up! A Mack truck could have run in here and we wouldn't have even turned over. The little fuckers doped us," I said to Lucy, who had walked in wearing a pair of Jimmy's pajamas and rubbing her eyes, still sleepy.

"Maybe we were just tired," Lucy said, shrugging and put some coffee on.

"Maybe trained monkeys will fly right out of my ass, too," I said angrily. "Fucking stupid little bastards." I was worried sick about them, which of course just made me want to kill them.

"How are your ribs?" she asked.

They were actually better. A lot better, which just made me sure that I was right and they had just been bruised or cracked, not actually broken. "Well I'm not going dancing any time soon, but they're actually pretty good. The little fuckers! They saw what the Lorcet did to me yesterday and they put some in that damn hot chocolate. If they come back alive I'm going to beat them to death, those stupid fucks."

"Actually that's pretty smart. They really are your boys," Lucy said with a laugh as she started to make breakfast.

"What's that supposed to mean?" I demanded.

"That it sounds like something you would do if you had to get around you."

I was sure that made sense on her planet.

She walked by me on her way to the refrigerator and I got a whiff of her. She smelled good, and I know she was wearing the same deodorant and using the same shampoo that me and the boys were because it was all we had, but it smelled different on her.

She looked at me as if she knew exactly what I was thinking, smiled, shook her head, and put the eggs and bread down on the counter.

"What?" I demanded.

"Nothing," she said, and just started working on making breakfast. I mostly mumbled shit about how stupid my sons were the whole time she was cooking and we were eating. She just listened, so I think maybe she knew I just needed to blow off some steam.

"They'll call if they get in trouble," Lucy said.

"They are huge dumbasses and... I'm cold. Is it cold in here?"

"A little."

"I bet the dumbasses didn't feed the God-damned stove, stupid fuckers." I got up with only a little twinge of pain, turned to Lucy and said, "My ribs are much, much better."

"Maybe they did you a favor, drugging you. Maybe you needed a good, solid..." she was counting, "...fourteen hours of sleep."

"Oh, I'm kicking their asses, Lucy. Just as soon as I get back to my full strength I'm going to kick their asses good. Don't even try to talk me out of it. And if I have to go after the little fuckers with my ribs all buggered up... Well they just better hope I don't have to go after their asses."

Lucy followed me into the living room and to the stove. I started to bend over to take care of it but I didn't feel THAT good yet.

"I'll do it, Katy," Lucy said. She opened the damper, stirred the coals, and threw in some wood. She let out a yelp.

"Damn," she said and shut the door.

"What did you do?" I walked up to her and she held up her finger there was... Well more a timber sticking out of her finger than a splinter. I took her hand and pulled it out with my teeth.

"Thanks," she said. She took her finger, which had a speck of blood on it, put it in her mouth and sucked on it. I swear I nearly came in my pants. She pulled the finger out, looked at it and said, "It's alright." And then she looked up at me.

Her face was right there, her lips. And she was looking at me *that way*; you know what I mean. *That way*. And suddenly I didn't care how my ribs felt or if she was straight. I bent down and kissed her gently on the lips and when she kissed me back I wrapped my arms around her and I really kissed her and... Well she kissed me like I'd never been kissed in my life. Maybe I still had enough Lorcet in my system that the ribs didn't hurt, and maybe I was just so fucking horny that over-rode even the pain, but in that moment I forgot all about my cracked ribs. I mean, come on, I couldn't even masturbate because she was in my bed, and someone was always outside the fucking bathroom door.

Our lips parted for a second, both of us just catching our breath. Her chest was moving up and down and my own heart was pounding in my ears. If I had ever wanted anything or anyone more than I wanted her in that moment I don't know who or what it was.

I just couldn't get my hands on her quick enough, and the more I kissed her the more I wanted her. Before I was aware I'd done it I had her shoved against a wall and my hands were up her shirt. When my hands caressed the flesh of her breasts she shook, and my blood ran so hot I swear I could feel it pumping through my veins. I moved my mouth to her neck and just started nibbling and kissing her throat.

"Oh my God," Lucy said, and her hands grabbed my ass and pulled me tightly to her and then she was grinding herself against me.

My hands left her breasts and ran down her body till they were on the top of her pants. Elastic, elastic is a horny woman's best friend. I was in her pants in seconds and then my fingers were caressing her. Then they were in her and her hands, which had moved to my shoulders, grabbed me in a death grip.

"Do it, oh God, do it, do it!" she demanded, slamming herself against my hand hard. I started working my fingers in and out of her harder, faster, never forgetting to work her clit with my thumb. "Come on harder!" she yelled out. She was already coming and close to climax, so I knew two things. The woman was every bit as queer as I was and she liked it a little rough—which made her just about perfect.

We wound up in bed taking turns on each other till my ribs were pounding and I felt like there was no blood left in my head at all.

I was lying on my back looking at the ceiling just feeling like I'd really done something to be proud of, and Lucy was lying beside me making little circles with her finger on my stomach. "Christ! I never thought you were going to make a move on me."

"Me! You said you were straight," I said in disbelief.

"No I didn't," she said, a confused tone to her voice.

"Come on! You said you had a boyfriend. Same difference."

"Oh, come on, you never had a girlfriend you called a boyfriend just to keep people from asking questions you didn't want to answer?"

"No," I said truthfully.

"How could you not know?"

"Why didn't you just tell me?"

"I thought it was obvious. Besides," she sighed, "I had a girlfriend. In the beginning I didn't want to have sex with you... Well, that's not true because I did, but I didn't feel like it would be right. I mean... there was a chance she could have been alive. Maybe she still is. Then one day I realized that even if she is alive I'd still rather be with you, but you just would not make a move."

"God, you are such a fucking girl! I would have jumped your bones in a heart beat if I had even the slightest notion that you were even remotely interested in me."

"And you're such a guy! Why did I have to tell you? Why couldn't you just tell? I was spooning you every fucking night for God's sake. Besides you're a fucking top and from what I know about tops they always have to make the first move."

Was I a top? I really wasn't sure. I was just gay. I hadn't ever hung out in clubs, read gay magazines, or been in with the hip gay culture. I did like to be in control sexually, but then I liked to lay back and get done, too, so... I don't know. And does it really fucking matter? The truth was I'd always rather a girl made the first move because then I didn't have to worry about getting smacked down emotionally or physically.

"So... do you believe in fate?" Lucy asked.

"Come on, Lucy. Ten percent of the population was gay. The odds are really good that you'd be gay—a one in ten chance."

Lucy laughed. "So there is no magic then?"

"I didn't say that, and if I wasn't all crippled up, and if I hadn't already fucked you till my brain is numb, we'd make some more right now."

That was when the gate alarm went off. I was buck-naked, so was Lucy, and even though I'd been worried sick about them—until Lucy had taken my mind off of it—I wasn't ready for the boys to be home yet. I got up and walked naked to the office where on the monitor I could see Billy undoing the lock. I could see Jimmy, too, and two more people. So my boys were home safe and they'd done what they'd set out to do and... I was going to kill those little fuckers just as soon as they got to the house.

CHAPTER 8

Everything Can Have More Than One Purpose

If you weren't well prepared, or you were prepared but an unforeseen catastrophe took out part or all of your supplies, then you aren't going to be able to run to your nearest Wal-Mart and get what you need. And nine will get you ten you aren't going to find what you need just lying around on the ground at your feet. You're going to have to be able to take what you can find and make it into what you need.

Don't wait till the last minute to start seeing how things might be used in the future; start right now. Look around yourself at what you have in your house and what other people might have in theirs. What could be repurposed and how might you turn one item into another? What could your washing machine be turned into—part of a wall, storage for water, a wood stove?

Let's say a volcanic eruption is spewing ash. Well, ash is very heavy and you can't breathe the shit; it will kill you. You have to cover all your windows and doors as best you can. If you were smart you kept a store of plastic sheeting and duct tape. If not then wet sheets and use those. But here's the big problem—the one problem that people who aren't in that immediate blast zone don't think about. The weight of the ash will start to crush buildings if it gets too thick. Rooms with shorter spans may be safe, but the roof in say your living room is a long span. Unsupported it cannot stand up to the weight. With volcanic ash it doesn't take much—an inch or more can cause problems—but snow, if there is enough of it, can cause the same problem.

Don't wait till the last minute to start thinking about what might make good support pillars. You have books, you have furniture, turn them into pillars to support your ceiling then crawl into the attic and use the same sorts of things to shore up your roof joists above your pillars.

You'll have to think on your feet because even if you were ready for ten different scenarios you may get hit with one you never thought of.

Plastic bottles are and will be everywhere. The obvious thing is to fill them with potable water, but they could have hundreds of different uses. They could be tied together and made into flotation *devices, filled with sand and used as weights to hold down tarps, cut in half and used as scoops or bowls. You could flatten them, tie them to sticks, and use them for oars. They could be used as insulation, burned as fuel, any number of things.*

Think about what might be there and how you could use it. Most everything you are using today could be used as something else.

I greeted the boys in the shop—fully dressed even if we did it in a bit of a hurry—and before they could even get the shop doors closed thundered, "Which one of you little fuckers had the bright idea to dope mommy?"

"We didn't," Jimmy said.

Boy can look anyone else right in the eye and lie. He tries to lie to me, but he can't look me in the eye and do it so I know when he's lying.

"Which one?" I demanded.

"Mine, Mom, it was all my idea," Billy said. "It was just a couple of Lorcet. You needed the sleep anyway."

"Don't you fucking dare... and you doped Lucy, too. What the hell for?"

"Because I figured she would wake you up because she knew you didn't want us to go," Billy said.

"Fucking little assholes!" I roared.

"Mom, we're all freezing," Billy said.

"Alright everyone come on in but Billy. You can by God stay here and clean up all the gear." I glared at him through slitted eyes, daring him to defy me. "When I get better I'm going to kick your ass when you least fucking expect it."

Lucy took my hand and started leading me back towards the house, nearly skipping. I heard the boys giggle, knew they knew what had happened while they were gone, and my face turned red.

"Shut the fuck up!" I ordered them, which just made them both laugh louder.

Lucy looked up at me and smiled. I smiled back. "I want to kill them you know," I said to her.

"I know, but they're alright and we're more than alright."

I untangled my hand from hers and put my arm across her shoulders, not caring that it hurt. "I don't think I've ever been as alright as I am right now."

"Me either." She put her arm around my waist, careful not to hit my ribs.

The boys and the girls—who were so bundled up you couldn't see them at all—rushed past us and we stopped in the green-house to cop a quick feel.

"Mom!" Jimmy screamed down the hall at us.

"What!"

"Evelyn is sick. Can you come check her out?"

"Sure!" I sighed, and Lucy and I walked into the house hand in hand.

They stank to high heavens, no doubt because they hadn't had a bath since the apocalypse. They smelled like BO and bad breath and smoke and days of clothing-filtered bean farts.

Evelyn was running a fever; she was dehydrated, way underweight, and barely coherent.

"Diarrhea?" I asked the girl. She nodded. Too much cold, exposure sickness, it was a condition that used to only happen to idiots who tried to climb frozen mountains.

"Cherry, get both of your clothes—all of them—off and throw them on the floor outside the bathroom. Billy will take them and put them in the washer. Then get a good, hot shower, both of you. She needs help."

Cherry nodded.

Evelyn's teeth were chattering.

"Quick, girl. While you're showering I'll set up what we need."

I set up the couch in the living room to be Evelyn's sick bed. Well, actually Lucy mostly made up the bed because I was still having trouble bending over. I put up the pole and set up the IV.

"What's wrong with her?" Lucy asked.

"I can't be sure, but I think it's dysentery caused from prolonged exposure, dehydration mostly, maybe pneumonia."

"Why isn't the other girl sick then?"

"Well mind you it's hard to tell through the twenty layers of clothing, but I think Cherry is a little thicker than this girl." Which some confused me.

"What?" Lucy asked, reading my features.

"Well, Billy usually dates drop-dead gorgeous, total psychotic bitches with perfect bodies."

"And what sort of girls do you normally date?" Lucy asked with a sly smile.

"Breathing," I said truthfully. I'd never had a type. If I liked them and they were clean I could fuck them and enjoy doing it. Didn't matter what they looked like. I'd never dated any crazy-assed girls like my sons because... Well women, even most really butch women—yes, even me—are different than men. I never slept with anyone I wasn't considering for permanent residence in my life. And it's a fact that you can only have one really crazy motherfucker in a relationship and I had that sewed up.

"What about you?" I asked.

"I've always had a soft spot for butch dykes with head problems."

"See, we're perfect for each other."

"And yet you don't believe that some things happen for a reason or that anything can be fated."

I sighed, finished what I was doing, and looked down at her. "And you keep calling ME a hard head."

It was a good thing that I had so many clothes for Jimmy because getting to the clothes in the storage room would have been a royal pain in the ass and his clothes were the only ones that came close to fitting these two girls.

I was right about the girls' shapes, too. Cherry was about five-four and a little chunky with huge breasts and short, red hair. Evelyn was probably five-seven and thin as a rail, which made her look taller. From the looks of her I'd say she was probably borderline anorexic when this all started and weeks of tight rations hadn't helped.

I got the girl bundled up on the couch and then worked at getting the IV in. It wasn't easy. The girl was so dehydrated it was hard to find a vein. Hell, I was lucky I didn't get dust. She was so out of it she didn't even wince. I finally found one and got the drip going.

"We were fine," Cherry explained, "till our wood supply got low and we had to start rationing what we had because every time we tried to go out and dig more up out of the snow we just damn near froze. Well we were mostly cold all the time but it was bearable... mostly, until we had to use less wood. I didn't even realize she was sick till last night, I mean she hadn't stopped bitching since day one so I had no idea that she really was sick... We were just so cold all the time."

"Yesterday Cherry told me Evelyn was sick. That's why we had to go," Billy said.

"You didn't, and you sure as hell didn't have to drug Lucy and I," I said, glaring at Billy.

"Please ma'am, don't be mad at Billy," Cherry said.

"Don't worry about it, girl, and don't call me ma'am. Key-rist makes me feel like I'm a hundred," I said. "And don't worry about your friend. She's warm now. I'll put some antibiotics in her line, we'll get some warm chicken broth in her, and she'll be fine."

I didn't know that for a fact, of course, but having her sitting around worrying about the girl wasn't going to help either. Truth was Evelyn's pulse was thready and her lungs were rattley. She was suffering from hypothermia and I was pretty sure she had pneumonia.

"Mom was an EMT," Billy explained.

"Jimmy?" I called.

"Yes, Mom," he said, running into the room eager to please, no doubt because he didn't want any of the ass-kicking his brother had coming.

"Go in and make some dinner. We could all use a good, hot meal. Warm up some chicken broth for the girl."

He nodded and headed for the kitchen.

"I'll help him." Lucy started to leave and I took her hand.

"No, you stay with me," I said.

She smiled at me and I smiled back.

"Billy, stoke the fire and bring in more wood."

He nodded and said, "I'm sorry, Mom."

I smiled and patted his cheek. "No, but you will be. By God, you will be."

He made a face and started taking care of the stove. When he was finished he headed off to get wood, no doubt glad to put some distance between him and me.

Cherry sat down on the couch with a sigh, a look of relief on her face.

"Tough time?" Lucy asked.

"Awful," she said. "I never thought I'd be warm again. Thank you, thank you so much," she said to me. Then she started telling us what they'd been through.

When they heard about the storms that were coming she and Evelyn had filled the tub and a bunch of jugs with water. Cherry had already cut a piece of plywood to go over the tub so she covered the tub and piled blankets and pillows on top of it.

"I felt it was going to get really bad... I just knew it. Maybe I'd read too many of your posts." She'd managed a smile. "Anyway I didn't just have my survival kit in there when it hit because we'd moved all of the food in the house, all of it, in there and most of our clothes, too."

The house had been ripped apart around them, but the bathroom had been left intact. The rain had been relentless and it had leaked through the bathroom ceiling but they'd managed to cover themselves and their provisions with plastic sheeting from her survival kit and stay dry. In the morning she and Evelyn had surveyed the damage and gone to work. The bathroom was still standing and mostly whole and they had Cherry's car. Cherry figured that it didn't matter what happened to the car, so the first thing she did was to drive it up on the concrete slab and right up to the bathroom door, leaving only enough room between them to open the car door.

"... then it was all about rolling appliances around. We used the washer and dryer, washer on the bottom and dryer on the top, to make the wall on the north. Then we rolled the refrigerator over and used it on the south wall, using the door as the door to the outside and filling the inside of the fridge with wood. Then I started throwing two by fours over the gap between the car and the bathroom and on top of it. It wasn't hard to find stuff to work with—it was just torn up and thrown all around us. We stuffed couch cushions and pillows and that pink insulation crap under the car and then we just started throwing old clothes and blankets and stuff over the bathroom ceiling and the car and over the roof I'd made between it. We left the windshield—which was pointing south—uncovered and cut a piece of cardboard to go in it at night. We knocked the front seats all the way down into the back seats and threw in all the dry blankets we had."

She explained that the temperature had been dropping fast, so she'd realized there was no need in even finishing their shelter if they didn't have heat. It was an old house and the gas stack in the wall behind the toilet was metal so she'd unscrewed it. They'd each used the toilet one last time and then flushed and removed the tank and the toilet seat and baled all the water out of the bowl. She'd made a hole in the bathroom ceiling, found a piece of tin that had a hole in it almost the right size, and forced it over the pipe and then she'd nailed it to her rafters. They'd been careful to keep the blankets and old clothes they were using for insulation away from the metal. She put the vent pipe into the tank hole but then realized it wouldn't draft. This whole time Evelyn had been hauling bricks up. They got some mud in a bucket and stacked the bricks using the mud as mortar all around the commode till it was about a foot over the commode on the three sides and to the commode in the front then they set the toilet tank upside down on the back of the stove and connected the pipe. They found a piece of tin and used it for a top, sealing the cracks with mud and got another piece of tin to put over the door. They started a fire immediately and it drafted fine, so they were sure they were going to make it.

"...till then I just didn't think we had a chance. I was mostly just working because if we didn't try we didn't have a chance in hell, but once we had fire I knew we could make it, so we just started working faster and harder."

They had thrown plywood scraps on their roof over the top of the two by fours and stacked bricks and mud up to the bottom of the refrigerator door they were going to use to get in and out. They covered their whole shelter with the plastic sheeting she'd had in her survival kit and held the edges down all the way around with bricks. Then they threw some more two by four scraps on the plastic to help hold it down if there was wind.

"Then we just started hauling pieces of wood small enough that it would work in our stove or that we could cut up with my hand saw without much trouble. It wasn't hard to find—the twister had just flat shredded stuff. We just kept getting wood. We filled every space in the shelter and then we just kept stacking it outside the front door till it was too dark and we were too cold to go on. Then we went in the shelter, closed the door, and lit a couple of candles. When we heard from you... When I knew we weren't alone... I knew we could make it. But then when Evelyn got sick..."

"She's going to be fine," I said. Again I still didn't know that for a fact. Prolonged exposure, not enough food—once the body starts breaking down it can sometimes be hard to get it to stop cannibalizing its own organs and work right again.

Over dinner Jimmy and Billy told us about the group holed up at the high school. Seemed like they weren't nearly as inventive as Cherry. They were mostly some teachers and students who'd been working on getting the school ready for a dance when the storm hit. Other people had joined them, seeing that it was one of the only places standing, and they'd all brought supplies. They'd spent the morning after the storm finding everything they could and moving it all into the home-ec room. Amazingly, most of the high school complex had been left intact.

"It looked like someone had rolled the chain link fence up and the activity center looked like it had exploded. Everything else was whole. They made a stove in their shop, but they didn't get much wood. I think they thought it was a lot till they had to start burning it. They were having trouble running their wood stove, so they've just been scrounging for gas and running generators to run a few electric space heaters, so it's cold in there. I told them how to build a damper and how to keep the fire going. I had to explain it like I was talking to some idiot. When I told the guy who has put himself in charge that they could use the tools in their shop to rape the rest of the building to make themselves more comfortable, that they could tear desks and shelves and stuff apart and cut them up to heat with if they ran low on wood, it was pretty obvious that he had never even thought of it."

"You shouldah seen this guy's face, Mom." Jimmy laughed. "You would have thought Billy made him eat a turd. They hadn't even thought of burning the text-books."

"They were surely glad for the supplies, and when I hauled out that bag of chocolate I liked to thought I was going to have to shoot them to keep them back," Billy said.

It had been a dangerous thing to do. You'd think bringing people like that some food they wouldn't likely try to do anything but thank you, but likely as not if the boys hadn't been heavily armed they would have had some sort of trouble. See, people always want more. We gave them something when we didn't have to give them anything, but they had to know that meant we had more, and human nature seems to never be happy till they have it all.

"The new super center was mostly intact, too," Jimmy said. "Stuff all over outside, though, and only a few cars in the parking lot. Didn't see any people."

"Let's hope some of the survivors were smart enough to go there to get supplies."

The government and the news had been calling it looting and the National Guard—where it had been able to be deployed—had been told to shoot to kill. Stupid. The fucking government couldn't think outside the box. They knew, they had to know, what was about to hit. What they should have done was order stores to give ten items to each customer who walked in, but NO, they never believed it would be as bad as it was. They couldn't because if they did they had to admit that the all-important corporate America was going to fall apart. Since no one acted to control them, the corporations had upped the prices on basic items. Then the government sent out what sparse National Guard troops we had—not to help the people to prepare, but to stop them from looting.

God Bless America. Of course if more of the troops had been here when the shit hit the fan there might have been some hope for people trapped in the cities, but probably not much. Most of the bases got wiped out one way or the other, too. See, just because you're in uniform doesn't mean you can't die from mundane things like flood and ice and fire. People expected police and firemen and the military to risk life and limb to save them no matter what was happening. It never dawned on them to learn to take care of themselves. Civil servants have families, too, and when the shit hit the fan the smart ones left their posts and went to take care of their own business. It's not disloyal to save yourself and yours first. Further you have to wonder about the real integrity of someone who would actually shoot looters at a department store instead of taking care of their own families.

Let's face it, when the world fell apart the military did what it could to help people up till they realized just what was happening, and then like every other sane person they worked on saving themselves and those they cared about. After all, they'd all had survival training.

"Huge sections of Fort Smith and Van Buren are still on fire," Billy said. "Broken gas lines I guess."

"Or people trying to get warm. Hell if I were stuck there I'd be real tempted to just start lighting all those damaged houses, stay by one till it burned out then move to the next one," I said.

I shifted in my chair; my ribs were starting to protest all the ways I'd twisted them while I'd been having marathon sex with Lucy.

Lucy got up from the table and when she came back she had a bottle of ibuprofen that she put on the table in front of me.

"Thanks."

"You're welcome." She kissed me on the cheek, my face turned bright red, and she sat down.

Jimmy and Billy exchanged a look and giggled.

"Fuck you boys!" I said angrily. "It isn't any of your damn business what I do. If you don't stop riding me I'm going to grab you and kiss you right on the mouth and you know damn good and well what I've been doing."

"God," Jimmy said, holding his hands over his ears. "I'm pretty sure I'm never going to get that image out of my head."

Billy just looked at me, his face blank.

"What?" I demanded.

"I can't believe you said that," Billy said, making a face. "I'm pretty sure that your mom isn't supposed to say things like that."

Lucy laughed, and I just kept eating. About the only way to stop those fuckers from teasing the living shit out of me when I have a girlfriend is to say something that will just completely gross them out. To tell the honest truth I don't think the boys have ever been comfortable with me being with anyone who wasn't their mother.

When they were younger they'd just flat tell me they didn't like... Well anyone I dated. As they got older and their own hormones started running their bodies I think they realized that I was never going to be happy unless I had a woman, but it still made them uncomfortable. They wanted to be alright with it because they knew it was stupid to expect me to be celibate, but part of them was always going to feel like I was cheating on their mom so they teased me and teased whoever I was with because to them that said they were alright with it.

"So, did you wind up sleeping in the car or in the bathroom?" I asked Cherry, changing the subject as I downed four of the ibuprofen.

"The stove worked good, but it smoked pretty bad, so we slept in the car wrapped around our rocks and each other right up till our wood started getting low and we realized we couldn't stay out in the weather long enough to get enough wood to make it worth getting that cold. Then we moved into the bathroom and of course the smoke wasn't as bad only because we couldn't afford to burn much wood to make smoke. The last few days have really sucked and then Evelyn got sick and it's..." Her voice broke. "If they didn't come get us we wouldn't have made it."

And this was no doubt why Billy had insisted on going today. And here was the thing—Cherry had used her head. She'd worked hard and done everything right. There just hadn't been enough time to get enough wood to carry them through. And this was here where it wasn't nearly as bad as it was up north. Other places might not have had tornados, but there was no area of the country that hadn't been hit with something, and now there was this blizzard, this cascade of ice and snow. A lot of people who did everything right still wound up dead because— short of spending your whole life getting ready like I had—you just couldn't be prepared for something like a winter that will not stop.

And we weren't done with the winter weather, not by a long shot. The alarm went off and we all jumped. Someone was at the gate.

CHAPTER 9

The Barter System

In the post-apocalyptic world. paper money won't be worth shit and all those people that hedged with gold or precious stones might as well have collected river rocks and turds. The only things that are going to have value are the things people really need— the things that will help them survive.

Food, matches, hand tools, nails, screws, bolts, generators. If you know someone has extra of something you need, don't try to take it by force. Find something they might need that you have and offer to make a trade. Then everyone is happy. Make allies not enemies.

That will be the new world, a world run on the value of an egg and a hammer head—necessities not bullshit.

The generation of people who always cared more about the way things looked than the way things really are, well they will have been wiped completely out and ALL that's going to matter are things that are exactly what they seem to be.

I went to the monitor and there was Matt Peters on his tractor.

"Jimmy, it's Matt. Gear up and go down to the gate and let him in. Take your gun just in case. Bring him round to the front door."

Jimmy grumbled some but turned on his heel and started for his coveralls and the four-wheeler in the shop.

"How can you tell who it is?" Lucy asked, looking at the image of the bundled up man on the monitor.

"Honey round here you know a man by three things his truck, his dog or his tractor."

Billy went back to the table to finish eating. "So... are they going to be alright with... us?" Lucy asked at my shoulder, I didn't pretend I didn't know who she was talking about.

"They're fine." I wasn't about to tell her what I just told you. Besides let me tell you something. People pretend to be alright with something long enough they wind up really being alright with it and it didn't matter anyway. I wasn't going to quit having sex with Lucy just because it made the boys a little uncomfortable. In fact the way I felt about the little shit heads right in that moment that just made it all the more appealing.

"What's he want?" Lucy asked, and while she didn't come right out and say it, you could hear in her voice that she hoped it wasn't to live here. It was a small house and with today's additions I was already starting to feel the squeeze. Even if I wasn't, it was for sure that Lucy was

"He's not staying," I said, and she let out a sigh of relief. "I like him, but not that much." I watched as Jimmy let him in the gate then kept him on camera till they got to the house. I grabbed my gun, stuck it in my pocket, and went to the front door. Lucy followed. "All this crap is sort of ruining our honeymoon isn't it?"

Lucy laughed. "It's a little annoying, but after all you are the king of the world now."

"King of the world... I think I like that." I made Lucy stay inside when I went to open the air lock door. When I did Matt came lumbering in. "Leave your rifle and your gun here," I told him. The part that was his head sort of nodded and he put the rifle down as I closed the airlock door. He mumbled something I couldn't hear through the layers of scarf he had wrapped around his head and then he took off one of his gloves, pulled his gun out of his pocket, and laid it on a shelf there. I saw he'd worn sunglasses to keep from getting snow blind and felt some better about what I'd paid for those fog-proof goggles when I saw he actually had frost on his glasses—and remember this was the warm day. "Come on in and strip by the stove."

People have a tendency to want to strip gear that's snow or ice covered outside so that it doesn't get all over the house or because they figure it isn't doing them any good and they'll be warmer without it. WRONG! You expose already cold skin to super-cold air and it's a good way to destroy several layers of skin immediately.

He started stripping layers and when he got his head clear he said, "Looks like you've got a full house."

"Yep, no more room in the inn."

"What's she got?" he asked, pointing at Evelyn.

"Don't worry. Its exposure, nothing catching," I said. "So how'd you fair?"

"House didn't take a lick of damage. Neither did the barn. Fact my place didn't get hit as bad as yours did and me and my boys spent that whole first day cutting wood and stacking it in the boys' bedrooms—my wife just pitching a living fit the whole time she was helping us do it.

"I have an insane amount of hay because... Well, who's going to come buy it now?" Matt cut hay and had supplied every feed store in the area for years. "I'm missing a bunch of cows and I know some are dead because we've already found and butchered some but I think some just might have run off. I've got fences down everywhere. Damndest thing though..." He laughed; he's a big guy with a good sense of humor. "...I've picked up five zebras, two llamas, and four buffalo. Guess from up there on the road. They're mostly as tame as my cattle and they are just hanging around there with them eating hay. Took the cows a couple of days to get used to them but now they're just all laying around the feed lot together like it's normal. Drink a lot and I have to fill the water in the barn every day, but there's plenty of water in the well and it's good for me and the boys to pull water out of the well. Only takes us about thirty minutes a day to get enough water for us and all the animals and... Well it's about the only exercise we get and... Well if we run out of beef before the weather clears I figure we can eat those critters just as well and if not... Well might not hurt to have our new world have some of those critters in it."

There had been a guy with about eighty acres all under six-foot chain link with barbed wire on the top who had kept all sorts of exotic animals. I don't think there was any doubt that this was where Matt's refugees had come from.

"I've got all the cattle we had to butcher just cut up and sitting in bags in our garage, even with the door closed they are all frozen solid, so the garage makes a damn good freezer."

"So what can I do for you?" I asked.

"Well we're running low on human provisions... except for meat. When we heard you saying on the radio yesterday that there was going to be a break in the weather Jenny made a list and told me to get over here and see if you wouldn't trade me a butchered cow for it. The beef is in the trailer behind my trac-tor."

"Sure. What you need?"

He handed me the list. It all made sense. Sugar, flour, corn meal, salt, eggs, milk, cheese, flour. Then there was the last entry, "Gloves," written in someone else's hand in big block letters. Matt must have seen me smile when I read it because he said, "My oldest boy put that there. He has some jersey gloves but that really isn't enough in this."

"Not a problem, anything else you can think of that I might have that you might need?"

"Snow shovel," he said with a shrug.

"Done... Boys!"

Jimmy grumbled something about never getting to finish his dinner. Then there was a slapping sound and he let out a yelp and then Billy was muttering something about not making me mad because they were in enough trouble as it was.

Billy and Jimmy walked in the room, Jimmy rubbing his arm and staring holes in his brother's back.

"Boys get the beef out of Matt's trailer and put it in the cold room." It is what it sounds like—it's a small room I built into the north side of the storage room. It has an old freezer door to get into it. Inside is my freezer and there is a two-foot hole that is covered in screen and steel bars two feet off the ground that goes into a tunnel that goes to the outside of the complex mound where it catches wind. The room is always cool, the idea being that freezers have thermostats and the colder it is the less they work. My freezer, well it's on a switch and any time the temperature in that room drops below twenty degrees it shuts it off altogether. "Just put it in the room on top of the freezer. Then fill this order." I handed Billy the list. "Give them four pairs of the good, heavy gloves and a snow shovel as well."

Billy nodded and the boys took off grumbling at each other till I couldn't hear them any more.

"Matt Peters, this is Lucy Powers." They shook hands. He was looking at her like he thought she was familiar and couldn't quite place her.

"So how have you been really?" I asked.

"We're good, all mostly living in just the living room. Boys are fighting all the time so... About like you all," he said with a smile.

Lucy laughed and then patted me on the ass and went to the kitchen, no doubt to finish eating her dinner.

"That's new since I was here last," Matt said, warming his hands over the stove as he nodded his head towards Lucy's fine, departing ass.

I grinned, no doubt like an idiot. "Yep, got here just in time for the apocalypse."

"So... You were right about everything, feeling pretty smug?"

"You know just because I saw it coming doesn't mean I'm a big-assed fan of the end of the world."

"I know that, Katy, I was just kiddin' ya... Heard you ride off for Rudy a couple of days ago and heard you talking about it on the radio. You didn't say nothin' about having any trouble, but I found the Burkholder boys frozen dead in the middle of the road, and I notice you're gimping around a little bit. Want to tell me what happened?"

"Dirty sons a bitches waited for me and popped me in the ribs with a fucking tree limb. Sent me and Lucy flying off the ATV and screwed up my back and my ribs, so we killed 'em."

"I have to tell you the truth I was awful relieved to find those two fuckers dead. You can ask my missus next time you see her, I haven't really slept since the shit hit the fan for fear those turds were going to crawl out of their hole, try to kill us all and take our shit," Matt said. "I drug them off the road. They was froze solid; it was like moving a rock. You suppose those fuckers had mines around their place, trip wires?"

Now that was a damn good question and with fences down a real potential problem.

"Don't know. I guess when the smoke clears we'll need to go check it out."

"Stupid cows will doubtless walk over there and step on one if there are any," Matt muttered.

Evelyn stirred, made some mumbling sound, and then just went right back to sleep.

"How fucked up is this shit Katy? How fucked up? I wasn't like you. Katy. You know that I thought all the global warming stuff was a bunch of liberal hippie shit, but that's at least part of the problem, ain't it?"

"Yep, color you wrong, Matt. When everything's close to being the devil's own sperm anyway, it only takes one thing to make it all fall apart."

"Guess we'll have to start all over again."

"Why?" I said more than a little mad. "'Cause things were so God-damn good? Last thing we need to do is try to build things back to where they were. What we have to do is not make the same mistakes again. We don't need to try to cover the planet in people, or build things that tear everything up. We need to go in thinking how to do it cleaner, and then better and do it right this time. The fewer people there are the more there is for everyone. If we don't fuck things up in the first place we don't have to fix them. If we do things right this time... I mean it's not like we don't know where all that shit is going to lead us now."

"You're right, ain't no doubt about that. I can remember my father saying work smarter not harder and that's one of the things fucked everything up. Everyone so worried about breaking a sweat that they had something to do everything for them, and with everything they built to help us... They were really just putting another nail in our coffin."

And that's why, in spite of what he's said, he wasn't really like everyone else. Matt used his brain. Matt had two kids and stopped, and he didn't like liberal hippies but he hated right-winged idiots, too, so he'd been about where I had always been when I was voting—just vote for the rich idiot you think will do the least damage.

"You know, Matt, those folks down in Rudy have plenty of food, mostly just like you running out of what makes food good to eat. They could use some meat, and we all know it's easy to keep it cold enough. You might run some down to them if you have enough time after you get home."

"You know what, Katy, if you can help those assholes I can, too."

By the time Matt started back home my dinner was mostly cold. I ate it anyway. The boys had made themselves scarce and Lucy was just sort of watching me like she was thinking deep thoughts. "What?"

"I was just thinking that I knew so much less than I thought I did. I would have thought I was a good judge of character, but I didn't get you right at all. All these years I had you pegged for a real hard ass and a total nut job. The kind of person who only ever looks out for themselves. I thought you were like one of those hard-core survivalists you hate so much and you'd just kill anyone who came near you if the worst happened."

"Yet you ran up here anyway," I said, shaking my head and laughing.

"Well it wasn't like I had a lot of choices and the gate was down. I figured it was fate." She smiled then and I shook my head. got up and put my dirty dishes in the sink, thinking the boys could by God wash them.

"You're like a dog with a bone." I laughed.

"Is that a bad thing?"

"Not always."

"My point is you aren't any of the things I thought you were because you ran around in camouflaged cargo pants..."

"Hey, they're comfortable and they don't show dirt and I've been wearing them since I was sixteen—way before and way after everyone thought they were cool," I defended, turning away from the sink.

"The point is I thought I had you all figured out and it turns out that you aren't any of the things I thought you were—except clever."

"Thanks... I think." I smiled then. "You know what? You aren't any of the things I thought you were, either."

"What did you think I was?"

"A cold, self-serving, stupid, egotistical bitch—a bit of fluff."

"Ouch!" She looked wounded. "What do you think now?"

"There isn't anything cold, stupid, or self-serving about you, and surprisingly you are as tough as nails when you have to be and you know how to think on your feet."

"You still think I'm egotistical?"

"Well yeah, but you're hot as hell and you're damn smart so why shouldn't you be?"

She laughed and decided to change the subject. "How are your ribs?"

"Sore. Why, what did you have in mind?"

She shook her head. "I was thinking maybe we ought to actually do something for the ribs besides try to break them." She walked over and hugged me and it didn't hurt at all; it just felt good and I thought, *Why she isn't ruining the apocalypse for me at all.*

That night as the sun started going down and the cold started setting in I could tell we were in for another round of hell. Oh alright it had nothing to do with intuition, how dark it got, or how quick, or even a feeling in my bones. I was looking at all the satellite images and checking all my instruments and there was another huge storm coming down from Canada. I'd picked up signal from a couple of Canucks and they were saying this storm was worse than the last one.

I had the boys bring in a bunch of wood and we cranked the stove up. Evelyn was mostly unconscious and I wasn't at all sure that she was going to make it, but I knew it would help if we could get her warm enough. People will try to cool the body down when someone's running a fever. The truth is you only ever want to do that if the fever is so bad it's going to burn up their brain. Otherwise you want to warm them up. See fever is the body trying to burn the infection out. If you help the body stay warm—especially a body that's been so cold—it should help burn the infection out faster particularly since I had her on antibiotics.

My ribs were starting to throb. I really shouldn't have spent a big chunk of the day fucking like an animal, not that I was at all sorry that I had, just that it hurt.

I told Jimmy to do the evening report. He nodded and headed towards the office. Cherry was just sort of looking at Evelyn like she was sure the girl was going to die and that it was maybe her fault.

"Cherry why don't you go help Jimmy? When he gets done giving the weather report you should tell the listeners your story. It may give them hope, might give them some ideas, too."

She looked unsure but went anyway and Billy got up and followed her—no doubt because he'd tagged this one as his and didn't want her alone with his brother. Cherry for her part was too run down and too worried about her friend to have any romantic feelings for anyone at that moment.

I went and checked Evelyn. I put my stethoscope on and checked her pulse, which was still thready at best. Her lungs were full of fluid so I decided to shoot some Lasik into her line to help dry them out. I hated to do it because she was so dehydrated but as long as we had her on an IV drip she was getting rehydrated and we needed to dry those lungs out. I also went ahead and gave her a breathing treatment, which only works sort of half assed on an unconscious patient who's breathing shallowly.

"Well?" Lucy asked at my shoulder.

"Girl's got pneumonia and hypothermia. Add a big heaping portion of dehydration and malnutrition and... She's in bad shape."

"Is she going to die?" Lucy asked in a whisper.

"I don't know," I snapped back, a lot angrier sounding than I meant. "I'm sorry."

"No, I'm sorry. It was a stupid question."

"No, it's actually a perfectly obvious question, I just don't know. You know everyone was so obsessed with being as thin as they could be. They kept saying stupid things like you can't be too thin. Well the truth is we'd all be a lot healthier if we were carrying a little extra weight—just ten to fifteen pounds. I purposely always carry an extra twenty just to be on the safe side," I said, only about half kidding.

"You look great."

"Why thank you, but it's not about how we look it's about how we are, and it's fine to be just the exact perfect weight or even a little underweight until there's no food or you get sick. When I was a kid I got Russian flu. I was a little overweight when I got sick. I lost fifteen pounds in two weeks, which actually made me a few pounds below my medical chart's perfect weight. I was convinced that if I'd been any thinner I would have died. I've just stayed twenty pounds over the charts ever since."

I walked away from the girl and Lucy followed. I lowered my voice. "I'm going to go out on a limb and say this girl was way too thin to start with so she just had nothing to lose and nothing to help her stay warm. That's why the other girl is still healthy and this one's on the verge of death under the same damn conditions. The other girl started a couple of pounds over the charts. Your body burns fat to stay warm; you don't have any fat there is nothing to burn."

Lucy nodded. "I fought my weight my whole life. I would fast if I gained a pound. Never ate what I wanted... It all seems so pointless now. I keep thinking about all the great, exotic food, prepared by some of the finest chefs in the world—food that I didn't eat because it might make me fat, and now I'm never going to get to eat it. Even if I could have done like these girls and survived out there—and believe me I don't think I could have lasted a night—I would have more than likely wound up like her. And for what? You're right. Our whole damn society was completely consumed with the way things looked. And me? I was right there in the big middle of it." She looked tired then.

"I'm going to go get a shower."

I nodded and went to check on the boys and Cherry. They were still doing the report. Billy was telling them about all he'd seen. How they had to be super careful because you couldn't be sure what the snow was covering. It was so deep that most of the time you just had to guess whether you were driving the right way or not.

If he hadn't gone those girls would be dead in this next storm, I had no doubt of that. Maybe those idiots holed up at that school, too, and they'd been through quite a bit. It didn't matter; I was still going to get Billy back when he least expected it. Why? Because that's who I am.

Jimmy was glaring at me—so obviously he'd either forgotten that he didn't want to make me madder than I already was or he'd decided I was going to beat his ass anyway so there was no sense in tiptoeing around me any more. I wasn't sure why. Maybe it was because Jimmy couldn't stand for me to be happy. He blames me and always has for everything that he perceives is wrong with his life. In fact, I'm pretty sure that to this day Jimmy thinks I had something to do with the apocalypse just so I could ruin his day. He was fine as long as I was brooding and didn't smile too much. Lucy had fucked me rotten most of the day so I was actually happy. I've never been good at hiding what I'm feeling, so Jimmy was pissed.

Or maybe he was mad because I asked him to do something. That boy will ask me to jump through twenty hoops for him then act like I'm asking for blood if I ask him to do the slightest thing. He'll ask me to do something for him and then when I do it he'll complain that I'm always interfering with his life. He once had this skank-assed girl he was living with. She had a kid and he asked me to paint a room in his apartment for this kid. I did and even helped him decorate it. Hell I liked the kid. Then Jimmy ran out of money as Jimmy is prone to do—especially when he has a woman because he just lets her spend everything he's got—and then the skank left—kid and all. Jimmy screams at me for thirty minutes about how I ruined his life and I'm just like my father—who he never met but he knew I hated him because I was always bitching about him—and how I just had to quit meddling in his life. He then spent an hour telling me all the stupid shit he had planned to do as if testing me to see if I would say anything at all.

I didn't. I went home and didn't talk to him for three months. Decided to let him see what it was like to be out there without my help. See how long he could go without asking Mom for money or help. Of course what happened was he hit his brother up instead and then I gave Billy the money but still... It's the principle, right? Jimmy didn't call me at all because he's a prick and I didn't call because he told me not to. The next time I heard from him... Well that was the phone call I got when his brother called because the world was ending and the real reason he kept screaming, "I'm sorry, Mom!" over and over again.

Life's too short to raise kids. It's a giant waste of your time. I just don't get people who willingly put themselves through that sort of total bullshit. Do you know why parents always want their kids to have kids? Because they know for a fact it's the only way the ungrateful, judgmental little bastards will ever know what hell it is to raise fucking kids and how no one! No one! Ever gets it right.

Anyway, Jimmy just kept glaring at me and I couldn't be sure why till he said, "I've got this covered," in his very best you-know-what-you're-a-moron-mom voice.

I smiled, in too good a mood to be thwarted, reached over and turned the transmitter off. "Fuck you, Jimmy. You know what? Don't give me any of your bullshit. All the things you blamed me for, all the crap you've laid on my head over the years, it stops right the fuck now. I was right, alright? I was right and everyone else was wrong, which means all the crap you say I put you through wasn't for nothing, it was for this.

"You're alive. Better than that, you're alive and actually help-ing other survivors, and millions... MILLIONS are dead, Jimmy. You drove over some of their bodies today. You were warm and fed in here while those girls were freezing to death hungry in their car. Have you listened to her story, Jimmy? Do you see that girl in the next room fighting for her life? You had better by God learn to love me, Jimmy, because I'm all that's between you and sleeping out there."

"I didn't say anything," he spat back. "You're always on my back!"

"A dead turtle could have told you were blowing me off. Now I don't know who you're showing off for or if you just feel like being a prick, but this house is too small and there are too many of us in it for your bullshit or one of mama's conniption fits, so cut it out right now."

"Mom," Billy said quickly. "He wasn't mad at you, he was mad at me because I took over."

I looked at Jimmy who was now obviously mad at both of us. "But you snapped at me and that's why I'm bitching at you."

Jimmy nodded silently and grumbled a half-assed apology.

"Now I can see you've got this under control, so I'm going to get a shower and go to bed. Billy, let your brother handle this." I looked at Cherry. "You sleep on the other couch in the living room and keep an eye on your friend, alright?"

She nodded silently looking at her feet and I smiled because she already felt like one of my kids.

"Anything goes wrong—anything at all—come and get me even if you hear noises coming from our room you don't want to hear."

"Christ, Mom," Billy said, turning red.

"Don't you give me any lip. I'm in a fucking good mood. Why can't you hateful little turds let me be in a good mood? And Billy I meant it, Jimmy knows more about the equipment than you do. You let him run the show."

I turned and walked out of the room and Jimmy immediately grumbled something the equivalent of na na na na boo boo at his brother. Which I ignored.

I was pretty sure my ribs weren't going to get a chance to heal. Not that I really cared right then. Lucy was just sort of passed out against me her head resting on my shoulder.

She sighed, a sort of pleased-with-herself sigh. "I can't imagine what this is going to be like when your ribs are healed."

"Let's hope better or you'll be very disappointed." I was actually feeling pretty smug my own self.

"You were right."

"Hah?" I said intelligently.

"You were right about me. I was a bit of fluff and I was a cold, self-serving bitch. I gave lip service to caring about the environment but I drove a too big car and lived in a too big house. I had the compact florescent bulbs and I recycled, so I felt good. I had no guilt, just like you said. I pushed my way to the top, then just kept pushing, trying to get higher. I thought being sent to report on you was way beneath me."

"I knew that," I said not really caring.

"My girlfriend Samantha she was crazy about me. She would have eaten broken glass for me. She wanted to go to Vermont and get married. She even bought me a ring. I'd been putting her off for two years. I was totally closeted; she was out. She wanted to get married and live together and I could never even fully commit to living together because... Well I loved her but I guess I loved my stinking job more, and lots of people had come out and some were alright but let's face it most weren't. So we lived between my house and her apartment and I never took her to any of my work or even social functions because I just didn't want to risk getting caught by... well anyone. And my family has known since I came out to them when I was sixteen, so it was all about work. It's hard to think about Sam now, knowing she's dead, laying out there somewhere in the snow... everyone is."

Alright here's something that sucks, having someone you've just made love to cry over their dead lover. There's no Hallmark card for that. There is nothing to say and you're naked, so you feel really vulnerable. When you've loved and lost, too, well you know how they feel and... Hello! Still naked! I sort of tried to pull the sheet up over me which I really couldn't between where she was laying on me and the sore rib. I gave up and just held her, patting her back, which wasn't good at all because she just cried more and I was still naked and I still couldn't think of anything to say.

Finally I said, "You know, some of them might be alive."

"No they aren't. You know they aren't. They were all in Atlanta. Atlanta was flattened and now it's under three feet of snow. No one not a single person from that area has made contact with you," she cried harder.

It was closer to five feet of snow but I didn't bother to tell her that.

I think sometimes having sex opens channels. It makes you a little more emotional. All the hormones racing through your body and all and well... when you get that close to someone, especially when you are talking about the love between two women, it just makes you closer—breaks down any walls between you. I didn't feel like there was anything between Lucy and me at that moment. Right then it was just us alone and all of the sudden I didn't feel so naked.

"I'm sorry Lucy," I said softly, as I kissed her on the top of her head.

"I know you are, Katy. And see? I think that's why I'm so upset because you were right about me, but I was all wrong about you."

"No I wasn't Lucy, no I wasn't. You didn't live the way I did, but you at least did something. If everyone had done even what you did, it would have made a huge difference. You at least admitted there was a problem, even if you didn't fully understand how bad the problem really was. And let's face it; everything would have probably been fine if those idiots hadn't started slinging nukes at each other. So you wanted to stay in the closet to keep your job, big deal! How many queers did that and some with a lot less high-profile jobs than yours. Did Sam understand?"

"Mostly, but she didn't like it."

"Well if it made her very unhappy don't you think she would have just dumped your ass a long time ago? I mean you're a fine hot mama and you give great head, but you know butches. We'll replace you in ten minutes if you're too damn much trouble."

She chuckled through her tears.

"Give yourself a break, Lucy. There are always things you wish you'd done or said different, whether you have a week together or twelve years. With me and Cindy I still loved her but the spark had sort of gone out. I'd sort of let it go out just too busy all the time and didn't spend enough time just being with her. There were boys to raise and houses to build and an apocalypse to get ready for and I just sort of let the romance go. Oh we still had a great sex life, I'm not saying that, but we had stopped making time to do the little things, just take a walk, go out to dinner just the two of us, go dancing, or just sit outside without the boys and have a glass of wine. Just talk about... well something, anything besides my building projects, her job, the coming Armageddon or the boys.

We just sort of forgot to talk about love and us and our dreams. It was all my fault, too, because Cindy... Well she was never romantic and never filled with ideas. I always had to be the one to say, let's do whatever and then she'd do it and it would be wonderful and... Somewhere along the line I just got tired of always being the one to say let's do because most of the time she didn't want to at first. She had to be talked into everything and it just... made me tired. I wanted to say let's go and have her be eagerly waiting in the car—or better yet have her say come on let's do something. I realized she didn't care. It didn't mean anything to her, she was happy to just sit and be with me and... Well I don't think she even missed it, the spark I mean. Who knows, maybe she never had it. Cindy... Well let's face it Cindy had been through a lot before I ever knew her. She wasn't a very passionate person, I was but she wasn't. I just got tired of dragging her along for the ride. I let my obsession become my passion and she was happy to just coexist and have sex two or three times a week.

"When she was dead, when there was no fixing it, then I wished I had done everything differently. Because I did love her and there was never any doubt that she loved me. But the fact is that I didn't know she was about to die, for all I knew we'd be together for the rest of our lives and then the spark might have just come back some day and everything would have been the way it was.

"You can't spend your life second guessing yourself. Who knows? Maybe if you'd come out it would have cost you your job and then you would have resented her and maybe she would have run off with some girl from her office, and right now you'd be dead. Maybe if I had continued to court my wife it would have become increasingly obvious that there was nothing left there and I would have wound up giving up in that 'get the fuck out of my house' sort of way and then the boys would have gone with her and they'd be as dead as she is now."

Lucy had quit crying. "Wow, you're really good at this."

"Yeah, well I've had a little longer than you have to try to rationalize my guilt away," I said, and I was only half kidding.

"Most of the time I just try hard not to think about it," Lucy started. "You know everyone and everything that's just gone. It's like I just got picked up out of my life and shoved into someone else's and everything here is so different from my old life that most days it's just easy to pretend like I'm acting out a part in a play or something and that somewhere away from the stage everything is exactly like it was when I left it."

She moved off of me to look down at me.

"But today... being with you, it's very real and I just... I killed someone the other day and it didn't even really phase me... I was so much more worried about you... and I've lost everything and everyone that ever meant anything to me and I should feel worse than I do... and I'm making love with you over and over... and Sam's dead somewhere and... What kind of person am I that I'm not more upset?"

So she was crying and upset mostly because she wasn't upset enough and... When someone figures women out I hope they write a book.

Yes, I know I'm a woman, but remember I said I'm a guy? Well this is why I think that. When guys are sitting around talking about the things they don't understand about women... Well I can't help them because I don't get it, either.

"Lucy, that has got to be the stupidest thing I have ever heard." Yep that's what I said. See? Now do you get it? I'm a guy.

"What?" she asked in disbelief.

"That's stupid. It's over; close the page. You either adapt—which you seem to be doing very nicely—you go crazy here, or you die. You know why people don't get over their grief? Because society tells them that it is their duty to show their love for their dead loved ones by dwelling on their death and wallowing in their grief. Why? Who does it actually serve to be miserable forever over something you can do nothing about? Life runs in cycles, cycles end, and other cycles begin. You're always talking about fate. Worse than that, you want me to believe in it. But now I'm going to ask you, do you believe in fate?"

"Yes," she said.

"Then everything you just said is utter bullshit, because according to your way of thinking, you're *supposed* to be here with me now, and if everything that happens is destined to happen then why dwell on what brought you here now and..."

Well I don't really know what I said or why she reacted like that but she was just all over me kissing me and kissing me till I was kissing her back.

Maybe having sex made her forget all the stuff she didn't want to think about. Maybe I was just being used.

I wasn't worried about it either way.

CHAPTER 10

Even Colder

Cold and water, that's what will kill most people, not lava, or earthquakes, or noxious gas streaming from a volcano, or even tons of ash and mudslides. The real killer during this apocalypse will be the weather and mostly the rising water, lack of potable drinking water, and cold.

People fail to understand that increasingly cold winters are also caused by global warming. I mean most people don't get it, but we're getting worse winters because the planet as a whole is getting warmer. Any of a half dozen different disaster scenarios will sling God alone knows how much debris into the atmosphere and on a planet already badly out of balance... We're very likely to have a mini ice age.

You can have all the food and potable water you need for five years and outrun the flood or the fire, but if you don't have a way to get away from rising water or to keep warm you will not live through this apocalypse.

Learn to build a fire and keep it going now. Don't think you know how to do this. Don't assume any idiot can make a fire and keep a wood stove going. This is not true. Spend even one weekend trying to keep a fire going and you'll figure out just how easy it isn't. Buy extra warm clothes and extra warm blankets even if you live in an area of the country that has never been cold enough to need them and put them back just in case.

Do not take down insulation or other modifications you make to your shelter that make it easier to heat until all the snow and ice has melted and you're sure warm weather is on it's way. A warm day does not necessarily mean you are looking at a warming trend.

Cold kills painfully and not so quickly, and it's a good bet that when you think it can't get any colder, it absolutely will. If you aren't ready, this will be what kills you.

And, brother, did it get cold that night! When I woke up it was still dark, and it was cold but when I looked at the clock it was seven-thirty.

I say it was cold because I was in bed with Lucy with blankets wrapped all around me and my feet were still cold. I probably would have panicked right then if I didn't realize that: a) I was naked, and; b) we had forgotten to open our bedroom door. We had been more concerned with our privacy than opening the door to let in heat. See I have vents to the barn and greenhouse because they are far away from the heat source. Our bedroom is less than thirty feet from the stove so if the door is open it's plenty warm in there and at the time I built it I didn't plan on having a woman.

My ribs hardly hurt at all and since Lucy had a fist resting on top of the bruised area I figured they were already mostly mended.

Still the room had been toasty when we went to bed and like I keep telling you this house is half way under the ground and it has two eight-inch walls of concrete one foot apart with sand between them between us and the outside. The snow had once again covered the window, which blocked the outside light—if there was any.

I tried to get up without waking Lucy but... I've never really been good at that. "Where ya going?"

"It's seven-thirty. I'm going to open our door, let some heat in, go tend the fire, and check on the girl."

"Alright," she let me go. "Can you come back to bed?"

I thought about it for only a second, why the hell not. "Sure."

I pulled on my forgotten pajamas and walked across the room. When I opened the door I was hit with a blast of hot air that felt damn good.

When I got to the living room Evelyn was sleeping. Her breath was raspy but she was breathing. Cherry was on the other couch asleep and the stove was blazing, so I guessed the boys had taken care of it in the middle of the night. A little light was coming through the sky light—not much because it was coming through I couldn't tell how much snow. I decided to check the "air lock." Out the door I could see we'd had probably six more inches of snow. The temperature outside was seven below zero; I took a double take. The wind chill was twenty below and that was here in the south. A lot of people would have died last night. People who like Cherry and Evelyn had made it by their wits and by the skin of their teeth would have lost their fight last night.

I decided not to think about it and headed back into the house to check on Evelyn and then go back to bed, which just seemed really decadent to me. When I walked back in the living room Evelyn was actually sitting up. "How do you feel?"

"Better," she said in a choked voice, and then proceeded to start coughing—which was actually a good sign. "I... I need to go to the bathroom."

I nodded and helped her get herself and her IV bag to the bathroom.

Cherry appeared at my side looking sleepy. "I'll take care of her, I'm sorry. I was just so warm and so full and I just slept so hard."

"No problem." I left her to it and went back to my room and started to crawl back into bed. Lucy looked up at me and made the cutest pouty face I have ever seen.

"You're leaving the door open?"

"It's cold, baby."

"It's warm enough now."

I closed the door.

I started to get in bed again and she made the face again. "You're wearing your pajamas?"

I took them off. Yeah, no doubt about it, I was being used.

Several of the people I'd kept in touch with over the last few weeks couldn't be reached, and here's the thing—the ones with radios that could actually still talk to me were the ones that were set up pretty well. I knew there were thousands of people who could hear me that couldn't get in touch with me. If the ones who were set up were going, what hope did that leave for the others?

In Rudy they were having trouble keeping it warm enough, but they were doing it. I had given both Roy and Matt a ham radio, and Matt reported they were doing alright but burning a lot of wood and sort of wondering if with even as much as they had it was going to be enough.

"The cattle and all those other critters are all in one corner of the small barn so even they know it's easier for more bodies to heat less space," he told me. "I closed the door. Figured they weren't going out in this shit anyway and might as well keep it as warm in there as I can. Like I said I got plenty of hay and I'll just keep throwing it on top of their shit. Should be clean enough and a hell of a lot better than freezing."

In Fort Smith at Northside High school they weren't doing so well. It had gotten so cold there had been ice in their water jugs only a few feet from where they were sleeping. The real problem was they were running out of wood. They'd burned every desk, shelf, and chair they could find and they had started tearing rooms apart to burn the wood. They had already burned most of the gym floor, all the bleachers, and every single plastic thing they could find. They had started burning books and whatever else they could find for fuel, but they had very little actual wood left. Books will burn, but they won't put off much heat doing it. They were reduced to melting snow for water, and I can tell you right now that doing that brings a big bunch of the cold in with you. They were running the electric heater off the generator, but the two of them together weren't enough.

See, like I told you already, they made their wood stove in their shop and it was adequate but not too efficient. Even with a damper half their heat was likely as not going right up their chimney. And it was just that cold.

I told them to quit stuffing so many books in their stove at one time. All they were doing was smothering their fire. A smoldering fire doesn't produce much real heat. I looked on my maps and saw that the new Wal-Mart the boys said was mostly intact was only a few blocks away from them. I instructed them to make snowshoes by tying metal tennis rackets from the gym room to their feet, to cover themselves in sunscreen or lotion if they had it—'cause it holds in your body's heat. I more ordered than told them to hike to the Wal-Mart, make sleds from the hoods of cars they would doubtlessly find there, and then look for those fireplace logs in bags, charcoal briquettes, wooden furniture—anything that would burn.

They told me the Wal-Mart had been hit by the tornado. I wanted to just let them die in that moment because I decided they were too stupid to live. I explained that hit or not it was mostly standing and with a little effort they would find these burnable items. Three of them bundled up and went out into the sub-zero weather, understanding that they didn't have a choice and that they might not make it back alive. They came back with three car hoods loaded with fireplace logs and charcoal briquettes. They even had some lighter fluid. They told the others there was tons of it and where it was. They had built a fire there at the site and had warmed up good before trekking back out into the cold.

Yes charcoal briquettes emit carbon monoxide and you're never supposed to use them indoors. Here's the thing—it's a wood stove, a closed system, and the pollutants are going up the pipe. If not you're mostly screwed any way because I'm sure you've all heard of smoke inhalation. Also if the choices were dying of carbon monoxide poisoning and freezing to death I'd pick poisoning every time.

They got their wood stove roaring again, and then they took turns going in groups. They made a total of six trips that day and they didn't stop till they had everything burnable they could find, a whole car hood load of those memory foam mattresses, pillows and blankets—till then they'd been sleeping on wrestling mats and covering themselves with clothes and coats they'd found in the lockers. While there they grabbed some rifles and ammo and killed the half dozen dogs that tried to attack them when they raided the meat department. Everything was frozen completely solid, so they knew it would be good and they were all hungry for some protein that wasn't canned since they had eaten most of the frozen meat out of the cafeteria in the first couple of weeks. The effort cost one of the teacher's two fingers—frost bite—but proved to me that they did deserve to live after all.

The storm was horrible It stretched across most of the US and Canada all the way into Mexico. Europe and what was left of the Middle East and Africa looked bad, too. Australia looked mostly alright. Lucky Aussies.

I got a call from a guy I'd been talking to on the radios for years. He was in Arizona, an Indian living in a Hogan with his wife, mother, three sisters and a bunch of kids. "We are out of wood, we are out of any fuel at all and it is getting colder. We are huddling together for warmth but it isn't enough. My mother died last night and my baby is sick, too cold."

"I'm so sorry, Solomon. Is there nothing you can burn?"

"Only our clothes and we are wearing all of those, we need them."

So many people in such a small, well-insulated space, and they were still all freezing. It showed just how cold it actually was.

"Can you go out and cut wood?"

"The snow is five foot deep here."

"Do you have an out-building close by?"

"Yes, a shed it is..." He seemed to understand where I was going. "I can take my chain saw and cut it up, burn it."

"The storm will move on in two days. It will still be cold and the snow will still be deep, but you may be able to get out and cut wood then. For now dismantle the shed."

But for everyone I saved that day another one disappeared and the radio got quieter as the day progressed. The people who had bunkers and who were damn near as prepared for it as I was were doing fine, but people like Solomon who had just done the best they could to prepare with limited funds were all struggling. I tried not to think about it, but it was hard. Another on-line friend, Bob who lived in Michigan, radioed to tell me that he had plenty of fuel but he was still freezing. He had lived with his aged father and his father had died a week ago.

See cold and heat will kill off the weak quick. You have to be hearty to withstand constant harsh elements. It was why Evelyn was barely alive and Cherry was healthy, because Cherry had been in good shape going into it and Evelyn hadn't.

"I just don't care any more, Katy," Bob had said. "I'm tired of fighting it. Nothing is going to be left when this is over, nothing and... it's just so cold and I'm alone and... I've just got my dad stuffed in his bedroom, which we haven't heated in weeks and he's frozen stiff as a board and I'm alone. Alone and... No body can be alive out there and what's the point? I haven't seen one more chimney belching smoke in two weeks. No lights out there at night. Nothing, they're all dead. They have to be."

"Just stay next to the stove, Bob. It will pass; it's just going to take time. When it's over you can leave there, come here, there are people here."

He'd laughed then. "Katy... You don't understand how cold it is here. I've done everything you said. I've closed off all the other rooms. I've hung blankets—not just over all the windows and doors and stacked furniture over them—but I've done it over all the walls, too. I've got lots of wood and plenty of food and water and it still got so cold in here my father died. He died, and he wasn't even sick. When I stand next to the stove I only get warm on the side facing it. Last night I slept two feet from the stove under six blankets in all my clothes and I was so cold I shook all night. I'm tired of being cold, tired of being alone. I'm just tired." There was a gunshot and then silence. I shut the radio off and got to my feet. Lucy had gone to the bathroom a few minutes before and I was glad she wasn't there because I just suddenly needed to get way away from everyone. Suddenly it seemed to me that there were people everywhere, and of course it didn't help that I wasn't wrong.

The boys had taken care of the animals that morning because my ribs still stung and I figured I might as well milk it for all it was worth. They owed me for the whole drugging me thing.

I just wanted to be alone with the animals, not be around people or on the radio. I just wanted to not have to think for a minute. I was tired of solving problems, tired of everyone's problems becoming mine, tired of feeling like I was responsible for everyone. Like Bob I was just tired.

Of course I wasn't in the barn five minutes, hadn't even finished sweeping all the goat shit into the methane tank when there was Lucy. "You alright?" she asked quietly. This was the point in time that Lucy first got to see me act really crazy because I just didn't want to have to explain anything and I didn't like that she seemed to have figured out that my suddenly leaving the office and going to the barn meant that something was wrong. My brain was over loading and I needed to just not have to deal with... Well anyone or anything for at least ten minutes.

"Not really." I snapped back and then I started sweeping really hard, slinging goat shit all the way to the other side of the barn, which wasn't helpful at all but was something I suddenly wanted to be doing.

"What happened?" Lucy asked. She wasn't intimidated at all by my screaming or shit slinging, nope she just moved a little to the left out of range.

"Leave me the fuck alone!" I threw the broom down, turned quickly and headed into the hall that lead to the shop, slamming the door behind me. Damn it was cold in that hall. Of course not even that stopped Lucy who followed me into the cold-assed hall and shut the door. "God-dammit! Don't you get it? When I storm off into this cold-assed hallway I want to be alone!"

"Tell me what's wrong," she demanded, but didn't sound angry or hurt just maybe a little concerned.

I turned around, got two inches from her face and yelled as loud as I could, "What?! Are you still fucking reporting?"

She didn't back down just said, "No I'm not fucking reporting. I'm worried about you because when you went stomping out of the house you were obviously upset."

"If I wanted to talk about it, don't you think I would have done that instead of trying to be alone?"

She just looked at me then and she wasn't even a little bit afraid of me and she wasn't angry. It was infuriating and so was what she said next. "It's awful cold out here." Alright I don't know why that was so infuriating, it just was. Maybe because I had been in the barn where it was warm till she showed up, invaded my space, and forced me into that cold-ass hallway. Maybe because Bob had just killed himself because he couldn't get away from this cold and I could just by walking back in the barn.

"Why don't you state the fucking obvious? It's cold everywhere, Lucy." I started kicking at the pile of fire wood that lined the walls of the hall then, intermittently jumping up and down slinging my arms around and making noises that weren't really words. Somewhere in the middle of all that I managed to say, "Stupid people! Stupid people and all their stupid shit and now they're all dying. Even the ones that made it are dying in the hundreds now because it's just too fucking cold for humans and... It was easier to just be crazy Katy the nut job who said all the stupid shit about doomsday but never had to really deal with... Well what I said was coming actually being here."

"It's not my fault! I didn't do it! I didn't do any of it. They did it; they did it to themselves. I didn't do it and I'm just... I'm just so fucking tired of having everyone expecting me to be able to fix it all. It took centuries to make this mess. I can't fix it; no one can fix it now. It's way too late for someone to come along wave a magic wand or let go some CO_2 eating fungus and save us all. I don't have a big bottle of Nukes-away just lying around. Or a spray can of snow be gone in the back of my truck. It just has to run its course. If anything is left when it's over it will be a miracle. It's not my fault it's cold, it's not, and old people die in the cold, it happens and..." I just stopped screaming and kicking the wood pile and all the other stupid shit I was doing and I looked at Lucy. She was just sort of standing there, listening. She still looked concerned but still not angry or scared. I was having an all-out, screaming, crazy-assed fit, and she wasn't judging me or cringing in fear.

Cindy... Hell, every other woman I'd ever been with always did one of two things when I was pissed off. Either they got mad and started screaming back at me—which by the way is a big mistake—or they started crying and ran off. Somehow they always managed to make it about them, but Lucy—who I basically thought was the most self-centered woman I'd ever been with just wasn't.

"I'm having a conniption fit." I told her in case she hadn't actually noticed.

"Yeah, surprisingly I was aware of that," she said with a shrug. "It's alright, baby."

"Aren't you even a little upset?!"

"Why would I be? I get it completely. I cry when I think about it and you throw a fit. It isn't all that different. You've been there for me. You're absolutely right. The world is all fucked up and everyone *is* expecting way too much of you, and there is only so much you can do and most people think they're carrying the weight of the whole world on their shoulders but they aren't and you really are." She smiled then. "It isn't like you're really mad at me... You aren't are you?"

I thought about it for a minute. It annoyed me that she had followed me out there, but no I wasn't really mad at her and I told her so.

"Then wouldn't you rather say what's bothering you to me than to no one? I mean come on we're in this together aren't we?"

"Yeah," I said and I actually felt better.

"Then can you tell me what triggered this? I mean you have every right to be upset, but just what happened?"

I told her what had happened with Bob.

"It's not your fault Kay, not even close. You are doing everything you can possibly do. You can't save everyone, so quit kicking yourself. It's cold in here." She took my hand and we walked back into the barn.

Billy was standing there with that look on his face. The one he got whenever I was throwing a fit. The one that said he didn't know whether to shit or go blind, hose me down or run and hide. "You OK mom?" he asked carefully, and you could almost see him cringe getting ready for me to come undone.

"Yeah I'm fine," I said, and I was. I didn't know how she did it, but she had completely defused me. Better than that I didn't feel like a big, open wound with no peroxide in sight. No one in my life had ever done that for me. No one had ever let me get my mad on and sided with me against the injustice of the world. I felt ten feet tall and bullet proof.

I slugged my son in the face as hard as I could. He whirled backwards clutching his jaw "Jesus Christ, Mom!"

"And now I feel even better."

"What the hell?" Lucy shrieked.

I pointed right at Billy's nose. "Don't you ever, ever, drug me again."

CHAPTER 11

The Importance of Entertainment

It will seem trivial as the world falls apart around you, but it's very important to find some way to entertain yourself and those you are with. Close, confined spaces and hardship have a way of stressing out even the most even-tempered person and eating away at your will to live.

Put a pack of cards, some books, board games, sketch pad and pencils, knitting, needle point—anything you can do to break the monotony—in your survival kit.

Practicality is all-important, but so are playtime, hobbies, and the arts. We want to keep these things alive because these are the best parts of our civilization—the parts of it we ought to save if we can.

Use your imagination. Keep your mind busy and don't dwell on what's going on with the apocalypse.

The next three days were brutal and it was hard to have any sort of conviction not to dwell on the apocalypse. Fewer and fewer people were on the radio every day; they were dying. I wondered how many had run out of supplies and how many like Bob had just given up hope.

When we weren't giving reports or talking to someone on the air I played music. I also had a bunch of books on tape and I started playing an hour of a book each day figuring I'd do it till it was finished and start another one. Those people who had some sort of renewable power source and could listen to the radio just for entertainment would appreciate it.

I woke up, rolled over, looked at the clock, saw it was eight o'clock, and started to roll over and go back to sleep. It was when I did this that I realized that my ribs didn't hurt. They didn't hurt at all. I got up walked over and shut and locked the door then crawled back into bed and crawled up too Lucy's back and started... well you know.

She laughed. "What are you up to?"

"My ribs don't hurt," I explained. Then she was all over me.

"Damn!" Lucy said looking at the ceiling. "I knew you were good, but when you aren't hurt... damn!" she said again.

"Yep, once you go whacked you'll never go back," I said and pretended like it was the first time I'd used the line as she laughed at my joke.

Then she got up on her elbow, looked at the clock, and her mood changed immediately. Now I need to explain here that I didn't just give lip service to keeping track of the date. That clock gives the date and the time to the second.

"What's wrong?" I asked.

Lucy sighed and flopped back on the bed looking at the ceiling again. "Nothing, nothing." She just tried to shake whatever it was off, but she obviously couldn't. I was just hoping it wasn't something I did, so I didn't push the issue because... Well I was in a good mood again and I didn't want anything to ruin it.

Billy had made two extra chairs for the table and Evelyn was finally able to eat with us so meals were a tight fit what with six of us at a table I'd built for four people, but we made do. Lucy was quiet. Evelyn hadn't said much and I didn't know if it was because she was still sick or if she was just quiet by nature. I should have been so lucky, but I'll talk about that later.

Cherry... well between that girl and Billy and Jimmy just talking about this music group or that one and other crap I couldn't care less about it would have been hard for Lucy and I to talk at the table anyway.

I went out to do the milking and take care of the stock and Lucy went with me. It turned out she actually liked animals, really enjoyed working with them, and wanted to learn everything about them. That morning though she was just withdrawn, which I didn't get because I figured we had started the day pretty good. She didn't really talk to me till she was getting hay to put in the feeders and let out a scream shrill enough that my otherwise-immune-to-yelling animals actually jumped.

I'd been cleaning the chicken pen and came running out to see what was wrong.

"Snake!" she shrieked pointing. "Snake!"

And let me tell you right now, that God-awful high-pitched screech that some women make when they get scared, I have never found that the least bit attractive.

I looked and saw the black, red and yellow tail disappearing into the pile of hay. "It's just Fred," I explained. "He's a king snake. He's not poisonous."

"What the hell?!"

"He eats mice and bugs," I explained. "The wire mesh on the chicken pen is too small for him to get in and steal eggs and he steers clear of the goats. He got into the river once and tried to get a fish but I beat him good and he's stayed clear ever since."

"Couldn't you have a cat?"

"You have to feed a cat and they shit all over and there's the fur and they don't eat bugs..."

"Why can't you have something just for fun? Why don't you have a dog? I mean this is a farm don't all farms have a dog?"

"Dogs eat a lot and they shit all over and they don't produce anything." Now the truth was that I loved dogs. The last dog I'd had I loved like one of my sons when he died of old age just three weeks after Cindy. I cried like a baby for three hours straight. I just never wanted to go through that again so... "They need food" was as good a reason not to have one as any.

"So you can't do or have anything just for fun. Everything has to have a purpose!?"

I have you, I thought, but was smart enough not to say it. I knew she was just upset about something and then getting the shit scared out of her by our nearly five-foot barn snake that wasn't cute and furry like a cat was just a little much. I kept my cool remembering how she had defused me just a few days ago and that she was really good in bed. And let's face it, what were the odds I'd find another good looking gay woman who would have anything to do with me any time soon?

"Why does everything have to serve more than one purpose? Is this your brave new world Kay? A world where practicality is everything and anything—everything that isn't practical is just a frivolous nuisance?"

Now I guess I could have blown right back at her. Let's face it, I'm a lot better at the crazy than she is, but even though I didn't know why I knew that she was hurting.

"I'm sorry about the snake, Lucy. I should have told you he was out here, but he doesn't bite and as you can see he'll just run away from you." I didn't try to hug her because when I'm mad—even just upset—I don't want to be touched. Like most people I figure everyone is just like me. "Listen, the weather has broken. It's still colder than a witch's tit outside but there is something that has to be done. I was going to do it myself but maybe you'd like to go with me just to get out of the house for awhile and... I promise it doesn't serve any real purpose at all."

Lucy seemed to start breathing then. "I'm sorry, Kay." She'd taken to calling me that and I liked it so I didn't tell her not to. "I don't like snakes."

"I don't either, but I've gotten used to him." Fact was I bought him. You never saw the pretty red black and yellow King snakes here, just the green and black spotted ones. There are at least two of them—a male and female in the barn. See, I hated snakes so much that when I found out that King snakes will kill poisonous snakes and eat them I got some. The pair had at least one batch of babies because I'd seen them out on the place. We called them all Fred. We don't have any mice in the barn or greenhouse—or at least we don't see any—and damn few bugs.

"Why don't you wait for me in the greenhouse, put some distance between you and Fred. I'll come get you in a minute and we'll gear up and go out to the bird house."

"Bird house?" she asked.

"You'll see when we get there."

We had on all our gear. It was still cold but not unbearable. I hitched the trailer to the four-wheeler we had left with its snow mobile kit on. Lucy rode behind me and we drove to the "birdhouse."

It's really the old barn and it's not far from the old house. Neither of which are far from the new house but over a rise so that you can't see either from the house. Both were the prototypes for what I have now and were built when I didn't have buckets of cash at my disposal. That both structures made it through doomsday shows that the new house is really overkill, and that you didn't need a bunch of money to get set up to survive, but it sure didn't hurt any.

We drove up close to the "birdhouse" and got off the ATV, immediately sinking up to our knees in the three-and-a-half feet of snow. By the way, when I say we had a break in the weather that means it was a balmy ten degrees with a wind-chill of fifteen below on that day.

I grabbed a bag of feed and started towards the "birdhouse." As we approached, I pointed to all the animal and bird tracks in the snow leading up to and at the doorway. We walked down the ramp to the barn floor. The opening—usually big enough for me to drive in on my four-wheeler—was barely big enough for us to crawl through because the snow had blown in to fill it up.

Inside there was a stir among the birds. They still spook when they first see me. They calm down after the initial start. After years getting fed here the raccoons, possums, and squirrels just got out of reach and watched eagerly as they waited for me to put out food. They never panic any more. To them I'm the candy man.

I put the feed sack down and removed the mask and goggles from my face. I didn't know if it was just a comparison thing but it actually felt warm in there.

"This is the birdhouse," I whispered as hundreds of birds swarmed overhead, finally lighting.

"It's huge," Lucy said as she stripped her face gear as well.

"It used to be the barn. It's the same size as the new one. Of course this one isn't half full of hay and feed. When I built the new one I decided to make this wild-animal habitat. I figured they'd need some place to ride out the storm as well." I started dumping the bag of corn into the old goat feeders. The last corn I'd put there was gone. "Wow, these guys have really started eating. There should have been some corn left," I told Lucy. I checked the salt blocks and they were still mostly whole, so they'd last a good long time.

When I was digging down to build the old barn I hit a spring so I had dug it out and walled it up. It had only actually gone dry twice since I built the barn. It is a little half-circle trough at the back of the building. When I checked it there was no ice on it. That meant without heat the barn was staying above freezing which sort of amazed me. I showed Lucy. Of course now I think of it the ground water from the spring may have actually been helping to heat the building.

"Watch the birds; they'll shit on you if they can. I suggest you don't look up."

She just nodded, her eyes focused on a coon who had jumped into a feed trough.

"They won't attack and they've all had shots," I added.

That was true. A couple of years before I'd decided that we didn't need rabies or other animal-born illnesses in the post-apocalyptic world, so I'd tranked all the critters and once a year I gave them rabies shots and booster shots for other conditions.

Now coons and squirrels will raid your bird feeders and coons and possums will eat birds and their eggs if they can, but because of the way the birdhouse is built and the way I hung the feeders they can't. The bird's roosts and houses are all hanging from the top of the dome some fifteen feet above the floor in the middle. The three mega-sized feeders hang on chains from that same ceiling and can only be reached by the ladder I keep there, so until the coons figure out how to use the ladder the birds are safe. I grabbed the feed and started back in and that's when I saw them: three does and a buck, all watching me and like me about knee deep in the snow. I now noticed the deer tracks going in and out of the birdhouse. I had a bale of hay because I had been throwing it in there for wild rabbits and to keep there from being something besides shit on the floor. I had wondered why it was all gone. Now I knew. The buck was coming closer and the does were following and I realized that like Matt's zebras, lamas and buffalo these must have come from the wildlife refuge out by the highway because they were obviously tame.

I went back inside and just put down the bag of bird food. I grabbed Lucy's hand and pulled her over to stand by the door. "Be very still and very quiet. I think I just figured out what happened to all the corn."

Lucy just nodded.

I went back outside, grabbed the bale of hay off the four wheeler, and started back into the barn and just like I figured, here came the deer. They followed me right inside. I heard Lucy let out a little gasp and saw the buck turn to look at her. Then he just followed me with the does to where I dropped the bale of hay on the floor and cut the twine.

"Are they yours?" Lucy asked at my shoulder in a whisper.

"They weren't but I guess they are now. The snow must be deep enough that they could clear the fence. I'm going to have to start bringing more feed and hay out here."

"Can you afford to do that? Will you have enough?" Lucy was already starting to think like a survivor.

"Yeah, I have plenty, and if I run out of hay I can get more from Matt."

We watched the different animals scurrying around eating. The deer were lean so I decided, weather allowing, I'd bring more hay and some rice bran in a couple of days. I pulled a bottle of antibiotics I'd mixed out of my pocket and dumped it into the water. This many animals in this small a space I figured it was a good precaution to just dose them every once in awhile. I'd dumped wormer in it the last time I was there. I'd worm them again in a week just to make sure the deer got wormed.

Lucy walked up and took my ungloved hand in hers. "This is great."

It is pretty, snow was mostly blocking the sun from coming through the windows in the dome, but some light was still getting through.

"Give me a second." I put my gloves back on and popped my goggles and mask back into place. I got the snow shovel out of the trailer and started clearing the windows even though Billy and Jimmy had cleaned it twice and I'd cleaned it once already it still took me most of thirty minutes and by the time I got done I was freezing but it was worth it when I walked back inside and Lucy was just staring at the ceiling, a huge smile on her face.

"It's beautiful. Is it what I think it is?"

"Yes, this is the barn that poverty built. Instead of two-foot thick aquarium glass and fibered reinforced cement the walls are just two regular concrete domes a foot apart and the windows are made of bottles with the necks pointed into the void."

How'd I do the domes? Wet sand—lots and lots of wet sand. I built the side walls and then I just filled the whole thing with sand, domed the top, and poured six inches of concrete on top of it. When it dried I took the sand from inside and spread it a foot deep over the whole thing and covered the sand with another layer of concrete. Where I wanted windows—in all my structures—I made boxes. When the second layer of concrete dried I took out the boxes and put in the windows.

I'd made four "windows," each four-foot across and each a different pattern using different colored bottles. One is a four-leaf clover, one a star, a yin and yang, and a double helix.

The deer looked up at us each with a mouth full of hay and Lucy chuckled. "I feel like Snow White." That was a picture... Lucy running around singing, little animals dressing her waiting for all the little men to come home... But of course they'd all died in the apocalypse. "It's like they're saying thanks."

"Well sure they are. Come on we better get back to the house."

Lucy seemed reluctant to go but geared up and followed me anyway.

The ride back to the house was easier because we had just been out and of course using the same tracks we used before we were making a sort of road in the snow.

By the time we got back to the house we were both freezing our asses off and nearly raced each other to get to the fire to start stripping gear.

"How's the birdhouse?" Jimmy asked before I had even gotten my coveralls half way down. Jimmy loved the birdhouse and converting the old barn into wild animal habitat had been the one project that we'd done that he'd been passionate about.

"Fine. We have deer now—three does and a buck. Tame, too. Followed me in the building to eat. They've been there for awhile, so I imagine the four wheeler scares them and they run off," I told him.

"That's way cool. How are the coons?"

"Counted five so they're all still with us," I said. "Jimmy has them all named," I told Lucy.

Jimmy would have made a great field biologist, and that's probably what he would have eventually become after he grew up if the world hadn't mostly blown up and the need for such things with it.

I went back to the bedroom to finish stripping because all my underclothes were sweaty. Lucy followed me in and then mostly just stood there and watched me strip, which made me feel really uncomfortable actually because well as I've said before she has a really great body and me... not so much. "Ah Lucy, do you mind?"

"Oh Christ," she sighed, disgusted like. But she turned her head away. See we'd already had this argument at least once. "We do it all the time, I've seen you naked dozens of times." Alright so we're still having this argument.

I put on a robe. "Alright," I said. She turned back around and just sort of made this face which was a cross between a smile and a thought, the thought being I was sure at the time, What the hell is my fine ass doing with you, oh it's the whole end of the world and you being the last dyke around thing. "You're right. I'm sorry."

"The stupid thing is that I like your body, dumb ass."

I just shrugged. "I'm going to get a shower."

Which I did and when I came back to our room to get dressed Lucy was just laying across our bed still half dressed, just staring at the ceiling and looking close to tears. I sighed and then asked what I guess I should have made her tell me that morning. "So... What's actually wrong?"

"Nothing." She forced a quick smile that just looked like she had no acting skill at all, which I knew she did 'cause I'd seen her use it already.

"Fuck that, Lucy. Like you said, who else are you going to talk to? Now what the fuck's wrong? If it's something I did then I need to know or I'll most likely do it again, probably twice. Of course I'll probably do it again any way 'cause I'm a dumbass, but I'd at least try not to... for awhile."

Have I mentioned I'm really too honest for relationships with... well anyone?

"You didn't do anything," she said and then she sat up on the edge of the bed.

"I'm fine just tired." And then her eyes started to fill with tears.

I walked up to stand in front of her and looked down at her. "Listen... I know I'm not the most lyrical speaker and I just sort of bumble through the whole comforting thing not really knowing how to do it, but I really care about you, Lucy, and I can't stand to see you so unhappy."

"I'm not unhappy Kay, and I'm certainly not unhappy with you. It's just..." she wrapped her arms around my neck and lay her head on my shoulder—yes the bed is that far off the floor—"Today is my mother's birthday, or at least it would have been her birthday if she were alive."

"Oh baby, I'm sorry," I said, and patted her back. See what I mean? That's about as good as I get with the comforting.

"She's just dead, Kay. They're all dead and I don't know how. I could have talked to her one last time and I called the fucking network instead. I was really close to my mother. I loved her. I could tell her anything. Anything. And now I have no one to talk to."

"You can talk to me, Lucy."

"I can't talk to you about you."

"You could but I'd probably get pissed off."

She laughed "I don't want to say bad things about you. I'd

love to be able to tell her about you, about us, all I've been through. I miss her." She started to cry and I just held her and rocked her and let her say incoherent things against my shoulder till she was finished.

CHAPTER 12

Keep the Calendar Updated

I can't express enough how important it is not to lose track of the hours and the days. Even if all you can do is take a crayon and make a mark on the wall, keep track of the passage of time. Knowing that a new season is coming up and maybe a break in the weather—whatever the weather might be. Knowing that a loved holiday, a birthday or anniversary, is coming up will give you the heart to go on. This is especially important to kids. Knowing when it's day time or night time will be all-important if you're stuck somewhere there is little or no light. You need to keep these simple rituals going, keep the clock or watch wound, mark the days off that calendar. If you have lights and can afford to use the energy, turn them on during what would be day light hours, and turn them off at night. This will help your internal clock keep on track.

Know when it's your birthday, Christmas, Chanukah, Kwanza—whatever you celebrate—and do something different that day even if it's as simple as hanging pieces of aluminum foil on a piece of firewood or sticking a candle on a can of spam.

We mark the seasons and the time and have holidays for a reason, it's these things that make life worth living. In the post-apocalyptic world it will be more important than ever to celebrate these special events.

There is a reason why there are so many holidays in December. It's because this is when the nights are the longest, when it's coldest, when everyone was huddled into too=small spaces and were forced to stay indoors.

There will likely be more than one month of this sort of crap so maybe we should all make up even more winter holidays.

We dug a downed Cedar tree out of the snow—still all green—knocked the snow off of it, pulled it into the greenhouse and decorated it. It looked more or less like our tree did every year because... Well I was still in my house and I still had all our old family decorations—the ones we'd had all the boy's lives. I even had them hang their "baby's first Christmas ornaments" on the tree the way they always had—a tradition Cindy had started not me.

Yep, except for the nearly four feet of snow outside and all of the animals being stuck in the barn my life really hadn't changed much. In fact, let me be honest. My life was better than it had been in years, maybe ever. For years... hell all my life, I'd done nothing but obsess about what was going to happen. I'd spent my whole life worrying and preparing for the worst while people ridiculed me and my own kids thought I was a nut job. Now I didn't have to worry about dumb fucks tearing up the world anymore; it had already happened. So far it was nothing I wasn't fully prepared for.

In addition, both my sons were back home and one of them was as good as married to someone I actually liked, and I had a gorgeous woman who—since there was really not much else to do—was fucking me rotten at least twice a day.

I still have a little guilt because the apocalypse has been so good for me.

We each had a gift under the tree wrapped in bright paper. As was our tradition, the gifts had to be hand made, which was just as well since there were no stores. Of course I had plenty of crap out in the shed and I had made the trip out there to get some decent clothes—you know that would actually fit them—and arctic gear for the girls and had wrapped them.

Lucy, Evelyn and Cherry had all complained that me and the boys had an advantage since we all knew how to use tools. But let's face it, there really wasn't a choice and I was more than happy with the gifts Lucy was giving me every day—most times twice.

Between what we'd made for the kids in Rudy proper and what we'd made for each other and the girls, me and the boys had spent most of two days in the shop with the tools just a-going, the methane generator running on high, the wood stove blazing, and I think we all had fun playing Santa's elves. It was nice not to be in the house or the barn and to have something to do besides cook, clean house or mess with the garden and the animals. It wasn't as good as sex but you can't just do that all the time and working with wood has always been a pleasure of mine.

Of course none of us were really surprised by what we got because we'd all been working in the same shop at the same time, but it was still nice to sit and open the gifts.

Evelyn still didn't talk much. Still weak and overwhelmed I guessed. I had no idea what a blessing that was till it was over, but I'll talk about that later.

Cherry talked constantly, but not ever really to me. In fact when I think back on it now, everyone but Lucy seemed to avoid talking to me as much as possible. I won't pretend to know why, though Lucy has said more than once and the boys agree that I'm more than a little intimidating.

Which, duh! I'm crazy. That is a little off-putting for most people I suppose.

Lucy told me that Cherry told her that Evelyn was really depressed and couldn't quit talking about her family and friends all being dead. Of course I never heard Evelyn say this. If I had I'd have told her to shut up.

Does that sound like I'm harsh and unfeeling and just a total bitch? Let me tell you something, if you dwell on something you can't do anything about... Well that's one of the things that made me crazy. If you choose—and it is a choice not like sexual orientation which isn't—to just think about everything you've lost you will never get over it. People need time to grieve, that's true. But wallowing is a whole different story and making your friends listen to you go on and on about everyone you've lost when they've lost just as many people if not more than you have? Well that's just selfish.

Maybe this is why they weren't really talking to me at this point, I mean it was pretty close to the beginning of the apocalypse and maybe all any of them wanted to do was sit around and talk a bunch of morbid shit and they knew I'd tell them to shut the fuck up.

The whole, *this has ended, that one has died, we have to start all over and look at all we've lost.* Well if you're still doing that as you read this then you just need to kill yourself because you aren't ever going to get over it. Every ending is a new beginning. Everything that dies makes room for something new, maybe something better.

I for sure think the world is better now.

Let's face it; the world sucked. It especially sucked for everyone who wasn't rich. Our country was never able to come back from what the rich idiots and those that blindly followed them had done to it. We were never going to convince people to stop killing each other and the world till they just did it and got it out of their system. There would have always been some religious hoo-haw wanting a jihad to kill all the infidels—which was never, ever them.

The apocalypse was the ultimate do over. Quit crying and plow your damn field, plant your corn, plant your beans, tend your chickens if you're lucky enough to have any—and build a better shelter.

In short get the fuck over it already!

The only thing I still get really depressed about is that I know as hard as some of us will try people will fuck everything up again, because it's what people do. We'll build a really cool little self-sufficient world for ourselves without wars and religions and governments and huge pollution-spitting factories, and then somewhere someone will decide it's not enough and they'll create new religions and build new factories and governments and we'll have crap again. It's human nature to question things. When we can't answer questions that can't be answered people will once again look for something besides what they see to explain it... like Lucy and her damned fate thing.

Anyway, as soon as we'd opened our gifts and had some breakfast me and the boys loaded the sled with all the presents for the kids and a bag full of candy canes. Then we loaded up some milk, eggs, cheese, five pounds of sweet potatoes, sugar, rice, some fresh tomatoes, squash, carrots and lettuce from the greenhouse, flour, and half a dozen butchered rabbits for the adults. I even threw in a small can of coffee. I have to tell you this last was huge because I had done the math and, at the current rate of our personal use, I was going to have to die by ninety or I'd be out of coffee. And if I ran out of coffee and toilet paper I wasn't going to care if I died anyway.

Now let me tell you the God's honest truth right now, I don't think I would have been nearly so generous if I hadn't been silly in love with Lucy. I was in love with her, too, even if I hadn't yet told her that I was. She'd said it to me a couple of times after we'd made love but I mean come on you can't take anything to heart that someone tells you when they're still gasping from the orgasm you just gave them.

How did I respond when she said she loved me in those moments between great sex and falling asleep? I pretended I didn't hear her.

Yes, I'm well aware that's a chicken shit thing to do, so shoot me!

The point is I was being really generous and it had nothing to do with the spirit of the season and everything to do with the fact that I was in love and happy and just wanted to share that happiness.

If I'd had a Santa suit I'd have made Billy wear it and go with me and play the big guy, but since I didn't I took Lucy with me because... Well I'd rather have Lucy's arms wrapped around me and at that point in time having realized I was mad in love with her I just didn't want to be separated from her at all. You guessed it; just as she was getting to a point where she didn't have to follow me around all the time I reached a point where if she wasn't right there with me I immediately went and found her, so I'm pretty sure I didn't have to say it because she knew I loved her.

It was really cold and our fogless goggles still fogged up but I hardly noticed I was excited about playing Santa Claus. Hell, if I'd had the suit and a fake beard I would have played the jolly old elf myself.

As we pulled up outside the old church most of the adults were already outside waiting to help us carry stuff in. The tree they'd brought in was small for a good reason, space was at a premium. They'd decorated it with ornaments made from craft paper, beer cans, and old plastic bottles. Paper chains hung around and cards that different people had made for each other and that the kids had made were hanging everywhere. The minute we brought the food in the adults went right to work preparing what would be the group's Christmas dinner. When the kids saw Lucy and I walking in with the feedbags full of presents, you could see that it was all they could do to keep from knocking us down and mugging us for toys.

Everyone watched as Lucy and I moved to the front of the building and the kids followed. I let Lucy make up the story and do the talking because: a) she's better at that shit than I am, and; b) as it has been pointed out, folks seem to think I'm intimidating.

"Hey kids," Lucy started, and the kids crowded her so fast I was afraid they'd knock her over. She pulled a note from inside her coat that she'd apparently written the night before. "We found these bags of toys on the other side of the bridge with this note." She cleared her throat for effect. "Dear children of Rudy, I'm sorry I couldn't stop in but the reindeer have been acting really funny. Seems even they are too cold, but you've all been really good kids this year and I wanted you to have your presents." She started pulling the wrapped toys from the bag. She would call out a kid's name and then a kid would yell out and start hurling themselves through the crowd and grab the package greedily. When they'd opened their gift and screamed it was just what they wanted, Lucy would grab another and start the process all over again. I smiled when she called Karma's name and she bounded over those other kids, just as greedy for her gift as all the rest were. You'd have never guessed she'd been at death's door just a few weeks before.

Too soon all the presents were opened and the kids were just playing and sharing toys. You know, the whole "you can play with mine if I can play with yours" that starts with toys when you're a kid and... Well you know where I'm going.

The smell of cooking food flooded the building and to me it smelled like happiness. I must have just been grinning like an idiot because Lucy walked over to me and punched me playfully in the shoulder. "You look awful dammed pleased with yourself."

I laughed, "Is that bad?"

"No." She smiled back at me then raised up on her tiptoes and kissed me on the lips. There was sudden silence and I knew why. I just stared around the room at all of them and thundered. "Oh don't even start that shit." There was a general nodding of heads and then everyone went back to what they were doing. Working at not looking at us. Lucy gave me a curious look and I shrugged and mumbled. "We weren't standing under the mistletoe." Lucy seemed to realize what she'd done then and she blushed. See, you have to remember Lucy was the one who'd always been in the closet, not me.

"I'm sorry," she said.

"What the hell for?" I said loud enough that everyone could hear me. "It's a new world and we aren't going to start it with any stupid shit." Then I looked around the group. "Isn't that right?"

"Right," Roy Jr. said and most of the others agreed.

Someone was jerking on my pants leg. I looked down and there was Karma.

"Crazy Katy?" Around the room I saw the adults all cringe. I ignored them.

"Yes honey?"

"Thank you for making me better and thanks for my bear," she said holding it up.

"Honey you're welcome but I didn't get you that bear, Santa did."

The little shit winked at me and motioned for me to bend down so I did and she whispered in my ear, "I know there is no Santa. My parents told me. There's no Santa Clause except for you." She then hugged my neck smacking me in the head with that bear and then she let me go and ran off to play.

I laughed and stood up, and just to make sure they all knew I wasn't going to hide just to make them comfortable I took hold of Lucy's hand and held it tightly. Ken Porter glared at me, and that's when I knew he was going to have to die.

One of the older kids walked up to us then and held out a homemade card. "We made this for you." I took it, read it, and it nearly brought a tear to my eye. "Thank you very much." I folded it and stuck it in my shirt pocket. "Well, we're out of here. I want to get home way before it gets dark. Roy, would you and Ken help me get everything tied down to go?"

Roy and Ken followed us into the vestibule, which was cold but not unbearable, and Lucy and I started putting our gear back on. "Katy, we can't thank you enough..." Roy started.

"You want to thank me, get Ken to quit preaching."

Both Roy and Ken looked shocked and Ken said, "I didn't say anything in there. Didn't want to ruin everyone's mood, but you shouldn't be doing your queer thing in front of the kids. As for me preaching it's our faith which is sustaining us..."

"Fuck that. I'm the one sustaining you. Listen and listen. good asshole, 'cause I'm only goin' to say this once." I punched him in the chest with my finger hard. "You are a withering piece of shit. Religion destroyed the world; it was nothing but trouble. You aren't being saved by God or sweet baby Jesus, you are being saved by my godless, sinner, very queer ass, and by your own will to live."

"Now you listen here..." He got right in my face and that was when I put the barrel of my gun against his nuts and he shut up.

"No, I'm *not* going to listen to you at all. I've heard all the hateful crap you and your kind spew all my life. It ends here."

"Now, Katy, calm down," Roy said.

"I'm crazy, remember? I don't calm down. Without my help, there is no way you'd be alive right now and certainly no way that you will make this winter without running out of food. If you think you and yours will storm me and take my stuff..."

"We'd never do that, Katy," Roy said quickly.

"No, you wouldn't, but he would. And after he convinces all those idiots in there that the whole world ended not because idiots like him thought God wanted them to wipe out the infidels, but because God wanted to kill out all the horrid gay people, that's exactly what they'll do because religion always allows, even condones, people doing what they otherwise simply would not do."

"Godless people brought down the wrath of God..."

I moved the barrel of my pistol to Ken's nose.

"You stupid fucks. What has to happen to make you let go of your hateful rhetoric? Everyone's dead, dumbass. Everyone's struggling except for me. Now why would your hate-mongering God do that? If I didn't help you, you'd all be dead and me... Well, I'd have more supplies. If I pull this trigger right now your God won't save you. You think their faith is sustaining them?" I nodded my head back towards the interior of the building. "They know that's crap even if you don't. If you think for one minute that because of my generosity today that I won't let you all starve tomorrow then you're dead wrong. Now get out of my face."

He practically ran inside, and behind me I could hear Lucy start to breathe again.

"I'm sorry, Katy, really sorry. You're right; we'd all be dead without you. I just don't know what to do about him and..."

"It's simple. Tell everyone that if they continue to let him run his mouth trying to turn everyone against me, that I'll not bring them one more ounce of food. I'll not help in any way even to give you information. Why should I help you to live, to thrive, only to have you all try to kill me and mine for our trouble? You live on my doorstep. If I can't trust you then I won't let you live much less help you do so." I put my gun back in my pocket. "Of course *try* would be the operative word there because any of you try to come after us and you won't make it past the gate. Truth is, Roy, we only put our lives in danger if we continue to help you, and I'm not going to do one more thing to help any of you until you can prove to me that you don't all secretly feel the same way Ken Porter does."

"We don't, Katy, I swear it."

"Yet the kids still call me Crazy Katy, and they had to hear that someplace. I'm serious, Roy, you better all decide right now who you're going to trust—Ken Porter's hateful version of God or me."

"Katy... We all appreciate everything you do. Ken... We'll deal with him, Katy. I promise you we'll shut him up."

"Good. Merry Christmas." I left and Lucy followed.

"Are you serious, Kay?"

"About what?" I asked as I started the four-wheeler.

"Abandoning them."

"Well, I'm certainly not going to continue to help them if they're just going to hate me and try to over-run us later."

"It's just one man, Kay."

"They let him talk, Lucy. They wouldn't let him talk his crap unless they at least in part believed him."

"But... Kay what about the kids?"

"It's up to them, Lucy, not me. I don't believe any of them besides Ken have enough hatred left in them that they'd rather starve than change."

She nodded, though I could tell she wasn't happy with me. Which is what happens when you tell someone something they know is probably right but they just don't want to hear or think about it.

We went to Matt's, wished he and his a Merry Christmas, dropped off some supplies and got some more beef.

It wasn't till we were alone in our room changing our clothes with the door closed that Lucy said anything else about the altercation at the church.

"Katy... you don't really think... you don't think they'd really come after us?"

"They will if Roy can't shut Ken up."

"And you're just going to let all those people—those kids—starve? You aren't going to help them anymore?"

"Not if they don't prove they've shut Ken up. But don't worry about it because I've had some time to think about it and if they can't shut Ken up I'm going to kill him myself. I kill him for spouting shit, then none of the rest of them are going to be in any hurry to spout the same sort of shit." Surprisingly, this didn't seem to make Lucy happy.

"Kill him? Kill him Kay?!" Lucy screeched.

I looked at her like she was from Mars. "Well, yeah."

"It's just that easy for you?"

"If he's going to try to get me, turn the town against me and build an army to come after me and mine? Yep, it's that easy for me to just kill him."

"Surely there is some other way."

"What would that be, Lucy?"

"Maybe he'll just shut up on his own. I mean I would, you had your gun in his nuts... up his nose..."

"You really don't understand religious nuts, do you? He's not going to shut up on his own. He's convinced God wants him to spread *his* truth."

I didn't really understand why we were having this fight, and I guess Lucy didn't either because she just let it drop right there. Believe me, if she'd been really sure what she was mad at me about she would NOT have let it go... ever. I realized that Lucy wasn't really mad at me. That like me she was mad at Ken. Maybe more than me because first he must have reminded her of all the reasons she'd never been able to just be herself and second he was forcing my hand. Finally, somewhere in her brain she knew as well as I did that the only way to deal with Ken Porter and people like him was to kill them before they could spread their venom.

For the record, I didn't have to kill Ken Porter. Roy told the group what I'd said in front of Ken, but Ken wouldn't shut up. In fact, as most preachers had always done, this just seemed to give him more fuel for his fire. You know the whole, "See how the devil runs from the word of God? See how the sinner turns to violence and wants to raise their hand against God's servant? They want to shut me up; therefore, I must be speaking the truth."

Well apparently they all tried to shut him up for about a week, but he just would not shut up till every last person in the building wanted to kill him. Let's face it, you're being told that if this guy doesn't shut up that you're all going to die. You already didn't really buy his shit anyway because... Well a church full of praying people get killed by a massive tornado and you're all huddled in one room and the only reason you're alive at all is because of some godless, lesbian heathern, then your faith in whatever higher power you may have believed in has to be a little stretched. Then this guy just keeps spouting the same shit you've been told is going to kill you all, and you're most likely tired of hearing it anyway because it just doesn't ring true to you anymore even if you believed the crap in the first place. Well it's only a matter of time till he walks out to the outhouse and he just never comes back.

Roy said even Ken's wife told him that she thought it would be best for the group if Ken just died. And he said she winked and added, "If you know what I mean." Apparently Ken was just flat a bastard. It reached a point that every time there was a moment's silence Ken started flapping his jaw. Everyone told him to shut up, but the more they told him to shut up the more he wouldn't. They beat the living crap out of him twice and that didn't help. Then one day... Well, he went to the outhouse and he never came out, at least not on his own. Someone had stuck a knife in his liver. To this day no one will say who, but I think it was Roy because after that he became the kind of guy who says it's my way or the highway and no one ever questioned his right to lead again.

We had each picked a dish and made it and then ate a huge Christmas dinner buffet style. We butchered a rooster, and as I ate it I started to wish I'd raised some turkeys because the truth was except for what wild or lost domestic animals happened upon places like our birdhouse or Matt's hay barn, I doubted much wildlife—much less domestic stock—would survive this winter. Too cold, nothing to eat, snow for water, and no one to take care of them—which is why domestic stock, especially, was doomed.

I noticed at one point that it got very quiet, and when I looked around I realized that I was really the only one eating in that good ole glutinous style that the holiday demanded. As I looked at them they all looked a little blue, which pissed me off no end because I was in a really good mood, such a good mood that even my run-in with that preaching idiot—I'll speak ill of the dead if I want—hadn't dampened my spirit.

At first I tried to ignore their obvious mood, but then Evelyn started crying. She jumped up and said, "I'm sorry. Excuse me." And then just ran out of the room. That's right; it turned out the girl wasn't quiet at all. She was, in fact, a huge drama queen.

"Jumping Jesus on a pogo stick," I muttered.

"Katy, for God's sake," Lucy snapped at me. Then she got up and went after Evelyn and Cherry went after Lucy. That's fems for ya. All have to go be as miserable as whichever one appears to be the most miserable.

I looked up at the boys, smiled, shrugged and said, "Women."

As if that answered everything and then I went back to eating. Jimmy nodded, smiled and then he started eating, too. It was Billy who just couldn't leave things alone.

"They're upset, Mama. It's the holidays and our family is still all together except for Mom, but theirs aren't."

"That's not my fault," I said, plainly around a mouth full of food.

"Mama... Don't you remember what the first Christmas after Mom died was like?"

Well of course I did, and he succeeded in ruining the good happy I had going on because I *did* know why they were all upset, I had just been avoiding thinking about it. Even the boys had lost friends in this thing. I'd lost friends, too, and it wasn't that I didn't occasionally think about them, but let's face it I'd been so obsessed that I'd distanced myself from my friends years before. And the truth was I'd always been too busy and too crazy to make any really close friends anyway. There were people I'd miss from time to time but it just wasn't the same.

I remembered clearly that first Christmas after Cindy died. I made a big dinner just like the one we were sitting down to that day—except we had a turkey. I really miss turkey. We sat down to eat, I took one look at her empty chair at the table, and I just lost it. Of course when I did the boys did, and by the time we quit crying our dinner was cold and it just ruined the whole day.

"Son of a bitch." I muttered, quit eating, and stood up from the table. I went to find Lucy. Frankly I didn't care about the other two. Let them cry on each other. I found them in the greenhouse all three just talking in incoherent sobs in a manner I was sure would make all the plants sick and put the goats off their milk. Seeing Lucy cry made me feel bad. I just couldn't take it, and if I hadn't already known I was in love with her I would have known it right then because before when she cried I tried to comfort her but I didn't feel anything except maybe a little annoyed and now when she was crying it just about broke my heart. It literally hurt me to see her so unhappy.

Of course all that said I still had no idea what to say or do. I walked up to them and, ignoring the others, put out my hand to take Lucy's. Before I could take her hand she threw her arms around my neck, grabbed me in a death grip, and just started sobbing loud, raking sobs.

"Come on, baby." I half-pulled and half-carried her back to my room where I shut the door. Then I just held her and rocked her and patted her back and... felt completely useless and helpless and sort of sick to my stomach.

"Everyone's just dead, Kay," she cried out.

Now we'd been through this a couple of times already, so

you would have thought I could have come up with something better than, "I know, baby. I'm sorry."

"I feel so alone today. Everyone I loved is dead. Everyone that loved me." She sobbed.

"I love you, Lucy."

She sniffled, signifying the crying might stop soon. "You're just saying that to get me to stop crying, Kay."

"Is it going to work?" I asked with a smile. Then she just started crying hard again and I felt like a shit so I said, "Come on, Lucy. You know I love you."

"Do you?"

"You have to know I do. If I didn't love you, I'd hardly even care that you were crying much less feel like I'm going to hurl."

"I love you, too." She sniffed again and I just knew she was covering yet another of my shirts in snot and tears, but this time I really didn't care.

"I love you, Lucy. Have you not noticed that I just sort of stand around grinning all the time? I know it's wrong because everyone else just feels like a big, raw nerve most of the time and you've all lost so much, but I'm happy. I'm happy because you're here and I love you and you love me. I'm sorry that I'm not all chewed up like everyone else is, like you are, but the only thing that has made me feel the least bit unhappy for days was when I saw you crying. Before when you cried it just annoyed me." I thought this explained everything.

Lucy actually laughed a little then. "Well thanks, honey."

"You know what I mean, Lucy."

"Yeah, I know what you mean."

I handed her the handkerchief out of my pocket. Once again it wasn't really clean, and once again she didn't seem to mind. "I'm sorry about all the drama."

"First off, you didn't start it. You know what, Lucy? When people cry for no reason that's drama. When they cry over the death of everyone they knew and loved—that's not really drama. I just forgot for a minute that you can't always keep your grief locked away. That some things push it out of the place you stick it. Billy reminded me."

"I was alright till Evelyn lost it, and then I went to just comfort her and then Cherry came to help and we all just wound up crying." Well yeah 'cause that's what chicks do. "I'm sorry we all ruined Christmas dinner."

"Oh, I'm going to go eat my dinner, and so are you. Then we're just going to come in here, listen to some tunes, and just lay in our bed in our room..."

"Our bed, our room?" Lucy asked with a smile.

"Yeah ours. Not mine any more—ours. We'll just lay here,

listen to some tunes, and talk and then later if our food settles and we have the urge maybe we'll make love. **B**ut maybe we'll just hold each other..."

She pushed away from me looked up and smiled. "Oh... we're doing it, bitch."

CHAPTER 13

Making the Most of What You've Got

Just because you're short on cash doesn't mean you can't be better prepared for the apocalypse. You can't afford bottled water? Make your own. Take your empty juice bottles, or even those old liter bottles everyone tosses out, clean them and fill them with water. If you're afraid the water will get stale—some idiots believe water goes bad I think they're full of shit but to be on the safe side—change the water every three to six months. Keep a lot of bottled water—at least five gallons for each member of your family—this should hold you over till you figure out how to make the water you find drinkable. Store it under your bed, under your furniture, in the bottom of a closet, wherever you have room.

And people, if you're sleeping on a waterbed guess what— hundreds of gallons of potable water—just don't put that treatment shit in it. It turns green, who cares? A little algae never hurt anyone. Hell, some people eat the shit on purpose.

Start saving plastic bags—all those stupid little sacks you get every time you go to the grocery store, all those plastic dog and other animal feed bags. Find a place in your house or in your yard and just start collecting stuff that would normally be considered trash, stuff that could be used to fill cracks or cover holes, build a shelter. Here's an idea—get rid of all that useless crap that you've been hording that fills every space in every home in America and start filling those spaces with the things you will need to survive.

Build your survival kit a piece at a time. Don't try to buy it all at once and it won't tax your income as much as that soda you buy every day or that candy bar you get every time you go to the store. As for food items, every time you go to the store buy a bag of dried beans, some canned food, or some jerky. Put it back and pretend you don't have it.

As I've said before, start seeing everything as something else and start putting back those things that might be useful if the worst happens.

Poverty isn't an excuse to be unprepared. Poverty is the mother of necessity, and as they say necessity is the mother of invention. Stop waiting for the government to fix things and get to work. Even *if there isn't a full-blown apocalypse, there's a damn good chance that some disaster will hit your community and would it really hurt anyone to be prepared for that?*

Stop worrying about things that don't really matter and start worrying about what really does. Stop thinking your kids need a new video game and start thinking about putting back the stuff you'll need to get them through the end of the world as we know it.

Of course the real problem is that too many people spent most of their time trying to find ways to get other people to do their work. They wasted all their time trying to make a job easier instead of just doing the job that needed to be done. They kept waiting till they had the money to do it right, but since they never had the money to do it right they spent all their money on brightly-colored plastic crap and useless electronic bullshit and they didn't do anything to prepare. *That's* why so many people died.

Well that and the coldest, longest winter humans had seen since the little ice age.

It had been three weeks since the New Year dawned in the age of the apocalypse. We all stayed up till twelve and made lots of noise. The girls all cried again and I began to wonder how long it would be before we could celebrate a holiday without them just having a complete breakdown.

Lucy and I were working in the greenhouse. I was taking out some of the old lettuce and planting new seeds. The plants didn't seem to mind that ninety-five percent of their light was artificial; they were thriving. No doubt all the CO_2 from all the animals and six humans was helping, and of course I was still side-dressing the plants with compost I was making in a fifty-five-gallon turn-style compost bin I'd moved into the barn before the shit hit the fan. I had to keep the plants producing at peak because I was beginning to think winter might never end. The sun hadn't penetrated the cloud cover in weeks, and the temperature just kept dropping. We'd had another small snowfall, but the big problem wasn't more snow, it was just the lack of sunlight and the cold. I had the fake sunlight bulbs all through the house because I'd been afraid of this, and they was supposed to help keep you from getting the winter-time blues. Even that wasn't the real problem in our house, the real problem was six people living in a house really built for three and everyone's different personalities clashing into each other.

Of course, as is often true one person was making most of the trouble. Evelyn was the real problem. Her passive-aggressive, narcissistic, bullshit was driving me and everyone else to thoughts of homicide.

Cherry and Billy never seemed to stop talking except when they were screwing which they were doing about six times a day. Can we say Nuvo-ring? Last thing we needed was anyone getting pregnant. God, heterosexuals are a pain in the ass!

Jimmy was withdrawn and sullen and... Well, basically Jimmy.

The only one who wasn't annoying the living piss out of me was Lucy. At that point in time I think if she'd crawled onto the middle of the kitchen table and shit I would have applauded and acted like I thought it was performance art.

We couldn't watch a movie or eat a meal without someone snapping at somebody else and we would all get so stir crazy we made excuses to go out into the freezing waste land just to get the hell out of the house.

But everyone else I could tolerate. No one else made me want to really kill them—except Evelyn. In fact, Evelyn was the reason Lucy and I were working in the greenhouse—just so we could get away from her.

"I see them," Lucy said, excitedly pointing down into the water. I knew what she was talking about. A bunch of fish had hatched about a week ago. I'd been trying to show them to her but this was when she admitted that she was a little near sighted and that she'd lost her contacts running to my house and her glasses had been in her purse in the car that had been sucked up and blown... Well God alone knew where.

I walked over to look and saw about twenty of the little fuckers. We'd already gone ahead and eaten about fifteen of the bigger fish. "We're going to have to eat five more fish if those all make it. The canal only supports about a hundred fish, so if twenty get born, well we get to eat twenty. If nothing else, if we don't get rid of some of the big ones they won't give the little ones a chance to grow." There wasn't a lot of fear of that, though, because the nursery is well planted with dense foliage, which gives them plenty of places to hide, and as I've said before the fish get plenty to eat. Cherry was doing the breakfast dishes and as we watched a piece of egg floated by. One of the little guys snagged it.

"Did you see that? It was nearly as big as he was," Lucy said. She smiled at me and her whole face seemed to glow. We were happy, or we could have been if we didn't have to live with my sons and those girls.

Mostly we all could have been happy if we didn't have to put up with Evelyn. Compared to her, even Jimmy seemed like a pretty even-tempered, easy-going guy.

Of course Jimmy was still trouble.

From the living room I heard Jimmy scream at his brother, "I'm sick of your shit!"

"Fuck you, Jimmy. It's your turn to get the wood. Get off your lazy ass and go do it."

"Make me!" Oh yes, so mature my boys.

Billy laughed. "You're kidding me, right? Boy I will fuck you completely up." Billy had a point; Jimmy is half his size. I heard someone smack someone, and I took off before the idiots could tear the reinforced concrete house down. I grabbed hold of Jimmy as he ran at his brother, who had obviously thrown him back onto the couch. Of course when I grabbed Jimmy the inertia of him moving knocked us both into the floor where I realized my ribs weren't quite as healed as I thought they were and my back popped out again. Jimmy jumped up and ran at his brother. Billy just sort of held his hand on Jimmy's head and held him at bay, which just seemed to infuriate Jimmy even more.

Lucy ran in the room, ran over to me, and put down a hand to help me up. She could tell I was hurt and there was still scuffling behind her so she yelled out, "Knock it off!"

With Lucy's help I got to my feet barely.

Jimmy shoved away from his brother and turned on Lucy. "Who the fuck do you think you are? You ain't no one to me, lady, just some bimbo who's fucking my Mama to stay out of the cold. We all know you wouldn't be with her in a million years if you weren't stuck here. Hell, you probably aren't even queer and..."

"Shut up right now, Jimmy!" I screamed, standing to my full height even though it damn near killed me to do it. "You've already said way too fucking much. *Way* too much. You ever talk to her like that again or you ever talk about me like I ain't standing here again, and I will rip your head off and shit in the hole. This is my house, *mine!* You are *all* living here because I say you can, but all this willful crap is going to stop right now. Things need to be done around here. Everyone's going to pull their own weight. No one is going to sit around and watch movies all day. No one is going to use up supplies and contribute nothing, and I'm tired of having to tell people to do things. You're all grown people; I shouldn't have to treat you like little kids."

"You've always treated me like a kid. I'm so tired of Billy always being the perfect one and me always getting treated like a bastard. I'm the one you and Mom made."

"That's right, dumbass, you were always mine, but Billy doesn't go out of his way to piss me off most of the time and you do."

"I don't have to stay here and put up with this shit. I'm going to go to Rudy and live with them."

"Have a nice walk, 'cause you ain't taking one of my four-wheelers, and I'm pretty sure right now your brother ain't gonna let you have his."

"Fine!" he screamed.

"Fine!" I screamed back. I started for our room and Lucy helped me. She helped me into bed, and then she fixed my back. The whole time I could hear Billy mumbling and Jimmy yelling he was going.

"You should go talk to him," Lucy said as she continued to rub my back. My ribs were alright—just a momentary twinge for which I was thankful.

"Why? Fuck him!"

"He's your son."

"Tell him that. He has always treated me like the devil's own sperm. I'm sorry about what he said to you, Lucy."

She kissed my ear and whispered, "He was mostly using me to yell at you." Lucy's pretty smart. "He wanted to hurt you and he figured what he said would do that. But you know he's wrong, right?"

I didn't, not really. I mean Lucy was a lesbian, no doubt about that, but Jimmy was right that if the world hadn't gone to hell in a hand basket she never in a million years would have been with me. That was just the truth and played right into my insecurities. You want to believe that the person you love loves you and would no matter what the scenario... or is that just me?

"Why did he want to hurt me? What the fuck did I do to him?"

"I don't have a clue. Most likely just stir crazy like the rest of us, and from what little I have seen he has a very father/son-type relationship with you."

"What's that mean?"

"Only that men seem to have a complex relationship with their fathers, always slipping between wanting their approval and rebelling against everything they stand for. He never had a father, so you fill that niche. That's all I'm saying."

She was right. I knew she was. Jimmy lost his mother when he really wasn't old enough to not need her, and let's face it in the boys' life I was a sad replacement for Cindy. I was obsessed with doing my own thing. I took care of them and I loved them but I never did all the little things that she did for them.

"Nature or nurture?" I asked.

"What?" Lucy asked, momentarily stopping my massage.

"Don't stop rubbing. I'm asking do you think it's all about who your biological parents are or do you think it's who and how you were raised?"

"I'm not like my father was, and as much as I loved her, I'm not like my mother, either. Billy was already a toddler when you started dating his mother, but he acts a lot more like you than Jimmy does. Hell, Billy walks the same as you, he talks the same way you do. Every once in awhile I'll see your facial expressions on Jimmy, but I see it all the time on Billy. So who can say? I don't think Jimmy is anything like his father, if that's what you're worried about. I just think he's..."

"Sort of a jerk."

Lucy laughed. "I didn't say that."

Billy slung the door open then making us both jump. "Mama, Jimmy really left he really did."

"I figured he would," I said calmly.

"You want me to go after him?"

"No."

"Are you going to go after him?"

"No."

"Mama, that dumb ass can't walk all the way to town in this cold. At least let me go get him on one of the four wheelers and take him to Rudy."

"He wouldn't get on with you right now; you ought to know that. And I'm not going to go and kiss his ass to get him to come home because if I do then he'll show it the rest of the apocalypse and just ruin it for everyone."

"Mama... He could die out there."

"Could but won't," I said.

"Mama, I really think..."

"Then stop."

"I feel like this is all my fault."

"Because you asked him to get off his dead ass and get some wood? It's not your fault, he was in a mood. He just wanted to throw himself a hissing fit and..." I smiled then and turned to look at Lucy and said proudly. "He *is* like me." I turned my attention back to Billy. "Look, he'll either make it to town or to Matt's, or he'll come home, or he'll freeze to death in the snow and ice. If he does that will be completely his decision. We have to let it be his decision, Billy."

Billy nodded, his shoulders slumped, and he started to leave.

"Shut our door on the way out."

Which he did.

Lucy started rubbing my back again. "Maybe you should go after him, Kay."

"No, I meant what I said. Whatever he's going to do needs to be his decision or he's just going to make himself and the rest of us miserable. That's good, baby." I rolled onto my back and looked up at her. "So, you're stuck with me—screaming adult kids, bad back and all. How do you really feel about that? You might as well tell me because, seriously, what's it really going to change? You don't really have any choice."

She smiled and kissed me gently on the lips. "I'm happy with you, Kay. He's wrong, and you know why I think he's wrong."

"Because fate brought us together." I laughed, but grabbed her and drug her down to me and hugged her—probably too tight. "Whatever you want to think, baby."

Now I know what you're thinking—that Jimmy didn't come back right away because he got hurt, and Billy and I had to risk life and limb to save him and from that day forward he just stopped being a jerk. Or you're thinking that he makes it into town, turns them all against me, and winds up leading them in a battle against me—which I of course win only by killing my youngest son and as he dies he says poignant words of apology to me and I forgive him and he forgives me and then I cry into the snow, my tears turning to little icicles. Or he gets found by some renegade group of military survivalists and brings them back to kill me, and he finally does kill me only to realize that I was right all along and now he has to lead and leading isn't as much fun as he thought it would be and...

This ain't a work of fiction people!

About an hour after he left he comes back home, his clothes packed with snow, his teeth chattering, and just runs in the house and starts stripping by the stove.

"Cold?" I ask as Lucy and I walk in from the kitchen as if nothing of interest had taken place that entire day.

"Yeah... I'm sorry, Mama," he said.

I nodded.

"I'm sorry, Lucy."

He couldn't look at her, so I'm thinking he was more sorry about screaming at her than he was for screaming at me.

"That's alright," she said.

"No it wasn't all fucking right," I snapped at her. She just shrugged making a face that said that she knew at this point in the game there wasn't much she could do to really piss me off— which, by the way, is never a good place to be in a relationship unless you're the one that can do no wrong.

"It was a crappy thing to say," Jimmy said, "and I shouldn't have said it."

He had stripped all his gear off and some of the chill was coming off. "Can I talk to you Mama... alone?"

I nodded, and when he'd had a few more minutes to warm up we went into the office and closed the door. "So... what's with all the shit?"

Jimmy was obviously trying to think of some more intellectual way to say what was on his mind but then he just let it out. "You're getting it at least twice a day and Billy and Cherry are just fucking all the time and my wrist hurts from jacking off and I'm starting to think Harriet is sort of pretty." Harriet was one of the goats. "And Evelyn... Well she isn't really my type and she obviously doesn't like me, and well it's like she's the last girl on earth and she doesn't want anything to do with me."

"Look... Right now that girl can't think about anything but dragging around feeling sorry for herself and your type was always tight-assed, mean and crazier than a shit house rat... and I'm thinking she's all of that and more. Even if she's not your type... well as that old song goes... if you can't be with the one you love, love the one you're with. After all, that's obviously what Lucy's doing."

"I said I was sorry, Mama. I was just mad and just said the first shit that jumped into my head. Anyone can see she really does like you. What am I going to do, Mama? There isn't really anything to do all day and I just sort of feel alone. I know we're all stacked up in here like cord wood, but I don't think I've ever felt this lonely in my whole life."

"Why don't you try talking to the girl explain the whole we ain't got nothin' else to do we might as well screw thing."

"I've never been good at talking to women, you know that, Mama."

"Well, you could start out by telling her that there are all these people in here and yet you still feel all alone because I'll bet a dollar to a doughnut hole that's how she feels, too. Just talk to her. You got nothing to lose; it's not like any of us can seriously get away from each other." I stood up from where I'd been sitting. I started for the door and was just going to leave him with his thoughts but then that mother thing kicked in and I turned around.

"You know why it always seems to you like I favor Billy?"

He shook his head no.

"Because you were mine. I cut your cord. I was the first one that ever held you, and you were MY baby. I had to work very hard to never let Billy know that you were just a little more special to me than he was." He got up, ran over, hugged my neck, and just started crying, so I rocked him like I did when he was a baby. For just a minute he didn't seem like such a giant pain in my ass.

Just for a minute.

CHAPTER 14

Hording and Scavenging

Most doomsday scenarios will include a long, *very cold winter. Unless you are near the equator this is what you'd better prepare for. You can't have enough fuel for heat or enough food. Look, even a normal winter without utilities and not being able to go to the store to get groceries will be the hardest thing you have to go through. Realize that communities used to spend most of their time getting ready for winter, and that there was a reason for it. You have no idea how much food and fuel it takes, so when you think you've put back enough—put back some more. You will be able to get water from ice and snow, but food is going to become scarce fast. Know where every possible source of food is, every grocery store, every quick pick, every restaurant, any place where you might find food, and don't wait till your food is getting low to go on scavenger expeditions. Do them in any break in the weather— but only if it is above freezing or better—and before fear of starvation can even think to come into play.*

If you didn't put them back you can make snow shoes out of nearly anything—tennis rackets, wicker baskets or chair bottoms, pieces of fencing, anything you can tie to your feet that isn't too heavy and that will make your foot wider and keep you from sinking up to your ass in the snow. Make a sled—easy to do out of any number of things—old street signs and car hoods or trunk lids, or garbage cans. Plastic kiddy pools, come to mind, not to mention you might be able to find actual sleds in department, hardware or sporting goods stores—don't make more than one trip and make that trip count. Load up with everything you can haul.

Face it, most of the people who made it through were the people who, like me, had been preparing mentally and physically for years. Strengthening their homes to stand up to whatever might happen, putting back lots of supplies. But there were lots of people who made it who did it by the skin of their teeth like Tom in North West Texas who had hunkered down in the basement laundry room of the apartment building he'd been living in. The town had been hit by a twister and hit hard and like they had in Fort Smith most of the residents had buggered out. But even though he hadn't done a damn thing to prepare, he'd faithfully listened to my podcast, and when the shit hit the fan he'd been in that basement with every container he could find at the last minute full of water, his toolbox, a two-way radio, and all the food in his apartment. The basement had been all that was left of his apartment building and as everyone else—who wasn't dead already—was running as fast as they could to get out of town to someplace else, he was scrounging food and fuel anywhere he found it and dragging it into that basement. He made a heater out of one of the dryers—ingenious really. The place he found the most food had been what was left of a pizzeria. At one point he told me he was down to eating a soup he made by boiling water and throwing in two packages of Parmesan cheese and one package of crushed red peppers.

We weren't in any fear of running out of food. I had already figured it out and even with the extra mouths to feed and if for some reason everything in the greenhouse suddenly died and we had to eat all the animals we still had a five-year supply of food. While this winter was bad and we hadn't seen the sun in weeks and I didn't plan to see it soon, you could still clearly define day from night. So as bad as this apocalypse was it wasn't as bad as it could have been if say the Yellowstone or Krakatau calderas had done their worst.

Since they had tapped the Wal-Mart for food and other supplies, the people at the school in Fort Smith were just fine. Plenty of food and plenty of fuel, and they had found ways to make themselves ever more comfortable. In short, they were learning to think like survivors instead of people waiting for someone to come and save them.

The folks in Rudy, though, were running really low on supplies. Here was the problem; if I was going to let them starve then I should have done that to begin with. As long as I was feeding them and helping them out they weren't going to come after me and mine no matter how much more we had. How did I know that? I told you I studied history. People only ever rose up to fight the "power" when the power had all and gave them nothing. As long as I was sharing with them, as long as their bellies were full, they weren't going to risk almost-assured annihilation by coming after us. I was in a position where I was sure I had more than enough food and supplies to be able to make it through and keep feeding the people in Rudy, but tapping my own stores to feed them without really knowing when the winter might actually end was breaking about a dozen of my own rules.

And it's not just the winter you have to get through but the growing season, too. Then you have to hope the crops are going to come in good enough to feed everyone. I was thinking we'd see thawing and the sun by June at the latest, but even with all the imaging equipment I had and all the different weather machines and bullshit I don't even know the proper names for, I couldn't be a hundred percent sure that we weren't in for a three-year winter. I was damned if me and mine were going to starve along with those dumbasses who... Well, do I have to remind you that they all thought I was a nut job because I kept saying the end was near?

But I couldn't just not feed them because that made me like the hard-core survivalists that are sometimes called military survivalists even though most of them had never really served in any military and were about as disciplined as cats. These guys thought the end was going to be a liberal, communist-backed government coming after them to take their guns. As such they were armed out the ass and ready for a full-fledge attack—or at least they thought they were. They were most of them like the Burkholder boys, dumbasses whose biggest fear had been losing their right to bear arms, which they of course thought would lead to the end of everything. They hadn't counted at all on what happened. You know, the Middle East going nuke crazy, setting up a chain reaction with Mother Nature just kicking our asses, and I doubt they were ready for it. Must have been a huge let down for them not to get to use all those weapons, and that's why I was always worried about them.

Truth was I had no idea how these guys were doing because none of them had ever tried to contact me either before or after the apocalypse.

Anyway... I didn't want to be like them and worry about me and mine and screw everyone else. I mean I did, but I didn't.

There had been a railroad damage and overstock store up on the highway called All 'n More, and that was about true. They had a little bit of everything including tons of food items, and here's the thing—in this cold nothing was going to go bad, it was just going to freeze.

It was only about two, maybe three, miles from the town's center, but in this crap we had no idea what might lie between us and them. Then Matt remembered that ole man Kent had a D-6 bulldozer and he always kept a couple of tanks of diesel. Also, there had to be a tank of diesel at the new truck plaza on the way to All 'n More.

It was February sixth and there was a break in the weather—a window that was going to last about three days and bring us high temperatures of a whole thirty-two degrees. There wasn't much could tear up a D-6 dozer, so Lucy and Billy and I geared up that first "warm" day, grabbed a bunch of tools, and headed over to the old man's place.

It took us about an hour just to get there and considering it was less than a half-mile away that lets you know just how much damage there was. There were trees down everywhere. They weren't just snapped through, either, here most of them had been pulled up and were just thrown around, root ball and all. Because of the snow you couldn't really be sure what you were driving on, so you just avoided mounds that were probably downed trees and hoped for the best and that the holes they left weren't big enough to swallow you four wheeler and all.

Old man Kent's place was gone; just a pile of snow on what was left of the foundation. But as expected there was a dozer-shaped mound of snow right in the middle of what used to be the guy's farm. Lucy and I started shoveling the snow off the bulldozer as Billy grabbed the engine blanket, started the generator, and wrapped the bulldozer engine in it. You see in that cold you aren't going to start a diesel motor until you can warm it up. Hell, in that cold you couldn't start anything unless it was warmed up. When Lucy and I had removed all the snow I thought was necessary from the dozer we went off—wearing snow shoes now because the snow was too deep to do more than walk a few feet without them—to look for the old man's diesel tanks.

Problem was they had been on stilts, and those were obviously gone. We stomped around for the better part of an hour, occasionally telling each other how fucking cold thirty-two degrees still was. It was the wind chill off all the ice and snow that was the killer. We didn't talk too much because bundled up like that you just can't and... Well, walking around in that much snow in the cold even with state-of-the-art snow shoes will just wear you right completely out. Even if we were all working out for at least thirty minutes a day, stuck inside it's just not the same as really working all the time. I have to admit I was a little out of shape.

By the time we found one of the tanks half way down a small hill a good two-hundred feet from where it had been and found that it had been crushed and was empty, I was ready to just scrap the whole idea. After all without enough fuel to at least get us to the truck plaza—or rather what was left of it—we weren't going to be able to do what we planned anyway, so what was the point? Then Lucy spotted a similar tank-looking bump in the snow about fifty feet away, and that one was intact and full. Now I'm not stupid. You don't want to run back and forth back and forth in the cold, so I'd brought five five-gallon gas containers and a hose with me. I siphoned the fuel into the containers—yes of course I got a mouth full of diesel which is the nastiest shit on earth and of course—after she found out it wasn't going to kill me—Lucy laughed every time I spit and cussed for the next thirty minutes.

Now I'm not lugging five-gallon containers of diesel some two-hundred feet uphill in the snow. I tied a rope to three of the containers, ran up the hill—alright in snow shoes you don't run anywhere and certainly not uphill—got my four-wheeler as close as I could, pulled the winch line out as far as it would go, and I had just enough rope to tie on to. I switched the winch on and walked along behind the sliding containers making sure they didn't get stuck on branches or rocks. No, it wasn't easy. Lucy didn't get the winch turned off in time once and the rope got snagged in the reel. I had to cut it and then fiddle around for ten minutes. Without gloves on because you can't do things like tie or untie knots with battery-operated heated gloves on and here's the thing you gottah love the damn things and how warm they keep your hands no matter how damn cold it is, but then when you have to take them off that just makes it seem that much colder.

Anyway, eventually we got the fuel into the dozer with five gallons to spare, and we got it started. Billy has always been very mechanical. In fact, if it has a motor Billy can make it run and drive it. Hell before the apocalypse Billy used to drive heavy equipment for a living.

Lucy drove his four wheeler and I followed her because she still wasn't really comfortable driving it. Though following the bull dozer even as slow as it was going—because he had the blade down and was clearing the road—it still didn't take us as long to get out of old man Kent's place as it had to get to it. We went straight over to Matt's, but by the time we got his big hay trailer hitched to the back of the dozer we all decided there was no way we could get to All 'n More and back before nightfall. So we covered the bull dozer's motor with an old hay tarp Matt had laying around and secured it hoping it would keep the engine warm enough that it would start easier the next day and we went on home. I was exhausted and I know Billy and Lucy were as well.

When we walked into the greenhouse from the hall Cherry was waiting for us. She hugged Billy and then started helping him out of his gear. I guess Lucy was the first to realize that something was up because the minute she pulled off her facemask she asked Cherry, "What's wrong?" And let's face it, right after the apocalypse if anyone acted the least bit different or if they wanted to tell you anything you just naturally assumed it wasn't going to be good.

"Nothing's wrong it's just... Well, weird." She looked from Lucy to me then said, "Jimmy's been on the radio most of the day with someone who is claiming that he's the President of the

United States and demanding that he be rescued."

"Well fuck that shit. I'm king of the world. You don't demand anything from the king of the world," I said with a laugh, and finished stripping my gear.

"Jimmy thinks the guy's for real. Stupid, but for real," Cherry said.

"Doesn't really matter," I said. I shrugged as I headed for the wood stove to warm up my face and my ass, which were still freezing. No matter what I wore that winter my face and my ass were cold when I'd been outside for any length of time. I would strip my gear and my face warmed up fairly quickly, but it could take my ass hours to warm up. Jimmy said it was because my ass was so big it took it hours to get cold and even longer to get warm.

What a smart ass.

Anyway that's why I call it the cold-assed winter.

"He says he needs access to all of your equipment so that he can run the country," Cherry said.

I just kept warming myself by the stove, unconcerned with what this so-called "president" wanted. In a country where I'd been a second-class citizen without any rights just because I didn't want to sleep with men, I hardly thought I was the one anyone should assume wanted to save the president so we could preserve the American way.

"He's on the radio again," Evelyn said, running into the room.

I could tell by how excited these girls were that I wasn't going to get any peace till I told the "president" to fuck right off. So I pulled my still-frozen ass away from the stove and headed for my office. Lucy was right behind me but she wasn't excited about talking to the president, no, she was grumbling about being cold and just wanting to warm up, and what the fuck did he think he was president of anyway, and such sweet things as that. Yep, the more she was around me the worse her mouth got. Of course I had no idea why she thought she had to leave the warm stove to follow me except that in those days we both sort of acted like we were joined at the hip.

"My mama's here now," Jimmy said. As I walked in he looked at me and rolled his eyes. He got out of my chair and I sat down. I patted my legs and Lucy smiled, walked over and sat in my lap. She wrapped her arms around my neck and I felt warmer instantly.

"What you want, Mr. President?" I asked, just a tinge of laughter to my voice.

"Look, Kate, you have..."

"Folks call me Katy, my woman calls me Kay, but no one who wants to live calls me Kate. Also, I don't have to do anything 'cept die 'cause there ain't no taxes no more. Just who the hell are you anyway because last I heard DC got ate by a hurricane and no one could get in touch with you..."

"I'm speaker of the house, Tip Waverly..."

"You ain't speaker of nothin' any more, and you sure as hell ain't president." Because of course the madder I get the thicker my Southern drawl gets.

This was when the "president" lost his cool. "Listen you, every grade-school child knows the chain of succession is President, Vice president, Speaker of the House..."

"Well, shucks, Mr. President, ain't no one here so smart on stuff like that. We been way too busy buildin' bunkers and storin' food in case there comed a 'popacolypse. Weren't none of you fellows ready up north with all your fancy book learnin'?"

Lucy laughed. Probably more because until then I hadn't taken out my good-ole-boy Southern accent for her to hear than at what I was saying.

You could hear him expel a big batch of air that said he knew he'd gone too far. "Katy, I know you aren't stupid. I'm sorry, we seem to have gotten off on the wrong foot, but I am the President of the United States, and this country has got to get it's government up and going if we're going to survive this catastrophe."

I laughed loudly, looked at Lucy and rolled my eyes before addressing the *president*. "Only a dork like you would want to be president of an arctic waste land. And only a total idiot would think that he could vote for a constitutional amendment to ban gay marriage and then ask the dyke—who for all intents and purposes is the only authority anyone is listening to anymore—to help *him* be president. Look, buddy, the last thing I want right now is any kind of government, much less one run by your right-winged, ultra-conservative ass..."

"We... We're running out of supplies..."

"You're all holed up in some government-made bunker somewhere, right?" I asked, thinking he was full of crap.

"We're in Nevada. There are forty-three of us..."

"And it took you all this time to get a radio working?" I asked. From the look on Lucy's face it didn't make much sense to her, either.

"We... We didn't want people to know our location."

Of course not, because they'd been sure they had enough supplies to last them till this blew over and if they'd radioed out where they were and what was going on then people might find them and try to take their supplies, want to share their shelter. Then I started thinking—the president and vice president bite the big one, then what this guy flies out to some secret bunker in Nevada... Why hadn't there been enough food there for thousands of people to live for fifty years?

And why were there only forty-three people there? What sort of government installation wouldn't have just had thousands of people milling around making any chance at real security nearly impossible?

It just didn't make any sense unless... "Gee, Mr. President, what did you do? Did you get you and a bunch of your peeps into the bunker and shut everyone else out?"

There was silence and then he spits out the sort of double-talk shit politicians always spill, "Someone had to protect the installation... The nation must be preserved." And no doubt that was what they told all the military personnel guarding that place when this guy and his political buddies and all their wives and kids went into the bunker and locked all of them outside. See, military personnel are trained to follow orders without question, and let's face it, how many people actually thought the end of the world was coming even when it was? So it's not much of a stretch to see how this played out. He told them to stand their posts and they did, not expecting... Well what happened. Then, once the bunker doors were closed he didn't have to let them in and so he hadn't.

But where were all the supplies?

"Why don't you have enough supplies to last you a hundred years?"

I didn't ask that, my partner the reporter did. I just nodded so that she'd know I'd been thinking the same thing.

There was another one of those long pauses—you know the kind politicians always take while they're getting ready to double talk you some more, or making up a good lie.

My mind started working. What could they have done to use millions of dollars worth of supplies? And that was the answer—it would have been millions of dollars worth of shit. I laughed again. "Some crooked bastard said they fully stocked the bunker and stuck enough stuff down there so that dumb asses like you would think it was a huge stock, and then they stuffed the rest of the money in their pocket."

"Worse. They filled the space with barrels full of toxic waste." He sighed. "We thought we had enough food to last longer than we could possibly need it, and then... Well, we opened a barrel and there was this green goop and most of them were full of that instead of food rations. We need you to send someone to evacuate us immediately."

"Dude... Don't you get it? Even if I wanted to I couldn't come save you. There is no one to rescue you. This is it. You and people like you said that everyone who said there was a problem with climate or with starting wars everywhere was a mistake were crack pots or bleeding-heart doves who wanted to stand in the way of free enterprise. We were unpatriotic assholes who hated God and country. I can only rescue a few people. Only a few. And I'm not about to use my network or waste my time to try to find someone who may be able to help you and then convince them to do something I know is absurd. In case you haven't noticed, nearly everyone is dead. They're dead in part because the government never made any plans for what to do if the worst happened. You idiots filled your bunker with toxic waste to get even richer, and now you've got nothing to eat but... well, toxic waste..."

"None of us were responsible for this travesty."

"A whole world full of people passing the buck. People like you playing with the facts, tinkering with them till they fit your needs. You are up to your ears responsible for this, and even if I'm wrong, you sure as hell didn't do anything to stop it. And I'd bet a year of rations you've done as bad if not worse than filling a bunker with toxic goo instead of K-rations. Look, you left all those people outside. They're all dead. Get out of your bunker, dig them up, and eat them."

"You've got to be kidding. We couldn't cannibalize the dead."

"But you could and did leave them out there to die in the first place for no reason better than to stretch your rations—and that would have been way before you knew how short your rations really were. What's worse? It's really your only choice. Peoples who lived in harmony with the land, who were constantly being pushed onto less and less land, they all believed one thing—you should never kill something and not use every part of it. Most of them will die now. Their climate will shift, nothing they have done for centuries will work any more, and they'll be just as dead as the guys you shut outside. What did the Hadza people do to deserve their fate? They lived on the land for thousands of years and left hardly any foot print, but they're going to be dead if they aren't already because of shit none of them even knew about much less did. You and people like you did this. You'll have to excuse me while I don't give a good damn what happens to you."

"Won't you at least try to help us?"

"I just did. I told you to eat what you killed. Look, I'm doing all that I can do. You just aren't as important to me as the people who are struggling out there who are taking care of themselves. We don't need a president, we don't need a government. We certainly don't need one run by people who did what you did to survive. You didn't have any trouble killing those people; you shouldn't have any trouble eating them."

I turned the radio off. Jimmy and Billy and the girls were standing outside the door. "If he calls back, shut him down. We don't have time for him."

They all nodded and then made themselves scarce.

I fully expected Lucy to at least be a little annoyed with my cavalier attitude towards the "president" and his people but she just said, "What a dick." And then she started kissing me so that I knew we were going to have to either close the office door or move to the bedroom. Who knew what turned her on in those days? It didn't take much.

You know what? They say power is sexy and I'd just told the president—in not so many words—to go fuck himself. Maybe that was it.

For the record, two years later people found that bunker when they were scavenging for supplies. It was obvious by what they found that the politicians and their families in the bunker had resorted to cannibalism, but it hadn't saved them. They had all obviously died from some disease—most likely from being stuck in that bunker with tons of leaking toxic waste containers. The scavengers sealed the bunker and put up a warning sign.

Oh how the mighty have fallen.

The next day went as planned but that didn't mean it was any walk in the park. We had to warm the dozer engine anyway then once we got it started Billy plowed on ahead—literally. Now see a D-6 dozer was built to tear up huge trees and dig great big holes in the earth, so pushing a few feet of snow and some tree branches, pieces of houses and cars out of the way was nothing. Still, the going was slow because it has a top speed of about fifteen miles an hour. It pulled Matt's big hay trailer, Matt pulled the small one with his tractor behind that, I followed on the four-wheeler with my small trailer behind that carrying more fuel for the dozer. The truck plaza was gone but we could see where it had been. One of the men with us had worked there and knew right where the tanks were, so using an electric fuel pump Billy had rigged for the purpose—and later gave to the Rudy crew so that they could more easily get gas from the tanks at what used to be the grocery store—we refilled the dozer to make sure we'd have enough and then we moved on.

Matt's boys and Jimmy came with us and we picked up five more people in Rudy to help us. Matt said that by God he was going to take first pick of the food, and I said I reckoned on how that was fair enough since we were using his two big trailers and his tractor.

It was cold, but I think everyone that went didn't notice so much because it wasn't as cold as it had been. Let's face it, we were all just really tired of being all cooped up inside, and it was nice to have different people to talk to, even if most of them seemed to purposely avoid me most of the time. I even let Lucy drive part of the way there just because she wanted to I was in that good a mood.

When we got to All 'n More as luck would have it—the good kind not the bad kind we were all sort of getting used to—it had been completely missed by the tornados but immediately covered with snow, so the roofs on most of its big, expansive steel buildings had buckled or fallen completely in. The grocery store was a smaller building but the roof had still sagged and was mostly being held up in the middle by the shelving system inside. So precarious to say the least.

We decided we'd come back when winter ended and get anything worth getting from the entire complex. No one, including the owners, were there because there was no smoke coming from anywhere and that year... Well if you didn't have fire you were dead. No one else had claimed it, so I figured that meant it was all ours.

Right then all we were interested in was the food, and as much of it as we could haul off. Of course we had to be careful because like I said the roof was mostly caved in and the whole thing could come down at any minute. In fact, I gave Lucy the job of watching the roof for any sign of immediate trauma, any shift. She mumbled that I just didn't think she was competent to help do anything important, but I just ignored her.

It was weird because there was a lot of snow that had blown in once the roof gave, but for the most part it was pretty clear inside and we were able to shore up the roof with a few well-placed metal struts we'd found. Cans had frozen and were all pushed out but that didn't matter because they hadn't had any chance to unfreeze and it wouldn't be hard to keep them that way. They'd be fine to eat, at least until they thawed out.

Most of the stuff in glass bottles was ruined except for the oil and an entire pallet load of honey—both of which I had them load first. Matt immediately said he and his crew were getting a case of each. I took a case of each, too, even though I had plenty of oil and I have my own hives that I rob and so far my bees were fine—I'll explain this more later. The dry goods were all fine, even the stuff packed in paper, because the snow was what had taken the roof out and it hadn't been warm enough since it started to fall for it to thaw enough for anything to get wet. We just brushed any snow we found on the sacks and containers off and loaded them up. There were huge walk-in freezer units all stuffed full of every kind of frozen food, and of course none of it had thawed out.

We loaded up everything we had room for and headed back for Rudy. You did NOT want to be out after dark. Even though the daylight hours weren't warm, night was as dark as anything I have ever seen—no light to reflect off the snow, and the minute the sun went down the temperature plummeted by twenty degrees and kept falling. So we rushed to unload. I took my small trailer full of what I wanted and Matt took half a trailer full of supplies for himself and his family. Everything else we left in Rudy in a garage that had been mostly still standing and that the Rudyites had shored up and fixed for the purpose of storing food.

Now I know what you're thinking, why did I take anything at all? I mean what kind of greedy bitch am I? I probably had more food than we needed. Hell, I had animals and plants still giving us fresh food every day. Well, I'll tell you why, because I had given a lot of my stockpile away and like I said there was no way to know how long this little ice age was going to last or if what I'd put back would in fact be enough. Our growing seasons were bound to be shorter for years which meant we weren't likely to be able to grow all the crops I would have liked to.

I figured without me those folks would all—every last one of them—have frozen or starved the first week, and I didn't owe any of them a God-damned thing. Hell, none of them had ever even been nice to me before this, just ignored me and took their children's hands and pulled them close when I walked by. I was always just that crazy bitch who built the fortress because she thought the end of the world was coming at best. At worst I was that heathen dyke who they wanted God to smite. Part two of that was that I couldn't trust those people to ration the way I would have done. They might use everything that should have easily lasted them another six months in two and then I'd have to feed them again, and if I did... Well, I just needed to hedge my bets.

I helped them more than enough. I don't feel guilty for restocking my larder. Hell, it was my idea.

By the time we had knocked all the snow off ourselves and the four wheelers and had put up the supplies we'd taken we were all just freezing and exhausted. I was sure glad that Cherry had kept the fire stoked in the shop as well as the house because it made the whole knocking-the-snow-off process a lot more comfortable.

We all stripped off our outerwear by the stove and bitched about how cold we were.

"I have no balls, none," Billy said, and he wasn't referring to some sissy thing he'd done. "I swear they have crawled all the way up in my body. All the way."

"Ah... mine, too," Jimmy said, as if his brother had insinuated he had balls and it was a bad thing. At that point in time I had no idea whether he had finally talked Evelyn into having sex with him or not, but Evelyn wasn't sleeping on the couch and he had been less annoying, so I assumed he had. But when Jimmy bitched about his balls and Evelyn brought a blanket in and wrapped it around his shoulders I knew by the huge idiot smile he smiled that they were doing it.

I'd laid in enough rubbers and KY to last an army a lifetime, and I said a little prayer that these idiots were going to be smart enough to use them. Imagine being a huge obvious dyke and walking in and ordering twelve cases of assorted condoms. The least the horny bastards could do was use them.

Now you might be wondering why I didn't buy a bunch of birth control pills and IUD's and such. Well I'll tell you why. Rubbers are the only thing that helps protect people from STDs, but guys would rather die than use them. Why? Because they can't get off? Bullshit, a guy always gets off. They didn't use them because it meant they had to actually think about someone and something besides their dicks. They were embarrassed to have to stop and put one on, such silly-assed shit as that.

If women faced with the apocalypse didn't have enough sense to make a guy put a condom on, then they deserved to die in childbirth. Survival of the fittest.

Is that harsh? Look, if you haven't found a doctor who can perform a C-section for your community, then chances are very good that if you get pregnant you'll end up dead. See, for most of the history of humankind if a woman couldn't give birth to a baby vaginally she died, which was awful but it meant that women who couldn't have normal births didn't reproduce. In two generations modern medical science managed to make a situation where nearly as many births were C-section as were vaginal. They undid generations of selective breeding.

And we over populated the planet and destroyed our world and had to start all over again because men didn't want to wear condoms. So, in the new world women will learn to tell men no or they'll die in child birth. It's that simple.

Of course fear of death has never made women tell men no, so it likely won't now. I'd brought a huge box of them to Rudy hoping they'd be smart enough to use them there, too, and they all acted like no one was having sex, which was just fucking stupid and I didn't believe it for a second. People—well most people—we at least want to believe we have some privacy when we are doing it. The people in Rudy were saying they weren't doing it and pretending that they didn't know that everyone else was out of common courtesy, and then I come and bring them a huge box of rubbers.

I don't expect people not to have sex. Hell, I think they ought to get as much as they can but wear a damn condom. This time, everyone replace themselves and stop. It shouldn't have taken an apocalypse to make people protect themselves and each other, to realize that they should have two kids and stop. Two is enough for any couple—three's pushing it, and anything more than that in a world already bulging with people is just selfish and stupid.

In the future when people look back at this time they will realize that the whole thing crashed only because men wanted to have all the sex they wanted and didn't want to wear condoms or do anything at all to stop the spread of VD or unwanted pregnancies. Come on, men invented religion. Why do you think there was all that shit about women coming from men—by the way how the hell did they figure that happened, a rib? Come on—and be fruitful and multiply—what dumb ass thought that was a good idea? I mean maybe when there are only two of your species, but when there are so many of you swarming across the face of the planet that you can't fart without someone else hearing it?

Everything has always been about serving a man's fucking penis. I'm not just saying that because I'm a dyke, and as I've told you before I'm no man hater. The truth is the truth. Money and power—it's all just the means to the end—which is more sex, which is really all men care about. Which there is nothing wrong with that but—wear a damn condom!

Before women get to thinking they're so superior I think the shit women care about is a lot stupider than sex. Everything comes down to "Do I look good in this?" And not for the opposite sex, no they have to look better than other women, they have to make other women say, "I wish I looked like that," or they're not happy with how they look. When they have sex they aren't normally physically satisfied so they do it for two reasons and two reasons only—to get control of a man or to have babies—and half the time when they want babies it's only to control some man.

This is why I believe that all women are basically queer. Men are a means to an end, and they don't care what men think only what their girlfriends think and...

Well I don't give a damn what I look like or what anyone thinks of me. In fact, let's just tell it like it is and say that I care a lot more about sex than just about anything else.

But I digress... Anyway I was standing there just warming

my ass, listening to the boys' sudden argument about whose balls were the coldest and hoping that they were both using rubbers to have sex when I noticed Lucy wasn't by the fire. I saw her cover-alls hanging on a hook but she was gone. I shrugged and started to just stand by the fire but then something told me to go check on her. I mean after all at that time I usually couldn't pry Lucy off my ass long enough to go to the can.

I found her in the bathroom and the door was locked. I wondered how long she'd been in there and then something made me knock on the door. "Honey, you alright?"

"I'm fine." It was a lie; I could tell by the sound of her voice. "What's wrong?" I demanded.

"Nothing." Another lie.

"Open the door."

"Dammit, Kay..."

"Open the door or I'll break it down." I wouldn't really. I had the key, I'd just go get it and unlock the door, but you never want to yell, "Open the door or I'll go get the key where it's stuck in the back of the silverware drawer and unlock it!" It lacks any sense of urgency.

"What's wrong?" Billy asked.

"Go away; I've got it," I ordered. He nodded and walked away. "Lucy, open the door."

"Kay..." She sighed and then I heard the latch twist and I pushed the door open.

She looked some startled and hid her hands behind her back.

"You hard-headed little dumbass," I said, knowing exactly what was wrong. See she'd told me the batteries had run out in her gloves about half way through the day. I should have packed extra gloves and batteries and normally I did but I'd flat-ass forgotten. I'd offered her mine, even suggested we swap back and forth, but the silly little bitch kept insisting her hands weren't cold.

"Let me see them," I ordered.

Lucy held out her bright red, slightly-swollen hands and just started crying. "I really was fine until I got wet."

I started the water in the sink going, got it luke-warm and stuck her hands down in it. She flinched. "How did your hands get wet?" Because you see when you're wearing water-proof gloves and it's so cold that unprotected water will freeze solid in ten minutes, it's sort of hard to get actually wet.

Lucy was quiet except for the crying.

"You little dumbass, how did your hands get wet?!"

She cried louder but still didn't answer.

"In a second I'm going to leave you here alone to thaw and

go find your gloves."

"I put them on the heater." She cried still louder.

I'd brought a kerosene heater with us so that everyone could take turns warming themselves up. Lucy had taken her gloves off to warm her hands by the stove because the gloves will keep your hands from freezing but they can still get cold. Without thinking she'd sat her gloves on the heater. See, people who have never been around heat that didn't come out of a register in the floor didn't always understand that fire burns. They caught fire and she had to stomp them out. It not only burned up the heating unit in the gloves—turns out there was never anything wrong with the batteries and she's damn lucky they didn't blow up—but it burnt the rubber-proof coating off and actually put holes in her glove. Once that happened any time she touched snow her own heat melted it till her hands were wet and every time the wind rushed through those holes it had been miserable. At least she wasn't stupid enough to take the gloves off. Of course she didn't tell me any of that till later. She was too busy crying and I guess it was then that I realized why she was so upset.

"Oh, honey." I took a second to kiss her cheek. "There are degrees of frost bite just like there are degrees of sunburn. This is actually pretty minor." I turned on straight hot water then and kept it on till the water in the sink was almost too hot. "It's going to hurt like hell, but you aren't going to lose any fingers."

I left her there and filled a dishpan with warm water and Epsom salts and moved her to the living room. The kids were smart enough to go away for which I was glad. I bundled Lucy up in a blanket, sat her close to the stove, set the dish pan in her lap and stuck her hands in it.

"Why the hell didn't you just tell me?"

"Because you already think I'm a dumb ass." She cried. I handed her a pill and a glass of water and she took the medicine without question.

"I don't think you're a dumbass," I said. She just glared at me. I went over what I'd said in the last few minutes. "Well it was a pretty stupid thing to do, Lucy. You're damn lucky it's not a whole lot worse."

"You were busy. Everyone was so busy and I was mostly just in the way and then I do something stupid and you want to share gloves with me and... Well the minute you would have seen them you would have known what I did and I didn't want you to see that I'd burnt up my gloves because I knew you'd think I was just a huge dumb ass and... I used to be smart, Kay. Everyone used to say how intelligent and informed I was."

"You are."

"No I'm not, not any more." Lucy cried again. "Is it supposed to hurt this much?"

"Let's see, the blood in your hands started to turn to ice crystals and now you're thawing it out. I'd say yes, it's supposed to hurt a whole lot. The Vicodin should kick in soon. Give it a minute."

"You didn't want to take me with you in the first place and then I did something stupid and... I just didn't want you to know."

"That's not true." I smiled at her. "I did want you to go with me, but I have to say that I don't so that it won't be my fault if you do something stupid and wind up with frost bite."

Lucy laughed then so either the Vicodin was working its magic or her hands were starting to warm up. Lucy stopped laughing and looked up at me. "Is it ever going to warm up out there?"

It was a good question. There was just no telling how long this was going to last. Everything had been perched on the edge for so long and then well everything just seemed to get pushed over at the same time. The little ice age had lasted several hundred years—though climatologists and historians were always arguing over just how many hundred—but if you're living in it all you care about is that it's cold. I knew it shouldn't stay this bad, I knew the world should start to right itself, but all that equipment I have and limited knowledge of how it works and what I'm looking at will only get you just so far.

"A few months at the most..."

"Liar," Lucy said.

I laughed then stopped. "I don't know. I hope months, but realistically... it could be years."

"How long can we last here?"

"Indefinitely if we can keep the animals and the greenhouse going. Of course eventually we'd have to thin our herds down, maybe eat that snake you love so much... We should be more than able to make it through this, Lucy."

She nodded and didn't push it. "I'm sorry, Kay," she said looking at her hands.

"No I'm sorry." And I was, too. "I should have kept a closer eye on you. I should have known."

"You can't take care of everyone and watch out for my stupidity as well."

"You're the only one I should be worried about taking care of at all." I moved a stray strand of hair out of her face and kissed her cheek. Then I put my arms across her shoulder and whispered in her ear. "If you ever do anything stupid like this again I'm going to kick your ass."

She laughed. "Why Kay, you do say the sweetest things."

"I'm serious, Lucy. I'm not some ogre. You're hurting, you tell me and let me fix it before it turns into something like this. I'm crazy. Everyone knows I'm crazy but what's the worst I was going to do? Scream at you for being a dumbass? Big deal, Lucy, so what? Isn't it better for me to be a little upset than to have all your fingers fall off?"

"You said I'd be fine."

"You will be, but you didn't know that."

She nodded and laid her head on my shoulder. "Now I do feel really stupid."

"Good, you should."

She looked at her hands where they lay in the bowl of warm water. "They're starting to feel better."

"Good."

It turned out it really was pretty minor. In a few days she lost a few layers of skin, but except for a couple of days when she could hardly use her hands she seemed to be physically fine. She was sort of quiet and a little withdrawn, though. I couldn't tell if it was because her hands hurt or if the meds were affecting her, or if it was something else.

We were in bed—which face it was really the only time we were free to talk to each other because it was the only time we could be sure of being alone. She had her back to me and I has holding her, just smelling her hair because let's face it she didn't feel up to any sort of hanky-panky.

"You ok, baby?" I asked.

"Yeah. Getting hurt, letting myself get hurt in such a stupid way, it's just got me thinking about things. Believe it or not it's got me thinking about the future. What's it really going to be like, Kay?"

It was a good question. I wasn't completely sure, but I knew what I hoped for and found that I was happy to share my ideas with her.

"Well I think the sun will start to break through the dust and debris in about three months. There will be a lot of flooding, a lot of mud. Deep mud. But once the thaw starts in about a month the ground should start to dry out. We'll release our stock from the barn, plow our garden, and plant. I'm thinking to feed the population in Rudy we should plow up the old airfield and plant it. Of course we'll finish cleaning out everything of use from All 'n More and the people in Rudy will need to build personal shelters for themselves. I'm going to send my boys and the girls to live in the old house and then you and I will have our house to ourselves and..."

"That's great, Kay, and I know you've got that all planned out because you're brilliant, but I was thinking about the world as a whole. Will there ever be shops again? Are we going all the way back to the wheel? Am I ever going to get up and have to decide what I want to wear to a party or is our whole life just going to be work and practicality?"

"I don't think so. I think you'll find you're going to have even more time to pursue hobbies and things you care about."

"That's just it, Kay. I didn't have any hobbies and all I really cared about was my stupid job." She wasn't close to tears, but she was pretty upset. "We haven't been able to make love for two days because I stupidly screwed my hands up and... well what else is there to do to pass the time?"

"I think it's a pretty good way to pass the time."

"Oh I'm not saying it isn't but... We can't just do that all the time and since I haven't been able to help get the wood or take care of the animals or work in the greenhouse... what do I do?."

"You could do the news cast on the radio," I suggested. After all wasn't that her real passion? Wasn't that the same job?

"But I'm mostly useless there now, Kay, because I don't know anything. I don't even know enough to keep from getting frost bite. I'm not like you I don't know how to tell them what they need to do. Hell, I can't even read the satellite images and tell them what the weather's doing, which let's face it in my old life if I'd had to be the weather girl it would have been a huge demotion and now it turns out that if I could be the weather girl I'd be one of the most respected people in the world right now. When people listen to their radios they want to hear your voice you comfort them and give them hope. When someone radios here they want to talk to you, they want you to answer their questions. I couldn't do it. Half the time I don't have a clue what they're talking about. And we're out there in the cold and everyone is working and I'm watching to make sure the roof doesn't collapse like I don't know you aren't just making up something for me to do to get me out of the way and..."

"Geez Lucy, that's the whole thing isn't it? Lucy, you dumbass. That wasn't a nothing, made up job. It's true that I didn't want you in the building in case the roof did collapse. There really was a good chance the roof could go at any minute even after we shored it up. Snow is heavy, heavy enough to damage the roof in the first place. I needed you to watch the roof because my sons mostly do what I tell them to do and I don't have to explain to them what I mean so they were my best help. I didn't want any of the others on look out because, to tell you the truth, if me and my sons had the roof fall on us then they might think that would save them all a lot of trouble because then they could just ride on out here and take everything we have. I needed you to watch out for us because I know you wouldn't let the roof fall

on me or my boys, you wouldn't let it fall on anyone and you...
Well you have the keenest eye I have ever known. Even without
your glasses you see more than most people. I knew that if that
roof would have shifted you would have screamed your head off
and we would have had time to get out."

"I... I thought you just wanted me out of your way. That you
took me just because I wouldn't stay home and then told me to
watch the roof just to keep me out of your way."

"Lucy... do I make you feel like you're in my way?"

"You did at first."

"That's because you were at first," I said with a laugh. "You
aren't in my way now. I love you. Look, just because I don't
believe in this fate thing you put so much store in doesn't mean
I don't think we belong together. Lucy, I wouldn't want to do the
apocalypse with anyone but you."

Lucy leaned her head back on my shoulder almost purring,
"Oh honey that's the nicest thing you've ever said to me."

CHAPTER 15

Deal With the Dead

Never assume the worst is over. In fact, the more it seems like spring is just around the corner, the closer you better watch those food stores. Just because the waters start to subside or the ice starts to melt doesn't mean you can start to plant, and even if you can plant, you can never bet on a crop coming in. You've all heard the saying "Don't count your chickens till they hatch" well you'll come closer to being right about how many eggs will hatch into chicks than you will how much food bare land will produce.

You will be better off if you were able to stay where you live and you already have a garden, but let's face it; most of you will not have been raising all of your food so you'll need to plant more land.

Continue to ration till you run out of food or the crops come in. Even then remember that you can't eat everything you get; you have to put some back. In the post-apocalyptic world no one should be fat. Everyone ought to always be eating just the amount of calories they need to eat. Have canning jars and lids and drying racks put back so that when the time comes you can actually store your food safely. Buy garden seeds even if you don't have a garden and don't need one right now. Then be sure to put a bunch of fresh garden seed back and replace them every year with new seed. If you do keep a garden, buy double what you need every year and use half the seeds from last year. Rotate out your stock and always be ready to plant twice what you need. After the apocalypse **never** plant all your seeds at once. Read some books on how to save seeds because after the world ends you won't be able to go to the store and get them any more.

If you make it through the worst of the shit and can make the land work for you, then your space will become a little oasis of humanity. That's all the world will be for quite a while—just small villages where a handful of families live. There won't be cities anymore. When and if you walk up on what's left of the cities, you'll see them for what they are—the dried-up bones of a dead era. Their husks will be the dinosaur bones our children's children find.

As soon as you can leave shelter safely you will need to take *care of the dead. All of the dead—animal and human—must be gathered up, burned, or buried, preferably away from your population center. Rotting carcasses are a sure way to invite disease and predators—if there are any left. Make sure you don't get rid of bodies in your watershed area and continue to boil your water ALL of your water. When possible, get your water from ground sources like natural springs, old wells, or dig new ones if you can. Remember that if you are getting your water from a river, stream, or creek, unless you are at the headwaters you have no idea what that water is running over, around, and through.*

It was a damn good thing we got those supplies when we did because the next day we had a storm come in worse than all the ones before—more snow and even colder temperatures. Roy said the snow had banked up past their windows on the west side of the church. I told them to leave the snow alone because at this point it was breaking the wind and actually helping to insulate the building. It was a rock building, so it was safe to just leave it alone.

I knew what we were in for, so I had already brought extra hay and feed and a whole fifty-five pound bag of rice bran to the birdhouse for the wild critters. We had dug some downed trees out of the snow and replenished our wood supply as well, and it was a damn good thing, too. For the next two weeks straight there was always a light snow falling and the temperature never rose above zero.

We had plenty of food for the animals and for us, and the plants in the greenhouse were still producing well so we had fresh vegetables for everyone. In fact, we had a batch of peas that were just coming off as the snow started to fall and the temperature started to drop and they kept making all through the blizzard.

I noticed it first with the goats and chickens. They were used to running the whole place and now they were basically stuck in the barn. It's a big barn, but it isn't outside. They had artificial sunlight twelve hours a day, clean water and plenty to eat, but they were getting bored. In part I was sure that it was because I had finally run out of pumpkins. The chickens loved to have me take a machete and open a pumpkin for them. They had all sorts of vitamins and nutrients and they would pick on one pumpkin for a week.

I'd chop one a week up for the goats, too, and they would happily eat it. It was something different, something to break the routine and now... Well, we were out of pumpkins. There were six of us and the greenhouse easily fed us but there wasn't a whole lot left over for the animals.

The goats and chickens weren't the only things getting rest-less. We were all tired of being cooped up inside and way tired of each other. We spent less and less time in the living room as a group and more and more time in our separate rooms with our respective mates. I noticed that Evelyn and Cherry would gravitate towards the kitchen or the greenhouse just to get away from the boys or each other, and Billy and Jimmy would start a fire out in the shop and find some project they just had to work on alone or together for the same reason.

Lucy and I spent a lot of time on the radio. This weather front—even though it was the worst one yet—didn't kill many people. See... Well let's just tell it like it is—by then anyone who wasn't a real survivor had already died. The people who had made it this long they were hard-core people like me who had prepared way in advance. They'd had a plan from the beginning and had over-stocked everything they could just in case. Or they were people too damn stubborn to just lie down and die, who were also smart enough to problem solve their way through just about anything.

These people still occasionally needed help, but more and more they had the same problem our group did—they were all going stir crazy, too.

One night as Lucy and I lay in bed after doing it till our brains were numb I said, "You know what's saving us?"

"Huh?" Lucy didn't understand what I meant.

"The reason we aren't all trying to kill each other. I mean it's tense but nothing like the people we've been on the radio with."

Lucy laughed and wrapped herself around me. "Tell me ole sage of the apocalypse. Why aren't we all trying to kill each other?"

"None of us really knew each other till this thing started. I mean there are three couples in this house and none of us were couples when this started. We aren't bored with each other be-cause everything is still new and we still have lots to talk about. Imagine if we were like Fred and Belva." A couple we'd talked to that morning who were on the verge of killing each other and who said the only thing keeping them going was listening to the books on tape we broadcasted. "They've been married thirty years. They don't even like each other any more and they know every damn thing about each other. They've heard each other's stupid-assed stories and jokes thousands of times already and now they're stuck in an eight-by-sixteen-foot living space where they can't get away from each other and they realize that they actually hate each other."

"It could also be that we have more room than they do and... Well there are six of us so we aren't stuck with just each other for company," Lucy said. Then she made an unhappy noise and I would have almost bet she was about to talk about she-who-was-a-thorn-in-everyone's-side. "Then of course there's Evelyn."

"That girl... She's like a caricature of a human being." I laughed without much humor. "I have never in my life met someone as... as..."

"Selfish, self serving, self centered and devoid of any redeeming qualities." Lucy supplied with a smile.

"Exactly," I said.

"But she gives us all someone to hate, which keeps us from maybe taking closer looks at each other."

I looked at her with raised eyebrows. "What are you trying to say?"

Lucy laughed. "That maybe we'd want to kill each other, too, if we were stuck in an eight-by-sixteen bunker and we only had each other to talk to with no Evelyn to annoy us."

"You have a point. Daily I think about just sticking that girl out into the cold."

"I think everyone does, even Jimmy."

"Maybe especially Jimmy," I mumbled. "Of course the one thing that Evelyn accomplishes on a positive note is that she makes Jimmy look resourceful, bright and hardworking—by comparison of course."

That was when the screaming started. Billy and Jimmy were fighting again, and then I heard something crash to the floor. I jumped up, pulled my pants and a shirt on, and ran out of the room. The boys had broken a bookshelf in the living room and were trying to break each other. Of course Billy was winning. "Knock it off!" They didn't listen to me, so I picked up the fireplace shovel and knocked them each in the head. They went reeling away from one another, rubbing their heads and said at once.

"Ow, Mom!"

"Stupid little pecker heads tearing up my shit!" I was pissed, too. It was just a shelf; it could be fixed easily enough, and none of the books looked damaged. That didn't matter not to me. "What the hell could be so important that you'd risk fighting in here? Maybe break something important, something we can't replace fucking around like idiots!"

"He started it!" they both screamed at once.

"I don't give a shit who started it. Don't you get it? We're, stuck in this house together. There is no place else to go. We **have** to get along; it isn't a choice, not a suggestion. You think you two fuckers and those two air-headed girls don't get on my last nerve? I built all of this by myself. You dumbasses didn't help me do it. Hell, you thought I was as crazy as everyone else did. Jimmy even wanted to have me committed at one point just so he could clean out my bank account... Oh don't look so surprised, Jimmy. You guys didn't take a dump that I didn't know about it 'cause I had you followed by detectives. Yeah, that's right. Why? Because I could afford to and you've always been a couple of dumbasses, that's why. What the hell were you fighting over anyway?"

"He was flirting with my woman!" Jimmy accused.

So... he started it. He decided his brother was flirting with his "woman," and so he hit him and then Billy had to kick Jimmy's ass.

"He's a retard!" Billy screamed at his brother.

"Yeah I know," I said with a sigh. I noticed Cherry and Evelyn were just sort of standing there. Cherry looked mortified, like she couldn't believe the huge idiots would actually hit each other, but Evelyn she had this look on her face that I knew meant there had been flirting but it wasn't Billy who was flirting with her. No, Evelyn had been flirting with him—no doubt because she wanted the big, good-looking one not the little, scrawny ugly one. Cherry wasn't worried. She knew where Billy's heart was. He was totally and completely in love with her and she with him.

I glared at Evelyn, who I would come to refer to as the fly in the ointment of my life—well actually that was a bit of a mouthful so I just called her fly girl which she never understood and which made Lucy laugh every time I said it because she **did** know what I meant.

"Look, no one expects anyone as self centered and egotistical as you are to like the way we have to live right now, but this could literally go on for years and we're all just going to have to get along. I don't have the time and none of us have the patience to put up with all your little game playing, drama bullshit. Now I realize you're used to whining your way through life and getting everything you want by manipulating everyone around you because normally you hold all the cards. Well guess what? You don't have any cards. Here you aren't special at all, and we're all tired of your crap. You know what I mean, all that crappy little passive-aggressive shit you keep saying about all of us and our home and... Well everything from the cheese we eat to the wood heat. Up till now we've all just sort of ignored your crap because you were so sick and sad, but from now on every time you say or do something that annoys me or anyone else I'm going to tell you."

This would be when the stupid bitch started screaming at me like she had some right to do so. She was, of course, trying to turn my stupid-ass, already-looking-for-a-reason-to-hate-me son against me.

"Me, me! It's you always pushing your weight around thinking you're king. Telling Jimmy what to do all the time. Telling everyone what to do all the time!"

"You ungrateful little bitch," Lucy said. "Katy saved your miserable life."

"Shut the fuck up, Evelyn!" It was Cherry who shouted it. "I am so tired of your shit!" She looked at Jimmy. "Sorry, Jimmy, but she was all over Billy not the other way around. I saw what happened, not you."

"That's the truth, Jimmy, I swear it," Billy said.

Cherry looked at me then. "You want the truth, Katy? Before everything went to hell in a hand basket I had every intention of kicking her out and getting a new roommate. All through the crap we went through I could hardly get her to help and she bitched non-stop, twenty-four/seven just like she has done ever since she got well enough to talk."

Evelyn looked truly shocked.

"And you know why I wanted another room mate?" Cherry continued. "Because you're never happy until you make everyone around you miserable. We would have all been way ahead if you'd just died."

See I hadn't realized it, but apparently the girl had been pressing Cherry's buttons for a long time. I'd thought they were good friends. It had never dawned on me that they were just room mates thrown into this thing together not because of a bond between them but just bad luck.

I smiled smugly down at the girl. "Look, sugar, in the old days... You know a few months ago, people lived by a different code and people like you just did your shit and made people unhappy and no one ever put you in your place because they really couldn't. You'd push people's buttons and push them and push them and when they finally snapped and pushed back then to people who didn't really know you *they* looked like dicks. You know how you *should* act because you do it in the beginning when you first meet people and don't let the bitch out of the box till people are stuck with you in one way or the other. Society never allowed us to deal with nasty little pieces of crap like you because you always have a reason for what you've done, don't you? A bad childhood or some other half-assed excuse for bad behavior. You always had a way to make it look like it was someone else's fault and when you wore out one group of people or a boyfriend well you just said it was all their fault and you moved on. Well now there ain't no place else for you to go except down to the church in Rudy and... Well, they killed their last troublemaker, didn't they? Here in the new world—you know the one where I think I'm king—you'll either start acting like a human being and quit trying to stir up shit, or I will put your ass out in the snow."

She looked at Jimmy thinking he would come to her rescue because she was little and cute. But little and cute can only get you so far and Jimmy... Well Jimmy never liked to put up with any form of shit whether he deserved to or not, and he knew he didn't deserve this. She'd just made him look like a jack ass in front of his whole family. While he often did this all on his own, he wasn't about to let her do it to him. And while he could do or say, and often did, whatever popped into his tiny little mind to and about me, no one else was allowed to do so.

He curled his lip at her, laughed cruelly—something he did almost too well—and said, "Oh don't even look at me, bitch. I'm sick of your shit, too."

He looked at his brother then. "I'm sorry Billy."

Billy just nodded.

Jimmy glared back at Evelyn and then right before my eyes Jimmy, whose balls had always been two sizes too small, grew six sizes that day. "You better apologize to my mother and my brother and Cherry and Lucy, and then you better start kissing my ass, or I'll let Mama... Hell *I'll* put your hateful ass out in the snow myself."

I smiled proudly but stifled the laugh that wanted to come out of my head.

Evelyn's face became a mask of hate, and it was obvious that she really wanted to spit out some more crap. See, she was a classic narcissist and as such she was never wrong and anyone who thought she was needed to be killed. She was totally incapable of caring for anyone else longer than it took her to realize they couldn't make her happy. Of course nothing could ever make her happy because the thing that always brings people the most happiness is loving someone else. Loving yourself will only ever get you just so far physically or emotionally—if you know what I mean.

She really wanted to be able to tell us all to go to hell and leave to find other people to torture as was no doubt her habit. But of course there were very few other people to torture and no place she could get to before she froze to death, so she swallowed the ball of hatefulness that wanted to come up her neck and spill out of her mouth and apologized to all of us—including Jimmy.

"Go to our room and stay out of everyone's face for a while. We all need a vacation from you," Jimmy ordered her.

She obviously wanted to tell him to eat shit and die but instead she hung her head and went to his room.

At which point I heard Lucy chuckle at my shoulder.

"What?" I asked in a whisper.

Lucy got on her tiptoes and whispered in my ear, "I think that was the first ever bitch intervention."

I laughed because it really was funny.

"I'll clean up this mess and fix the shelf, Mama," Jimmy said.

"Good boy." I walked up and kissed him on the cheek then I walked over and kissed his brother on the cheek, grabbed Lucy's hand, and started back to our room.

For the next couple of days things were mostly peaceful. But then, of course, Evelyn started her shit again, just complaining about this and that and crying a lot and saying how everyone hated her, and all her friends were dead and... Well this time we all knew what we were dealing with so every time she said anything that stuck in anyone's craw, no matter how small, we either just told her what a crock of shit it was or we told her to shut the fuck up. It was damn near as good as putting a shock collar on the bitch and within just a few weeks she actually started acting like a human, doing her fair share of the work, adding things to the conversation that had nothing to do with how bad she felt or sticking little pins in any of us. So it turns out that passive-aggressive, narcissistic behavior **can** be cured. You just have to remove them from all of the people who just let them get away with their shit because it's easier than arguing with them. Then you have to be relentless in training them and not let them return to bad habits—just like you would a dog.

By the time the blizzard stopped we had five and a half feet of snow and the drifts on the west side of the dome completely covered that side of the house. When we finally got to the bird-house it was obvious that nothing had been out in days because we had to dig snow out of the doorway to get in. I had taken Billy with me because I wasn't at all sure that anything would have lived through all the cold and the sight of a room full of dead animals would have crushed either Jimmy or Lucy.

But there was nothing dead in there and they even had a little feed left. The deer sort of looked at us warily at first, but by the time we had fed everything and brought in all the hay one of the does walked right up to me. It was clear that she wanted to be petted, so I did. Truth was that between the spring and all the animals while it wasn't warm in there, it wasn't freezing in there, either. The coons and possums—even the rabbits—had gone into hibernation mode, the birds were mostly still conserving energy, and the deer huddled together for warmth as soon as they had eaten what they wanted and got a drink. But all-in-all they were doing alright.

"Mom," Billy started, as he put a new mineral block in one of the feeders. "Is it... Is it ever going to clear and warm up? Is the sun going to come out and is all this shit ever going to melt?"

"Sure it is," I said.

"You know what I mean, Mom. Are we going to be alive when it clears?"

"Sure we..."

"Don't blow smoke up my ass, Mama."

"We should be." I started throwing a five-gallon bucket of wood ash I'd collected from the stove over the layer of animal shit on the ground. That should work as a disinfectant as well as keep the stench down to a manageable level. "I'm thinking it will clear off by mid-summer, but that could be wishful thinking. It could be longer, might even be years. A lot of crap got thrown into the atmosphere. Now a lot of it has fallen, driven to earth by rain and snow, but a lot of it is still floating around up there as is evident by the fact we haven't seen full sun since the day after it happened."

"Can we make it that long? Can anyone else?"

"Yes and yes," I said. He nodded but got real quiet. I just thought it was because it was a lot to digest.

A couple of weeks later the boys and I had been working in the greenhouse when Lucy called us in for dinner. When I walked in Cherry looked close to tears, Lucy was looking worried, and was tight-lipped and Evelyn—well she had this mean little smile on her face like the cat that ate the canary without getting caught. I knew that anything that made Lucy and Cherry unhappy and thrilled Evelyn couldn't be good, so I mostly ignored it.

I've found that you can almost always wait to hear bad news. There are exceptions like when a problem has to be addressed right that minute, but for the most part if it's bad sooner is never as good as later.

I pretended not to notice all the tension and sat down to eat. I got half way through my dinner when I saw Billy looking at Cherry. Then Cherry nodded in Lucy's direction. Then Lucy shook her head and gave Billy a dirty look after which Billy mouthed the words, "You tell her" to Lucy and I realized they weren't going to let me just ignore them.

"What the fuck is going on?" I asked Lucy.

Lucy looked at Billy. "Your son has something to tell you."

Well, Billy turned white and looked like someone had slapped him in the face with a fish.

"Spit it out, boy, you're ruining my dinner."

"Ah... I ah... I think Lucy should tell you later. Not at dinner."

"You mean when you aren't in the room."

Any number of stupid-assed things he could have done that he didn't want to tell me about ran through my head. Left a door open somewhere, left the methane generator running too long and emptied the tank, broke the heating stove, pissed in the water supply, but when I looked around the table at everyone and read their different expressions I knew instantly.

I sighed and said, "Key-rist! I put back enough rubbers to last three apocalypses and you couldn't use them for one."

"But I did," Billy said. I glared at him my very best don't-lie-to-me glare. "Only a couple of times..."

"A couple of times... You dumb ass, it only takes once."

And this was why he was asking when the ice might clear why he was so worried, because he'd knocked his girlfriend up and I was the only thing close to a doctor that we had. He was about to be the father of a child born into a world he knew nothing about, that none of us knew anything about. Hell, the kid could wind up living the first three or more years of his life in the bunker. Or things might never get better and the greenhouse and animals might not make enough to sustain us and he might live and die here with the rest of us. It was a lot to comprehend. Kids are a huge responsibility at any time but bringing them into the world right at the start of the apocalypse... It was a lot to think about, and all because you didn't want to take a few seconds to wrap your winky.

My first instinct was to be spitting mad, but what good would that have really done? Not that I don't often throw a huge fit even though—like then—it would be like shutting the barn door after the horse gets out. I guess right then I just had one of my few moments of clarity. It was done, she was pregnant, and short of doing a chop shop abortion there was no undoing it.

"How far along are you?" I asked Cherry.

"Two, maybe two and a half months," she said. She looked like she wanted to cry.

I nodded. "Well I have brought quite a few babies into the world; it should be a snap. Were you a C-section baby?" I said all this very conversationally, mostly I have to admit just to watch all of the wind taken right out of Evelyn's sails.

"No." she let a part of a sob out.

"Then odds are good you won't have any trouble. If you do, well I have the books that tell how to do just about any kind of delivery," I said. I hoped I sounded a whole lot more confident than I felt. Truth was I'd delivered and even pulled dozens of goats but I'd only delivered one infant in my time as an EMT and that child was the fifth child the woman had given birth to so he just sort of slid out. I'm not even sure she had to push. I must be a better actress than I think I am because Cherry seemed to calm right down, Billy was obviously just glad I wasn't going to scream at him, Jimmy and Lucy looked puzzled, and Evelyn just looked totally deflated—which made the moment a perfect score.

I just went back to eating my dinner as if nothing were wrong. "Hopefully the snow will melt by mid-summer at the latest, we'll put out some crops, and the baby will be born before the snow starts to fly again."

Because you see, best-case scenario, I knew for the next few years we were in for shorter growing seasons and longer colder winters.

"I'm sorry, Mom," Billy said.

"It was a stupid thing to do, Billy, but you didn't do it by yourself. We'll get through it and it's not like I don't love babies."

That's the truth by the way. I know it doesn't fit my persona, but I love babies. The truth was that since my boys had grown up and I'd been branded the craziest woman in the world I hadn't been able to be around many infants. Part of me was really looking forward to being a grandmother. But I looked at Jimmy and I meant it when I said, "You... a rubber every time." Last thing I needed was a grandchild with fly girl for a mother.

He nodded, and the look on his face told me that if he hadn't been being careful before he had just for sure gotten the wake-up call he needed. He was in no hurry to have the responsibility of a child and certainly not with Evelyn. So the truth is Jimmy was a whole lot smarter than I had given him credit for.

I had dried the goats up in the middle of February because they were due to kid in April. We had made plenty of cheese and had frozen plenty of milk, enough to last us, Matt and his clan, and the folks in Rudy till the goats came fresh again. My barn was full of hay again because I'd been trading Matt milk and eggs and such for hay. I didn't know if I'd need that much hay but I wasn't going to take any chances.

It was mid-March, and though we had settled into life inside and had fallen into familiar new patterns, we were all a little more worried about the future than we had been before Cherry and Billy had stupidly gotten pregnant. Something about that baby maybe being born and never seeing the real sun, never being able to run through grass, really got us all to thinking about what the future might really be like for all of us. We didn't talk about it as a group, but Lucy and I talked about it a lot when we were alone and I figured they were all doing what we were. Why? Because it's human nature to think that everyone handles things the same way you do. It isn't true, but it's what we all think.

The animals were all acting off. The billy goat was bored and depressed in his eight-by-sixteen pen, and the chickens were tired of their coop, and it wasn't just us that were going stir crazy. So one day I stuck the billy-goat in the wood hall just to change his scenery. Then I opened the chicken coop and let the does run in and out of the buck pen and chicken pen and let the chickens and guineas have the run of the whole barn. Now I had to hang out in there with them to make sure the two roosters didn't fight and that the does didn't get into too much mischief because there are few things that goats delight in more than doing something you absolutely do not want them to do.

Now some of you might be asking why the buck wasn't running with the does. After all, they were already bred so what real harm could he do? Well a billy-goat is one of the most cantankerous things on Earth, and it's not beyond a billy to beat a doe and make her abort just so he can breed her again. Even though I was watching them, he weighs in at about two-hundred pounds and I try to stay out from in between him and what he wants to be doing. If he'd given me too much trouble that cold-assed winter I would have butchered him. I had a freezer full of frozen goat sperm from several different sires and I didn't actually need him. So why did I keep him at all? Because I don't like doing artificial insemination at all, and I sort of liked the asshole.

There was another reason for keeping him separated from the does. Billy goats have scent glands and they piss on their heads. When they're in rut they are the foulest-smelling things you can imagine, and even when they aren't in rut they don't smell too pretty and will make the milk smell and taste off. So I just always kept him penned separate from the does except for the one month a year I ran him with them to breed. Normally he lived in a one-acre pen and had his own small pond and an out building to protect him from the weather. I usually even let him have an extra rooster for company, but we had eaten his extra rooster for Christmas dinner because I couldn't afford to feed extra mouths that weren't producing.

Yet I was feeding that billy goat. I know it doesn't make any sense.

So now you're asking why did I have to stay out there to keep the two roosters from fighting. Two reasons really. First, what if you only had one roster and it died? Well eventually there would be no chickens at all because I have to tell you that except for me and a few of my cohorts who managed to keep flocks alive through the apocalypse—one of them by moving the chickens into the house with them—there were no chickens, no live ones after the snow cleared. Not in our part of the world anyway. Also I have two different kinds of chickens—Production Reds for eggs—so I have two-dozen hens and a rooster at any time. And I also keep four silky hens and a rooster at all times because a silky will set on a golf ball. See I want my laying chickens to lay all the time, and with the light in the barn making sure they always have at least twelve hours of daylight they do always lay. I'm tricking them but I don't care. What I don't want my laying hens to do is to go broody because you see when they go broody they stop laying and they set on the eggs. It's just a pain in the ass to try to break them up, so they bred the setting gene out of laying hens. However I still need to raise chicks and I don't want to screw with an incubator—though I do have one—so I have the Silkies who lay about a dozen eggs and decide it's time to set. I take all but one of their eggs and give them the Production Red eggs to set on and hatch. That's how I get new hens and extra roosters to eat and to keep the billy-goat company.

Any way, I was just sitting in the barn with a stick pushing it between the roosters every time they started to fight and watching the goats sort of running in and out of spaces they hadn't been in before. The goats kept screaming to tell me that I should notice they were doing things they weren't supposed to, which I mostly ignored while I wondered whether I could talk one of the boys into cleaning up the goat shit out of the wood hall or if I was going to have to do it myself.

Then I... Well I felt it before I saw it. See, I was leaning against the door to the greenhouse, and like I said before the top part of it is wire, when all of the sudden for the first time since November I felt the warmth of sunlight on my back. When I turned around there was full sun in the greenhouse. Let me tell you nothing feels like sunlight—nothing.

Oddly enough, all of the animals stopped what they were doing, walked to the middle of the barn, and just looked up at the sun shining through the glass of the greenhouse—well at least the part we had managed to clear after the last blizzard—I swear they did. I figured this was how Noah and the animals must have felt when the clouds parted and they saw dry land.

I quit worrying about the roosters fighting and even the goats getting into things they shouldn't. I opened the door to the greenhouse, walked out, closed the door behind me, and just looked up at the sun rushing in. The equipment had showed a front of warmer weather, but I hadn't dared to hope the sun might actually come all the way out.

"Lucy come here!" I yelled.

She was there in seconds. I could see the word "what" form

on her lips and then it vanished and she was looking up. I saw the sun hit her face and she smiled. I think it was the first time I'd seen her—to actually look at her—in real sunlight. She walked over and hugged me and I hugged her back.

"It's the most beautiful thing I've ever seen," she said. Her voice choked with emotion.

I just nodded then kissed her forehead.

Of course then the roosters got into it back in the barn and I had to go break them up. Lucy had followed me into the barn. "Kay, is it over?" she asked, her voice hardly above a whisper.

I knew what she meant, and for some reason I just knew it was. "I think so, baby. I think the worst of it is over. The dust, or at least most of it, has to have settled or we still wouldn't have full sun."

And we might have had us a real moment right there if that wasn't when all the animals decided to show their asses at once. Then I was just trying to get everyone back where they belonged and none of them were cooperating and Lucy I guess was suddenly so happy that she just couldn't stop laughing—which wasn't much help but was the most amazing thing I'd heard in a long time. You know—just uncontrolled bliss.

Of course it was a couple of weeks before the temperature actually got above freezing, and then the melt was slow—which was actually a good thing because as it was I was afraid of massive flooding and had warned everyone who wasn't already above the flood lines to be ready to head for higher ground.

Surprisingly, having all that sunshine made us more restless not less so. We could almost see the end and we were all ready, way ready, to be out of that house and away from each other.

I had a guitar and all the books to learn to play. I had always wanted to learn but was always waiting for that magical time when I had plenty of time to devote to it. So I had been trying to play off and on since the end of the world because—let's face it I finally had the time. After months of mangling the guitar and putting everyone in the house through agony every time I tried, I finally admitted the awful truth—I was never going to be able to play the guitar. I just didn't seem to have any ability to do it. I had always thought I could do anything I put my mind to but I had to admit that I was wrong about that. Playing guitar was simply something I couldn't do. However Lucy learned to play in just a few weeks and Lucy became not only really obsessed with playing but she got really, really good quick.

So there are some things you are meant to do and some things you aren't and the best way to see what you're good at is to try everything and see what you can actually do instead of just always saying I can't and never seeing if you can.

I can't play guitar. Now I know it for sure.

Is it really sappy and sort of a chick thing to say that listening to and watching Lucy play the guitar just makes me incredibly hot? Of course I think that's why I always wanted to play guitar... You know, because chicks would think it was hot.

Lucy and I were in the office one night. She was playing guitar and singing real low and I was checking the charts. She was playing that song about fire and rain and such which I thought could be taken as sort of apocalyptic, but still I waited till the song ended to say something, which was even more a sign of the times.

"We're going to have to go dig up all the bodies in Rudy and get rid of them." 'Cause let's face it that's not just something you break up a song to say.

Lucy sighed. "Just when I thought there was no down side to the snow melting."

Because you see that's why the bodies had to be dug up and gotten rid of—because the snow was melting and the last thing we wanted was to try to move the bodies after they had thawed. They sure had to be dealt with way before they started to rot. Now I'd had the town's people knock down a bunch of bamboo, tie cloth flags to the sticks, and drive them into the ground at the armpit of every dead body. There are two kinds of bamboo around Rudy, the small cane that was native to the area, and giant, hardy, tree bamboo which I had bought and planted along the creek because bamboo can be used for everything from animal food to clothing and planting it along the river bank would help stop erosion.

Why the arm pit? Because then when you dig down around the flagpole you aren't likely to hit the body in its face or its groin, which just seemed wrong to me. I purposely hadn't looked at all those little flags flying above the snow every time we'd traveled to Rudy but it became really apparent that Lucy had.

"I counted over a hundred and fifty flags one day as we were driving through town." She put the guitar down. "Roy made a map of where the corpses are. When I told him how many flags I counted he said there were at least seventy-five in the other church, the one that took a direct hit from the tornado, but that they'd only planted one flag there. Kay... Why do we have to help? I mean couldn't they do it themselves? Haven't you done enough for them?"

"You don't have to go, Lucy. Actually, I don't want you to go."

Lucy smiled. "Is this yet again another time when you say you don't want me to go with you but you do but don't want to be responsible if I do something stupid and get frost bite?"

"No this is a time when I really don't want you to go because I don't want you to have to deal with dead bodies. It's something I'd like to protect you from."

"I'm going if you're going, Kay. Hell, I didn't know any of those people. If you're tough enough to do it, then so am I."

"Yeah, but I hated most of them," I said. But I didn't argue with her. I'd sort of learned that didn't really do me any good anyway.

No one expected it to be an easy job and no one was looking forward to it, but it was one of those things that had to be done and could no longer be put off. The sun was out and the snow was melting. Billy used the dozer to push the debris and snow off the ground around the ill-fated Assembly of God on all four sides. Since the most bodies in the area were in the church, it seemed to make sense to bury everyone else there as well. And then... Well, there were seventy-five bodies we didn't have to dig up.

Matt had a blade on the front of his tractor and since the tractor was smaller and easier to maneuver Matt would pick a flag and start pushing snow. I would follow with a team of three of the Rudyites with picks and shovels in my four-wheeler trailer. Matt would scrape most of the snow away and then we'd go to work digging till we got the bodies up. Then we'd load them on the trailer behind my four-wheeler, take them over to the church, and go to the next flag.

We swapped out every hour who was driving and who was digging. After her first body I was able to convince Lucy that she'd be more help watching the kids and letting other people come work. She agreed, not because she thought she needed to be harbored from the horrors of the truth as much as because of the frostbite. You see she was fine but having had it her hands now got colder quicker, and having had it she had a very real fear of getting it again.

When Billy had cleared all of the snow and debris from around the church foundation—because let's face it the foundation was really all that was left—I had him start clearing the snow and debris off the roads. Not an easy task mostly because it was hard to find them. It helped that he knew about where they were supposed to be.

Now this might seem like a frivolous waste of fuel and time, but here's the thing. There was five foot of snow when the melt started. We'd only lost about a foot of it when we started this project and there were little rivulets of water running everywhere. That water needed to be able to free flow somewhere away from Rudy. It needed to be directed towards the creek if at all possible, and the town needed some protection from the rising water from the creek when all this snow melted. So Billy used the snow and debris he cleaned off the roads to make temporary levies.

It took us most of three days to dig out and move all the bodies. Then Billy used the dozer to dig a six-foot deep trench around the church foundation and then he used the dirt to bury the bodies good and deep. See the trench should keep the composting bodies out of the ground water. Of course I was hoping the cement slab and what was left of the church walls would help do that, too.

By the time we were done I think everyone was a little numb. Weird stuff went through my head the whole time we were doing it. When my shovel had been the one to reveal old lady Hubert's face, just for a second I could see her working in her yard on a summer day in her stupid bonnet tending her roses with a look of concentration on her face—not unlike the look that was frozen on her face as we chipped away the snow from her body and loaded her into the trailer.

As we drove our four wheelers back over the river on the last day I could hear the ice crack a little and knew it wouldn't be long till that river was running again. We were going to have to build some sort of bridge, but I couldn't even really think about that.

As I drove home with Lucy's hands wrapped tightly around my waist all I could think about was why I didn't feel sadder. I admit to being crazy, but was there something more wrong with me that I could treat something like digging up and moving the dead like just another job that had to be done? And wasn't it just that? Just another job that had to be done? Even the thing with Mrs. Hubert's hadn't left me feeling like we were moving a person. They were dead bodies; that was all. Whatever had been people about them wasn't there anymore, and they were just a biohazard that had to be dealt with properly. Matt and I had even had to dig up the Burkholder boys from where he'd put them and brought them down to bury. We actually made jokes the whole time we did it about how much better they smelled and looked.

There would be more bodies. There were houses all through these hills and people in or thrown around most of them. Not just people but cattle and other animals. But we had no way of knowing where those were and we'd have to wait for a full thaw to go looking.

It was a morbid thought—the whole we'll pack a lunch and go looking for the dead thing.

I must have been more upset about the whole thing than I

thought I was because when it was my turn to shower I just kept the water going. The melt had the cisterns spilling over and the waterfall was running so there was no reason to conserve water, but I was so used to taking a quick shower that I normally did. Not that day.

Lucy walked in. "Honey, you alright?" she asked. So apparently I was in there even longer than I thought I was.

"I'm fine." I grudgingly turned the water off. I got out and grabbed a towel.

"It's alright to be upset, Kay. It was a horrible thing to have to do," Lucy said.

I nodded. "You alright?" I asked.

She smiled. "I was after I took a really long shower. Seriously, Kay. I dug up one person. You dug up dozens. It's alright to have a meltdown."

Wow! Permission to have a meltdown. Is it any wonder I was crazy about Lucy Powers? "Actually, honey, I think I'm more upset that I'm not more upset," I said. As if it made sense.

Lucy nodded like she understood that, even though I was pretty sure she didn't. In that moment I was pretty sure that Lucy was perfect in every way.

CHAPTER 16

Don't Do Anything Stupid

When the sun finally comes out and the snow starts to melt you're going to think the worst is over and want to just relax. There will be no time for that unless you're well away from any lake, river, stream, or even a wet-weather wash.

Don't do anything stupid. Rushing water and extreme cold are two things that will kill you quick. Use caution in all things you do; you can't just run to the hospital if you get hurt.

It's going to be a lot of water. An incredible amount of snowfall means an incredible amount of water crowding frozen rivers and streams which are probably already full to capacity.

All that snow melts and the world will turn to mud. Don't try to plant in mud. You will have to wait till the ground is dryer and remember—whatever the time of year—that what you are dealing with is early spring. So plant only crops that do well in early spring—greens peas, beets, carrots and such.

Keep rationing your fuel; it could still get ugly cold at night.

As soon as it is safe to do so, start trolling your area for everything you can scavenge. Take everything you find because you'll find a use for it later and if you don't it still didn't hurt anything to take it. Do NOT try to take stuff from another survivor. If they have something you want, see if they will trade for something you have. If not, then move on. This will be an odd time in which wars could start over a shovelhead.

Here's a good and inexpensive way to hedge your bets to make sure you have stuff to trade that will be really needed. Start hitting yard sales, flea markets, second hand stores, and buy any hand tools you find even if they don't have handles. Handles can always be fashioned from sticks if nothing else, but metal working... Well it might be awhile before some areas can get something like that going and some never will, so those things will be the gold of the future.

The rain started falling hard and warm one afternoon and you could almost see the snow melting. It fell for just three hours but when it finished we only had about a foot of snow left. I wasn't too surprised when I got the panicked call from Roy telling me that the creek was almost to the top of the levies. It was a lot of water, but it shouldn't have done that—not this quick. I knew what that meant. An ice dam had formed somewhere downstream.

See, the river was frozen solid and then as things start to melt those giant sheets of ice start to break free, float on the water, shift and then they float away... Till one of them get's caught on something and then others back up behind it and it forms a dam. Then the water starts to back up, too.

There were lots of things to impede the flow of the river. Trees were down everywhere, hell most of the bridges were out. The Rudy Bridge was down and I imagined that was where this problem originated.

I was wrong, of course. The Rudy Bridge had already been washed completely out of the creek by the force of the water. There was so much water in fact that I could barely make out Roy and some of the other people on the other side of the creek. Roy had his walkie-talkie.

"We're screwed, huh?" he asked. Because he was right. If they had to run from the water at this point, they'd have to bug out in a couple of hours, on foot and without most of their supplies and no real destination in mind.

"Look, if you have to bugger out bundle up good and just head for All 'n More. You know there is plenty of shelter, food, and everything else there. It's a long hike, but you can make it," I told him. "I'm going to ride down the creek and see if I can find the ice dam."

And by me I meant me and Lucy and Billy and Jimmy. The going was rough because the snow that was left was wet and super slick. I wished a couple of times that Lucy wasn't on the four wheeler with me because I would have taken a lot more risks if she hadn't been. Which of course was probably her reason for always wanting to go everywhere with me.

We were riding along the top of the ridge looking down towards the creek. Since Lucy was the only one not trying to drive through the torturous shit, it's not too surprising that she was the one who spotted the ice dam. In a narrow spot in the creek a big tree had gone down. It had lodged side ways and the water hadn't budged it. Now about forty bazillion pounds of ice had built up behind it. And millions of gallons of water.

We stopped the ATVs, got off and huddled together.

"We found it; now what we going to do about it, mama?" Jimmy asked.

It was insane, what I was thinking I mean, but really the only way I could think of to do it. I looked at the huge ice dam and scratched my head trying to think of some better way and didn't come up with one. I went to the toolbox on my four-wheeler and opened it.

"Kay... What are you doing?" Lucy asked carefully.

"I gottah blow it up."

"They could just evacuate..."

"Not really. I told them that because it's better than nothing, but that five miles might as well be twenty in the dark with kids. This shit is slicker than it was before it started melting. They couldn't make it before dark and the temperature is going to drop again."

What I said got punctuated by the sound of another huge piece of ice crashing into the dam of ice already there, making an ear-pounding noise and piling the dam even bigger. We were running out of time.

I took three sticks of dynamite and a lighter and headed for the ice dam. Lucy stepped in front of me, blocking my path.

"What the hell are you doing, Kay?" she demanded.

"I'm just going to light them and toss them on the middle, towards the bottom of the back side of the dam. You guys take the four wheelers and go higher."

"So we'll be safe while you do this stupid-assed thing. I don't think so." Lucy shook her head no, and the boys who had moved in behind her were doing the same thing.

"I'll do it. I have a better throwing arm," Billy said.

"No. I'll do it, dumb ass. You're going to be a father," Jimmy said.

"Neither one of you dumbasses know anything about TNT. I do." Cause... Well remember my job with the road crew? Well I knew all about how to blow stuff up.

"No, Kay. No. It's too dangerous; it's crazy," Lucy said. "At least think of a safer way to do it."

But there really wasn't a safer way. The right way to do it would have been to go to the bottom of the ice dam on the back side, pack a charge in just the right spot, and then set it off with a detonator. But that would take hours to rig up and, well it would actually in a lot of ways be more dangerous.

"Look we're wasting time and we're running out of daylight." As if to prove my point another huge chunk of ice slammed into the dam. "Now take the four wheelers and head for higher ground."

"Mom I don't think..."

"Then don't!" I told Billy.

"I'm going with you," Lucy said.

"No you're not," I said. "That's the most ridiculous thing I've ever heard."

"Well here's the most ridiculous thing I've ever heard." She tried to do an imitation of me that was just too cute. "I'm just going to get really close to all that crashing, crunching, ice shit and slush and then throw dynamite at it till it goes away."

I laughed, which just really pissed her off.

"Dammit, Kay, if you do this and you don't get your stupid ass killed I'm going to cut you off."

But she must have decided there was no sense in really fighting with me because she got on the four-wheeler and headed up the hill. The boys must have decided that if she had given up there was no reason for them to even try because they got on their four wheelers and followed her.

I walked over to a ledge that sort of jutted out over the creek. I wrapped the three sticks together with tape then wrapped the wicks together. I found the spot at the foot of the dam I wanted to hit, figured out which direction I was going to run after I threw the thing, then I lit it, gave it a toss, saw it land damn near right where I wanted it to, and then I took off running uphill. Of course like I said the ground was slicker than shit. I hadn't run four maybe five feet when my steel-cleated boots slipped on the shit and I fell sliding downhill about three feet. I covered my head with my arms, lay prone and braced for impact. There was a huge *caboom!* and then small pieces of ice, water and tree rained down on me. Fortunately, nothing was big enough to hurt me, so I just lay there and waited for everything to quit moving and shaking. I heard the water release as the ice dam disintegrated into the shards of ice that covered me. The earth didn't quit shaking so I just lay there face down in the snow waiting till I thought it was safe to move. That was when someone flipped me over and started smacking me in the face hard, and I was glad for my ice mask.

"Kay, Kay, can you hear me? Are you alright?"

I grabbed her hands. "I was till you started hitting me."

She started crying then and she didn't get up from where she was sitting on my hips. "I thought you were dead. God, Kay! You were there and then you were gone and there was the explosion and..." Her words got drowned out by her tears and she threw herself down on me and was hugging my neck so tight I thought she might do damage, so I knew there was no way she was actually going to cut me off. Finally Billy and Jimmy were helping both of us up and I was just watching the water rush by feeling pretty proud of myself.

"Damn, Mama, you scared the shit out of me," Billy said.

"You know, Mama, I thought I could run. But Lucy... Well she was down here before I could get off my ride." Jimmy and Billy both just looked at Lucy with amazement and any animosity they'd been harboring against her because she wasn't their mama just vanished in that instant.

I popped my mask and got on the radio. "Roy, you there?"

"Yeah, heard the boom. You guys alright? Water's already going down and quick. Thanks, Kay."

"We're fine and you're welcome."

Lucy was still crying. She'd popped her mask and her goggles so I reached up and dried her tears with my gloved hand.

"It's alright, baby. Now calm down; you're going to freeze."

Just because it was warm enough to melt the snow didn't mean it was really warm. Forty-five feels balmy for a little while when you've been dealing with sub-zero weather, but it isn't warm by any long stretch of the imagination. I kissed her gently on the mouth.

"I'm sorry I scared you."

"You're such a crazy piece of shit, Kay," She cried. "I love you, and you're not going to be happy till you get yourself killed doing some stupid butch-ass shit."

Billy laughed and I turned on him. "What's so damned funny?"

"Nothing." He shrugged, but when I looked at his brother he was smiling, too.

"What?" I demanded.

"Mother told her the same thing," Jimmy said to Lucy, not to me.

"That was like twenty years ago and she ain't dead yet," Billy said. He patted Lucy on the back.

On the ride home Lucy suddenly started pointing to my right, making gestures, so I pulled over. I popped my mask as the boys pulled in beside me.

"What?"

"I think that's my car... Well the rental car."

I stopped the motor and got off the four-wheeler.

"I didn't mean we had to stop. I was just saying... I mean we're miles from the house."

"We can scavenge the radio right now and come back for other useful stuff later," I said.

I figured the radio thing would make sense to her. I walked over to the car, which was sitting on its side in the dead middle of a field. I climbed up on top of it. I didn't want to tell her why I was bothering to check the car out because I didn't want her to be disappointed if I didn't find what I was looking for—or did and they were ruined.

With the help of a pry bar me and the boys managed to get the door open. Then I climbed inside. The car had been tossed around and nothing was where is should have been. I found an American Tourister bag still in good shape but was about to think I wasn't going to find what I was looking for when there it was, stuck up under the front seat. I pulled the purse free after three tugs and inside found what I was looking for—still in perfect condition.

I grabbed the purse and the bag and climbed out of the car. I held up the purse and yelled down to Lucy in a triumphant "who brings home the bacon" kind of voice. "Oh, honey! I just found your glasses."

Lucy was ecstatic, but we were all cold and it was getting dark so we loaded the purse and her bag into the tool box on the back of my four-wheeler—you know all safe and sound with the rest of the explosives I'd brought and didn't have to use—and we headed home.

Lucy had stripped her outer gear by the stove quick then grabbed her bag and purse and hurried to our room without a word. I knew why. She'd come here with even the clothes on her back basically all but ripped off of her. She'd come here and her past, every bit of it, had been stripped from her. As small as this might seem to us, those two bags must have seemed huge to her right then.

I let her have a few minutes to herself before I knocked on the door.

"Who is it?" Lucy said.

"Kay."

Lucy laughed a little. "Honey, you don't have to knock on the door."

I walked in and Lucy was lying in the big middle of our bed on her belly wearing her glasses—which I thought made her even hotter—and looking at stuff she had spread out all over the bed.

"I can actually see," she said with a smile.

"That may not work so well for me," I mumbled.

"You're the best looking thing I've ever seen," she said. "I'm never going to get it, the way you think, how quick you think. I just saw the car. I never in a million years would have thought to look for my glasses. I never would have thought that all of this stuff might have been in there and... Kay, none of it's even wet, not even dirty! It's just like it was when I packed it."

"Too bad they'll never be making that add. You know 'My car was thrown into the middle of a cow pasture by an F-5 tornado, but my luggage was fine,'" I said with a smile.

She patted the bed next to her and I crawled up there and lay on my belly beside her, careful not to move any of the items she'd so carefully laid out. A manicure kit, a bunch of make up, brushes and combs, deodorant, a pair of dress pants, a red silk blouse, a short blue skirt, a blue and white polished cotton blouse, a pair of stiletto heels, pictures—lots of pictures—more than most people carried. Then I realized why. Lucy had been very close to her family but she was gone a lot so she took them where ever she went.

"When the girls got here I just felt so sorry for all they went through. Then one day they were both going through their family pictures just having a good cry, and I was really mad because I had nothing. My family was just gone and I had nothing." And then she introduced me to her family. She was a little weepy which was understandable, but she was happy, too, because now it didn't seem so much like they were something that she just made up.

"What about the girlfriend?" I asked.

I shouldn't have asked because she frowned. "I never carried her picture with me in case someone would see it and ask who she was. I didn't want to have to lie about it. I wish I had one now."

She looked at me quickly, no doubt to see if I was upset. Which I wasn't. I wasn't jealous of some dead chick any more than I expected Lucy to be jealous of Cindy. And I guess I should have expected the next question.

"Kay, why don't you have any pictures of Cindy?"

"I do have," I said.

"Why aren't they out? I mean I've seen pictures of her because both of the boys have them hanging in their rooms but why don't you have any pictures out?"

"Really? You really want to know?"

Lucy nodded.

"You aren't going to like it."

She smiled. "Try me."

I sighed. "It's just going to ruin your good mood about being reunited with your own photos."

"No it won't, Kay. It's not that I don't care what you think, but I don't feel like we have to share a brain, like we have to believe the same shit."

"Alright, but remember that and remember that you're the one who wanted to know."

I have to tell you that right then I thought about just telling her a lie because I was afraid it really would ruin her mood.

"I have pictures and occasionally—not very often—I even look at them. Those pictures... They never look the way I remember my boys looking when they were little. Cindy never looks the way I remember her looking. Looking at them well it just makes me wonder if I remember anyone or anything the way it really was. See I tend to see people more as who they are than what they look like. Pictures always look close, like I know who it is but... that's not the way I remember them. I don't like pictures because they make me question my own judgment of people and of the time in which they were taken. My parents were the worst sort of dicks, but in pictures they always looked like happy, easygoing, even loving people. People pose for photos or maybe even worse a photographer waits for just the right moment to snap a picture. Pictures are all about what things look like and not what they really are. It's all about making what's ugly pretty. Or making someone look plain when they really aren't plain at all because their spirit shines when they speak. You take a picture of a place and it's always prettier than it was when you saw it. It doesn't really look like the place you saw at all. I never saw a picture of me and said, wow that looks like me, and there is not one picture that I have of Cindy which I think looks like her."

"Wow." She moved to kiss the back of my head and then she messed my hair all up. "That really is some pretty dark shit."

Apparently she was in too good a mood to let my very negative take on pictures bring her down. She got up and started to pack her things away, not in her bags but into her drawers in the dresser. She propped a picture of her mother up on top of it.

"I can make you a frame for that." I told her just so she'd know I didn't have a problem with her pictures. Then I rolled onto my back and looked at the ceiling. I didn't want to admit it to anyone but my ribs were sort of smarting no doubt from falling on my face followed directly by the percussion of the blast.

"That would be great. I'm going to go get a shower."

She left and I just lay there in my thermal underwear looking up at the ceiling and poking at my ribs where they hurt. It wasn't bad just the old wound smarting because yet again I'd done something insanely stupid. I wondered if maybe the women in my life weren't right and I did have some sort of death wish.

I must have fallen asleep because I didn't wake up till I heard one of the boys wolf whistle. They were always making some sort of noise so I turned the right way in bed—just because once I realized I was sleeping on it backwards I just couldn't do it—and started to go back to sleep.

Then the door opened and when Lucy walked in she was all dressed up. I would have said I didn't care about things like that, but when I saw her in that tight black skirt with stockings and heels on, in that red silk blouse which was almost-closed across her boobs, her face all made up and her hair pulled back with earrings and the whole works... My heart started pounding, and I was instantly hot. I got out of bed and stood there just looking at her.

"So you like what you see?" she said, and winked seductively.

"Uh huh," I said intelligently as I came in my pants. I just wanted to throw her right on the bed and have my way with her but... "I haven't even showered yet." Because of course I'm really way too neurotic for actual spontaneity.

She laughed. "Well good because I sort of wanted to wear them for more than a few minutes."

I started past her, stopped and just looked her up and down. "Damn, baby, I..."

"Yeah. Go get a bath and we'll talk," she said, and kissed my cheek.

When I walked to the bathroom Billy met me in the hall. He smiled knowingly at me. "I'm guessing from the way Lucy looks she forgot that she was going to cut you off."

"Ha, ha," I said. Mostly because I couldn't actually think of anything else to say. Let's face it; as much as kids don't want to think about their parents doing it, well that's how much we don't want our kids to know that we're doing it. I ducked into the bathroom and shut the door, trying to think of something—anything that I could do that would be special. I mean, come on, she had gotten all dressed up for me and she was hotter than hell and what did I have to bring to the table? I'd been lying there in my sweaty thermal drawers. Even after I showered I'd basically have a fresh clean scent and minty-fresh breath and my old, slightly-flabby, drooping body to offer. And not a whole lot more.

I probably would have spent more time trying to think of something, anything, that I could do that might be the least bit special but seriously what could I have thought of anyway? Besides, I just wanted to get back to my room, look at how good she looked, then strip her naked and just rub my body all over hers and... Well you know. I threw my robe on and practically ran to our room.

When I opened the door she was just sort of standing there striking a pose. She started slinking across the room towards me while I fumbled around closing and locking the door. I started towards her but she put up her hand indicating that I should stop where I was. Which I did, wondering if she had remembered the whole cutting me off thing and had just gotten all dolled up to make it that much more of a punishment. Then she started walking slower and unbuttoning that blouse till I could see her nipples and... Why was it so sexy to watch her take her clothes off? I take my clothes off; it's not sexy at all. Hell I think everything I just said sort of explains that I didn't have a clue how to make it sexy, but Lucy sure did. By the time she actually let me touch her she had next to nothing on and I could hardly breathe.

Afterwards as she was just lying all over me in bed and I was holding her so tight she couldn't have gotten away if she tried. I whispered so low I'm surprised even she heard it. "God forgive me, Lucy, I have never loved anyone the way I love you."

She was quiet for just a minute and then she managed to turn so that she could see me. "Today... just for an instant... I thought you were gone and... I just felt like I was going to die, too. All I could think was that the last thing I'd told you was that I was going to cut you off. The last thing I said to you was hateful and God, Kay, I love you so much I sometimes feel guilty because it's like... If I had to choose between having the world back just the way it was or being with you now I know I'd rather be with you."

"I'm sorry I scared you," I said, but I really wasn't because I don't think for a minute she ever would have done what she did that night or said what she said if she didn't think just for a minute that I was dead.

By the end of April all but one of the goats had kidded. Outside the snow was all gone and... Well the world was mud, so I still couldn't turn the animals out. But I think we all breathed a sigh of relief when we went outside in our winter gear and got too hot.

We had work to do, and with the daytime temperatures climbing into the fifties it was plenty warm enough to do it. We just wore muck boots and tried to stay out of the low areas as much as possible. The high spots were mostly dry, but the low areas... Well in the right spots you could sink in damn near to your knees. That's what freeze/thaw does to the ground—turns it into mush.

I put the windmill and solar panels back on line, which was good because we needed most of the methane to run our four wheelers which we were using all the time. There were trees down everywhere and they had to be cut into firewood-sized pieces and hauled back to be stacked beside the houses.

One afternoon I had grabbed Lucy and gone off to see how the old house was doing. Mainly checking to see if it was going to be good enough for the boys and their mates to move into right away or if we were just going to have to put up with them a few more months while we repaired it.

From the outside the house looked fine, no bottles broken, no concrete cracked. The top of a tree was down on part of it, but when I checked even that didn't seem to have done any real damage—just a question of cutting it and hauling it off.

I'll admit I spent a lot longer looking at the outside of the house than I really needed to because I was more than a little apprehensive about taking Lucy into the house I'd built with my first wife. The house that was mostly exactly the way it was when Cindy died. It was one of those things you knew was going to happen and that you just needed to have done, but there is just this dread.

The worst thing I could see from the outside was that the garage floor was muddy. Of course that would be because there were no doors on the garage and the snow had blown in and then melted. Nothing a little dry weather wouldn't take care of.

Finally I opened the front door. The house smelled a little stale and it was colder than it was outside because... Well, the house is well insulated and it had been really cold for a long time and there hadn't been any heat in here the whole cold-assed winter.

The first thing I did was start a fire in the heater. All I had to do was open the door and put a match to the fire I'd already built there God alone knew how long ago. In just minutes the living room was warming up.

"It's... Well it's mostly like the other house," Lucy said, a little surprised.

"This one was the prototype. When we bought the property there was an old house place on it that had a hand-dug well on what used to be the back porch. So we knocked down what was still here and we built this on the old cement floor, pushed the dirt up around the outside. Turns out it would have been just as good as our house. Which is good because it means the boys can winter here next year, no problem."

Of course it wasn't as set up as we were—no greenhouse, no connecting buildings—but it had its own solar cell banks and windmill, which I had installed when I installed the ones on my house. Though it didn't have huge cisterns full of water under-neath the house, it did have the well, which had a pump in it that fed a fifty-gallon tank so that the house had gravity-fed wa-ter. Of course I'd drained all the water lines years ago, so the whole system would have to be primed and put back on line.

"You're in a hurry to have them out of the house?" Lucy asked. She was looking at an afghan Cindy had made that was lying on the back of the couch. Then she moved to look at the pictures hanging all over the walls.

"Aren't you? Christ, we've never gotten to be alone. I'd like to do it just once and have it not be the topic of someone else's conversation."

Lucy sighed. "Yes, that would be nice."

"They'll probably still be around a lot more than we want them to be."

"Cherry's really starting to show."

"Yeah, I told her to stop eating so much. Last thing I need is to try to deliver some forty-pound baby," I said.

"It's a really nice house," Lucy said. There was a hint of wistfulness to her voice.

"What's wrong?" I asked.

"Nothing, it's just that it's the same basic floor plan as your house but it feels more like a home and less like a bunker. I love your home, don't get me wrong, but it's just sort of bare necessities—all functionality. This place is well... decorated."

"It's our house, not just mine anymore. If you want to decorate it then by all means do so as long as you don't move the shit I need and it doesn't get in my way—go for it."

See, that kind of shit is something important that I didn't even think of. Everything doesn't have to be functional. You need a little whimsy in your life. I understood the importance of celebrations and music and art as things to pass the time, but I didn't understand how important a simple thing like decorating your house or putting on special clothes was until that night Lucy had gotten all dressed up and it made something we did all the time seem so different, even more special.

I sat down in my old recliner, which was close to the wood stove, which wasn't nearly as nice as ours but was still a good one. Lucy walked over and sat in my lap and she wrapped her arms around my neck. "I have to tell you that I thought I'd feel weird coming in here because the boys told me you hadn't changed anything since their mother died. I was sure I'd feel like an interloper, that it would make me feel like the boys do when I can tell they're looking at me and thinking 'she's not my mother'..."

"Baby, you aren't old enough to be their mother," I said with a laugh.

"You know what I mean, Kay."

I did, so I just nodded silently.

"But I feel good here, like I can tell that this is where a family lived. You were happy here with her and with them. I don't feel threatened by that."

"The boys had never lived in the new house till after the apocalypse... You know we need to think of something besides 'the apocalypse' to call it because that's a big word and I get tired of saying it all the time. But what else can we really call it? Just saying 'the shit hit the fan' or 'the end of the world as we knew it,' well that's just as long and I'm just as tired of saying those things, too."

"I know what you mean. What about we abbreviate it? How about TP short for the apocalypse," Lucy suggested.

"Good idea but I don't think TP. I mean that's also short for toilet paper." I thought for a minute. "I've got it! We'll call it BS cause that's when everything took a big shit and it was all caused by a bunch of stupid bullshit which then caused all of us to deal with bullshit, so BS fits."

So in case you wanted to know that's why everyone now calls the apocalypse the BS. That's also why everything before the end of the world is referred to as BB—before bullshit—and everything that's happened since the apocalypse is ABS—for after bullshit.

When we got back to the house the last of the kids had been born. I was sort of disappointed because all four does had normal births, which didn't really let me test my skills as a midwife at all. I was some worried they'd have trouble giving birth or that the kids would be malformed just because they'd been cooped up for their entire pregnancies, but every doe had twins—which is sort of normal—they were all giving good milk, and all the kids were perfectly normal. The only thing to bitch about was the doe to buck ratio. We needed to be able to repopulate at least our part of the planet with livestock and of the eight kids we'd gotten only three does—the rest were bucks. The folks in Rudy would take one of my old does and two of the young ones and a buck for their herd. The rest of the bucks would be weathered, fattened up, and butchered for food. But I didn't tell Lucy or the girls that when they were feeding them with bottles and talking baby talk to them.

We managed to get through all of April and May without any bad weather. The usual tornado season seemed to have given the whole country a break—well except for New Mexico which just seemed to get pounded by just about everything. The people who had decided New Mexico was a good place to hunker down and ride out the BS had long since decided they'd taken a wrong turn at Albuquerque. Many of them had gotten out while the getting was good and taken up with groups in west Texas and Oklahoma.

That's what happened when the winter finally ended. People who'd barely hung on where they were or who were all alone were moving into groups that were well-established somewhere else or getting together and forming their own groups in places they felt could sustain them better. Most of my time on the radio was spent putting this group or individual in touch with that group or individual, guiding people to places like old army camps, parks and schools that they would be able to turn into communities.

By mid-May it was still really muddy in the low places but all our fences had been fixed and I'd noticed the deer running around the property with three new fawns. Now that the snow was gone they couldn't clear the fences so they were ours—not that they seemed like they were in any hurry to go anywhere—and I figured if the deer thought it was alright to be out I could let the goats out, too.

We moved the billy goat to his pen first. He looked lonely in that big pen without his rooster, but we'd get him a new one soon enough. At least he could actually run for the first time in months—which he did so much I began to worry he was going to keel over from a heart attack if he didn't calm down. Then just before I was going to go get him and pen him up again he just went up to his shelter, found a wall in the sun, and stood there sunning himself.

I closed the top of the barn door between the solarium and the barn so that the barn was once again closed off from the house. I then opened the barn door to the outside and let the does and guineas out. The kids stayed in the kid pen in the barn where it was warm. Now I have a big door that I load hay into the barn through, but the goat door is only two feet by four feet. When I first opened it there was a big push for who was going to get out first. There was no grass yet, but there were lots of downed trees and they wasted no time going and chewing on the tips of the limbs and the softer bark towards the tops. The whole world was just sort of brown and gray till sunset. That first year after the BS the sunrises and sunsets were just vivid and gorgeous. I let the chickens into their respective runs outside and they went crazy digging and scratching and running around even though there was nothing but dead grass in their pens. The guineas just ran out—they normally only come in the barn to roost and spend their days just flying and running around the property eating bugs, there weren't any bugs, so they were mostly just flying around making that ungodly noise they make and causing me to seriously wonder why I'd let them live. There was still ice on the ponds, but there was water at the edges and when one of the does found this water she drank it like it was the greatest thing she had ever had in her mouth.

I knew as soon as I was able to release the animals that it was time to start hunting up the dead. There were no vultures circling, so I knew vultures hadn't made it through the BS—at least not here. Animals tended to run from bad weather when they could find places where it wasn't so bad—some place where there was food and shelter. Like the deer and wild animals and the birds that knew about it had all come into our old barn, and the llamas and zebras and buffalo had gone to Matt's hay barn. The problem was for most there would have been no place to go. Even if they could have found some place there wouldn't

have been anything to eat, and even animals that hibernated...
Well the winter would have been too long and too cold for most
of them, too.

Cherry and Lucy stayed with the kids in Rudy and the rest of
us all loaded onto four wheelers and tractors with trailers and
we headed out in different directions deciding that we'd all steer
clear of the old Burkholder place just in case there were mines
planted out there. Now that the snow had cleared we could see
where houses used to be and clearly see where dead animals
lay... and people. I had insisted that Evelyn help because I
thought it would be good for her to see death up close and personal. She acted like everything that had happened had only
happened to her. It might do her some good to be reminded
what lay under all that pretty white snow.

Of course the first time we came up on human remains—it
was still getting cold enough at night that most of them were still
frozen in the core so no rot which was good—she had a complete melt down, blubbering and whaling and... useless. So I
sent her home because I figured the last thing those kids needed
was to listen to her retell her horror over and over again. No way
she was smart enough to not say anything in front of them. Like
I told you, as far as Evelyn is concerned everything is about
her—always.

A whole country full of Evelyns—that's what had screwed
the pooch. Everyone just trying to get everything they could for
them and NEVER thinking about anyone or anything but their
own personal desires.

I'll beat the dead horse if I want to!

We spent three full days just dragging in human and animal
bodies and throwing them in the pit Billy had dug on the south
side of town before we decided we'd done enough. We'd cleaned
enough of our area that we should be safe, and the truth was I
don't think any of us had the heart to just keep looking. It was
like a really morbid Easter-egg hunt. Billy pushed the dirt back
over the hole and we didn't even bother to mark where it was. It
wasn't likely anyone was going to forget any time soon.

The number of dead animals had been staggering. I found
myself wishing I'd thought to keep some ducks, some sheep,
that some horses had made it to Matt's. It felt like the only animals that had lived through the BS did so at mine or Matt's
place, and for our part of the world at least that was true. Matt
and his wife had a pair of Welsh Corgis that they'd kept all through
the BS and as far as we knew those were the only dogs that
made it through the BS in our entire area.

There was a lot to be done and no one bitched much about
the work because we were all just so glad not to be stuck inside

stacked on top of each other any more.

I was of course still talking to the little groups I was in contact with all over the world, helping them through whatever problems they were facing and answering any questions, but for the most part I was worried about making sure me and mine continued to thrive. For some odd reason Matt and his family and those people in Rudy had all become mine, too, so I was pretty damned busy.

For a couple of days after we finished getting rid of the dead we all just needed to be busy and do something positive, so we all went to the other house, cleaned it up and got everything running. Then we moved the boys and girls from our house into theirs.

Did I think they'd all get along and live well together? No, I fully expected that Evelyn would make them all nuts and that Jimmy and Billy would keep right on fighting about everything, but I didn't care because I wasn't going to have to listen to it.

I also expected that as soon as things calmed down one of the boys would build another home and move out. Billy would probably be more than willing to help Jimmy build just to get rid of him and fly girl. Of course I was sure that as soon as he could find a way to ditch her Jimmy was going to shake her off like you shake shit off your boot and hook up with anyone who wasn't her. Maybe that was just me hoping.

Now the truth is that first night it was just Lucy and I alone in the house I think we both felt a little strange. Like we just didn't know what to do with so much space, so much privacy, and so much quiet. But after we had done the newscast for the evening and eaten dinner we made a point of just running around naked and making love in every room in the house. Sort of like you might do a cleansing ritual with sage and cedar to get the evil spirits out of the house, only we just had great sex all over to disperse the image of having four nosey-assed, idiot adult children in the house.

Those first couple of weeks after the kids moved into the other house was really the first time I'd ever been with someone that I didn't have to worry about anyone else.

Oh I'm not saying that I didn't still worry about my sons, or that I wasn't still worried about the coming grandchild and everything that could go wrong. But Lucy and I were able to just be alone together and not have to get a kid to sleep first or step over and around them all the time. I didn't have to spend every waking minute thinking how I was going to save myself and my sons from the BS. It had come, we were alive, the snow had melted, and there was now no doubt in my mind that we could and would make it and do well. So I was just sort of relaxed, like all the stress I'd ever had was suddenly gone and even when the boys and their girls were around and they were bitching about this that or the other thing it didn't matter because when I got tired of hearing their shit I told them all to go home and then... the world was quiet again and Lucy and I had the whole house to ourselves and life was amazingly sweet and good.

We cut and stacked enough wood from trees that had fallen just on our property to heat both houses for three more winters just like the one we'd just had and our winters were going to be bad for a few years but not like that one. I had reseeded the whole property as soon as it was dry enough to do so. Even as I was doing this I noticed that the grass was starting to come back up. See it just *looked* dead, it wasn't actually dead. The snow protected the plants from most of the serious cold and kept them alive. They'd gone dormant but they were coming back fast. I'd planted flower bulbs and garlic all over the place over the many years I'd lived there, and I could even see the hint of these plants breaking the surface of the ground.

Our orchard had taken some damage from the wind but we'd only completely lost two trees. While some of them had to be cut back pretty far just to save them I was sure it would be back in full production given a year or two to recover. By the time we'd finished clearing the debris and trimming up the damage I could see buds starting to form on the ends of some of the branches. Life was returning to the land.

As soon as the water had receded and the creek was down closer to its normal banks—we knew it was likely it would be higher indefinitely—we took the dozer and pushed the old bridge around to make a new bridge. Now the bridge was a rough ride in a truck, but we didn't plan to run a lot of them over it any time soon, and it was perfectly good for tractors and four-wheelers.

The snow levies still hadn't melted completely and the small airfield I hoped to turn into a community garden for the Rudyites was mostly still a couple of feet of mud. So we worked on taking everything—and I do mean **everything**—from the old railroad damage store. We took all the merchandise, the buildings, the freezers—everything.

Now some of the others had thought this was ridiculous. They didn't understand why we couldn't just go up and get what we needed when we needed it. Some of them even wanted to all just move up there. I explained that the store had been on a main road. We didn't want to be on a main road. That there was no readily-available water supply and that Rudy still had a viable water tower and a running creek.

They wanted to know why it would be bad to be on the main

road because... as I've said before people are stupid! Like I was talking to kindergarteners I told them that we weren't likely to be the only people looking to scavenge for stuff—and some of the people, likely all of the people who went hunting for stuff— would be armed. We were. And we weren't the only ones knew the store was there. I also explained that there wasn't going to be any way for us to just manufacture the things we needed for a long time so we needed to get all there was to get and horde it.

It's amazing how fast a group of people can get things done when they are motivated by survival. We stripped the entire All 'n More complex down to the concrete slabs in a little over a week. In Rudy we used what we'd scavenged from those buildings to build several warehouses to house all the stuff we got there. Billy cleared the old general store and the damaged buildings next to it to the slabs with the dozer and we built three huge warehouses there. In one we put the foodstuff that was still viable. In another we put all the paper goods and cleaning products. And in the last one we put all the tools and fasteners we'd gotten from their tool store. We built another one at the end of what used to be Main Street, well away from all the others, and we put all the combustibles in there.

The whole time I'd been scavenging the place I'd wondered where the people who owned the place were. See, their house had been right in the big middle of the complex and like I said the tornado had missed them. Let's face it; they never would have run out of supplies. Hell, we'd had to fill their semi truck— hey we'd cleared the roads so why not use the big truck once Billy got it started—*twice* just to haul off all the cans of Coleman fluid, kerosene, and thousands of bottles of lighter fluid, lamp oil, and so many candles it was crazy.

In short they could have lived fifty years easy without breaking a sweat... Or you know starving or freezing to death. Their house hadn't lost but maybe two shingles off the roof. It didn't make any sense until I noticed a tree had blown over in the back yard. It was a big one, and when I went to take a closer look I realized that the trunk was lying across the door of their storm shelter. I'd called Lucy over to me and pointed.

"There's the answer to the question 'where the hell are the owners'? Harsh irony—their home and all the dozens of buildings that made up their business were basically untouched."

"The roofs on all the big buildings caved in," Lucy pointed out.

"But that was the snow, baby, not the tornado. And if those buildings hadn't been so quickly and cheaply shucked together they would have been fine."

"Are you sure they're in there?" Lucy asked.

"Would you like me to get the crew over here with some chain saws to see?"

Lucy shook her head no.

"Where else would they be? They ran in their storm shelter to get away from the storm and the only damage from the storm that I can see is that damn tree blew over on top of the door to the storm shelter, trapping them inside."

Lucy got that look on her face—the one I've come to expect will be followed by her saying... "But you don't believe in fate."

"Christ Lucy," I said. I started walking away to go back to work moving boxes of something or tearing something down so that it could be rebuilt somewhere else. I don't really remember what I was doing at the time only that Lucy followed me so that she could go on and on with her rant about fate.

"We find my car and my glasses, and everything else I had with me might as well have been stuck in some time capsule they were so pristine. That's not fate. These people had everything. If they had lived they could have been the king of everything instead of you. We sure as hell couldn't just come here and take everything. It's got to mean something."

I laughed. "Yeah, it means they had some really shitty luck. That's what it means."

She stomped off to do something away from me because she was pissed off that I wouldn't just agree with her stupid-assed fate bullshit. I just didn't get it. I was the crazy, irrational one. Wasn't she the investigative reporter? Wasn't she supposed to be all-logical and crap? If anyone was going to believe in fairytale bullshit it should have been me. She was creeping onto my turf insisting that things were meant to be and happened for a reason and such utter crap as that.

When we left for the last time having taken everything from furniture—which was the last load and got left in the truck—to sporting goods that we thought might be remotely useful I looked at the main house that we'd left intact... and that tree on the top of the storm cellar.

As if reading my mind Lucy said, "You can't just explain that away even in your own mind can you, Kay?"

"I already did. Now shut up and get on the four wheeler," I ordered. But I was smiling when I said it.

As soon as we were all through salvaging stuff, I had Billy take the dozer blade, tilt it, and rip a six-foot ditch in the middle of the road. See I was still worried about survivalists. We ditched every road, paved or dirt, coming into Rudy in the same way. If we wanted out we could take the dozer and smooth it out for the day. Otherwise we were closed off.

I drew up plans of simple, one-family homes the Rudyites

could build using the best storm cellars they could find as a base. See the idea was to still have that 'fraidy hole because... Well, all of those who had made it through the storm had done so in their storm cellars. I figured that if they each built small, efficient homes over storm cellars, they would never have to run outside if a storm headed our way. It also meant the storm cellars were much less likely to fill with water. The houses were built to hold no more than four small rooms and a bathroom. A wood stove went in the middle of each house.

The plans were simple: two steel walls were held up with metal posts—usually metal T-posts every two feet, then the space between was filled with a layer of brick, rock, or other such hard, broken debris six inches deep, then six inches of dirt was thrown on top of that and pounded down. Up to six foot. We had lots of windows because while a lot got broken just as many didn't. Hell, at the time we started building the new homes there were still houses that had that weird tornado look where the whole house was gone but this one wall with a window still intact. Three feet of windows—or as close as what we could find would allow—two thick, were set on top of the south wall, framed out, and topped with a good, strong header. We made shutters that accordioned on either side of the windows made from the metal shelving we'd taken from All 'n More. Close the shutters when a storm was coming and I was fairly sure the houses were more or less tornado proof.

The roofs were a simple lean-to job. They were constructed by laying steel across the whole thing then laying the joists out on top of that. We had plenty of wood to work with. There was torn and blown pink insulation everywhere you looked so we "harvested" this and we would fill the spaces between the joists completely full of it and then lay another layer of steel over that. When we had finished the shell of the house as a community, the individual families went in and put in the interior walls and fixed it the way they wanted it. This included putting in a floor, which most of them did out of bricks—because we had loads of those—but a couple of people did theirs out of stone.

To figure out who got digs first they all put their names into a hat and they built the houses for the families in the order they drew them out of the hat. There was more than enough building materials between what was left of the steel buildings we'd salvaged at the railroad damaged place and all of the materials that could be scavenged from the trashed houses the tornado had left behind in Rudy and the surrounding area. Eventually they wound up gathering up everything else that was useful as they cleaned and stacked and covered it to use later.

I have to give Roy and those other people there in Rudy

credit. They got their water system up and running themselves using the town's huge storage tank and all the old plumbing. They all busted their asses that first summer and just worked at working well together. By the middle of summer—with our help of course—they had not only put in and tended the huge community garden and built a barn and pens for livestock which they'd be getting from me and from Matt, but they'd also all built their own homes and had managed to clean up most of the wreckage of their town. They made the church into a recreation center. They put the pews back and they were still watching movies there, but they were also getting together to play instruments and sing together and they were talking about trying to do a play. So far no one has talked about starting a church, thank God.

They salvaged what they could and put both the baseball field and the playground back together.

Oh we still had lots that needed to be done and lots we wanted to do but even if winter slammed us early and hard we'd all be alright. We helped Matt fix up some stuff on his place and rigged him up with a windmill. We were working on a hydroelectric plant for Rudy. For the time being we still had plenty of gas to run generators—and more generators than we'd ever be able to use—to run power tools, chain saws and such. But eventually even I would run out of gas, and I had a bigger tank than the one that had sat damn near under the store.

You don't wait till you're down to your last gallon of gas to work on alternate energy. You do it when you have the time to screw up a couple of times before you get it right.

That's something we learned the hard way.

Eventually everything would need to run on electricity created by the wind, sun or water. Things like trucks and four wheelers and tractors would have to be converted over to run on methane.

We had all the stuff to do it with. We just had to get it done.

It had always been my experience that a good snow in the winter meant good crops in the summer, but I'd never seen plants grow before or since like they did that summer. Matt said the same thing. No doubt all of that crap that had been in the air and had fallen to earth helped the plants grow. I checked and... Well, it wasn't radioactive and no one died from eating the food so it must have been alright.

One night Matt and Jenny had come over on the tractor to trade us some sweet potatoes for some chicks. He'd built him a hen house and said he was ready for them.

See, I'd hooked that incubator up and me and those Silkies were just cranking out chickens. The town needed at least three dozen chickens of their own, Matt and his family needed four hens, and there were a couple of other groups I was talking to that were close enough to trade with who wanted some, too.

We'd had dinner together and then all walked outside to sit in some lawn chairs in the gazebo by the pond.

"No fish in the creek," Matt said, no doubt seeing a fish jump in the pond.

"I noticed. There were a lot of dead ones in all my ponds, but a few lived, and I re-stocked them from the river in the house. I get back up where I need to be fish-wise and I'll sling some in the creek," I said.

"No mosquitoes?" Matt said.

"A few, not many. Not many flies either," I said. "Enough they'll come back. Can't hardly get rid of bugs. They were here before us and they'll be here after us, though I haven't seen a tick or had a single chigger bite yet, so hope springs eternal."

"Bees seem to have done just fine," Matt said. He looked some puzzled. "I mean bees were in trouble before the BS and now they're everywhere all over my crops. Which I'm glad about, but I don't get it."

"They're my bees," I explained. "They've already swarmed twice this year. I've started two more hives—one between my place and yours and one down in Rudy."

"Bees. How the hell did you keep bees through all that shit?"

It was a good question. Years ago I went in this honey shop down in Van Buren and this guy had a beehive in his wall. It had little tubes to the outside that the bees came in and out of and he had this glass door and you could watch the bees. I built a similar hive between the cement walls of my dome. I used the door from an apartment-sized refrigerator on the outside. The bees actually have two access tubes into the hive—one that goes to the outside and one that goes to the greenhouse. When the BS happened I stuck a cork in the tubes to the outside. The bees got sluggish and went into a near-hibernation state that bees go into when the weather is cold, but every once in awhile you'd see one or more of them in the greenhouse getting nectar from one of the blooms on the plants or getting a drink of water. The minute it warmed up they were all over the greenhouse, and when Lucy got stung I went outside and took the cork out. They'd gone crazy ever since. I'd put back a bunch of hives and when they started to swarm I'd just put on my gear, smoked their asses good, and put them in a new hive with a new queen. When I was sure we had enough hives to keep the Rudyites in honey I'd just let the swarms start filling the woods.

When I'd explained all that to Matt he'd just laughed and said, "You had the whole thing figured out didn't you?"

"She's extremely clever," Lucy said. She reached over and took my hand. I have to tell you I blushed a little.

"I miss the birds. There are so few of them now," Jenny said sadly.

"Most of the ones I'm seeing I think came out of our birdhouse," I said. "Of course every time we go out there I think a new batch of birds has hatched. The birds will come back slow, but they will come back. The bees will come back, too, and in time there will be fish in the creek again. The world will repair itself."

"You'll just help it out a bit," Matt said with a laugh.

Jenny smiled then and shrugged. "We're the only ranch I know of that has zebras, llamas and buffalo."

"Yeah, our llamas come up to the house the other day and they had a calf," Matt said. "Is that what they call the little ones?"

I just shrugged.

"Act mostly like cows the lot of them, if you ask me." Matt told me.

"Yeah, I have deer that act more like goats."

"You see any wild ones?" Matt asked.

"Only the dead ones we picked up when we were looking for dead stuff. Too cold too long and nothing to eat. No time to adapt."

"I've been wondering about breeding the dogs," Matt said. See, he and Jenny for as long as I had known them had raised cattle and Welsh Corgis. The pups had gone for five-hundred dollars apiece. "I mean, there aren't no dogs except ours that I've seen alive but maybe we don't need dogs..."

"You know what, Matt? Breed the dogs. They're small stock dogs. They don't eat much and you have plenty to feed them. Most people are going to keep small stock because that's mostly what made it through, so you'll be able to trade them."

Matt nodded, seeming pleased that the dogs he and his wife loved so much they'd kept them in the one room they were sharing with their two sons for the whole cold-assed winter might still be worth something.

"It all happened so quick none of us really had time to adapt," Jenny said. Then she added to Lucy, "I sometimes miss my old life, so I know you've got to miss yours."

Lucy was quiet for just a minute but she didn't let go of my hand and then she said, "I miss my family and my friends, but I don't miss my old life at all. I like it here being close to the earth, being with Kay. Sometimes you don't know what you want till you have it. All my life... I was never really happy. I was always looking for something that would make me feel complete. I always felt like there was something I should be doing that I wasn't.

I don't feel that way anymore."

Yep, I had it all right then. Everything was absolutely perfect.

Now hold that thought.

CHAPTER 17

I Hate It When That Happens

People are stupid. That's why it's all going to end and that's *why so many people are going to die. People will watch the weather. They'll hear that there is going to be a record-breaking cold front and that it has busted main water lines in some small town that isn't theirs. What do they do?*
Nothing.
They don't do anything. That isn't their town so they think they're safe.

Would it kill them to fill a couple of bottles so they have drinking water, fill the tub so they have water to flush the commode with, do a load of laundry so that if the water lines freeze they have clean clothes?

Knowing that people can freeze to death they will live someplace and have only one source of heat. Your house is all-electric and the power goes down because of ice. Guess what? You have no heat. How smart is that?

Look, you live someplace prone to flooding you ought to be moving right now. If you don't want to move just on the chance I'm right that the world's going to fall into catastrophe then at least have an escape plan mapped out. All over the country there are remote areas that have small cabins in the mountains by a lake or a running stream. Make plans to pack your survival kit, get in your car and go there. And don't wait till the last minute, either. The second you think there might be trouble—go. What's the worst that will happen? You'll miss a couple of days work and have a nice vacation.

These cabins are small which makes them easy to heat. Try to find one that advertises fireplaces or wood stoves. They're secluded, away from big cities, and comfortable.

You can't leave your brain at the door and think you will survive this apocalypse.

Do you know why I never say anything about surviving fire? Because you can't. You just have to run away from the flames. Every kid learned in school about not opening doors, crawling on the ground, stop drop and roll. If there is a catastrophe that includes fire you have only one course of action—run away from the fire. I shouldn't have to say it because it should be obvious to anyone, but if I don't it's a sure bet someone will run into instead of out of the fire and then as they're burning to death scream out that they didn't know.

People are going to die by the millions not because there is no hope of surviving the apocalypse but because they're stupid. Don't be stupid; make a plan. If you're someplace you don't want to be then try to ride out the worst of it and then move on. But move on to someplace you already planned to go and make sure you can actually get there.

Lucy and I were up early for no apparent reason, so we'd decided we might as well have sex. Which we did until we needed a nap—which I would have taken, but then I heard the radio.

I got up and ran in to hear Roy saying, "Katy, dammit! Can you hear me? There is some idiot buzzing us in a plane!"

I grabbed the mike up and pressed the button. "What did you fucking say?" I asked, really not sure.

Since I'd answered Roy calmed down some and said in a much clearer voice, "Some idiot has been flying over us for about forty-five minutes now."

This was when I knew what had made us wake up to begin with. We must have heard that plane; it just didn't register. But we hadn't heard one in so long that it had roused us from a sound sleep. Of course once we got... busy, well then we weren't likely to hear anything till we finished.

I tried for ten minutes to make radio contact with the plane without any luck, so I thought the worst but I wasn't even close. We got dressed, got our flack jackets and rifles, jumped in the pickup truck and headed for town.

That's right the pickup truck because I didn't want to be all-out-in-the-open like if there was some kind of trouble.

We got to the bridge just as the idiot in the plane decided to land on Main Street. Needless to say this had everyone in town running around like idiots, waving guns in the air and shouting.

It looked like the plane was going to run out of road before it could stop and then it just stopped. I drove up close to it and jumped out, rifle in hand.

"Stay in the car."

"Dammit, Kay..."

"Stay in the car!"

I took the safety off my rifle and walked towards the plane. Roy and a big guy named Bobby Jack joined me.

The door on the side of the plane opened and came down with a crash that made us all jump and then an arm was stuck out and it was waving a white handkerchief.

"I come in peace. Seriously," a young female voice said. And then she stepped out of the plane. Short, but well built, bronze skin, blonde hair and dark brown eyes.

Lucy obviously hadn't listened to me because I heard her say at my shoulder even as I lowered my rifle, "Samantha?"

"Lucy!" The woman jumped down from the last step to the ground, ran over and embraced my woman.

"Son of a bitch!" I said.

It sucked; if anything in my life had ever sucked more than Lucy's girlfriend coming back to life and showing up on our doorstep did then I don't know what the hell it might have been. And just why hadn't Lucy told me that her dead girlfriend could fly a fucking plane?

Lucy was still hugging that woman and then they were kissing on the mouth and I just screamed out accusingly towards her, "I knew it! I knew you were going to ruin the apocalypse for me!" Then I stomped off in the direction of nothing.

"Kay, wait! Kay!" Lucy called after me. In seconds she had caught up to me but I just kept walking fast, making her run to catch up. "Kay, seriously wait."

I didn't so she jumped on my back, her arms around my neck.

"What the hell!" I said. But I kept walking with her hanging on my neck like some deranged little monkey.

"Kay please don't be crazy for a minute."

"That's a lot to ask." I quit walking and grumbled. "Of all the crappy luck. Bazillions of people dead and she's fine. Better than fine, she's hot."

Lucy let go and walked around in front of me. She looked up at me. "Kay, I don't know what this means. What's going to happen..."

"You kissed her on the mouth, Lucy. In front of me and God and everyone else you kissed her on the mouth," I said accusingly.

"She kissed me. I kissed her back. I wasn't thinking. Kay... what are the odds?"

"Oh great, I guess this is fate, too."

"Of course it is, Kay."

I looked to where Samantha was obviously trying to come after Lucy and where a bunch of the town's folks were making sure she couldn't.

"Beautiful. Fucking beautiful!" I started stomping around, waving my rifle and my hands in the air. "Where the fuck does this leave me, Lucy? Huh? Where does this leave me?"

"I don't know, Kay. I don't know. I haven't even had time to process this, but don't treat me like this is something I did to you. Please, Kay, think about it. What if that was Cindy who stepped out of that plane?"

I quit stomping around, tried to put myself in her position for a minute, and then just said the first thing that popped into my mind. "But it's not Cindy who came back and well... I'd still pick you Lucy, I would."

"We don't even know what she's doing here. What she wants..."

No idea? Really? I have no idea why that made me so much madder than I already was, but it did. I went from calming down to being hyper-enraged in like ten seconds.

"Oh I know what she wants, but I'm damned if she's going to get it," I said. I started back towards the plane and Samantha.

"Kay, Kay, don't do anything crazy. Kay, let me at least tell her about us before you..."

But I was already back to the girl and her fucking plane by then.

"What's going on?" Samantha asked Lucy, not me.

She was so sane sounding, so together, that I instantly hated her guts.

"Sam I think..."

"What!?" I yelled in my usual I'm-about-to-kick-someone's-ass style. "You just shorten all your lover's names? Isn't that fucking cute. Not **special** because that would mean you only did it to one of us!"

I stuck the barrel of my rifle right in Samantha's face and she froze.

"Listen, Lucy's my woman now. Mine. And no one is going to come swooping down from the sky and take her away from me."

"Kay, for God's sake!" Lucy grabbed the barrel of my rifle and pointed it at the ground. Lucy has never actually been afraid of me one bit which is probably why I've always been crazy about her.

"Don't you call me Kay. You call me by my full name, Crazy Katy, ain't that right!?" I said.

I was glaring at everyone because well I was just mad at the whole world right then. They all pretended to be looking somewhere else which made them all look a little ridiculous and me even madder. I mean let's face it, BBS those people had never done anything but ridicule me. This was bound to give them all a good laugh or at least something to talk about. In an instant I had gone from someone they looked up to, the person who had saved and sustained them, back to that poor crazy lesbian that lived in the bunker.

I pulled the barrel of my gun out of Lucy's hand and slung it over my shoulder in a less menacing pose. I looked at Lucy. "I'm not going to be played like some fucking moron. If you want her then get on the plane with her and get the hell out of here. If you want me get in the fucking truck."

I looked at Samantha. "Either way I want you out of here."

I started for the truck but Lucy ran around in front of me. Like I said, Lucy wasn't afraid of me. Everyone else yes, Lucy no. "Kay, please calm down."

"I can't, Lucy," I said. I realized only then that I was actually working really hard not to break down and cry like a fucking little girl in front of everyone.

"Yes you can, Kay, you can. You aren't as crazy as you want everyone to think you are. You're upset and I understand that you're upset and why. But when you aren't upset you're the most rational person I've ever known. Please listen to me. I didn't do anything to you. Sam..."

I glared at her.

"Samantha didn't do anything to you, either. We don't even know how she found me yet. I'm not trying to do anything to you and neither is Samantha. I don't want to go off with her and leave you and I don't want to send her off without even talking to her. I can't tell you what's going to happen one way or the other. I haven't had even a second to process it. She's alive and she's here and I... we... just have to deal with that in a way that we aren't going to have any regrets about later."

Dammit all, she was right. If Lucy had to choose right then and she chose to go with Samantha I'd be kicking myself in the ass the rest of my life. And if I just made Samantha go without letting Lucy really have a chance to decide where she wanted to be then she was always going to wonder if she'd made the right choice and...

Well sometimes being rational just sucks. I nodded that I'd calmed down and the next thing I knew everyone had loaded all Samantha's gear in my truck and Lucy was sitting in the cab of the truck between me and her old girlfriend. Though I was glad to see that she was closer to me. In fact, she seemed to be trying hard not to touch Samantha, which made me feel good till I realized she was probably just doing it to keep me from killing Samantha which was after all my first instinct.

The cab was real quiet and it was hard to know what either Lucy or that freaking dwarf were thinking. But I know what I was thinking. Come to think of it, we were ALL probably thinking, "Well this didn't turn out like I wanted at all."

Because let's face it—not that I cared—but it had to suck for Samantha at least as much as it was sucking for me. I mean she obviously managed to survive somehow and had found a plane and flown here no doubt because she'd heard Lucy on the radio. She'd been expecting to come here, be reunited with Lucy, and have some really good catching-up sex and now she must have known I wasn't likely to let that happen.

I figured Lucy was trying hard to think of a way to keep us both because the bitch was just that horny.

"Promise me you won't kill Samantha," Lucy said to me.

"Oh come on..."

"Promise. There are other ways to deal with people and with problems."

"Wow," Samantha said. There was an obvious hint of anger to her voice. "That's sweet. I'm a freaking problem. I fly halfway across the country in a taped-together plane and all I am is a problem?"

"Way I see it," I spat back.

"Kay, I'm serious." Lucy just ignored what Samantha had said because of course you always have to deal with the seriously crazy one first.

I glared across the seat at Samantha. "You touch my woman and I'll fucking kill you."

"Your woman. Christ, Lucy, I realize there are slim pickings in this BS world, but Neanderthal woman, seriously?"

I pulled the truck over, stopped it and started to jump out. Lucy grabbed my arm, hanging on tight and trying to keep me from getting out of the truck.

"Calm down, Kay. Samantha has a black belt in taekwondo."

"Let her go. I'm in an ass-kicking mood myself," Samantha snarled out.

I shook Lucy off then. "Black belt my fucking ass. I don't give a good shit. Taekwondo my ass," I mumbled as Lucy ran behind me, hanging onto the back of my shirt. By the time I reached the other side of the truck Samantha had struck some stupid-assed fighting stance. I shook Lucy off, walked right up to the fucking dwarf, blocked her half-assed kick and slugged her in the face hard enough to drop her to the ground. Then I was just jumping around like an idiot mainlining steroids.

"Get up you fucking weenie!"

She tried a couple of times, but I'd obviously given the little bitch a concussion because she was just sort of wobbling around. Now I have no idea whether Samantha was any kind of black belt in anything or if it was just some shit she made up to impress women like Lucy, but I grew up in a family full of boys where if you couldn't fight and fight well you'd likely as not wind up giving birth to your cousin's retarded baby by the time you were thirteen and... Well, when you're a big, huge dyke in a part of the world that hates homosexuals as a part of their religious practice, someone's always wanting to pick a fight with you over some bullshit. You know what will teach you to fight faster than any kind of lessons you can take—where let's face it most times you were sparing with someone who didn't want to get hit any more than you did? Getting your ass kicked a half dozen times, that's what. One hell of a teacher. You really get your ass kicked you learn exactly how it happened and how to keep it from happening again. Plus... Well I'd studied several martial arts as well.

Think about it. You're crazier than a two-peckered goat you better be a world-class scrapper.

Lucy ran up to Samantha to help her up, as if I hadn't hurt my fist on the bitch's face. Where was my compassion? "Sam! You alright, Sam?"

"I'm fine." She tried to shove off Lucy's help but couldn't actually stand by herself so gave up.

"That was completely unnecessary, Kay," Lucy said in a scolding tone.

"You're taking her side? She was talking shit about me. I'm not going to let her talk shit about me in my own truck."

"That really was uncalled for," Lucy said to Sam. Which let me know just how on the fence Lucy was because she couldn't really decide whose fault it was.

We got home without me killing Samantha mostly because she kept her fool mouth shut.

At the house Lucy got some ice for Sam's jaw and sat her at MY kitchen table while I started to make dinner with my hurt hand. I mean... well it wasn't all that bad, but Lucy might have at least asked if I needed some ice.

The girl was in good shape, almost too good. As if she'd spent the apocalypse in a spa and that got me to thinking. I didn't say shit, though just kept making dinner.

"How'd you find me?" Lucy asked Sam.

I was liking this shit less by the minute because it was more and more obvious that Lucy was glad to see the dwarf who I now realized was at least five years younger than Lucy—which was not helping me with my insecurities regarding the future of my relationship at all.

The radio started making noise and I went to check it, more than a little pissed off because I didn't want to leave them in the room alone together. It was Billy. He'd heard because of course with the two-way radios and nothing else to do news traveled really fast ABS. Gossip became everyone's favorite past time.

"I'm really sorry, Mom," he said, after explaining that he'd heard about our visitor from the sky.

"Sorry... You just naturally think she isn't going to choose me," I said. I was pissed as hell because I was thinking he was probably right.

"I didn't mean that, Mom," he said.

"No you're right, she's young and good looking and she can fly a plane. I'm just screwed 'cause if I kill this girl Lucy is never going to forgive me and short of that I just don't see how I can come out of this a winner."

"Lucy loves you, Mom. I know she does," Billy said.

Did she? Hell I didn't know. I usually thought she was just with me because I was the only queer chick around. Because I was the one who had saved her. I got off the radio with my son and started back for the kitchen. I could hear them talking so I found a good place, hid and listened.

"...you don't know anything about her," Lucy said.

"Come on, Lucy. She wants to kill me, you know she does. And she's like a hundred years old! What is this like Stockholm syndrome or something?"

"She's not old and I don't have to explain it to you, Sam."

"Look. I've been through hell, Lucy. I probably would have just given up if I hadn't heard your voice on the radio. The only thing that kept me alive was thinking about you, about being with you again."

Now I ask you, how do you compete with crap like that? That's just what it was by the way—all crap—because there was no way that girl could have gone through all the shit she talked about and looked the way she did, just no way.

"I'm sorry, Sam, but... If it wasn't for Kay I'd be dead. We've been through a lot together and I have a real connection with her. I love her."

So that made me feel some better.

"What about me?" Sam asked. Her voice was choked. "What about me? Did you even think about me when you were fucking her? You thought I was dead, but did you even wait for my body to cool off before you started banging her? I've been fighting for my life out there and you've been here in basically the only truly safe place in the world and did you think about me even once?"

"Of course I did, all the time at first, Sam. But I learned that you just can't dwell on what's gone." She stopped then no doubt listening to see if I was on the radio, which I wasn't. "Kay, are you listening outside the door?"

I stepped out of my hiding place, walked into the kitchen and just started cooking again. Sam glared at me and I glared right back, daring her to start something I knew I could finish.

It was a crappy situation for everyone involved. I know that now, but at the time I didn't even care how Lucy felt about it; I only cared how it made me feel. You know like everything that came out of Samantha's mouth was correct and that Lucy was only ever with me because she was extremely horny, I was there, and there weren't any options. Now that there were options I couldn't hope that Lucy would choose me unless I killed Samantha and then... Well then Lucy was just going to be pissed off for the rest of our natural lives and she'd never forgive me. So the way I saw it I was just screwed.

They kept whispering to each other at the table the whole time I was cooking and I could only make about half of it out but they were mostly fighting the way a married couple did and that certainly wasn't doing anything to make me feel better about what I was more sure by the minute was just going to be me alone for the rest of the ABS.

Then I was eating my dinner the way you do when you're angry and sad at the same time. You know, picking at my food for a few minutes not wanting to eat anything, and then just stuffing food in my mouth as hard and fast as I could hardly chewing it and mostly swallowing it whole just because I wanted everyone at the table to know I was mad.

Maybe that's just me.

It was pretty quiet and then Lucy just had to ask the dwarf, "So, where were you when the worst of it hit. How did you make it?"

"I was in the basement of my apartment building doing laundry when it hit. I grabbed a blanket, covered myself up, and just lay in the floor under the table. I heard it tearing the building apart and I could hear transformers blowing up and everything was... It was so dark. I'd never seen dark like that before. I just lay there trying to call people but my phone didn't work."

"But you had a satellite phone," Lucy said. She sounded a little confused since some of the satellite phones we had worked for weeks after the BS. Frankly, everything the girl said from that point on just made me even more certain that she was full of shit.

"Don't know what to tell you; it wasn't working." She shrugged. "I couldn't see or hear anyone or anything. So I just lay there till the sun came up in the morning and then I got to work. I turned a dryer into a wood stove using duct work for a chimney. I crawled out the window because the stairs were covered in debris and I started dragging everything I could find down in there with me. Wood for the fire, food, bottles and bottles of water, blankets, clothes, a bed and then..." She pretended to choke on a sob and no, I'm not just being a cynic now. It was fake; I could tell it was fake. "I had a radio and when I heard you were alive then I knew I just had to live."

"What a bunch of crap." I said. Then I got up and rinsed my

plate.

"Kay, come on," Lucy said.

I nodded and sat down again.

The show wasn't for me. It was all for Lucy, so Samantha just kept going on and on and on building a web of crap so thick my fat ass could have danced on it. How she'd tune the radio to my station every single day for just the few minutes of battery that she could spare to try and just hear Lucy's voice. How she'd had to ration her candles and how dark and lonely her days had been. How she'd dug her way out at the end of the longest winter ever and immediately gone in search of a plane she could fly with one goal in mind—to reunite with Lucy. How she had struggled and worked to get the plane running and then had to keep stopping to find fuel.

On and on and fucking on telling this bullshit story which was punctuated every few minutes by how she'd done it all for Lucy. How much she loved Lucy.

You know like I wasn't even there. And Lucy, well she was eating that shit up like a chemical toilet.

I finally left them alone and went to take care of the animals. I don't think either of them had noticed I'd gone.

The goats could tell there was something wrong and seemed very sympathetic, so I told them all my troubles.

The rest of the evening I just did my chores and talked on the radio, giving out the weather reports, answering people's questions, and all basically knowing just exactly where Lucy and Samantha were and what they were doing at any given moment but ignoring them at the same time—which wasn't easy.

While talking to the goats I'd realized that nothing I was going to say about all the lies Samantha was telling was actually going to help me. I loved Lucy; I wanted her to be happy. That being the case I had to let her make whatever decision she was going to make on her own. She'd been going with this girl for years. She knew her, and by now she knew me.

Samantha was lying out her ass. Lucy wasn't stupid, so if I gave the bitch enough rope she'd hang herself. I was sure of that.

I was going to work at being rational and fair and letting this whole thing be truly Lucy's choice.

Of course you can want to act like a grown up and be sure that you're going to and then. Well the minute Lucy walked into the office and closed the door behind her to indicate that she wanted to be alone with me the first words out of my mouth were, "You were really with that dwarf?"

Lucy smiled at me, no doubt because she'd already figured out that I was easily defused by her smile. "She's the same height as I am."

"That's different, you're a girl."

She laughed and shook her head. "You're so weird." She walked over sat on my lap and wrapped her arms around my neck. I held her because well the truth was I didn't think I'd be able to hold her much longer.

"I love you, Lucy." That was all I could get out with out crying, and I sure as hell didn't want to be crying with Samantha in the house even if I'd wanted to cry in front of Lucy, which I didn't.

"I love you, Kay. I just... I have to figure this thing out. I have to see what it means."

"It means she came looking for you. That's all."

"But why is she alive, Kay? How? Billions dead and..."

"She's here to screw up my life, Lucy. That's why she's here. Just send her away."

See all my very good intentions just gone.

"I can't, Kay, any more than I can just walk away from you. I have to know."

"Yeah, well I don't want you to find out that you love her more than you love me."

"I could never love anyone the way I love you, Kay." And then she was kissing me and I was kissing her and then she broke down crying on my shoulder. The jist of it all was that she had put Samantha in Jimmy's room and she was going to sleep in Billy's and I was going to be sleeping in my room alone because apparently she needed to think and if she was in bed with me we'd have sex and then she couldn't think. Which would have worked for me, but wouldn't work for her at all.

My bed felt way too big and too lonely and I figured I'd better get used to it because this was probably how it was going to be for the rest of my life. I got really depressed and fell asleep and had a nightmare that I was living in a basement knee deep in water and floating ice and Samantha and Lucy were living in my house. Of course they were fucking and I could see it all on the big screen TV in my basement.

Dreams are weird.

When I woke up in the morning I immediately jumped out of bed to make sure Lucy was in one room and Samantha was in the other.

They were both still asleep, so being crazy I screamed at the top of my lungs, "This is completely fucked up!"

Which it was.

Everyone loved Samantha. She was pretty and bright and out going and not crazy and she taught the kids in town to play some stupid-assed game with the playground equipment. It was obvious to me that Lucy was really having trouble deciding between us and even more obvious that everyone who should have been rooting for me since I had saved their sorry butts all thought Lucy should be with Samantha because she was pretty and fun and I wasn't.

Samantha spent a lot of her time down in Rudy she said she was working on her plane but I was pretty sure she was spending all her time turning the town's people against me just like she was trying to turn Lucy against me.

She contradicted her story at least twice but it was in small ways. Lucy didn't seem to notice, and I would have just looked like a *shmuck* if I'd pointed it out, so I didn't. I just kept working at being a grown up and letting it be Lucy's decision. Which was getting increasingly harder to do because I hadn't had sex in a week and I hadn't had any real sleep because I was too busy sleeping with one eye open trying to make sure Lucy didn't sleep with Samantha which I was more or less sure would seal the deal and make Lucy leave with Samantha. Because I meant what I said and there was no way she could stay anywhere near me and be with Samantha.

I was cultivating my garden when Samantha came up to me. I was minding my own business, way busy, and so I was immediately pissed off. I killed the engine on the tiller knowing it was time for some sort of show down which by the way had happened almost daily for that whole week she'd been there ruining my life.

"What?" I asked.

"Look Kate...

"My name isn't Kate, it's Katy. You can call me shithead, but don't call me Kate again or I'll rip your head off and shit in the hole," I hissed at her. See, my dad used to call me Kate when he was drunk and pissed off just before he beat the dog shit out of me, so it was a trigger for me.

"Look, I'm not here just to rain on your parade."

"Bullshit. That's exactly why you're here. Save your bullshit for Lucy." I laughed at her then. "Who do you think you're kidding? Bitch I'm the queen of the Apocalypse and the shit that spews forth from your mouth about how you lived? Hell, most of it's right out of one of the survivor's mouths. It's not even funny."

You guys remember Tom, the guy who made the soup from complimentary pizza parlor packets? Well that's about the only part of his story she didn't use.

"You see those folks in Rudy? According to what you've told us you lived a whole lot worse than they did, and there isn't one of them that didn't lose too much weight over the winter. They still don't have any color to speak of. You're tan and you weigh exactly what you did when it all started, I heard you tell Lucy so. And... Well you're not fucking crazy, so if you'd really lived through what you say you've lived through you would be shaking like a dog shitting peach seeds. And let's just take a second to wrap our brains around this—you can find and fix a plane but you couldn't find or operate a radio—which would have been a hell of a lot easier to find—to try to contact Lucy. Idiots in Uganda with a can and a string I can hear, but from you not a peep. Nope, not a peep. Even when you're getting ready to land you don't bother to tell us what's going on."

"Why would I lie?"

"Because you've been using every time Lucy's left town for the last few years to go get you a piece of strange."

I smiled at the shocked look on her face. I held the rest of my cards to play later if I needed them and just said, "I told you, I'm the queen of the apocalypse."

There are very few people out there who lived who I hadn't talked to because let's face it anyone smart enough to live through the end of the world was also smart enough to figure out radio communication. Certainly anyone who could fly a fucking plane and had access to the communications in a plane could have contacted me at any time. So I listened to her little story, took into account how good she looked, figured out which group she'd been stuck with, and asked their leader some questions.

Remember I told you that one of my biggest supporters was a lesbian couple that owned a very successful bed and breakfast in the foot hills of Kentucky? They believed me and they'd gotten ready for the BS in a big way. Underground bunker with enough food for twenty people for two years, pool, hot tub, *tanning bed*, all powered by their own personal natural gas well... Which was of course how the bitches got so rich in the first place. At any rate they had six lesbian couples staying with them when the BS went down and they all went into the underground equivalent of the Ritz and spent it there. One of those lesbian "couples" was Samantha and some blond-headed bimbo my friends had nicknamed Tramp Stamp. In short, Samantha started trying to make time with everyone else's woman and she'd been voted out of the tribe.

So the little shit head had Lucy thinking that she wanted to commit and that the only reason they hadn't been together BBS was because Lucy wouldn't come out of the closet, while all the time she'd been playing around having Lucy and whoever else she wanted. That didn't sit well with me.

"It doesn't have to be like this; we could share her," Samantha said.

236

I made a face. "No we couldn't. I mean she'd probably love that because she's such a horny little shit, but I ain't sharing."

Samantha looked at me like I was crazy. "Horny? What's wrong, old woman? Two times a month too much for you?"

I laughed then. "Oh, dude, we couldn't be talking about the same woman. 'Cause Lucy acts like she's afraid it might close up if she doesn't get it at least twice a day."

That bugged all shit out of her. I could tell from the look on her face.

"Look, can we at least agree that it needs to be Lucy's decision?" she said.

"If it's going to be Lucy's decision then you at least ought to tell her the fucking truth, you lying little shit. She ought to know just exactly what she's getting if she chooses you," I hissed.

"I need to spend a little time with her alone, just to talk. Is that really too much to ask?"

No I guess it really wasn't. I smiled. "Tell you what, Jack. You go down to the pond by the gazebo and I'll go get Lucy and send her down to you. You have your talk and then I want an answer. One way or the other it's over today."

She nodded that she understood and headed for the pond. I left the garden and headed for where my truck was parked.

Son Su once said, "If you wait by the river long enough the bodies of your enemies will float by." Me, well I've never been that fucking patient. I grabbed my thirty/thirty off the gun rack and walked to the end of the chicken run where I had a clear shot at the gazebo and the dumb-assed dwarf who stood in it. I took aim and then I heard someone clear their throat at my shoulder.

"Kay, what the hell are you doing?" Lucy asked calmly.

I didn't lower my gun. In fact, I went ahead and lined up my shot. "I'm going to keep the woman I love no matter how mad it makes her."

She grabbed the barrel of my gun and pushed it down. "You don't have to do that. I'm not going anywhere." She stood on her tiptoes and kissed my cheek. "Remember when we first got together I told you that I'd decided that even if she was alive I'd still want to be with you? Well she is and it turns out that it's true."

"Oh you're just saying that to keep me from killing her," I said.

"No, Kay, I'm not. The truth is I don't want you to kill her, but even if you did I don't think it would change the way I feel about you."

"Really?"

"Really. You know I never realized what a lying little shit she was."

I looked at her in shock.

"Oh come on, Kay. She couldn't have called? She can fix a plane but she can't figure out how to use a radio? And she just kept changing her story. What's she doing down there?" Lucy asked.

"I told her I'd send you to talk to her."

"Well then she's going to have quite a wait." She took my rifle away and took my hand. I was pretty sure I knew what she was after and I was game but...

"Honey, I'm all slimy and..."

She grinned at me seductively. "Then we're going to have to give you a bath."

Which she did.

We'd made love for a little over an hour and Lucy was just lying all over me the way she normally did. She moved a little and kissed me gently on the lips. "You had to know it was always going to be you, Kay."

I grinned no doubt like an idiot. "What about fate Lucy? I mean what are the odds..."

"You know what, Kay? You're right about fate; it's a crock. She was out of town because I was out of town. She was there because it was a lesbian bed and breakfast just far enough out of town that she wouldn't get caught. Then when they kicked her out where else would she go? I mean everyone knows right where I am."

"You... How did you know?"

"I overheard you telling the goats yesterday morning. But you know what, Kay? I'd already made up my mind. I don't think there was ever any doubt in my mind I just... God I missed you, Kay."

And then she was all over me again and I know what you're thinking—wasn't I glad I didn't kill that girl? But seriously to this day I still sort of wish I had, just on principle.

Samantha gave up waiting at some point and came up to the house. Lucy and I were drinking wine. I was in boxers and a tank top and she was wearing nothing but one of my old flannel shirts and sitting in my lap watching some movie. We'd completely forgotten about Samantha. That must have been obvious to her, and the look on the bitch's face was just priceless.

"This is seriously your decision?" Samantha asked in a defeated tone of voice.

"Yes," Lucy said simply.

"I could hardly sweat you for twice a month. She says twice a day." And of course that would be the one thing of everything I'd said and done to the little bitch that got right under her skin.

Lucy smiled at me, "She does this thing."

"What's that?"

Lucy looked at Samantha, smiled smugly and said, "She loves me."

"So what happens to me now?" Samantha asked. Because let's face it with people like her it always comes down to them.

"There's a group in Fort Smith. They've decided to scavenge instead of farm right away. They could probably use a pilot to scout things out for them," I said.

She nodded. "You going to take me to my plane or make me walk?"

"Geez it's only a couple of miles," I said.

"Come on, Kay," Lucy said standing up.

"Well fuck." I got up to go pull on my boots and grab my keys. I was damned if I was getting dressed again. Lucy and I had a lot of catching up to do.

"Will you at least come and say good bye?" I heard Samantha ask Lucy.

"We can say good bye here. I think Kay has put up with enough shit, and frankly I'm done with you. I'm sorry, but I was done with you years ago. I just didn't know how to let go. The truth is I don't believe it's fate that you're here; I just think it's a pain in the ass. So good bye, Sam." As they say, hell has no fury like a woman scorned.

As I walked back into the room she turned on her heel and started for our room. She stopped, leaned in and whispered in my ear, "I'm going to take a little nap. I'll be here when you get home."

"Come on, chick, let's go. Places to go and Lucy to do," I said, shoving her towards the door.

CHAPTER 18

Your Survival Kit

Regardless of whether you think I'm completely out of my bird or not, would it really hurt you to be better prepared? People die all the time in minor things like power outages, snowstorms and heat waves.

There are some things that should be in everyone's survival kit. Water—at least five gallons for each person in your household—non-perishable food items—at least enough to last a week. Blankets, a flashlight, some kind of self-contained heating source.

But the truth is that a survival kit will be different for everyone depending on where you are, what you are most in danger from, how many people are in your family, whether you have a good, sturdy bunker on high ground or just a house that may flood.

You live somewhere in a flood plain then an inflatable raft might be a good idea. You're house isn't well built for bad weather conditions, you may want to put back the materials to cover windows or strengthen roof supports or doors or if you can afford it don't wait—do house repairs today that may insure your house will make it through a disaster.

Some great items for your disaster survival kit that everyone should have besides the essentials are baby wipes, paper towels, paper plates, duct tape, plastic tarps, rope, fasteners of all kinds, and hand tools—the more the better.

I can't take your hand and lead you all the way. I can answer your questions and give you advice but when it comes to the moment you'd better have personalized that survival kit to meet your own needs or you just flat won't make it.

That will be the future for those of us who survive to tell about the apocalypse. People will have to work together to survive but they won't have to toil to make an asshole rich any more. Individuality will be important again. We'll all find something at which we excel and we'll trade in the things we love to do that we're good at. There will be balance in the world again.

Well I don't know if that turned out to be true for everyone everywhere but that's the way it worked out here in Rudy. Balance is all about working with what you have instead of constantly against it.

I was right about our area and it being a good place to ride out the BS. There are more small communities here than just about anywhere else. There are groups of survivors who have thriving communities in Mountainburg, Chester, Kibler, Russellville and of course Fort Smith.

Let's face it; most of the people who lived through the BS were the ones who had the best survival kits, structures they'd built specifically to withstand a disaster, who'd stored up huge amounts of water and food. Mostly it came down to who had hoarded enough of whatever sort of fuel they used to heat and cook with. It didn't matter how much food people had. At least here in the US if you didn't have the heat you didn't make it.

Some people still bitch and moan and dream of the old days. They think we got bombed back to the Stone Age, but that just isn't true at all. We have managed to hang onto things like electricity all of ours is just clean now. We still use vehicles. Hell, most places people still use gas because let's face it there are hardly any people and gas stations everywhere with underground tanks mostly full and easy to access if you have half a brain. Gas goes stale it's true, but you pop a little additive in it and it will still run a truck.

People came together all across the world and formed little villages not unlike the one in Rudy. Usually built around the best shelter of one of the members. There were plenty of materials to build with and people knew what they needed now. That's another thing—we didn't lose the knowledge of how to build good, tight, energy-efficient, storm-resistant homes.

People didn't elect rulers because they mostly handled their own affairs. Oh there was always someone like Roy who sort of shepherded the village, but mostly people made their own decisions and ran their own lives. They worked together to raise stock and tend fields, scavenge, and build each other's dwellings, but people were truly free to find their true callings and follow them.

Roy's wife Belinda does nothing all day but make sure that no one takes more than their fair share of the things we scavenged from the railroad damaged store and keeps an inventory of who got what and how much is left. She marks what comes in from the field and rations it out accordingly to each family. She has become one of the most important people in town.

The whole town works in shifts to cut enough wood to last the winter, to grow enough food and then preparing and storing the food in the warehouse. When people get along, when ego gets forgotten and they all work for the common good, it really is a beautiful thing.

One of the men in town has become a writer. Now it turns out Raymond had always wanted to be a writer but let's face it that was never an easy field to break into. Now he writes in his spare time using a computer. Lucy proofreads his work and then he prints enough copies for everyone in town and trades the books to them for anything they might have or a service they can provide that he wants. It turns out the guy is an amazing writer, and when people can't just run in and turn on the TV they are more than happy to read a book. He comes in to the radio station—that's what we call the office now—every day and reads a chapter on air. That's right; he's the most famous writer in the world.

One of the Rudyites paints pictures, mostly of scenes from the world BBS, and people are only too happy to trade her whatever they do for her work. When Lucy got to decorating she traded for several paintings, but surprisingly Lucy didn't want BBS pictures. She had her paint pictures of flowers and landscapes.

By the way I like the way Lucy decorated and painted the house. It's all bright colors and the place is a lot less bunker-ish these days.

Getting back to what I was talking about... In a world with so few people being famous and respected is something everyone can accomplish simply by hard work and perseverance—both attributes that had been completely dismissed in the world BBS.

Down at the Rudy rec-center different members of the community give different classes on what they're good at. This can be anything from animal husbandry and medicine to sewing lingerie which... Well I've got to tell you I'm never sorry when Lucy goes to one of those classes.

People are learning skills they never thought they'd need like weaving cloth, sewing, and making paper. And they're finding out that they like doing it. That there is a lot more satisfaction in saying "I made this" than there was in "I bought this."

A couple of guys found out they were pros at metal working, and they not only finished building the wheel for the hydro-electric plant but they built the town its own methane-generating plant which is inside a huge greenhouse the town built. The plant makes methane to run all their vehicles and while doing that it also makes compost for the greenhouse. The process even heats the greenhouse. They now work daily tearing cars apart and making windmills which they trade to other communities for the things Rudy needs. Around here and in the ABS they are very rich men.

Some communities have been smarter than others about what they build to export. There was a paper mill in Russellville and they got the plant up and running. Now they do nothing all day but make toilet paper, and let me tell you people will travel far and wide to trade with them. They don't have to work the land or raise livestock. All they have to do is make toilet paper and everything else is happily given to them.

Cherry gave birth to a seven and half pound, twenty-one inch, screaming baby girl that she and Billy named Cindy. The baby came easy and I delivered her without a hitch. She is the light of me and Lucy's life and a bit of a pain in the ass at times, so a normal, healthy baby. Billy and Cherry help us run our farm and take care of our stock, and of course Billy does dozer work for anyone who asks when the need arises. 'Cause in the if-you-find-it-first-it's-yours world, that dozer belongs to Billy.

There are lots of new people being born all over and lots of them are being named after me. Just in Rudy alone there is a girl named Katy and two boys named Kay. I was a little weirded out at first, but I guess as long as there isn't a population explosion I'm alright with it.

Evelyn took up with Matt's oldest son, Randy. Did I tell you that Matt has a weird sense of humor? Named his younger boy Philmore. That's right, Randy and Philmore, and with a last name like Peters. Anyway, every time Randy bitches about her to Jimmy he laughs and says he ain't taking her back. I figure it's only a matter of time till Evelyn heads to the out house and just never comes back. In the ABS no one puts up with her kind long.

Jimmy has mostly been playing the field—which is pretty limited in Rudy—but seems to be pretty serious about the woman he's dating now. He built his own house in Rudy proper and lives there. He comes out almost daily to help me run the radio show, but spends most of his time doctoring animals and is considered our town's vet which seems to suit him really well.

Samantha took my advice and went to Fort Smith where she quickly became one of their most valuable players. The group in Fort Smith grew a little as people who dug out joined them. They worked non-stop that first summer making Northside High School into housing that could be more easily heated. Surprisingly no one worried about it being too hot any more. They dug out the building's old, abandoned boiler system, rigged it to run on combustibles, and reconnected it to serve the main building. Classrooms became apartments, and they scavenged the entire city for what they needed. They filled every space they weren't living in with anything useful they found.

They started raising crops the second year, but Sam went out to Fort Chaffee, found an old army troop-carrying type helicopter, and started taking a couple of guys with her. They would fly around looking for things to scavenge, so they are still by-

and-large a scavenging and trading community.

There were four doctors, some staff and some patients who had ridden out the BS in a hospital basement in Dallas. Because of the hurricanes that had been slamming the Gulf Coast, the hospital had filled its basement with K-rations and survival gear, including a massive back-up generator hooked up to propane tanks. The hospital got hit by one of the hundreds of tornados that basically cleared a huge swath through the middle and south of the country. Fortunately for them, one of the survivors was the maintenance guy and he got the power shut off to the damaged part of the building and was able to get everything running to just the basement.

Remember that people—thirty-five people, most of them doctors and nurses that we desperately needed in the ABS—were saved because of the janitor.

Sam went and got these people and distributed them throughout the country to the different groups. We wound up with a very competent RN who it looks like may be my new daughter-in law.

Sam found love, too, in the form of a huge bull dyke who could carry her in the palm of her hand. She found her on one of her scavenging expeditions, which seemed appropriate. It was weird to me that she could go from someone like Lucy to someone like that, but Lucy explained that Sam was a switch and I pretended to know what that meant.

Lucy and I are in the middle of our third winter together. I think we've gotten closer every year. It's for sure that each winter has been a little less brutal than the one before, but they're still long and cold. They give Lucy and I plenty of time to make love and lay around reading, watching old movies, eating popcorn, and talking about the BBS.

To me the world is better now. But then for me nothing really changed except people quit treating me like a pariah, I got a really hot woman that I love and who loves me, and my sons grew up and became the men I hoped they'd be instead of the men I was afraid they'd turn into.

Some people say I'm egotistical.

Some people call me a prophet.

Some people say I'm their savior.

Karma still calls me Santa Claus.

Lucy always calls me Kay.

But most people around here still call me Crazy Katy. As long as they smile when they say it that doesn't bother me at all.

ABOUT THE AUTHOR

Selina Rosen's short fiction has appeared in several magazines and anthologies including *Sword and Sorceress, Witch Way to the Mall, Fangs for the Mammories, Strip Mauled, Turn the Other Chick, Anthology At the End of the Universe,* the two newest *Thieves' World* anthologies, *Aoife's Kiss,* and *Here Be Dragons.*

Her novels include *Queen of Denial, Recycled,* the *Chains of Freedom* trilogy, *Strange Robby, The Host* trilogy, *Fire & Ice, Hammer Town, Reruns,* Sword *Masters, Jabone's Sword,* and *Black Rage.*

Her mystery novel, *Bad Lands,* was the first Holmes and Storm Mystery and was also co-written with Laura J. Underwood. *Bad City,* also co-written with Laura J. Underwood is due out late fall, 2011.

Check out her website (www.selinarosen.com) for her continuing series, *The House.* It's posted in episodes—approximately two per month.

In her capacity as editor-in-chief of Yard Dog Press, Ms. Rosen has edited several anthologies, including the five award-winning *Bubbas of the Apocalypse* anthologies and two collections of "modern" fairy tales including the Stoker-nominated *Stories That Won't Make Your Parents Hurl.*

If you haven't already looked for her on FaceBook, why not?

ABOUT THE COVER ARTIST/DESIGNER

Mitchell Bentley has shown his creations from coast to coast and border to border, though mainly throughout the Midwest or plains states—often at General or Literary Science Fiction Conventions. Mitchell has been honored with several guest positions and has won many awards. He currently works on a variety of speculative pieces, commissioned work and publications.

You can view—and purchase—much of his fine artwork at http://www.atomicflystudios.com/.

Yard Dog Press Titles As Of This Print Date

A Bubba in Time
A Man, A Plan, (yet lacking) A Canal, Panama, Linda Donahue
Adventures of the Irish Ninja, Selina Rosen
The Alamo and Zombies, Jean Stuntz
All the Marbles, Dusty Rainbolt
Almost Human, Gary Moreau
Ancient Enemy, Lee Killouth
The Anthology From Hell: Humorous Tales From WAY Down Under, Edited by Julia S. Mandala
Ard Magister, Laura J. Underwood
Assassins Inc., Phillip Drayer Duncan
Bad City, Selina Rosen & Laura J. Underwood
Bad Lands, Selina Rosen & Laura J. Underwood
Black Rage, Selina Rosen
Blackrose Avenue, Mark Shepherd
The Boat Man, Selina Rosen
Bobby's Troll, John Lance
Bride of Tranquility, Tracy S. Morris
Bruce and Roxanne from Start to Finnish, Rie Sheridan Rose
The Bubba Chronicles, Selina Rosen
Bubba Fables, Sue P. Sinor
Bubbas Of the Apocalypse, Edited by Selina Rosen
The Burden of the Crown, Selina Rosen
Chains of Redemption, Selina Rosen
Checking On Culture, Lee Killough
Chronicles of the Last War, Laura J. Underwood
Dadgum Martians Invade the Lucky Nickel Saloon, Ken Rand
Dark and Stormy Nights, Bradley H. Sinor
Deja Doo, Edited by Selina Rosen
Dracula's Lawyer, Julia S. Mandala
Dragon's Tongue, Laura J. Underwood
The Essence of Stone, Beverly A. Hale
Fairy BrewHaHa at the Lucky Nickel Saloon, Ken Rand
The Fantastikon: Tales of Wonder, Robin Wayne Bailey
Fire & Ice, Selina Rosen
Flush Fiction, Volume I: Stories To Be Read In One Sitting, Edited by Selina Rosen
Flush Fiction, Volume II: Twenty Years of Letting it Go!, Edited by Selina Rosen
The Four Bubbas of the Apocalypse: Flatulence, Halitosis, Incest, and... Ned, Edited by Selina Rosen
The Four Redheads: Apocalypse Now!, Linda L. Donahue, Rhonda Eudaly, Julia S. Mandala, & Dusty Rainbolt
The Four Redheads of the Apocalypse, Linda L. Donahue, Rhonda Eudaly, Julia S. Mandala, & Dusty Rainbolt
The Garden In Bloom, Jeffrey Turner

The Geometries of Love: Poetry by Robin Wayne Bailey
The Golems Of Laramie County, Ken Rand
The Green Women, Laura J. Underwood
The Guardians, Lynn Abbey
Hammer Town, Selina Rosen
The Happiness Box, Beverly A. Hale
The Host Series: The Host, Fright Eater, Gang Approval, Selina
Rosen
Houston, We've Got Bubbas!, Edited by Selina Rosen
How I Spent the Apocolypse, Selina Rosen
I Didn't Quite Make It To Oz, Edited by Selina Rosen
I Should Have Stayed In Oz, Edited by Selina Rosen
In the Shadows, Bradley H. Sinor
International House of Bubbas, Edited by Selina Rosen
It's the Great Bumpkin, Cletus Brown!, Katherine A. Turski
The Killswitch Review, Steven-Elliot Altman & Diane DeKelb-
Rittenhouse
The Leopard's Daughter, Lee Killough
The Lightning Horse, John Moore
The Logic of Departure, Mark W. Tiedemann
The Long, Cold Walk To Mars, Jeffrey Turner
Marking the Signs and Other Tales Of Mischief, Laura J.
Underwood
Material Things, Selina Rosen
Medieval Misfits: Renaissance Rejects, Tracy S. Morris
Mirror Images, Susan Satterfield
Mirror, Mirror and Other Reflections, James K. Burk
More Stories That Won't Make Your Parents Hurl, Edited by
Selina Rosen
Music for Four Hands, Louis Antonelli & Edward Morris
My Life with Geeks and Freaks, Claudia Christian
The Necronomicrap: A Guide To Your Horoooscope, Tim Frayser
Playing With Secrets, Bradley H & Sue P. Sinor
Redheads In Love, Linda L. Donahue, Rhonda Eudaly, Julia S.
Mandala, & Dusty Rainbolt
Reruns, Selina Rosen
Rock 'n' Roll Universe, Ken Rand
Shadows In Green, Richard Dansky
Stories That Won't Make Your Parents Hurl, Edited by Selina
Rosen
Tales from Keltora, Laura J. Underwood
*Tales Of the Lucky Nickel Saloon, Second Ave., Laramie, Wyo-
ming, U S of A*, Ken Rand
Tarbox Station, Rhonda Eudaly
Texistani: Indo-Pak Food From A Texas Kitchen, Beverly A. Hale
That's All Folks, J. F. Gonzalez

Through Wyoming Eyes, Ken Rand
Turn Left to Tomorrow, Robin Wayne Bailey
The Twins, Selina Rosen
Wandering Lark, Laura J. Underwood
Wings of Morning, Katharine Eliska Kimbriel
Zombies In Oz and Other Undead Musings, Robin Wayne Bailey

Double Dog (A YDP Imprint):

#1:
Of Stars & Shadows, Mark W. Tiedemann
This Instance Of Me, Jeffrey Turner

#2:
Gods and Other Children, Bill D. Allen
Tranquility, Tracy Morris

#3:
Home Is the Hunter, James K. Burk
Farstep Station, Lazette Gifford

#4:
Sabre Dance, Melanie Fletcher
The Lunari Mask, Laura J. Underwood

#5:
House of Doors, Julia Mandala
Jaguar Moon, Linda A. Donahue

Just Cause (A YDP Imprint):

The Bitter End
Selina Rosen

Death Under the Crescent Moon
Dusty Rainbolt

The Ghost Writer
Selina Rosen

It's Not Rocket Science: Spirituality for the Working-Class Soul
Selina Rosen

Meditations of a Hoarder
Melinda LaFevers

Not My Life
Selina Rosen

The Pit
Selina Rosen

Plots and Protagonists: A Reference Guide for Writers
Mel. White

Vanishing Fame
Selina Rosen

Non-YDP titles we distribute:

Chains of Freedom
Chains of Destruction
Jabone's Sword
Queen of Denial
Recycled
Strange Robby
Sword Masters
Selina Rosen

Three Ways to Order:

1. Write us a letter telling us what you want, then send it along with your check or money order (made payable to Yard Dog Press) to: Yard Dog Press, 710 W. Redbud Lane, Alma, AR 72921-7247

2. Use selinarosen@cox.net or lynnstran@cox.net to contact us and place your order. Then send your check or money order to the address above. *This has the advantage of allowing you to check on the availability of short-stock items such as T-shirts and back-issues of Yard Dog Comics.*

3. Contact us as in #1 or #2 above and pay with a credit card or by debit from your checking account. Either give us the credit card information in your letter/Email/phone call, or go to our website and use our shopping carts. If you send us your information, please include your name as it appears on the card, your credit card number, the expiration date, and the 3 or 4-digit security code after your signature on the back (CVV). Please remember that we will include media rate (minimum $3.00) S/H for mailing in the lower 48 states.

Watch our website at
www.yarddogpress.com
for news of upcoming projects
and new titles!!

A Note to Our Readers

We at Yard Dog Press understand that many people buy used books because they simply can't afford new ones. That said, and understanding that not everyone is made of money, we'd like you to know something that you may not have realized. Writers only make money on new books that sell. At the big houses a writer's entire future can hinge on the number of books they sell. While this isn't the case at Yard Dog Press, the honest truth is that when you sell or trade your book or let many people read it, the writer and the publishing house aren't making any money.

As much as we'd all like to believe that we can exist on love and sweet potato pie, the truth is we all need money to buy the things essential to our daily lives. Writers and publishers are no different.

We realize that these "freebies" and cheap books often turn people on to new writers and books that they wouldn't otherwise read. However we hope that you will reconsider selling your copy, and that if you trade it or let your friends borrow it, you also pass on the information that if they really like the author's work they should consider buying one of their books at full price sometime so that the writer can afford to continue to write work that entertains you.

We appreciate all our readers and *depend* upon their support.

Thanks,
The Editorial Staff
Yard Dog Press

PS – Please note that "used" books without covers have, in most cases, been stolen. Neither the author nor the publisher has made any money on these books because they were supposed to be pulped for lack of sales.

Please do not purchase books without covers.

Made in the USA
Middletown, DE
03 July 2017